MADELEINE

Euan Cameron

MADELEINE

MACLEHOSE PRESS
QUERCUS · LONDON

First published in Great Britain in 2019 by

MacLehose Press
An imprint of Quercus Publishing Ltd
Carmelite House
50 Victoria Embankment
London EC4Y 0DZ

An Hachette UK company

A CIP catalogue record for this book is available
from the British Library.

ISBN (HB) 978 0 85705 859 1
ISBN (TPB) 978 0 85705 858 4
ISBN (Ebook) 978 0 85705 857 7

10 9 8 7 6 5 4 3 2 1

Designed and typeset in Caslon by Libanus Press Ltd, Marlborough
Printed and bound in Great Britain by Clays Ltd, Elcograf S.p.A.

For Jane,
and in memory of Kate and Alastair

"There were a few black and creole collaborationists, and there was at least one English *vichyssois*"

Richard Cobb, *French and Germans, Germans and French: A personal interpretation of France under two occupations 1914–18 / 1940–44* (1983)

[CHAPTER 1]

I HAD NEVER MET A SINGLE MEMBER OF MY FATHER'S
French family until I happened to be in Paris towards the end
of January 1999. The chamber group in which I play second
violin was due to give a couple of concerts in the city and I had
a free day between performances.

It was my cousin, Ghislaine de Valcros, who had prompted
our meeting: an envelope containing a New Year greetings card,
a reproduction of Lorenzo Lotto's "Portrait of a Young Man",
had arrived in the post at my London flat shortly after New
Year's Day, forwarded by my agent to whom the card had been
addressed. It expressed good wishes for the coming year in a conventional way, and enclosed the following note, written in English
on the letterhead of a well-known French weekly magazine:

Dear William

I hope you will forgive this sudden communication *à
l'improviste*, or "out of the blue" as I think you say. Our
family history is complicated and mysterious to me, but
I hope you will agree that it's about time we met and
tried to understand the past and our families' complicated

relationships after all these years of not communicating. I am particularly keen to do so because a few weeks ago my mother, Madeleine de Launay, received a letter and several packets of what she describes as "family archives" from Henry Latymer – your grandfather, she told me, and her first husband – who, it appears, has been living in Buenos Aires for some years. He wrote to tell her that he feared he had not long to live, and this has clearly upset her, for it brings back memories of what she calls a "personal tragedy" that she had hoped to leave in the past. She says she will now once again be obliged to confront certain matters relating to her younger life that she has done her best to forget, so she has suggested that I try to discover your whereabouts and get in touch with a view to deciding what we might do with these papers.

Making contact has not been easy; the only clue my mother could provide was the address of a Miss Latymer ("his sister, if she's still alive") of Bourne House, Much Birch, Herefordshire. Alas, my letter to her, posted three or four weeks ago, was returned "not known at this address". Through the British Consulate, I then managed to find out the name of the present owner of Bourne House and I wrote again. A Colonel Thwaite replied by return, informing me that neither Miss Latymer, nor her nephew Theo, who used to visit her there and whom he had met, was alive. Apparently, Lavinia Latymer had been a neighbour and a friend of his family, but she had died in a nearby nursing home shortly after he had moved to Bourne House in 1988. Theo, her nephew – and, I now realise, your father – had also died, but several years before her. He suggested I write to you ("I assume him to be the sole surviving offspring of that ill-fated family"), and although he had no idea of where you live, he was able to give me the name of the chamber group you play with because he said he had been to a concert given by your quartet last year in Hereford Cathedral.

Bref . . . it has involved some astute detective work, but I trust I have now tracked down the real William Latymer, and I very much hope that you will get in touch with me.

Affectionately, your cousin (as it were) Ghislaine

In her letter was her Paris telephone number and an address in the *6ème arrondissement*. I immediately rang my mother to find out whether she knew anything about my newly discovered relative, but she was not helpful:

"I never asked Theo about that side of the family, darling. Talking about the past used to upset him too much. I think it was due to his unhappy childhood, which he tried to forget, and to being brought up by his aunt in rural Herefordshire. 'Please don't bring all that up again, Jane,' he would beg me whenever I asked any questions, and so I didn't."

I telephoned Ghislaine, told her that her card and letter had just been forwarded to me, and that, as it happened, my quartet was scheduled to play in a chamber concert at the little church of St-Julien-le-Pauvre in a few weeks' time. Naturally, I would very much like to meet her and, should she be free, perhaps she might like to come.

*

After an absence of almost two years, I found myself in Paris. Glints of wintry sunshine were shimmering over the Seine and the dark towers of the Conciergerie were reflected in the eddying waters as I crossed the Pont Neuf and made my way to Ghislaine's office in rue du Louvre.

I felt light-headed, I remember; Paris has many moods, but the city was at its most intoxicating that morning. Passing the ancient church of St-Germain-l'Auxerrois, I looked in to offer a brief prayer and to examine the stained glass, but a choir of schoolchildren and their teacher were rehearsing, and I felt like an intruder.

Ghislaine's office was at the top of a six-storey building, her magazine being part of a long-established newspaper group. I should have made an appointment. She was in a meeting with the editor, her colleague informed me, but if I could wait fifteen minutes . . . I sat down and surveyed her office. There were shelves of new books, recently arrived from the publishers, to judge by their pristine state, which had been divided into fiction and various other categories. Jutting out of the top of each book's spine was a white card on which was written what I took to be the date of publication. Her desk suggested mild pandemonium: there was a clutter of papers everywhere, scribbled notes, press releases and letters covered every available surface, and more books were piled up in columns on the floor around it. One of the two telephones tinkled softly, but someone on another extension must have answered it. I stood up and gazed out of the window, which looked out over the Banque de France building.

"*Tiens!*" a voice said with a laugh. "You must be William Latymer. I had not expected you quite so soon."

I turned around. Walking towards me was a tall woman in her early to mid-thirties, I imagined. She was smiling and she held out both hands to me in a gesture of welcome. Large brown eyes shone beneath fair, almost blond hair that framed her neck and fell loosely over her navy-blue cardigan and square shoulders. She wore little make-up and her open lips revealed very white teeth.

I was taken aback and mumbled something to the effect that I was delighted to meet a cousin I never knew existed.

"I would have recognised you straight away. Maman has a photograph of your grandfather taken during the war," she said in very slightly accented English as we embraced and brushed cheeks. "There's a clear family likeness, one has to say."

Ghislaine wore tight black trousers that emphasised her slimness and she exuded an air of bustling vivacity. Beneath her simple white blouse she wore a gold chain.

"Well, I'm very pleased you got in touch," I stammered, still taken aback by the effect of her physical appearance.

Ghislaine picked up one of the two telephones on her cluttered desk and asked for some coffee to be brought.

"Yes, we are cousins, but it may be more complicated than that," she said. "Perhaps I'm also some sort of aunt. You see, you are the son of the child of my mother's first marriage, while I am the daughter of her second. Your father would have been my half-brother, in other words. What does that make us?"

Still standing, she laughed and patted my arm. Her whole body seemed to quiver in amusement and, looking back now, I'm convinced I fell in love with her in that instant. Her voice, her infectious laughter, her total naturalness, the delicacy with which she moved, her sheer physicality . . .

"William?"

"It's Will," I said. "Everyone calls me Will."

Her eyes held my gaze.

"Well, Will, can you spare a few days to come to Brittany to meet Maman? As I told you when I wrote, the letter my mother received from your grandfather – a man she had not seen since 1945, believe it or not – distressed her very much, and, since then, I am sorry to have to tell you, there has been a further letter from a woman friend of Henry's – Rosita Suarez, I think that was her name – informing Maman that Henry had died three weeks ago in a Buenos Aires hospice. So, sad news. Yet I'm sure it would give my mother great pleasure to meet you. And I could certainly do with your help sorting out these so-called family archives he sent."

Ghislaine raised her eyes to heaven in a gesture of disbelief.

"It seems that they consist of personal diaries and a few letters, all pertaining to the war years and their time together. You see, whatever Madeleine – that's my mother's name, by the way – whatever she may have once felt for this poor Henry, your grandfather, it is clear that she does not wish to be reminded about a chapter of her life – those sad and desperate wartime years – that she had successfully repressed. Over time, she has told me something about her past. She has told me a little about Henry and his life in France during the war, and also about their son Theo, your father, who, to her obvious sadness and shame, she barely knew. It's clear that she has always felt guilty about him and about so much besides . . ."

She paused.

"Anyway, she believes that if these archives deserve to belong to anyone, they should belong to Theo, but since you say he is no longer alive – and I'm sorry to hear this about your father – then they should be yours."

I told her that she knew more about Henry than I did. All I had ever discovered about my grandfather was the fact that he had been educated at the same school that both my father and I had been at, and also that he was somehow *persona non grata*, a so-called black sheep of the family, who had disappeared in South America some years before I had been born. I said that he had abandoned his English family and that his son had never received so much as a single letter or postcard from him.

"Neither Henry's name, nor my father's, Theo, was ever mentioned at home," I said, "and no records or photographs of them appear to exist."

My first meeting with my cousin was memorable for me, but it did not last long, barely half an hour. She was due to attend a literary prize-giving at a Left Bank restaurant and her taxi dropped me off at my hotel on rue de Seine. She agreed to come to our chamber concert the following evening, and I told her that I would be delighted to stay a few extra days and accompany her to Brittany next weekend to meet the grandmother I never knew I had.

I always stay at the Louisiane when I'm in Paris, if only for sentimental reasons. It is not the most comfortable of hotels, but I like to think of figures such as Henry Miller and Ezra Pound staying there in the years between the wars. There is still a lingering louche whiff of a *hôtel de passe*, and of what I imagine Paris to have been like in the immediate post-war period, with those cobbled streets, open-backed buses and the faces that you see in Brassaï's photographs. When I first visited the city, shortly after leaving school, there was an elderly White Russian who was employed there as a night porter. He had escaped from Minsk at the time of the Bolshevik Revolution and he would sit at his little kiosk in the lobby of the hotel that had been his home since 1921. He was an incorrigible optimist and in the evenings he used to strum melancholy tunes on his balalaika. He remembered *"Monsieur Durrell et Monsieur Miller, bien sûr,"* he once told me in his fluent but harshly guttural French, and he appeared to have known all that existentialist *beau monde* who had met Jean-Paul Sartre and Simone de Beauvoir in the late 1940s and '50s.

That afternoon and most of the following one were spent rehearsing at St-Julien-le-Pauvre. Once inside its walls, you step back eight hundred years and there are few places where the anxieties of modern life slip away quite so effectively as they do amid the mysterious silence of the church's thick, damp-stained walls and stout pillars. I tried to imagine the chant of medieval monks in the days before its Romanesque vaults and interior were altered, when scholars from the Sorbonne attended daily Mass here. I thought of Abelard and Heloïse. I wondered by what miracle it had survived the Revolution intact and how it came to be a haven of reassurance during those turbulent times and during the dark days of German military occupation.

That evening, however, no-one was at prayer. The ancient church was transformed into a modern temple of culture, and the audience was still scrambling noisily for seats as the four of us – our leader, Gunnar Lowenskjold, Jean MacGuire, who plays the viola, our cellist Celia Elmhirst, and I – took our bows. As we tuned our instruments, I scanned the church and the faces of the ninety or so people who had come to hear us.

I thought I could make out Ghislaine in the very back of the church, but her features were indistinct.

We played three pieces that evening: a Haydn string quartet, Shostakovich's rarely performed and starkly brooding 7th string quartet, and, after a short interval, the Mendelssohn B-minor quartet. The performance was received not rapturously, as is usually the case in London, but with polite, restrained enthusiasm.

Ghislaine was indeed in the audience and she was waiting for me after the concert. She took me to dinner at a small restaurant off rue des Écoles that was known for its *bouillabaisse*. The owner, a Marseillais, greeted Ghislaine like an old friend and sat us facing one another in a corner by a window. I felt elated: by the music, by the air of Paris on this wintry evening, but most of all by my newly discovered cousin. She sat very upright at the table, her hands in constant motion as she spoke in a light-hearted, dizzying flow of French and English phrases, switching from one language to the other for no apparent reason, using hybrid "franglais" words and interspersing her conversation with bubbling peals of laughter. Her manner was more urbane and self-assured than it had been when we met in her office, and there was a confiding intimacy about her conversation that I found intoxicating.

"Don't you love this city?" she asked, wiping the condensation off the window and peering out into the darkened street. "I love its moods and its constantly changing beauty, but I wish they would stop destroying it. Deep down, I suppose, it's the nineteenth-century Paris that I love. The city of the Goncourts, of Balzac and Flaubert. But it's still the most elegant place in the world, don't you agree, whatever they do to it, whatever the passing fashions."

She held out her hands and shrugged simultaneously. Then, in a flash, her mood changed. She looked me in the eyes and placed one hand on mine.

"What about you, Will?" she asked. "Tell me. You don't speak about yourself much. Tell me something about your life in London, about the music you play."

And so, flattered by her apparent interest in me and fortified by some good red wine, I held forth. Habitually gauche and introverted where my own feelings are concerned, that night I felt liberated and unburdened, for I found myself describing not just my daily existence as a musician in London, but revealing to her most of what had happened to me since my father's death during my second year at music college in London.

"So tell me about your father – this mysterious Theo, a half-brother I never knew. I want to know, I really do," Ghislaine urged.

My father had always been such a distant, remote figure to me. He never talked about the past or about his childhood. It was as if there had been some deep black hole in his early life over which he had tried to draw a veil. He seldom displayed affection and, disloyal though it may sound, I have never quite understood what it was about him that appealed to my mother, or why she married him. I suppose that in his quiet, diffident way he was a good father, but he always seemed to me to be a man who had had to re-invent himself, someone with no identity, or at least an identity he had succeeded in burying.

I told Ghislaine just about all that I knew of our family history, with all its gaps, that evening. I knew that my father, Theo, had been sent from Europe towards the end of the war by his French mother and his English father and taken to Britain as a baby from Copenhagen, where he had been born in 1945, by my great-aunt Lavinia. She more or less adopted him, treated him as her own son, and educated him.

Theo's early childhood, I explained, had been spent in the Herefordshire village to which Ghislaine's letter to me had been addressed.

"When he was dispatched at the age of thirteen to be a boarder at a Jesuit public school on the banks of the Thames, near Windsor – a school that I and, as I discovered at the time from photographs of sports teams in the school corridors, my grandfather had also attended – Lavinia moved north to Scotland, and only returned to Herefordshire in her late sixties. She had always loved the novels of Walter Scott and the Border country, and so she chose as her new home a stone-built Victorian villa on the outskirts of a former mill town on the banks of the River Tweed. Theo spent his holidays there, fishing, birdwatching, walking and – his chief passion – making music. He was evidently solitary by nature; his health was poor and he was a painfully shy and deeply introspective boy.

"In due course, Theo was accepted as a music scholar at Edinburgh University. He had taken up the French horn in his school orchestra and very soon acquired a reasonable mastery of the instrument that set him apart from his musical peers.

"It was as a student in Edinburgh that Theo had first met my mother while playing in the university orchestra. She was a competent violinist herself, and she was much more adept at drawing Theo out of his brooding introspection than anyone he had ever met before. She is one of those brisk, confident, no-nonsense women who always seem to be able to take a positive view of life's problems. She has a wide circle of friends, many interests, and she has coped all too easily with her comparatively early widowhood. She is never short of an opinion, and I've rarely seen her dismayed or crestfallen.

"Two years after Theo and Jane had graduated and played together in a farewell performance of Britten's 'Serenade for Tenor, Horn and Strings' that had elicited eulogies from the staff of the Music department as well as from the critic of the *Scotsman*, they were married. The ceremony was carried out at the pretty Jesuit church in Lauriston Place on a damp November morning, my mother remembered, when the wind blustered through the Edinburgh streets, rattled at the church doors during the nuptial Mass, and almost blew off her veil as she stepped into the bridal car. They spent their honeymoon on Iona.

"Should I go on?" I asked Ghislaine, aware that it was late and the restaurant was emptying.

"But you must, Will. I find this fascinating."

"By marrying into a respectable New Town family," I continued, "Theo took his place in Edinburgh society, and my parents set up their first home in the top-floor flat of an austere, soot-blackened Georgian terrace house that seemed to be inhabited solely by old men – 'solemn, upright former advocates and retired colonels who wore tweed caps, darling, you know the sort!' was how I remember my mother putting it.

"I was born in that stern, precipitous city, and whenever I return to what I still think of as home, I rejoice in a sense of belonging, a reassuring and consoling permanence, as I contemplate those mournful churches, the dignified squares and sober terraces, and feel the damp haar seep into my bones. There is a certain awe about Edinburgh, a weight of history, which we lack in our more sanitised southern English cities.

"Yet my father never belonged to the city in the way my mother and I did. Indeed, I doubt whether he felt he belonged anywhere. When she could be persuaded to talk about him, Mother always maintained that he was an orphan of the Second World War, a child who had been deserted and dispossessed, one of the casualties of mid-twentieth-century European history. He always bore the attitudes of a foreigner, of an outsider, she said. Despite his British education, it was as if, at an early stage in his life, he had decided to create a new persona for himself, to build a shell within which he could protect himself from what seemed to him to be a hostile outside world and from the buffetings that had shaped and damaged his early life. Although my father remained devoted to his surrogate mother, his Aunt Lavinia, throughout his short life, he never could understand why the God to whom both he and she prayed had deprived him of both his real parents.

"And when I look at the photograph of my mother and father that stands on the bookcase in my London flat, I see a man who must have been in constant retreat from life. Theo and Jane do not look like a couple who belonged together or who sustained one another: my mother's expression is set in an all-encompassing grin; her youthful dark beauty radiates confidence and faith in the future, she knows what she is about and where she is going; but my father does not look at the camera; there is a withdrawn, soulful air about him, and his hollowed cheeks and prematurely bald head suggest suffering and resignation.

"Perhaps music was his only real consolation. It was certainly one of the few interests he and I had in common, and it may have been the only true love that my parents shared. The sounds of strings and brass echo through my childhood and as I cast my mind back I can see that it was inevitable I should have become a musician myself. It was not that either of my parents was insistent about this; it was simply a foregone conclusion that I should persevere with a *modus vivendi* that each of them saw as a privilege and a duty.

"'Your talent with the violin is inherited from your mother, but it is God-given, boy. Use it!' was one of the few conventionally fatherly remarks I recall him making from the time that I used to attend Mrs Belinsky's violin lessons in a back street near the Royal Botanic Garden in the years before I was sent south to boarding school. Practice and music lessons were part of a ritual that I never questioned, at least until I left home, and when the time came to decide upon a career there seemed no sensible alternative."

I had rarely talked quite so much and I apologised to Ghislaine. She took my hands in both of hers.

"Poor Theo," she said. "My mother found it hard to say anything at all about him when I once asked her. It was as if her son, whom she had abandoned when he was a baby, belonged to another life. It is something that has always haunted her. He was her lovechild – a victim of history, like so many of his generation, I imagine. A victim of our century, at least. I don't mean the fact that he was illegitimate – no-one even uses that word any longer – it's just that the war damaged so many of his generation, emotionally, I mean. I hope I don't shock you, speaking like this about your own father."

"No, you don't," I said, pressing her hand in mine for a brief moment before we stood up to leave. I noticed that Ghislaine appeared to have settled the bill with a discreet wave to the owner.

The night air was cold but invigorating as we walked back to her car, which was tightly hemmed in between two others in the narrow rue St-André-des-Arts, a few minutes' walk away. It was past midnight, but I did not feel in the least tired. We agreed that we should meet outside her flat in rue des Saints-Pères the following afternoon, before driving to Britanny. Then she sped off in her small red Peugeot. It had been a marvellous evening. I pulled up the collar of my overcoat and set off towards the Louisiane. The water pumps in the street were sluicing away the debris left by the market stallholders earlier in the day. I was in no mood to sleep. It was a crisp, starlit night and, instead of going straight to bed, I decided to have a cognac – a *fine* – in one of the late-night cafés still open on boulevard St-Germain. Lighting a Gitane, I drank to the grandfather I had never known, whose death-bed letter had been the cause of my meeting Ghislaine.

∞

The next afternoon, at three o'clock precisely, I was outside Ghislaine's flat. I rang the bell marked Valcros, but the concierge told me that she had not yet returned and so I paced up and down the pavement opposite, past the forbidding door of the Ukrainian church and the unadorned concrete mass of the Université René Descartes. Ten minutes later her car drew up and, looking a touch flustered, Ghislaine emerged. She reached over to the back seat for her briefcase and, waving a large bunch of keys, embraced me.

"Will, I'm so sorry to keep you. It's been such a rush," she apologised breathlessly. "Come up. Give me five minutes to change and pack a bag and I'll be ready. We must be out of Paris by four or the traffic will be terrible."

∞

Our journey westwards was painless, however. Within half an hour, we had joined the autoroute near the Porte de Saint-Cloud. I offered to share the driving, but Ghislaine shook her head. We spoke very little during the journey. She asked whether I liked Bruckner, and before I could answer she had put on a cassette of his Seventh Symphony. Two hours later, we drew to a halt in the small town of Dol-de-Bretagne.

"I need some coffee," Ghislaine said, pulling up at the first available parking space in the centre of the small town. "We've only an hour more on the road and there are some pretty streets here. You're officially in Brittany now, by the way."

We walked past the cathedral, whose Gothic lines made it look more English than French. Ghislaine pointed up to a street name: Grande-rue-des-Stuarts. "As you can see, they remember the 'auld alliance' here,' she said, giving an absurd, supposedly Scots intonation to the words. "Let's try that café on the other side of the square."

I stretched and breathed in the cool evening air. It was a relief to be out of the city and to sniff that particular scent of certain French provincial towns at dusk. We crossed a square with a pretty fountain and nineteenth-century houses and entered a bar, where Ghislaine ordered coffee.

"Will," she said as soon as we had sat down, her expression suddenly serious. "I ought to tell you a little more about Maman before we get to La Tiemblais. She's a wonderful old woman, but she has her *manières* and perhaps I should warn you. She is not a Breton for nothing."

Ghislaine leaned forward and pressed her hands together in an attitude of prayer. For a second, her brown eyes seemed to hold mine.

"You realise, of course, that she's actually your grandmother?"

"Of course."

"Her husband, René de Valcros, my father – though I scarcely knew *him* either – was killed by the F.L.N. in Algeria when I was a child."

"I'm so sorry, I had no idea."

Ghislaine shrugged. "It was a long time ago, and time heals. I remember I had just had a party for my fourth birthday, and virtually my only memory of him is the moment, a few days before he died, when he revealed what my present was to be. I remember coming down to breakfast, my parents embracing me, and then Papa took me by the hand, led me outside and into a large sort of barn where we kept tractors and equipment for the farm, and there in a corner, munching on hay, was the sweetest, tiniest pony you could imagine. He was mine, all mine, and I adored him from the first glance. Three or maybe four days later, Papa was dead. They blew up his car when he was on his way to Oran. It was a senseless act committed by cruel, desperate men. I don't remember much else, but life must have been hell for Maman, coping with everything. And being made a widow in her forties, can you imagine?"

She paused to light a cigarette.

"You see, René, my father, came from an old, quite well-known family and although he was reasonably sympathetic to the demands for Algerian independence, his name represented the past, the old colonial tradition of the *pied-noirs*, and some members of his family had been linked with one of the O.A.S.

generals. It's all history now, and I don't want to bore you, but it's important that you know something of Maman's life after the time she knew your grandfather."

"When did she meet your father?" I said.

"Papa? I'm not sure, but I guess it would have been in the mid-fifties. I know she was born in 1921, because I once saw her passport, but she has always been very secretive. It's rather charming, don't you think? And typical of that generation of actresses and singers. You know she had a certain success as a singer?"

"No. I'm woefully ignorant of my family's French links, as I told you. But please go on. I'm intrigued, and I'm learning."

Ghislaine turned to look out over the now darkening square and glanced at her watch.

"Well, perhaps she *will* talk about her youth and your grandfather. I don't know. She never has done much up till now, but somehow the communication she had from your grandfather, Henry, before his death seems to have stirred up memories. She was actually very pleased to hear you were coming to visit her – slightly to my surprise, I ought to say – and she immediately telephoned an old friend in Paris whom she and Henry had both known in the war years to tell him the news. Have you heard of Sylvain de Gresly? He's a writer. Speaks perfect English. Now in his nineties, I should imagine."

I shook my head.

"It's not important." She gave a dismissive wave of the hand and paused. "You know, that period of the war is a very delicate subject for her generation of French people, as I'm sure you know, and we can never be certain what they felt about the Occupation and about Vichy, or the fact that so many of them were collaborators – though that's not how they see it, of course."

Ghislaine looked down at her cup. She flicked back her hair and played with a packet of sugar. Two elderly men, evidently regulars, came into the café and were soon in conversation with the owner. They spoke slowly in deep, raucous voices, their solemn conversation interspersed with bouts of laughter and the frequently repeated Breton exclamation: "*Dame oui!*"

"France is only now beginning to face up to that terrible time," Ghislaine said. "Pétain, Vichy, the 'New Europe' that they thought would emerge, and the Germans' occupation of our country. You mustn't make the mistake of imagining they were all Resistance fighters. That's a bit of a Gaullist myth. Our country suffers from what someone once called 'the bureaucracy of amnesia'. Though, when I think about it, I'm not surprised about this secrecy and reticence on the part of my mother's generation. People have their pride. We're fortunate, after all, to have been born when we were, you and I. No? I mean, we've never been tested in the way that generation was."

I nodded, vaguely aware of what Ghislaine was referring to. I was trying to conceal the fact that I was ignorant of much of recent French history. I was also fascinated by her intense manner of speaking, her capacity for seriousness that could merge into sudden, uninhibited laughter.

"My mother was known as Madeleine Lambert. That was her stage name, the one she used on her records. Her actual name was de Launay, her maiden name, which she reverted to after her husband, my father, was killed. You couldn't succeed as a singer or as an actress in those days if you were thought to belong to the *petite noblesse*. And she deliberately kept her stage name after the war, until she married, because her father, Jean de Launay, had been some sort of minor official in the Vichy administration. He used to write for the collaborationist news-papers, and he had been quite well known. He was tried by one of those kangaroo courts during what we call the *épuration* – a sort of purge of those who were thought to have betrayed their country – and he spent some time in prison after the war."

Ghislaine signalled to the barman to bring us two more coffees.

"So, you see, she has a complicated history, your grand-mother. I don't think she was ever really famous, but she had begun to acquire a certain reputation as a popular singer. She was beautiful, too, as you'll see from the photographs of her at home, and we even have an old 78 of her first big success, a song called '*À nos amours*'. I'll play it for you if I can find it. It'll make you fall in love with her voice. It always fills me with a sort of nostalgia for that old, pre-war world when people sounded so wonderfully innocent. Not that they were, of course. But they respected authority, had certain standards, went to church, and led their decent, ordered, honest lives."

Ghislaine laughed in self-mockery and pushed a lock of hair back from her forehead.

"Take no notice of me," she said. 'I'm beginning to sound like some sentimental old fascist politician. Maman is not at all like that, and I can quite see why your grandfather must have fallen for her. Anyway," she said, looking at her watch and draining her coffee cup, "we must be on our way. I said we would arrive in time for dinner, and Jeanne, Maman's maid, who is even older than her, gets very offended if anyone is unpunctual. Dinner is at eight o'clock. On the dot. Besides, it's very rare for them to have guests nowadays.'

Just over an hour later we were entering the tiny village of St-Éloi. It was dark, but the two or three street lamps briefly illuminated the walls of the village church, the *mairie* and a solitary café, now closed, as we drove by. Ghislaine turned right, past what looked to be the gatehouse to a larger property, after which we bumped along an unmade drive and up a slight incline until we rounded a bend and the lights of the nineteenth-century manor house came into view.

Ghislaine steered the car across a pebbled forecourt and brought it to a halt beside a doorway, above which a heraldic device had been set into the main wall. She switched off the engine, stretched and yawned, but seemed in no hurry to get out of the car. Dogs were barking.

"Jeanne will have spotted the car headlights and she'll open the front door," Ghislaine said. "It's just that she takes a little time to shuffle along from the kitchen. She's also a bit deaf, by the way. And one other thing: it might be diplomatic if you were to kiss Maman's hand when you first meet her. Absurdly quaint, I know, but those old-world courtesies still mean a great deal to her."

I must have looked anxious, for Ghislaine suddenly put her arm on my shoulder, ruffled my hair and kissed the side of my head. "My poor Will." She laughed. "You must wonder what I'm inflicting on you. Don't worry, she's not an ogress, and I'm sure you'll get on with her wonderfully well. Remember, you're *en famille* here. It's your own grandmother you're about to meet, as I keep reminding you."

A light had been switched on in one of the principal front windows of the house and, seconds later, an outside lamp lit up the drive where the car was parked. We approached the steps leading up to an ornate front door, which now opened. Ghislaine ushered me through into a hallway where a plump, elderly woman, dressed in black, wearing a white apron and with her hair in a bun, offered the semblance of a curtsy. "Monsieur," she muttered, before proceeding to embrace Ghislaine as if she were her own long-lost daughter.

"Jeanne, this is Monsieur William from London," said Ghislaine, reverting to French. "He's my . . . well, my cousin, you could say. *Enfin*, you know very well who I mean. He's the son of that poor Theo who died and whose name nobody ever mentions."

The old woman nodded. Her small, bright eyes scrutinised me for a moment, then she shook my hand enthusiastically. "He's the image of his grandfather when young, Mademoiselle. Just like the photograph on Madame's desk." Then she looked at me from another angle and chuckled quietly to herself. "Dinner will be served in ten minutes," she announced in a lilting Breton accent.

Jeanne led the way along a wood-panelled corridor lined with nineteenth-century engravings before stopping in front of a thick oak door. She knocked and then waited for an answer before showing us into a large, dimly lit drawing room hung with family portraits that seemed to merge into a background of red and dark-brown wallpaper. A log fire flickered in a wide, open grate and beside it, in a high-backed armchair, sat a woman with white hair. She wore pince-nez glasses and had a brightly patterned shawl over the shoulders of her black dress.

"Maman, please don't get up," Ghislaine said.

But the old lady rose stiffly to her feet and embraced her daughter warmly.

So this was my grandmother, as I was now determined to think of her; Madeleine de Launay, formerly Madeleine Valcros, and once the popular singer, Madeleine Lambert. It was too much to take in and my imagination reeled. She proffered her delicate, fine-boned hand, arrayed with rings and bracelets, and I bowed.

"*Mes enfants*," she said, her voice a fluting tremolo, "I am so happy to see you. So very happy . . . I sometimes think that the phantoms of our past come back not to haunt us, but to open our eyes and help us confront ourselves . . ." She paused and turned towards me. "I have been looking forward so much to meeting you, William," she said, taking my hand. "You are most welcome at La Tiemblais."

The Comtesse de Launay, to give her the title used only by those who had known her before her marriage to René de Valcros, spoke a sonorous, old-fashioned French. She was small, poised and elegant, and though I knew that she must be in her eighties, the impression she gave was one of agelessness. Her eyes shone with humour and it was not difficult to imagine her having once been an actress or a singer. To me, she still looked beautiful. She had a distinctly French style and grace.

We dined simply and well that evening but, before Ghislaine and I had finished supper, Madeleine stood up to bid us good-night. "You will forgive me if I leave you to yourselves. We retire early in the country, you know, and we have much to discuss tomorrow."

It was not long before we also retired for the night. Ghislaine led me up a creaking wooden staircase and down a long corridor to a sparsely furnished room at the top of the house that smelled of varnish and turpentine polish. Two oriental rugs were spread over the bare floorboards. A high, four-poster bed had been made up with linen sheets and an elongated bolster. A vase full of red and yellow flowers stood on top of a narrow chest of drawers.

Jeanne had already closed the shutters and Ghislaine was now drawing the curtains and opening the windows.

She then turned back the counterpane. I was touched by her gesture.

"I hope you'll be comfortable, Will. Tomorrow, we must go for a walk, and we shall try to encourage Maman to talk." She stood at the door and blew me a kiss. "Sleep well."

I washed and undressed, but I could not sleep immediately. The concert at St-Julien-le-Pauvre already seemed to belong to another world. Paris and London were an age away. I got out of bed, pushed back the heavy wooden shutters and let the night air into the room. Sirius shone brightly, low in the southern sky, and the constellation of Orion, his belt and sword eternally in place, gleamed out of the blackness. A breeze shook the branches of the tall trees that stood at the rear of the house, and an owl hooted in the woods nearby. I rarely thought of my unloved father and the parents he had never known, but I was compelled to do so now. I was about to fall asleep in a house that, had circumstances been different, he might have visited.

⌈CHAPTER 2⌉

A WOMAN WAS SINGING AT A PIANO AS I VENTURED downstairs at eight o'clock the following morning, stopping on my way to examine a series of framed sketches of a female nude on the staircase walls. The voice as well as the youthful body portrayed in the sketches were, I imagined, Madeleine's: I traced the high-pitched, gently quavering notes to a room next to the *salon* where Ghislaine had introduced me to her mother the previous evening. I stopped by the door, which was ajar, and listened. I could not catch every word, but the song was a sentimental one about a Breton fisherman who drowned at sea and the girl who loved him and was left to mourn him. There were several verses, each followed by a refrain which Madeleine delivered with feeling and a certain dash:

> *J'aime Paimpol et sa falaise,*
> *Son église et son Grand Pardon.*
> *J'aime surtout la paimpolaise*
> *Qui m'attend au pays breton.*

Her voice was both moving and strangely alluring. I wondered whether Ghislaine was in the room. Perhaps she was accompanying her mother at the piano. As soon as there was silence, I knocked and put my head round the half-open door.

"My dear William, please come in. You must make yourself at home here." Madeleine beckoned as she spoke, and I approached the piano ready to bow and respectfully kiss her hand once more, but she dismissed the gesture. "No need for such formality," she whispered with a smile. She was alone except for a black and white spaniel which lay drowsily at her feet, only stirring to cast a reproachful glance at whoever was responsible for this interruption to its mistress' singing.

"I used to sing a little when I was young," she said. "Perhaps Ghislaine has told you. And I still love our old Breton songs. Some of them are so sad, and I have become rather sentimental as I get older. My mother used to sing them to me. Mournful little songs about the sea and the brave fishermen who never return, and the poor girls who have to confront life without their loved ones. Just as in Pierre Loti novels. Did you ever read him?"

I shook my head. His was just one more name in the long list of French writers whose work I had yet to discover.

"I don't believe people read him much anymore. But he was very popular when we were young. *Pêcheur d'Islande* is a beautiful tale. And, what is more . . ." Madeleine hesitated, rose to her feet, and walked towards the bookshelves that filled one wall of the room. "It was one of your grandfather's favourite novels."

From a low shelf in a bookcase filled with motley leather and paper-bound volumes, she took a copy of Loti's novel. She handed it to me, and as she did so a sepia-tinted photograph fell to the floor. I bent to pick it up. I knew before I looked at it that it was a picture of my grandfather. Leaning against a wall, dapper and dressed in a white, short-sleeved shirt and baggy trousers tucked in at the calf, stood a fair-haired, decidedly handsome young man who must have been in his late twenties. He was smiling quizzically, and in his right hand, which was stretched out at an angle from his body and towards the ground, he held a pipe. In the background was a castle with a multitude of turrets, which looked as if it belonged to an illustration in a volume of Grimm's fairy tales. I looked up at my grandmother, as I now thought of her, but she seemed lost in thought. I turned over the photograph. In faded handwriting were written the words: "*Madeleine, les beaux temps reviendront. Ton Henry qui t'aime – à la folie. Sigmaringen, mars 1945*".

"Not bad-looking, was he? It's a copy of a framed one I keep upstairs on my desk. I didn't know I still had it. You must keep it. And the book is for you. It was his copy. I think he would have been pleased for you to have it."

I ran my thumb over the faded, deckle-edged, yellowing pages with their bold pre-war typography and their smell of must. The fly leaf was inscribed: "Henry Latymer, Bellerive 1940".

At that moment, Ghislaine entered the room. Her presence was instantly uplifting, like an exhilarating breeze on a hot summer's day, and it brought me back to myself with a jolt. Her presence exuded an immediate freshness and seemed to offer the promise of unimaginable pleasures.

"Maman, you must open the windows and let in the air. It smells damp in here," she announced as she embraced us both. "The weather's warm and beautiful and we should be having our breakfast in the conservatory. I've told Jeanne to serve it there."

Ghislaine's Paris clothes had been replaced by white jeans and a dark-green shirt and cardigan. She must have just washed her hair, and a scent of jasmine flowers wafted through the room.

After breakfast, Ghislaine and I remained in the conservatory, looking out over the garden at the back of the house. Madeleine had left us on our own after breakfast, but she soon returned.

"*Mes enfants*," she announced, walking over to us and holding up her hand against the wintry sunlight. "I have to tell you that events over the past few weeks have obliged me to confront my past and, painful though it is after all these years, I want to tell you a little about a period that concerns you both."

The sun dipped behind a cloud and a soft breeze rippled the leaves of the ivy outside. In the distance, beyond the garden wall and a tennis court that was in need of repair, hardy black and white cattle could be seen grazing in a meadow; a tractor engine throbbed; smoke rose into the chill, azure sky from the chimney of a nearby farm building.

Madeleine had drawn up a chair, and she now sat in conversation with her daughter. In profile, the shared features of the two women were plain to see: they had the same slightly domed forehead and there was a sensual softness that hovered about the corners of their mouths and shone from their dark-brown, dancing eyes. A chatelaine and her daughter, I mused, and in that instant I imagined them as belonging to some earlier period in French history: a late-nineteenth-century provincial countess and her daughter; a scene out of Flaubert perhaps, or a portrait by Manet or Mary Cassatt . . . This house, too, accorded with my passing flight of fancy: with its two somewhat absurd slate-tiled and spiked artificial turrets, built in imitation of a much grander building, it exuded an atmosphere of melancholy, though any pretensions to grandeur were offset by an appealing air of decay that had settled over the unadorned grounds and over much of the undistinguished yet comfortable interior of the house.

"I first met Henry in Vichy in the summer of 1940," said Madeleine, moving out of the sunlight so as to be in a position from which she could address both of us. "It was at an exhibition of his paintings at a gallery in one of the arcades that adjoined the park there. Those were tragic days for all of us in retrospect, but somehow life carried on as normal and the owner of the gallery had managed to organise a *vernissage* for him. Your grandfather was a fine artist, William, and in a small way he became something of a local celebrity. He was so charming, too . . . so well liked. I don't believe they thought of him especially highly at the art school he had attended in London before the war, but from the time he arrived in France in 1939 he attracted people's attention with his strong line and his wonderfully bold colours. He wasn't frightened of expressing himself and he didn't feel he had to comply with fashion or bow to the influence of surrealism as so many young artists did at that time. He was also rather clever at promoting himself, and he made friends easily . . . in Paris, as well as in Vichy, in Collioure, where he had stayed before I met him, and even in Germany, later on, when we had given up all hope of surviving . . . You know, in Paris he would think nothing of walking into those smart little *rive gauche* galleries and summoning the owner to inspect his latest work. He had panache and confidence, that very British, public-school self-belief that we French find so infuriating. When it's accompanied by the cosmopolitan savoir-faire that Henry had, though, it can be very attractive. He could be blinkered, your grandfather, but he was never obdurate."

From the sleeve of her cardigan Madeleine drew a small handkerchief with which she proceeded to dab her face.

"And then he loved our French landscapes. I don't have any of the work he did at Collioure or Vichy. It was impossible for us to take any with us, and besides, most of it vanished during the war. Sometimes, he would introduce figures into the landscape and he managed to make them merge into the background in an extraordinary way. He didn't believe that art should imitate nature, but he thought that an artist should obey the laws of nature. I can't really explain . . . All I possess now are those pencilled nudes that you may have noticed by the stairs." Madeleine pointed in the direction of the staircase and smiled. "Those were done in 1944, in our *pension* in Germany, when our lives had become rather desperate, but where was I?"

"How did you both come to be in Vichy, Maman?" Ghislaine asked. "With Maréchal Pétain, and Laval, and all those awful *collabos*?"

"We didn't use that word, Ghislaine", Madeleine said, bridling, "and people should be careful of branding us all as collaborators. At the time, we believed Maréchal Pétain to be our only hope. Papa worked for the government, so when it moved in rapid succession from Paris to the Loire, Bordeaux, Clermont-Ferrand and finally to Vichy, after the German invasion, we all had to go there too. We had no choice. For weeks we lived out of suitcases. For me, personally, it was a disaster.

I had begun to be noticed in a small way as an actress and a singer in Paris, young though I was, and I had made my first record too. I suppose I could have stayed there on my own, but Europe was at war, and Paris was occupied. Besides, my parents were strict and liked to keep a close watch on everything I did. So, although I was in my early twenties, being an only child I obeyed their wishes. We all lived together in the old quarter of Vichy, in a pretty apartment from which we could see the River Allier from our sitting-room window."

"But what was Will's grandfather doing there?" Ghislaine said. "He was an Englishman, after all, and his country was at war with Germany."

"Ah! That's more complicated." Madeleine brushed away a fly from her face and fixed her gaze on me. "Henry was an artist who had no desire to fight a war, but he was also – how shall I say? – politically quite *engagé* in those days. He was an early admirer of National Socialism. I don't say that he necessarily supported Hitler and Goering and that gang, but I suppose he was what you would nowadays call Fascist in his political sentiments, and he regarded what was happening in Europe as the dawn of a new age, of a revolution that would sweep away all the corruption and restore the old, civilised values. I always thought it curious that an artist should hold such views, but . . ."

The old lady stopped and drew breath. She dabbed at her forehead with her handkerchief again, and sipped from the glass on the small wicker table beside her. I felt proud to think that I was her grandson.

"France – and you must know Henry was a francophile to his bones – was in a mess, he used to say, but between the Germans and the Maréchal they would get us out of it and rid us of the menace of Communism. I suppose he was what you might these days call a little anti-Semitic, too. Many people were at that time, including my own parents. I remember Henry's deep shock when he realised that his good friends, the Aragos – though that wasn't their real name – were Jewish. I don't say that he would ever have hurt or insulted a Jew intentionally, and he would certainly have been horrified by the terrible things that went on in Germany, but he blamed – as many of us did, one has to say – the misfortunes of what he called 'the civilised nations' on the *Israélites* and the Freemasons.

"The Maréchal thought along the same lines, particularly where the Masons were concerned. I can remember his very words on the wireless, even now: 'The Freemasons are our *bête noire*,' he said. 'A Jew is not responsible for his origins, whereas a Freemason becomes what he is by choice.'"

Madeleine turned away. There was a silence. Ghislaine raised her eyebrows and looked at me as if she were expecting me to respond to her mother.

"Are you shocked, Will, by these revelations?" she said.

"I must admit, I am a bit confused," I said. 'I had assumed that my grandfather loved France and I knew he had been an artist, but I had no idea he was a Nazi sympathiser. So he really was the black sheep of the family..."

Madeleine held out her hands, palms upwards, and shrugged.

"You know, we cannot be held responsible for the relatives the good God gives us, can we? And, I must tell you, he was not an evil man. Far from it."

Ghislaine had got up from her chair while her mother was speaking, and she walked over to a potted plant and pinched off some dead heads with her nails. Madeleine adjusted her spectacles.

"Poor, dear Henry! But we didn't fall in love immediately. He cut a very romantic figure, of course, and I was dazzled by his charm and good manners that evening in the gallery, but it was no *coup de foudre*, no love at first sight, by any means. In fact, I don't believe we so much as set eyes on one another again until the following year. That was at the Grand Casino at Vichy. It must have been in late April, because I had been asked to sing at an afternoon gala organised for the Maréchal's birthday. Tino Rossi was there, I remember – you could not switch on the wireless in those days without hearing that tenor voice of his – and a group of children from the local *lycée* came to sing '*Maréchal, nous voilà*', which was a sort of Vichy anthem in honour of the old man. And then there was an orchestra playing 'Ramona', and some schmaltzy German tunes too, because Abetz had arrived. Does the name mean anything to you? Otto Abetz? He was the German ambassador to Paris, and a man we were to come across from time to time."

Madeleine sighed and shook her head. There was a far-away expression in her eyes as she mined these images from her memory.

"Anyway, after the entertainment, there was a cocktail party, a *vin d'honneur*, and we were supposed to mix with the guests. I went to join my parents, who were in conversation with a man who had his back to me, and when he turned around, I realised it was Henry. Papa tried to introduce us, I remember, and we both said simultaneously: 'But we've already met.' He looked just the same, and it seemed to me that his French had improved enormously. Well, he was almost fluent, with just a hint of the Midi accent that he had acquired – deliberately, I used to think – in Collioure. He was so handsome with his fair, Anglo-Saxon looks and his dark suit. And, to my astonishment, he was wearing the *francisque* in his buttonhole."

"What's a *francisque*?" said Ghislaine, who had changed places and sat with her face raised to the pale sun that shone through the conservatory window.

"It was the emblem of Vichy. A double-headed axe crossed with a marshal's baton. People wore it as a brooch or on the lapel. You were given one for loyal service to the regime. It was then, of course, that it first dawned on me that Henry was temperamentally a *pétainiste*. Well, he must have been, because later on he was rewarded for his support with French naturalisation papers. A personal gift of the Maréchal. I never really knew quite how he obtained them, but they enabled him to stay in France. He must have been the only Englishman ever to be honoured in that way. You see, Henry always knew the right people."

The old woman's voice trailed off and, for a few seconds, lost in her memories, she seemed to falter. Then she recovered herself and spoke with a new vigour.

"But all this was a long time ago, my dears, and I am jumping ahead. If it had not been for that letter and those packets arriving from Argentina out of the blue, I would never have allowed myself to dredge up these things. It's too painful . . . such a very different world – and such a sad one, it seems to me now. So sad, in fact, that in order to survive in 1946 I had to wipe the past completely from my mind and start life all over again. I cut myself off quite deliberately from any previous friendships or associations I had from those years, and I have to confess that I tried to obliterate Henry, and our baby, from my thoughts. It was the only way I could survive . . . By the time I married René – Ghislaine's father – I had begun life afresh. After the death of my parents in the early 1950s – my father never recovered from his brief imprisonment at the end of the war – we went to live in Algeria, where René took over the family farm, and I don't think I ever talked to anyone about my previous life or what France had endured during the war. I suppose we were unable to cope with what history had thrown at us, but that is no excuse. In the end, we have to confront ourselves. That is something it has taken until now for me to accept: we must all face up to our past, to our guilt – to our crimes, in some cases – or our existence on earth will have been meaningless. Before we are judged by God, we must judge ourselves. But it is something we do in the secrecy of our own hearts, not necessarily in public."

She covered her face with her hands and looked out at the sky before continuing.

"You know, I have been asking myself lately whether I would have chosen to live as I did were I to be given another chance, but the question is pointless. It has no sense. I am too old to contemplate what life might have been like had things been different."

Madeleine nodded to herself and seemed momentarily disconcerted. Then she reached down to the low table beside her and picked up two large brown envelopes, streaked with postal markings and Argentine postage stamps. These were Henry's "archives", she said.

"They are for you, my dear, if you can make sense of them, for you and Ghislaine, if either of you can be bothered to read them. Your generation will have to come to terms with all that we failed to do, but you are all so busy. I'll have them packed up for you to do with them whatsoever you will."

Then Madeleine rose to her feet and declared that she was going upstairs for her morning rest.

$$\infty$$

Ghislaine proposed we take the dog for a walk. The bright winter sunshine was too beautiful, she suggested, for us not to take some exercise. As we made our way briskly along a path bordering the shallow brook by the meadows that had been visible from the terrace, I asked about her mother's life immediately after the war.

"That part of her life she was describing just now was always a bit of a mystery. All that business about Vichy and the Maréchal, and her meeting Henry, is more or less new to me, too. Of course, I knew she had been a singer – by the way, I keep meaning to play you *À nos amours*" – and I knew that she had had a certain amount of success. I've seen pictures of her at the time, too. She was very pretty. But those years from the end of the war until the time she married Papa were somehow always veiled in secrecy. Haven't you noticed how so many people – in France at least – avoid discussing the war and the aftermath? There's a sense of shame at the gradual realisation that so many of their compatriots were collaborators in one way or another, though you can't always blame them. As I said yesterday, what would our generation have done in similar circumstances?"

"I never stop to ask myself such questions."

Ghislaine glanced at me. Then she shrugged and stooped to pick up a stick for Madeleine's spaniel prancing about at her feet. It was the first time I had noticed she was left-handed.

"*Vas-y*, Ariel," she called, and the dog lolloped off into the fields, its ears flapping.

"Anyway," Ghislaine said, "it was only when I was virtually grown up that I discovered Maman had been married before and had had a child called Theo. That was when I heard about Henry for the first time. I was about sixteen, and I was quite excited to think that somewhere in South America I had an older English half-brother. That was the reason, I suppose, why British History became my degree subject at the Sorbonne later. Relations are important if you're an only child. Even if you don't actually know them, you can imagine them, fantasise over them. The fact that they exist is a sort of comfort, a security."

I stooped to pick up another stick to throw for Ariel. Ghislaine walked ahead of me, her hands tucked into the pockets of her jeans, her hips swaying delicately. In Paris her elegant insouciance had seemed to make her unattainable, but here, in the sunshine, in these frosty Breton meadows, I thought of her differently. Supposing she had not been my cousin, I wondered, or my aunt, in fact, but I quickly dismissed such thoughts.

"Tell me more about your father?" I said.

"Well, Papa was killed in Algeria in 1961, so I scarcely knew him. René was his name. He was a tall, striking man as you can see from Maman's photographs of him; dark and olive-skinned. A typical *colon* of that period, I'm told. I take after my mother physically, as you must have noticed, and, to tell you the truth, I sometimes used to ask myself whether he really *was* my father . . . He had served in the Navy during the war and he was accustomed to being obeyed. He was one of the survivors of the Mers-el-Kébir disaster, when your Royal Navy destroyed the French fleet as it lay at anchor. It was one of the reasons my father could never abide the British. Can you imagine? Having residual feelings about your wife's former lover *and* recalling that appalling incident . . ."

Ghislaine stopped and looked up at me.

"Did you know about that terrible tragedy? I don't suppose that they include it among the heroic exploits of the Second World War in history lessons in your schools," she said with an ironic laugh.

I had, in fact, read about the British naval action in July 1940 that had destroyed a greater part of the undefended French fleet in the Algerian port and caused the death of hundreds of French sailors. The desperate rationale, from Churchill's point of view, was that the alternative meant risking these powerful ships falling into German hands. It must have been a horrific decision to have to take. An ultimatum was delivered, the French refused to hand over their ships, the Royal Navy fired salvoes and, in the aftermath, hundreds of red pom-poms were left floating on the surface of the bay that day, and many sailors perished. How, indeed, could Anglo-French relations ever recover after such a hostile action? It was scarcely surprising that although many of that generation of French men and women revered Britain for helping to liberate them, others would mistrust us for ever because of what happened at Mers-el-Kébir.

I shook my head. "Infection and the hand of war," I murmured.

Ghislaine looked at me. "What do you mean?"

"Nothing. Just some words from Shakespeare that came into my head. They're from John of Gaunt's great patriotic speech in *Richard II*."

A gust of wind blew up from the banks of the estuary a short distance away and ruffled Ghislaine's hair.

"Actually it's no wonder that we think of you as *la perfide Albion*, is it?" she said after a while. "And it's why we French have never felt able to trust you."

"I know," I said. "I feel guilty myself in retrospect. Though imagine if the French fleet had fallen into enemy hands. History might have been different. Besides, we might never have met."

Ghislaine glanced at me quizzically and smiled.

"Well, back to our sheep . . . As I was telling you, Papa was a *pied noir*," Ghislaine said. "And so am I, I guess. I was born in Algeria, after all. He and Maman were married in 1958 and after their honeymoon they settled down on the farm that had belonged to Papa's family. It was his second marriage. I think they had quite a happy life for the few years they were together – a sort of French equivalent of the colonial life you read about in Somerset Maugham stories . . . I was born shortly after they were married, just when the Algerian troubles began. The rest you know. I don't remember much about my early childhood, but they must have been difficult years for my mother."

"I wonder how she coped, alone with a small child."

"I can't imagine, but that generation had courage, whatever else. They had real problems to confront, unlike us. Maman sentimentalises it all a bit now. She sometimes speaks about the Arab servants and how loyal and kind they had been, and I think she genuinely loved that immense Algerian landscape."

"All I know about Algeria comes from Camus," I said, remembering the French novelist's rich and sensual descriptions of his homeland in his early essays.

"Of course! He catches that world like no-one else,"

Ghislaine agreed. "That sense he creates of the vastness of the sky and the majesty of the sea, and the burning sunlight. He's one of my heroes."

We had stopped walking and were leaning against a gate that opened onto a field. Ghislaine bent once more to pick up the stick that Ariel had laid at her feet, tossed it in the air and watched as the indefatigable spaniel scampered after it.

"So after Papa was killed," she said, "and all the interminable police investigations and legal business were over, and the farm had been taken over by the government, Maman came back to France. But after a few months in Paris, she returned here, as any good Breton woman would, to the family home. Her parents were no longer alive, but her aunt, Tante Catherine, still lived here then. If Maman was going to be a widow – twice widowed, I suppose – she wanted to spend the rest of her days among her own people, in her own *patelin*, as we say. And, to cut a long story short, apart from the occasional visit to Paris to see friends, this is where she has lived ever since."

After we returned from our walk, Ghislaine took me into the salon where we had sat the previous evening and put on the old record of Madeleine's song "*À nos amours*". The embers of a fire burned in the grate and I sank into the depths of a large, soft armchair and watched Ghislaine. She carefully took out the 78 r.p.m. record from its paper sleeve. It had a mauve Pathé label, I remember, with a motif of a crowing cockerel, and underneath: "*À NOS AMOURS, chanté par Madeleine Lambert, avec l'orchestre de Georges Vitoux*". Then she wound up the ancient gramophone, which bore the trademark *Le Voix de son maître* on its lid and the label beneath it depicted a fox terrier peering into the trumpet horn of an even earlier sound reproduction machine. The record was scratched and Madeleine's voice was high-pitched and thin though, to my ears, very seductive. The bitter-sweet little song told of a girl's last night with her soldier lover before he departed for the war, and for me it was suffused with a retrospective nostalgia, evoking a period in European history that seemed immensely distant. What had been the point of those wars, I pondered, as Madeleine's quavering, almost childlike voice echoed through the gramophone's tinny sound-box, those all-enveloping con-flagrations that had divided Europe, set nation against nation and destroyed so many millions of lives? In what cause, and in whose name, had those young men been sacrificed, killed or maimed, their families' lives destroyed, their peace and harmony distorted for ever, their expectations shattered, their hearts broken? Had their deaths in themselves determined the course of history? Did it matter any longer that this old woman, living out her days with such dignity in a corner of Brittany, whose voice was so redolent of a particular time and place, should have happened to side with Vichy? Did it change anything?

I looked around the room and my gaze fell on a portrait of a young woman with light-brown hair, wearing a calf-length blue dress. A glance was enough to tell me that the girl was Madeleine when young: my grandmother, as I was now determined to think of her, the mother of my dead father, the child she had not set eyes upon after 1945.

I could sense Ghislaine watching me as her mother's little song reached its poignant conclusion. The needle continued to whirr against the crackling bakelite seams of the record. She stood up, switched off the gramophone and nodded towards the painting.

"That's Maman at the age she must have been when she first sang this song. The melody always has an effect on me whenever I hear it. I try to analyse what makes it so appealing, but it's impossible. We can never really make sense of the past, can we, Will?'

Before we left to return to Paris on Sunday, Madeleine presented us with the two packets that Henry had forwarded from Buenos Aires and which she had put into a folder.

"And you must take this letter he wrote to me, Ghislaine," Madeleine said, pressing a blue-and-red-edged airmail envelope into her daughter's hand, "He only ever wrote one other letter to me."

We went to the kitchen to say goodbye to Jeanne, who had prepared a packed lunch for our journey. She hobbled out to accompany us to the drive where Madeleine was waiting by the car. The old woman embraced her daughter tenderly and it seemed to me that there was a particular warmth and intensity in the way she also clasped me in her arms.

"Come back and see us again, William. Your visit has helped exorcise some of my ghosts. It has been good for us to have you here . . ." Her voice trailed off. Then she turned and walked up the steps to her front door. Jeanne, in her black dress, stood beside her and both women waved as we drove off.

Two hours later, not far from Mortagne, we turned off the main road. We passed through a small village. Its one café was closed, but opposite was an apparently derelict small

Romanesque church. The carved figure of a medieval saint – mitred, so perhaps a local bishop – rose above the porch, his arms spread wide, as if blessing all who entered. In front of the gates to the churchyard stood a war memorial: two *poilus* – First World War soldiers – stood back to back, they wore helmets and their heads were lowered, their hands clasped over the rifles they held out in front of them. Above, there soared the carved figure of an angel, its wings half extended, the finger of its left hand pointing heavenwards, while the palm of the right hand was held in blessing over the bowed heads of the soldiers. Above the columns of names on the plinth, in large letters, were the words: À NOS ENFANTS.

Ghislaine and I walked into the little church, sat down on a pew at the back and set out what Jeanne had packed for us: baguettes with paté and salad, a bottle of cider and two glasses, and some fruit. There was a chill in the afternoon air. After a few minutes, Ghislaine reached for the deep leather bag that she carried with her and drew out the envelope containing Henry's letter.

"Will," she said, patting my hand, "I think we should read this together before we reach Paris and before you go back to London. It may help make sense of the contents of the packets Henry wanted sent to Maman. Do you mind if I read it to you?"

I nodded. Though I was unable to focus initially on what Ghislaine was actually saying, at the same time I felt I could listen to her voice for ever.

"It's in French, and it's dated 28 September," she said. "Henry gives his address as Arenales 2484, Buenos Aires. This is what he wrote:

Madeleine –

How very strange it feels to be writing to you and to be using French after so very many years apart . . . You will certainly be astonished to receive news of me, and I fear you may find what I write distressing. But when I tell you that I believe I have very little time left to me, I hope you will understand and may be able to begin to forgive me for the pain I once caused you. Late in the day, I feel I must write and try to wipe the slate clean, impossible though that may now be.

I will not ask your pardon for my unpardonable silence. I deserve your contempt for not returning to you and to Europe, just as I do for my cowardly behaviour in 1945. I do not beg for your compassion; there seems little point – the greater part of my life has been spent in regretting – but I want you to know that throughout the long years since we embraced and clung to one another at that railway station in Copenhagen more than fifty years ago, scarcely a day has passed without my thinking of you. All I do ask is that you should understand why I should want to entrust certain material, which for some reason I cannot bring myself to destroy, to you, rather than to anyone else, before I depart this life.

The fact is, this must be something of a death-bed confession, for I have a heart condition and the medics say it's inoperable. "You could live for another year, or you could go tomorrow," Bouteillier, an old friend – he's a doctor who grew up in the Auvergne and who arrived in B.A. as a child, a few months after I did, in 1946 – told me when I asked him to be honest with me. He's a good man, considerably younger than me, of course, but one of the few who knows about my situation and whom I can trust. It may not surprise you to know that I do not fear death. It never frightened me, not even in '44 and '45.

Where to begin? With these packets, which you may receive simultaneously – posthumously perhaps? – I suppose. I am inflicting them on you because they relate in part to the years we spent together and to a time when, for better or worse, and despite the increasing horrors of the final months, we lived for each other. There have been other women in my life since then, but you are the only person whom I could, and did, marry. I do believe, my darling, that if there had not been a war and had I not felt impelled to flee Europe in 1945, we might have lived a conventional life as husband and wife and brought up our little Theo ourselves.

I also consider that I might have become better known as an artist had I remained in Europe. It is true that I have had a certain following here in Argentina, where there are a few collectors of my work. And my exhibitions have generally been well received, as you'll see if you should ever look at the file of cuttings included with these papers and journals. In my heyday, I was known in B.A. as "*el expresionista inglés*", which is ironic when you consider that I arrived here with a French passport. However, with a name like Henry Latymer you cannot avoid people assuming that you are a member of the large Anglo-Argentine community here. Only the other day, at the Belgrano Club, I was asked whether I was a descendant of the English Protestant martyr. When I explain that I was a Frenchman until I took Argentine citizenship in 1952, that I am a Catholic, and yet I was born and educated in England, they look thoroughly bemused. The other night I was writing in my diary – I still keep one – and calculated that I have spent twenty-eight years of my life as an Englishman, ten as a Frenchman and the remainder as a citizen of la Republica Argentina . . .

I am rambling, but I feel the time has come for me to try to settle my accounts – "*faire table rase*", as you said we should do with our lives when we left each other on that bleak morning in Copenhagen, and you boarded the train for Paris. I shall never forget your frightened face at the carriage window . . . your tears . . . your baby held in my arms . . . our promises all those years ago. Believe me, all I ever wanted to do then was to return to you.

Of course, we never could have begun again – not after all we had been through – and it's only now, as the twilight fades, that I realise the slate can never truly be wiped clean either. "What's gone, and what's past help, Should be past grief," Shakespeare says, but memories come back to haunt me in a way I never thought likely, and in the last months I have experienced such mental torture that I have returned to the faith I relinquished so recklessly when I left Europe. I have even begun attending daily Mass. One Saturday in May last year, I walked into the cathedral on the Plaza de Mayo here. Scaffolding was being erected and hundreds of pale-blue and white Argentine flags fluttered in the breeze, in preparation for the great national feast day on the 25th of the month. I knelt in front of the high altar, and I must have remained there for half an hour, my mind blank, unable to pray or register a coherent thought, when I noticed a young priest walking towards me. He looked no more than a boy, handsome, angelic and with a true innocence about him, or so it seemed to me. He smiled as he walked past. He opened the door to a confessional box, kissed the stole which he placed around his neck, and closed the door behind him. Something within me, some atavistic urge, made me follow him, and I knelt down inside that box, in the darkness, unable to make out the features of the shadowy figure behind the wire-mesh partition. Struggling for the words, I confessed my entire life: the treachery, the deceits, the wrong turnings, the lies, the inadequacies, everything . . . How could any priest, let alone this cherub, give absolution for the sins of a lifetime? I struggled through the words of the Act of Contrition, that formula I learned by heart during my schooldays, and somehow, like pebbles scattered over the strands of memory, the words poured out. Since that time, I have felt comforted – consoled even. "I can give you absolution, but only God can judge us, my son," the priest said. "Go in peace. Beg for His infinite mercy. Pray for me as I shall pray for you." Since then, I have come back regularly and talked to him; prayed for him too. He's surprisingly wise for someone so young. Two weeks ago I told him I was ill and close to the end. He asked me to leave my address and telephone number at the presbytery and said he would give me the last rites when the moment came. I feel it cannot be long in coming.

I have given away the little I have. The paintings that

remain I have bequeathed to Rosita to sell. She needs the money. She has been a combination of housekeeper, mistress and companion to me ever since I found her – picked her up, actually, for she was a *fille de joie*, a poor peasant girl from Entre Ríos province – outside the tea rooms in Calle Florida in 1950. She is now a respectable, seventy-year-old married woman, leading her middle-class life, but she still looks after me. I sometimes think of her as my creation – providing for her may have been the only good deed I have ever done.

Did you know that my sister Lavinia, the last of my English family known to me and the last link with the land of my birth, died two years ago? I can never forget how much I am indebted to her for bringing up our little Theo. Whenever I could afford to do so – if I sold a painting, for example – I would send her a little money towards the boy's school fees and, with Lavinia's consent, I wrote to him for his fourteenth birthday. He had been sent to a public school, the same stern institution that I endured for five years. I never had a reply, but this was many years ago, and how can I blame the boy for anything? He grew up and married, and he makes his living as a musician, so Lavinia told me in her last letter. He and his wife have a son, who is also a musician. (Where does this musical strain stem from? From you, Madeleine, if anyone.) But I have no idea what has become of him.

And that is all I know. Lavinia and I corresponded intermittently; she was the only member of my family I have ever loved, and my lifeline to England. Of those former friends whom we knew in France and Germany only Sylvain keeps in touch. He has lived in a flat off boulevard Saint-Germain ever since he was repatriated and where, he told me, you sometimes visit him. One of his devoted young men looks after him, and he is still writing novels at the age of ninety. It was through him that I heard about you marrying again, as well as the tragedy of your husband's death in Algeria. I should have written at the time, forgive me.

Of Robert Worcester, the American friend from my days in Paris – you never met him, sadly! – I have not heard a word, but there is one other old friend who has been a source of consolation these past years, and that is Marie-Hélène. You never knew her either, but I must have spoken of her . . . We met when I first came to Paris to paint, and I would take her out from time to time, though our relationship was never as close as I wished it to be. She and her parents arrived in Argentina in 1947, like so many Europeans, and she soon met and married the son of a wealthy Russian émigré family who have an estancia out in "the camp", as we Anglos say, about three hundred miles south of B.A. I have valued her friendship more than I can say.

I hope you will understand why I want to send you my diaries – the ones I kept in Paris, in Bellerive and at Sigmaringen all those years ago – some letters and sketches, and other ephemera. I have simply thrown everything together. Do with them what you will, or destroy them. I cannot expect Theo to want them, but perhaps his family may. If you do not wish to be reminded of those days, perhaps your daughter will be interested. I know you have one, for Sylvain kindly sent me a copy of her interview with the English novelist Graham Greene in a French weekly. You will find it among these papers, with my jottings. I once met Greene myself, here in B.A., with his friend Victoria Ocampo. He was an enigmatic, but attractive man. I recall his tall, hunched figure, his easy laugh and a certain haunted expression about his misty eyes. Victoria had brought him as her guest to the opening of an exhibition I once shared with the Argentine painter Juan Pablo Castel (a man who was later arrested for murder) at a gallery in Lavalle. Afterwards, she invited us all to eat a *bife de lomo* at Pedemonte, for she did not want Greene to leave the country without sampling the very best Argentine steak. He was diffident, witty and extremely courteous, but I thought his mind was probably elsewhere.

But I ramble again, my dearest. It is as if in the course of a single letter I want to acquaint you with all that has happened to me in the years since I wrote to you last in 1945. How fond and foolish I have become! Do you ever wonder how our lives might have been spent? I do. I firmly believe that had there been no war we would never have been separated. I was young and lily-livered in those days, politically naive, too. I do not think I would make the same mistakes again. The Europe I dreamed of then was a romantic and dangerous delusion.

As I write, I have a sudden and vivid mental picture of those days and of that first afternoon when we recognised each other in the Casino in Vichy. Do you remember?

There was some sort of celebration for the Maréchal, and you were there, on your father's arm, dressed in yellow and looking so innocent and lovely. I think you may have sung, too.

"Poor Europe! Poor France! Poor us!" I mutter to myself, and then I have to pull myself together, for I know I am lapsing into sentimentality. Is it pointless to live in the past as I so often do these days? I cannot tell anymore, but I like to think that you may understand.

And now I must say farewell, dearest Madeleine. Rosita is coming at any moment to help gather up these papers and I shall give her this letter to accompany them. And with that, *je tire ma reverence*, as Jean Sablon sang on the old gramophone record I still play.

On my knees, I remain,

    your ever-devoted Henry.

∞

Ghislaine guided her little Peugeot through the returning crush of weekend traffic that had built up around Porte de Saint-Cloud, slipping through the solid, prosperous streets of Auteuil and up onto the Pont Mirabeau, where the Seine sparkled in the evening sunlight.

> *Sous le pont Mirabeau coule la Seine*
> *Et nos amours*
> *Faut-il que je m'en souvienne*
> *La joie venait toujours après la peine.*

Ghislaine spoke these lines of Apollinaire as we were crossing the river, her eyes seemed to gleam with intensity. It was the abiding image of her that I took back to London.

She dropped me at Port-Royal station and I took the R.E.R. line to the Gare du Nord, there to catch the train to London. I promised to telephone her the following weekend, once I had examined the contents of the packets from Argentina that we had divided between us. I did not tell her how much I was going to miss her.

[CHAPTER 3]

I FOUND I HAD SOME TIME TO SPARE BEFORE REHEARSALS
began for our next London concert. I decided to devote myself
to my grandfather's notebooks and diaries. Apart from anything
else, it was a way of extending my relationship with Ghislaine
and Madeleine.

Rather than quote verbatim from Henry's diaries, for the
purposes of this account I have edited them and interspersed
some of the entries with my own imagined reconstruction of
his life. I have based what I write on details gleaned from the
notebooks, press cuttings, letters from home and from a variety
of correspondents, scribbled memos, etc.

48 rue Gay-Lussac, Paris *5ème*
October 1939
Cheque and letter arrived from Jean A. today. I cashed
money at once and will at least be able to eat. God! this
vie d'artiste is a bit soul-destroying unless people actually
want to buy your work. I shall need more collectors like
Jean and his sister if I'm to survive, particularly if there
is going to be a war. Not that anything much seems to be

happening on that front. Jean writes from Bellerive that all the fuss will certainly be over by Christmas and I dare say he's right; no-one in their senses wants war. Went back to the Louvre after cashing cheque at bank and studied the Poussins; then I waited for Marie-Hélène at Café de Tournon, but she never arrived. I'm not going to let her distract me from my purpose though . . . Later, I walked in the Luxembourg for two hours. The trees are turning to gold and there's the first real nip of autumn in the air today. I stopped for a beer under the plane trees and read Prévert's poems, which everyone here seems to be talking about.

October 5, 1939
I had intended to write this new diary daily, but already I can see I'll not succeed. Everything is too confused and too uncertain. All I know is that I should remain in France, come what may. I shall stay here and paint, and work, and live life the way I want. In whatever way we can, we artists will help create a new Europe and a new future for my generation. We shall put an end to these squabbles between nations. On no account shall I return home – at least, not for some years – and if war does break out, which most sensible people seem to doubt, then I am NOT prepared to lay down my life for my country. Patriotism is for those who can no longer think for themselves – the last refuge of a scoundrel, as someone said.

I risk cutting myself off from my family, and Father would never forgive me for not "answering the call", as he puts it in his letter (opened by censors, I think) that arrived today. They don't appear to realise that I am twenty-four, an independent artist whose small talent is infinitely more likely to be recognised here in France than it ever would be in London. Nor can they appreciate that my political opinions differ from the comfortable, flabby illusions that prevail in middle-class Britain. My future has to lie here in Europe . . . in France.

Henry Latymer put down the spiral-bound school exercise book that served as his diary. He poured himself a glass of wine from the litre bottle he had bought at the Félix Potin shop around the corner, lit a cigarette and walked over to the window. It was six o'clock, and in the dimly lit street two storeys below, the shops were closing and Parisians were returning from their offices and jobs. He pulled open the tall glass-panelled doors that gave onto his tiny balcony. There was an autumnal chill in the air, and people had begun to revert to their winter clothing: hats or berets, long overcoats and scarves, and the occasional fur coat. Indeed, Henry had been surprised to notice Maria, the concierge who looked after all the flats and rooms in the building, wearing a luxurious light-brown fur muff as she set off last weekend, made up, bejewelled and exuding a sickly smelling scent, for her Saturday night at the pictures or "*ciné*", as she called it. The fur could have been mink, but was more probably fox.

"*Que vous êtes belle ce soir, Madame Gonzales!*" he had joked when he met her in the entrance hall, bowing in an exaggerated fashion and removing his beret with a dramatic flourish. She had giggled coquettishly and blushed. A little flattery, the occasional bunch of flowers, or a tip for her perpetually sullen Catalan husband, Javier – a Republican who had fled the civil war in Spain after being wounded at Teruel, and with whom he had political arguments in their respective forms of broken French – paid dividends whenever he had a favour to ask, or ran short of milk or butter after the shops had closed.

It was almost dark. The cars and the green and yellow buses had their headlights on and, over to the left, above the dome of the Val-de-Grâce hospital, the first of the stars were twinkling in the southern sky.

Henry closed the windows and wooden shutters, and drew the flimsy cotton curtains. Then he picked up the copy of *L'Ordre* that he had bought that morning, but not yet read. He skimmed the headlines: Europe had officially been at war since September that year, but you would be hard put to know it. "Frenchmen have no wish to die for Danzig," someone had said. It was a phrase he had often heard in recent weeks and he agreed wholeheartedly with whoever had said it – Paul Reynaud, or was it Marcel Déat?

He had tried to explain his way of thinking, his "political philosophy", as he had described it rather pompously in his letter home that week, though without much hope of either parent being capable of appreciating so unconventional a point of view. "Your mother and I are convinced," his father had written, "that war will soon envelop Europe again, just as it did in our own youth. Our world is once again in grave danger and we implore you to come home, for all our sakes. A state of war officially exists between Great Britain and Germany and young men of your age are being recruited everywhere. We refuse to believe that our own son will not answer the call. Indeed, you have a duty to do so . . ." etc., etc. They simply did not realise that their son's mind was made up. He was answerable to himself at last, obeying his instincts.

During the four months in which Henry had lived in Paris, he reckoned he had made more headway as an artist than in the whole of his two years at the Grosvenor School of Art. His ideas about colour, about the application of paint, about structure and form, were respected here, and he felt no shame or awkwardness in expressing himself, whereas in London he had always been constrained. And, as he kept saying, all he wanted to do in life was to paint.

Anyway, this so-called war, this *drôle de guerre*, as the newspapers and wireless commentators referred to it, seemed highly unlikely. The "spectre haunting Europe", to use another of his father's pet phrases, appeared to have its hollow eyes fixed firmly on Poland at the moment and showed little sign of wishing to use force against Great Britain or France. If there was anything to be alarmed about it was not National Socialism or Herr Adolf Hitler, but rather the Reds: Josef Stalin and his Komintern. Henry had said as much to Marie-Hélène when they had a drink the other night after watching a newsreel film showing German soldiers marching into Polish villages and rounding up peasants.

"Henry, you can't trust the Reds any more than you can trust that strutting little Austrian corporal," she had said, lighting her own cigarette with his and gazing at him with an enigmatic expression. "To my mind, they're as bad as each other. You may prefer the pan-German cultural heritage that Hitler represents – though I can't imagine that creature sitting through a cycle of Wagner's "Ring" or reading Thomas Mann without leaping to his feet and ranting every five minutes, can you? Stalin and he are both tyrants and megolamaniacs who lust for power and have no concern for their people. And besides, now that Messieurs Molotov and von Rippentrop have signed their wretched little non-aggression pact, who can you believe? They're all hypocrites and knaves. That's my view."

Marie-Hélène had tossed her hair from her forehead and fixed her eyes on Henry with an expression of amused defiance. She was the girl he had been pursuing in his dreams ever since he had summoned up the courage to approach her at a *vernissage* in a gallery in Montparnasse. Accustomed to English girls who were acquiescent and who listened to his theories without contradicting him or disagreeing with him, he was still, a month after meeting her, astonished by her sophistication and directness, as well as by her almost confrontational manner.

Laying aside his newspaper on top of his open diary, he stretched out on the divan that served as both sofa and bed and tried to construct a mental picture of how she had looked last night. Light almond eyes shaped like a cat's, a slender, slightly retroussé nose, high cheekbones, a wide, full mouth, and black, tumbling hair that framed a face whose complexion was paler than any he remembered painting. It was so pale, in fact, that he sometimes wondered if she might be anaemic.

Did she realise what a kick he got out of her; that she aroused and troubled him more than any girl had ever done before? How could she, another voice said, if he never allowed her to think so? He was absurdly timid, he admitted, and late last night, when he had accompanied her home, walking almost the length of rue de Vaugirard beneath a starlit sky that was designed for lovers, he had been on the point of trying to kiss her when she announced that she was late and that her parents would be worried. She embraced him hurriedly and was gone. Perhaps he was over-eager and a little premature in his expectations, he told himself, though his other voice urged him to seize the moment. There would still be one further opportunity in the days ahead for him to pour out his feelings, however, and he congratulated himself on his foresight in arranging to ask her to the theatre the following week. He had booked seats for Giraudoux's *Ondine*, which Louis Jouvet had directed and which had been praised by the critics. They would meet for an early supper at some nearby restaurant, and after the show he would propose a nightcap before walking her home.

∞

Henry Latymer had angered his parents and upset his devoted sister Lavinia when he left London for Paris in the late summer of 1939 to study at the École des Beaux-Arts on a part-time basis. He had also ignored the advice of his teachers at the Grosvenor School of Art.

His father, a retired colonel, lately of the Hampshire Regiment, who had fought at Vimy and the Menin Road before being wounded at Passchendaele in 1917, had always anticipated a military career for his son. Instead, at a time when young men of his age were recruiting for another war with Germany, he was "idling among effete artists and tarts" in Paris. Henry had reconciled himself to the fact that his failure to rally to the flag would mean he might remain a permanent outcast from the family, and in all probability he would be disinherited. Colonel Latymer, the scion of an old-established and proudly recusant family, was not a man to stand for recalcitrance, and the greatest sins in his eyes were laziness and lack of patriotism. The God of mercy and compassion did not seem to feature in his thoughts.

Henry's political leanings were not to the Left. He felt little sympathy with idealists like Orwell and the poets and writers who had set off to cross the Pyrenees in 1936 and 1937 to join the International Brigades in Spain; all his instincts in that desperately sad and bloody civil war had urged him to support the Nationalists, and he had secretly cheered their brave resistance in the besieged Alcázar in Toledo. Though rebellious in other respects, particularly where social convention and middle-class attitudes were concerned, Henry was drawn to the new political thinking, largely unfashionable among his contemporaries, he had first encountered in the stories and essays of Maurice Barrès, the first French writer he had ever read, lent to him while he was still at school.

He was closer emotionally to his mother, an altogether gentler and more subtle character. Her enthusiasm for the Pre-Raphaelite school had been responsible for his first interest in painting. Although untrained, she had become a sculptor, and her horses and greyhounds in motion were considered good enough to be included in exhibitions in several provincial galleries. Henry knew in his heart that his mother could not wholly disapprove of the step he had taken and he reckoned she might actually admire his resolution. "Let your imagination soar," she would say to him. "It's a true artist's right to free himself of the conventions of society." And yet her own upbringing, her sense of a woman's duty towards her husband and home, had made her incapable of living up to the maxims she preached to her son.

He had informed his family of his departure only the

evening before he was due to catch the boat train to Boulogne. He had waited until supper, by which time his sister Lavinia had returned and his father had driven home in his Alvis from the local preparatory school where, since his retirement from the army, he had worked as the bursar. Within minutes of the old boy saying grace and sitting down at table, Henry had announced his plans, whereupon his mother had turned pale and left the dining room without a word, Lavinia had burst into tears and his father, shaking visibly with rage, had done his utmost to force Henry to change his mind, even offering to repay the cost of the journey to Paris.

∞

The sound of a door slamming in the flat below roused Henry from his reverie. He poured himself another glass of wine, switched on his single-bar electric fire, and opened his newspaper again. The call-up was in full swing and there were brief reports of young men queuing at barracks and recruitment centres. A politician was forecasting peace in Europe once German troops had withdrawn from Prague and Warsaw, and on the leader page there was an editorial to the effect that France's Maginot Line, where General Gamelin had 106 French divisions, was "unpassable" and that, in any case, with the enemy's armies occupied mostly in Poland, they were at present confronted by a mere twenty-three German divisions. France's frontiers, the newspaper reminded its readers, were the most heavily fortified in Europe.

To fight, or not to fight, thought Henry, and he yawned. Only a few days ago, as he was setting off to the Beaux-Arts, the concierge's husband, Javier, who was sweeping the little courtyard below, had greeted him cheerily and asked him why he was not with the British troops in Belgium. "A young man of good family like you", he had said, and although he was joking, Henry thought he could detect a faint mockery in the remark.

∞

Two days later, Henry had written in his dairy:
October 7, 1939
Warsaw has capitulated. The voice of Hitler, speaking from the Reichstag, was broadcast on Radio Paris this morning: "Let those who consider war to be the best solution reject my outstretched hand." I reckon that the only way to understand this situation is to argue that Hitler has invaded Poland so as to stop the Russians getting there first.

Took the *métro* to Le Peletier to see whether Vollard's gallery in rue Laffitte might consider my work. Some of the carriages have actually been "fortified" as part of the preparations for war! At the gallery, I was shocked to discover that Ambroise V. had died following a motoring accident in the summer. The steering wheel of his car had suddenly seized up, the chauffeur braked, and a bronze by Maillol, thrown forward by the impact, had struck poor Vollard on the back of the neck. I was flabbergasted. What an absurd way to go! It seems only the other day that I saw him in a gallery decked up to look like some Middle-Eastern bazaar, and I can still recall his sphinx-like features and his kindly expression. Robert Worcester, a young American who helps out at the gallery, told me about Vollard's great friendship with artists such as Picasso, Cézanne, Bonnard and Maillol. Apparently, he was a creole, originally from Réunion. Various well-known artists have painted his portrait, as has Picasso. Robert told me that when they first knew each other Vollard refused to pay Picasso's train fare to Barcelona even though Picasso offered him two of his "blue period" works in exchange!

Robert, whom I like and who seems to know a lot about modern art and is keen to earn his living from it, promised to arrange for someone to look at my work. He also talked to me about the *vitalistes*, a group of painters and writers who held a banquet last week in a restaurant near the Odéon, presided over by Vlaminck (another of Vollard's artists). Apparently, they burned a portrait of Hitler in protest at the Führer's remarks about "degenerate" French artists! "As if Adolf Hitler, a former house painter, knows anything about art," scoffed Robert.

I told Robert about the occasion I was invited to the New Burlington Galleries this time last year to see Picasso's "Guernica", which Roland Penrose had brought to London. I did not tell him that the reason I was there was because we had arranged for a huge canvas by the Spanish artist Zuloaga, depicting the defenders of the Alcázar, to be displayed in another room. As a gesture, it was rather futile, for Picasso's work was extraordinarily powerful and the public took scarcely any notice of our propaganda efforts on behalf of the Nationalists.

Robert and I have agreed to meet again.

*

This was the first mention in my grandfather's diaries of Robert Worcester, the American in Paris who was to play an influential role in his life during the years Henry spent in France. I would meet him myself much later, during the course of my pursuit of Henry's past.

As autumn and the phony war dragged on, the pattern of Henry's existence in Paris became more settled. Encouraged by another new friend, Jean Arago, whom he had first come to know at the Beaux-Arts and who had just acquired a small gallery in Vichy, the fashionable spa town in the Auvergne, he produced a series of oil paintings – still lifes, townscapes and one or two portraits – which Jean promised to exhibit in his gallery over the Christmas holidays. Henry had planned to travel south in December to visit Collioure, the fishing port near the Spanish frontier but, much to his delight, along with a formal invitation to show his work in Vichy, there came a proposal that he should spend Christmas – and as long as he liked afterwards – at the house that Jean shared with his sister Chantal at Bellerive, on the opposite bank of the River Allier to Vichy, before returning to Paris.

"It will do us good to discuss France's woes with you," he wrote. "Besides, it will surely be beneficial to your peace of mind and your health to spend some time out of Paris and away from all the talk of war. You might even make some money and carve a modest reputation for yourself among our provincial art lovers. Can you manage another six or seven canvases?"

Arago had begun his final year at the École des Beaux-Arts in September 1939 when, within three weeks of the start of the new term, his sister had sent a telegram saying that their aunt, who had brought up Jean and Chantal after their own parents' death, had been taken ill and died in hospital in Clermont-Ferrand. He was obliged to return home to help Chantal run the gallery. With his dark, olive skin, his sharp features, his slender, chiselled nose and intelligent eyes, and his air of bearing the troubles of the universe on his slight, stooped shoulders, Jean immediately interested Henry and, within a few days of their first conversation, he had been taken under the older student's wing. After morning lectures they would meet at lunchtime in the vestibule, beneath the Roman torsos of Venus and Mars, before walking to the estaminet in rue Visconti for onion soup, bread and beer.

"*À nous deux*" Jean had said the first time they had done this, raising his glass of beer in a toast – "To the outsiders". But Henry had not liked to ask what he meant. For him it was enough to be accepted, to have made a friend and to be involved, whenever the two of them met, in conversation that Henry regarded as appropriate to the image he had of an art student in Paris.

Ten days later, according to his diary, at lunchtime on October 17, Henry set off to the Closerie des Lilas to meet Robert Worcester. The news from the front had been getting worse and, with the advent of grey skies after a succession of sun-filled autumn days, a mood of grim acceptance had settled over the city. For the first time in weeks, Henry felt unsure about whether he had made the right decision to remain in France.

Robert greeted him with a wave and stood up to embrace him as he approached the table by the window. Stocky, with sharp blue eyes and a shock of light-brown hair, Robert was evidently in a cheerful mood and, after ordering two coffees and a bottle of Vittel, he was soon elaborating on Europe's problems, making his political tendencies very clear in the process.

"I blame Blum and his Front Populaire for the mess this country's in. They've created a decadent and spiritually bankrupt society. Europe needs a strong man, Henry, if we're to return to the old values." He sighed and sipped his water. "You call this a Christian country after fifty years of rampant anti-clericalism? It's a joke. We need a guy like Francisco Franco. Look at what he's done with that pinko Azaña and the decadent Second Republic and all its woolly Marxist, idealistic nonsense! At a cost in human lives, I grant you. What we've got to do is restore moral order and self-belief, and if that means fighting, then I'm ready to do so, whether I'm a citizen of France or of the United States."

Henry made no comment. Robert's voice – an educated Princeton drawl – was loud, and when the tall, prematurely balding man sitting writing at the nearby table had glanced across at them, Henry wondered whether he had overheard everything that his new friend had been saying. There was a sinister aspect to the man's slightly bulging eyes, but also something alluring about his louche, decadent air and his nonchalant expression. A cigarette drooped from his lips as he wrote. Henry thought he looked distinctly ill.

Robert followed Henry's gaze. "That's the novelist Drieu ..." he said, lowering his voice, but Henry could not catch the rest of his name and did not like to display his ignorance to this cultured, urbane American.

"He used to work at *Ce Soir* with Aragon, a Commie poet who must be utterly flabbergasted at what Ribbentrop and Jo

Stalin are up to, carving up Europe between them," Robert said. "Of all the hypocritical . . ." He shook his head in feigned bewilderment.

"And your man Dieu, where does he stand politically?" Henry said.

"It's Drieu, not Dieu!" Robert laughed. "Pierre Drieu la Rochelle. He's to the extreme right, I guess. You should read his new novel *Gilles*. It's autobiographical and it speaks satirically on behalf of his generation of Frenchmen. It's about a young man who finds his salvation from the tedium of bourgeois life by setting off to fight for Franco. Drieu's reckoned to be a brilliant political thinker and he's a leading member of the P.P.F., the Parti Populaire Français, run by Jacques Doriot, a former fellow traveller who has seen the light, and who was once mayor of Saint-Denis. I reckon he's the right sort of man for our time. He believes that Fascism is the sole means of reducing the decadence that is taking root all over Europe, and he has a point, I'd say."

Henry could not help but be impressed by the ease with which Robert appeared to have assimilated French political and cultural life. He reminded him of a character in a short story by Ernest Hemingway he had once read; there was something of the frustrated man of action about him: the Ivy League man who yearned to cast off his academic veneer and step into the big ring of real life.

Later that afternoon, after they had digested what for Henry was a more substantial lunch than he was used to, he and Robert walked in the Jardin du Luxembourg. A breeze blew the newly fallen leaves in eddies over the ornamental flower beds, over the rippling waters of the pond and its fountain, and over the statues that adorned the pathways of the park. Mothers and nannies pushed perambulators or watched their children at play, while students ambled to and fro in earnest conversation or sat reading on chairs and benches. They stopped to inspect the statue of Delacroix, upon whose head a pigeon perched, while in the distance, from the far end of the terraced gardens, beneath the plane trees, a band could be heard playing a military march.

Before they parted that evening, Henry had suggested that Robert should join him and Marie-Hélène at the Théâtre de l'Athenée in ten days' time to see Giraudoux's *Ondine*; Robert agreed and said he would try to book a seat.

Half an hour later, as Henry entered the door into the little courtyard, Javier greeted him cheerily in his heavy Spanish accent.

"*Ça va les anglais?*" he enquired, handing Henry a letter, and then proceeded to inform him that, first of all, every flat in the building would shortly be issued with black curtains – "*c'est la blaquaoute, vous savez*" – and, secondly, that food rationing was now virtually certain and Henry should go home to England while he still could. "*Si j'étais vous . . .*", he continued somewhat impudently in his heavy Catalan accent. But you're not me, Henry thought as he climbed the staircase and, by the time he had reached his landing and unlocked his front door, he felt so subdued that he downed half of a large bottle of Postillon wine, piled three Mistinguett records one after the other onto the automatic feeder of his gramophone, and threw himself down on the divan where he tried to conjure up a visual image of Marie-Hélène's naked body.

When he woke, he opened his letter. It was from his mother.

There was little news in it apart from reports of a neighbour's husband, a naval officer, who was missing after the sinking of H.M.S. *Royal Oak* by a German U-boat that had broken into Scapa Flow – something he had not seen reported in the French press – and, on the domestic front, Lavinia was leaving her London flat to live in a village in Herefordshire where she would be safe from the air raids. Then there was, as always, the usual plea to return home by any means possible before it was too late.

Henry switched on the wireless. A woman with a softly appealing voice was crooning a wistful little melody:

> *Y a des cailloux sur toutes les routes,*
> *Sur toutes les routes y a du chagrin.*

Ten days later, Henry wrote in his dairy:

October 27, 1939
Mood of Paris gets grimmer by the day as people evacuate the city in their thousands. Perhaps there will be war after all. General Gamelin stated on the news yesterday that he had complete faith in the Maginot Line. Conversation overheard in a café this morning, one old boy saying to another: "After what this country has suffered in '*la guerre de quatorze*', she's too weary to contemplate another bloody confrontation with '*les boches*'."

Jean writes from Vichy: "I miss you, and I miss Paris, but we are working hard to make a go of this gallery. The late-autumn colours here fill me with melancholy. And so does the mood of France; the greys grow darker;

they will soon deepen to black, broken only by a few rays of light. And then what?"

Ondine was wise and witty, though a bit precious, I thought, and too full of literary allusions that neither Marie-Hélène nor I understood. Packed house; superb sets by Pavel Tchelitchev. Robert came too, but was obliged to sit in the more expensive dress circle, the only ticket he could get. He was much more enthusiastic about the play than either of us, but I sense he's more au fait with literary/cultural life here, and he appears to have seen every show that's worth seeing in Paris. After the play, we went to have a drink at a café near the Madeleine, and I could tell from the look in her marvellous dark eyes that Marie-Hélène was not especially impressed by Robert. He was showing off, but perhaps he felt ill at ease with a woman present? (Is Robert interested in women?) It was nearly midnight before I took M.-H. back by taxi to her parents' flat. "I would invite you in, but . . ." she said, half opening the front door and putting her finger to her lips to indicate that her parents were asleep. She kissed me on each cheek and told me I was "*adorable*" to have taken her to the theatre. Then she said goodbye with "*à bientôt, alors*", which gives me hope. I think I may be in love with her . . .

I decided to compensate for the expensive taxi fare by walking home. My route took me through Auteuil to the river, then over the Pont Mirabeau where I stopped and watched the reflection of the stars in the dark pools of eddying waters. Soon the sky clouded over and it started to drizzle. I had no mackintosh, but I didn't mind getting soaked. The city seemed deserted, even forbidding, as I walked up to place Cambronne, then across to Montparnasse, past La Coupole, down those narrow, dark streets that run alongside the dome of the Val-de-Grâce, and then home. It was nearly 3.00 a.m.

Even so, I could not sleep. I read a copy of *Le Petit Parisien* that someone had left on the shelf by the main door. There's talk of Maréchal Pétain being asked to join the cabinet, which is cheering. He may be an antique, but he stands for civilised French values. Pierre Laval is quoted as saying that Pétain would serve as "a mantelpiece, a statue on a pedestal. His name! His prestige! Nothing more."

∞

There were clearly a number of anxieties that exercised Henry Latymer during the weeks before he set off for Collioure and the Mediterranean ("for a change of mood, a challenge, some risks, some decent air, and – above all – to PAINT," he wrote in his diary) at the end of the first week in December.

Firstly, his work. If he was to fulfil his obligation to Jean, he needed to paint at full stretch to provide a sufficient number of canvases to merit a one-man exhibition in Vichy over Christmas. As a result, he painted whenever he could, attended scarcely any of the lectures at the Beaux-Arts, and saw no-one apart from Robert and Marie-Hélène. He wandered through Paris with his sketchbook, paints and easel, choosing scenes and buildings that inspired him for one reason or another: the figures of two angels on a doorway at the church of Saint-Thomas-d'Aquin, for example, the fountains in place Saint-Sulpice, the Château de Madrid in the Bois de Boulogne, the scornful expression of the huge white owl in its cage and a pair of mangy wolves in the Jardin des Plantes, groups of children playing in the Tuileries.

Secondly, he was concerned about having his papers in order; this meant several visits to the *mairie* of the *5ème arrondissement* in front of the Panthéon to procure the necessary renewal of his residence permit. This was not automatic, as had formerly been the case. Ever since war had been declared, the authorities had tightened up on the procedure for issuing the documents that were needed by a foreign national in France, and after a further six-month period of residence he would be required to apply for French citizenship or risk being deported.

And thirdly, he could not rid himself of the image of Marie-Hélène. Not that he wanted to; it was just that the thought of her not realising how he felt about her was almost physically painful. He tortured himself with jealousy whenever he tried to visualise her in a variety of situations: in a restaurant with some coolly attentive, ultra-sophisticated Parisian escort; playing tennis in the Bois, her limbs flexed, her body svelte, sensual and lithe; or sprawled provocatively in the grass beneath the shade of the plane trees in the Luxembourg. Mostly, he liked to imagine her in his own bed, lying on her side, propped up on one elbow, and naked, of course, her eyes closed, her black hair strewn over her sun-tanned shoulders. Or else he fantasised about her travelling with him to Collioure, he having plucked up the courage to admit that he loved her more than she could possibly know, and she melting into his arms and agreeing to follow him anywhere.

But such delusions were pointless as well as painful and he

knew that he would have to declare himself and find a way of confessing his feelings to her in a forthright manner if he were to make any progress. Instinctively, he began humming a snatch from whatever Gilbert & Sullivan opera it was that the hackneyed old line, "Faint heart never won fair lady", remembered from visits to the D'Oyly Carte during Christmas holidays from school, had come from.

He shuddered at the thought of Gilbert & Sullivan. What would the French make of such sentimental nonsense, of all that pretty, insubstantial, passionless jollity? "Iolanthe"? "Ruddigore"? The mere thought was anathema here in Paris. It was the abiding image of suburban cosiness conjured up by those Savoy operas, by hallowed old nineteenth-century paintings such as "The Light of the World" and "The Boyhood of Raleigh" and by stiff Victorian moralists like Charles Kingsley, from which he yearned to escape. The thought of that safe and secure, bloodless and phlegmatic England, with its tidy lawns, its cricket matches on village greens, its Morris dancers, and Punch and Judy shows on the promenade, and its Royal Academy Summer exhibitions, suffocated him, and it was only when he felt the cool, liberating wind from the French coast, as he had done when he stood alone on deck the day he caught the cross-channel ferry, that for the first time in his adult life, he had felt truly alive and free.

∞

November 10, 1939
Robert arrived at 12.30 and we lunched at the Dôme before spending the afternoon in the Luxembourg. Trees still tinted with autumnal reds and golds, and the smell of

bonfires in the air as we kicked through the dead leaves. Later, we were sitting on a bench by the Médicis fountain, when a man shuffled up and asked whether he might join us. He looked about sixty, but can only have been in his forties. He began telling us about how he had fought at Verdun and never wanted to see war again. Nowadays he had a comfortable life, he had worked hard to buy his apartment in rue de l'Égalité, and all he asked was the freedom to do what he loved: a little fishing at weekends on the canal, the occasional outing with his wife in their motorcycle and side-car, and being with his children. "France has had enough, Messieurs. We are too tired to fight any more", he said. Then, as suddenly as he had come, he stood up, doffed his hat and departed, saying: "May God go with you."

Switched on the wireless back in my room and heard reports of an attempt on Adolf Hitler's life – a bomb exploded in a restaurant only minutes after he had left. Communist sympathisers are suspected.

Friday, ?
Half Paris seems either to be mobilising or leaving the city – there are even fewer students. Today, I took my sketchbook with me to the Jardin des Plantes. Caught the *métro* to Gare d'Austerlitz, where the station was teeming with soldiers in uniform, off to join their regiments, and with Parisians migrating south.

No communication from M.-H.

Yesterday evening, I stood on the Pont Neuf and gazed down on the rushing waters, rolling seawards as they have done for centuries. It was windy, and the dead leaves were cascading off the trees. The city looks proud and beautiful, yet also, today, vulnerable; an image came to mind of a fashionable lady, dressed by Chanel, who, having fallen on hard times and been brutally used by life, had resigned herself to an existence of servitude and penury. Robert says I'm a sentimentalist and that if the Germans do come, Parisians will cope, and that it may all be for the better ultimately. I sketched the view of the river, looking west towards Île de la Cité, gave a few centimes to the beggarwoman I've seen before, standing by the entrance to the Jardin des Plantes, and then walked over to visit the animals whose cages border the far side of the gardens. My friend the white owl sat motionless on his perch, as he does day in and day out, blinking and surveying the whirligig that parades about him with a disdainful air. I don't believe he has ever stirred in all the visits I have made here. Next door is the pathetic spectacle of the pair of wolves, "bred in Pomerania", the notice attached to their cages reads, with their bedraggled, moth-eaten fur, loping ceaselessly up and down, like defeated soldiers returning home. They look decidedly menacing and would wreak havoc, I dare say, if they should ever break out of their confine. I sat and tried to study them, remembering Mrs Dent's anatomy classes at the Grosvenor, hoping to capture something of their raw wildness, those half-bared jaws, the unnerving expression of total blankness in their yellow eyes . . .

In the gardens, a sailor and a young army officer were sitting on a park bench, a very pretty girl in a red dress, with a fringe and black curls, squeezed in between them. A drama in miniature was developing, for the girl seemed to be paying more attention to the sailor, while the army officer, I surmised, was gradually becoming resigned to rejection.

After an hour or so sketching and then skimming through the Penguin Lavinia sent me – *Black Mischief* by Evelyn Waugh – I took a rather indirect route home: along the Seine, up rue du Cardinal Lemoine, past the Lycée Henri IV and the Panthéon, and then home. At one point, two elderly men, both dressed in elegant pin-striped suits, stepped out from a porte-cochère as I walked past. One was saying to the other: "Remember this, cher ami. France possesses two great men, Philippe Pétain and Charles Maurras. If Pétain were to come to power, he would crown the thought of Maurras. He would stir up this dream-locked bourgeoisie too and make us a proud nation once more." Words to that effect . . . Music to the ears of those like Robert, I imagine.

Maria, the concierge, tells me that eggs are now scarce, so I cooked myself an omelette while I still have some. She was sweeping the courtyard when I returned. As soon as she saw me, she scurried indoors and emerged with my post. "*La vie sera dure, vous savez, Monsieur Henri*," she informed me before advising me to stock up at the Félix Potin shop while I still can.

Charles Trenet is singing "*Je chante*" – "*jour et matin, je chante*" – on a wireless in one of the apartments below mine. Can't say many people are singing here. The song makes me long for fresh air and the countryside, but

I'll have enough sea air at Collioure very soon, and the freedom to roam at will.

A card, at last, from Marie-Hélène. She and her parents are leaving Paris – "temporarily, at least". She gave me their new address in Aix-en-Provence, "should you ever find yourself in the region". I felt desolate and am still numbed by the thought that I may not see her again if war becomes a reality. There was a letter from England too: Ma's writing, but clearly opened and inspected by the censors. She implores me to come home and join up: "For the last time, and for the sake of your family if not for your country. Every young man of your age is taking this war very seriously and I beg you, darling, to reconsider your plans."

What she doesn't seem to realise is that it's too late. If I caught the ferry from Boulogne, I'd be arrested instantly for desertion the moment I set foot in Folkestone.

∞

My grandfather's diaries were inscribed in a neat, careful and somewhat self-conscious copper-plate hand in foolscap exercise books and were interspersed with the occasional scribbled aide-memoire, address or telephone number (e.g. Marie-Hélène: JASmin 4206), and the odd sketch, such as those of the owl and the wolves. They are very much the jottings of a politically naive young man and someone who is in love with his own idea of France. Patriotism appears to mean nothing to him, and he is happy to have escaped from the uninspiring world of his middle-class parents. I have been to look, but I can find no record of his student work at the Grosvenor; the art school itself no longer exists, my mother claims never to have set eyes on any of her father-in-law's paintings, and I don't recall my Aunt Lavinia ever having any. All I have seen of his works are the nudes Madeleine showed us in Brittany.

Ghislaine and I agreed to divide Henry's papers between us. The packet I took back with me to London consisted of two further diaries written after Henry had left Paris: one is marked "Bellerive, June–November 1940", the other "Paris, Nov. 1940–May 1941". There were a batch of letters that are of surprisingly little interest (Henry was not a good correspondent): several from Jean Arago, mostly to do with plans for Henry's exhibition, and some enigmatic postcards from Marie-Hélène, the girl he pined for, and who spent most of the war years with her parents in Aix-en-Provence, in the "free zone" created after the Armistice of May 1940. The cards cease after Henry left Paris. There are more informative ones from Robert Worcester and two ornate, deckle-edged postcards, decorated with a family crest, posted in Paris in 1950 and 1951, from the writer Sylvain de Gresly. There are identity papers, theatre programmes, newspaper clippings that confirm Henry's political leanings, sepia and black-and-white photographs of friends whose identities one can only guess at, some cuttings from Argentine newspapers about his exhibitions, and his Argentine naturalisation documents. Evidently, when Henry applied for Argentine citizenship, which he appears to have done in 1962, he was applying as a Frenchman, not as a British subject, though how he achieved French nationality at a time when France was experiencing the agonies of occupation is a mystery that only becomes clearer later on; he was a man who was adept at making the most of his connections!

Henry did go to Collioure and got the fresh air he longed for: in my packet I found an artist's sketchpad with drawings of the sea front there. As I was to discover much later, one of the paintings shown at his very first exhibition in Buenos Aires was entitled "*Recuerdos de Collioure*", *Dec. 1939*. But I am moving ahead too quickly.

∞

I telephoned Ghislaine in Paris at least twice a week. The impact she had made on me was considerable and I felt happier than I had for a long time. Before studying and transcribing my grandfather's diaries any further, however, I told Ghislaine that I felt I needed to discover the precise circumstances of his death. I filled in various forms at the Argentine Consulate in London, and after three weeks I received a telephone call from a Señor Diego Garay asking if I would call at his office.

"There was nothing noteworthy about your grandfather's death, from what we have been able to ascertain," Señor Garay said with a shrug of his elegantly tailored shoulders. "It appears he had a heart attack one Sunday morning on the terrace of the Café Biela, a fashionable meeting place close to the gates of the Recoleta cemetery. He was having an apéritif and collapsed at the table. It was approximately midday. An ambulance was called. He was taken to a hospital in the centre of the city. He was conscious on arrival, and a close friend – I have the name here, a Señora Suarez, Rosita Suarez – was sent for. She was with him when he died that afternoon. She in turn summoned a priest, who gave him the last rites. He is buried at the Chacarita cemetery. I have no information about a funeral."

I thanked Señor Garay. He was an agreeable man in his late

fifties, with an amused twinkle in his eyes, and I wondered whether he could conceivably have heard of Henry's name before.

"No, I'm sorry," he replied to my question, "but I'm from Cordoba, not the capital. I'm not a *porteño*, as we call those from Buenos Aires. But you may be interested to see this obituary, which was sent to me along with the answers to my enquiries. It's from the *Buenos Aires Herald*, an English-language daily paper which serves the British and American communities in the city."

Señor Garay twirled one end of his greying moustache and read the cutting himself before passing it to me across his desk. He smelled strongly of brilliantine.

"Your grandfather, Mr Latymer, must have been an artist of some distinction."

The newspaper had reproduced in black and white a painting of a young woman sitting beside a broad sweep of a river. It was hard to distinguish very much detail. Beneath a small bold headline ("Henry Latymer: the art of expressing the inner self"), I read the following:

We regret to inform our readers of the sudden death of Henry Graham Latymer, the English-born artist whose work graced a number of exhibitions in the capital's galleries over the past forty years. Latymer was born in England and trained at the Grosvenor School of Art in London during the years before the Second World War.

He was resident in France from 1939 until shortly before the end of the war, studying initially at the École des Beaux-Arts in Paris, and during this time he took French nationality.

It was in Argentina, however, that his gifts as an expressionist artist came to be recognised. The first of his four major exhibitions at the Lavalle gallery was shared with Juan Pablo Castel, the infamous, if justly renowned Belgrano artist, whose melancholy semi-abstract works fetched high prices after he was sentenced to life imprisonment for the murder of his mistress. It was an exhibition that brought both artists to the attention of the city's *cognoscenti* in 1954.

Latymer's work was in stark contrast to Castel's. His heavily textured portraits and landscapes evoked a pre-war Europe, both in his use of vibrant colour and in his subject matter. A member of the English Club on 25 de Mayo, Henry Latymer became an Argentine citizen in 1972. He had no known family. A.G.-Y.

∞

My life in London soon reverted to its normal rhythm: the orchestral musician's routine of practice, rehearsals, gigs, lessons for the pupils I have, and the occasional recording session. In the fortnight after I returned, there was a weekend concert tour to Mallorca, a Sunday morning "Coffee Concert" for our chamber group at the Wigmore Hall, in which our performance of the Beethoven Quartet in F Major Op. 135 was described by the only critic present as "vigorous and ultimately rewarding". Music occupied my working life, but images of Ghislaine dominated my thoughts. Yet she could have had no awareness of my feelings for her. When we spoke on the telephone to discuss Henry's papers, I remained tongue-tied in this respect. The sense of intimacy that our trip to Brittany had fostered gave me no reason to think she might feel the same way.

I continued to be obsessed with finding out more about my grandfather and what sort of man he had been. How, I wondered, could he and Madeleine have possibly come to abandon their child – my own poor father – at the end of the war? Did they have something to hide? Were they no longer in love? If not, how could he have left Madeleine? It seemed to me that there must be some further mystery that neither Madeleine nor my father, if indeed he ever suspected anything of the sort, had ever revealed. My social life vanished as I devoted my few free evenings and weekends to deciphering those of Henry's diaries and papers which were in my possession.

My mother came down from Scotland to stay for a few days. I took her to two plays and three concerts. Over dinner at the nearby Polish restaurant one evening, I told her about Ghislaine and about my trip to France, and about Henry's wartime diaries, but she did not appear to be interested. "All that stuff about the war and the Nazis, Will, darling, I've had it up to here . . . It's over, past, finito. Your father never allowed the subject to be mentioned. We've all got to learn to live together, in the present, and look ahead, not backwards, he used to say. I'm for a new Europe based on our common futures, and I find there's something unhealthy in unearthing past secrets. Let the dead bury the dead. I mean, supposing your poor grandfather *was* a Nazi, a Fascist, a collaborator, what have you . . . Does it affect us one jot? Does it alter anything? No, it doesn't. Privately, I've always thought he sounded a bit of a shit . . . Don't be offended, darling, but I'd be far more interested in seeing what he painted, to be frank. That really would be interesting. As you know, neither your father nor his sister Lavinia possessed a single painting by Henry."

She scarcely drew breath, and her borscht grew cold as she held forth.

It was not until March that Ghislaine and I met again. She had been in touch with an old friend of Henry's in Paris, who apparently wanted to meet me and whose memories might be useful, she said, if we did decide to delve any deeper into my grandfather's life. "Who knows where it could lead us? Like you, I'm trying to find out as much as I can, but Maman is not always helpful."

∞

I went back to Paris a fortnight later. I happened to have six days free of musical engagements, and when Ghislaine telephoned to say that we had both been invited to dinner by my grandfather's old friend Sylvain de Gresly and his son, I was happy to accept. It was Madeleine, evidently, who was responsible for arranging the encounter. A stream of memories had been jogged by our conversations in Brittany and it was she who had got in touch with Sylvain. "You had better bring a suit," Ghislaine warned me. "The Greslys sound rather grand."

Sylvain de Gresly's novels are scarcely read these days, even in France where he had once been lionised, and nothing appears to have been translated into English since *Rivoli* in 1955. I had never heard of him, and the few titles of his on the shelves of the London Library had not been borrowed by anyone in the previous three years, though Ghislaine assured me that in the immediate post-war period, and up until about the time of the Algerian troubles, he had been a highly respected figure, with a number of prestigious prizes to his name and sales figures that were the equal of those of Jean Giono or Henri de

Montherlant, both writers with whom Gresly's name was frequently bracketed in the literary appraisals of that period. If he had never been elevated to the ranks of the *immortels* at the Académie Française, it was only because of his forthright political views.

"He's from the far right," Ghislaine told me on the telephone, "an unreformed Pétainist. If he hadn't been who he is, he would surely have been imprisoned after the war. From what I've discovered, I think I'm beginning to see why he was a friend of Henry's. Perhaps I should try to obtain an interview with him for my paper. Perhaps he's ready to be 'rediscovered'. We shall see."

When Ghislaine met me at the Gare du Nord, she looked even lovelier than I remembered. Her hair had been cut short and she seemed younger. The collar of her brown overcoat was drawn up against the unseasonal chill winds; she smelled of Amarige – fresh, wholesome, exotic.

"It's good to see you, Will," she said as we embraced.

As we neared the Seine in her car, the Institut de France was tinged a shade of deep pink in the late evening light; the sun was setting behind St-Germain-en-Laye to the west and as Ghislaine crossed the Pont de la Concorde, my mood changed and my spirits soared. Neither of us spoke, but inwardly I felt deeply satisfied.

"I have the impression from what de Gresly said on the telephone that we may not be the only guests tomorrow evening," Ghislaine said, breaking the silence as she searched for a parking space, "but it should provide an opportunity for us to try, if we can, to ask a few more questions about your grandfather. When you think of it, how did an Englishman manage to remain in France for most of the war, acquire not just French, but later Argentine citizenship and then end his days as a respectable Buenos Aires artist, or so we are led to suppose. It's just not possible."

"And what strange train of circumstances," I said, "led my grandfather to meet your mother, marry her, one assumes, produce a son who was born in Germany and then taken to Denmark, and then sent to England before he was six months old? Every family has skeletons in its cupboard, I know, but Henry's story is more puzzling than most."

∞

Ghislaine lived in a spacious, three-room apartment on the second floor of an early nineteenth-century *immeuble* on rue des Saints-Pères, overlooking a shaded inner courtyard. It had once been Madeleine's flat and she and her young daughter had lived here together briefly after her husband, René, had been assassinated in Algeria and before she had moved permanently to Brittany. The parquet flooring in the little salon was covered in Turkish or Afghan kelims of different sizes and, the occasional print apart, the walls were covered with sagging, over-filled bookshelves. I recognised a photograph of Madeleine when young – bare-shouldered, her face half-averted from the camera and undeniably attractive – that hung over the mantelpiece above a gas fire. She looked very like her daughter.

"Make yourself at home, Will. It's not exactly luxurious, is it? But it's central, four stops on the *métro* from my office, and it suits me very well. The divan becomes a bed, by the way, and you can spread out as much as you need. You won't disturb me. This is where all my friends stay, though you must be the first relative, and you are certainly the first Englishman. Anyway, it's better than Hôtel Louisiane, no?"

Ghislaine beckoned me to follow her.

"Now, come to the kitchen. I'll get you a drink and we must compare notes. There's so much to discuss. It's riveting. Perhaps you should write about Henry's life. Or maybe we should do so together. I'm often asked to write books by publishers here. I realise that it's professional flattery, of course. A *quid pro quo*, as they say: make sure our books are reviewed and we'll look after you. I'm sure you have the same sort of network in London . . . And ever since Modiano's early novels, people seem to be fascinated by those dark years."

Ghislaine has a habit of hopping from one subject to another, like a bee seeking nectar. Before one comment can be considered, she is moving on to something else.

"Why dark years?" I said.

"Les années noires. That's how we refer to that bleak period in our history," Ghislaine said as she poured out two measures of Cutty Sark. "The Vichy years really; from May 1940 – when France was over-run and Maréchal Pétain signed the Armistice – up to the Liberation."

She handed me a glass and a small jug of water.

"It's only now that we are beginning to face up to what happened then. Many of us like to think that we were trampled underfoot by marauding, jack-booted Nazis and that we fought back heroically. But I'm sorry to say that, given the choice between resistance and supporting de Gaulle and his Free French in London in 1940, or collaborating with the Germans, a large proportion of my compatriots chose the easier path. Not that it was so easy. There was enormous suffering."

Ghislaine paused, sipped her whisky and looked straight into my eyes.

"But perhaps this sad chapter of wartime France is familiar to you," she said.

"No, it's not," I said. "As I told you, I know as little about that period of history as I do about my father's childhood. I remember seeing a film called '*Le Chagrin et la Pitié*'. I must have been in my teens, but I don't think I grasped its significance at the time."

"It was a very important film for us – at least, for those of us who managed to see it – and it opened – how do you say? – a can of worms. *Et comment!*" Ghislaine whistled as if to add emphasis.

"I can imagine. Although I've always reckoned that if the Germans had invaded Britain in 1940, we would probably have been open to the same sort of accusations."

"Who knows? I'm not sure that I agree with you. Our peoples are very different, as I don't have to tell you. It's true that we endured appalling losses in the 1914 war, and that may help explain the mood of inertia and defeatism that swept through France in 1940. There's still a taboo about Vichy – too many unanswered questions. Some people want to eradicate the past, but it won't go away."

Ghislaine drained her whisky, shrugged, smiled, and raised her eyebrows in quick succession. I admired her ability to discuss such matters so fluently and to pass from the commonplace to the serious in a matter of seconds.

"Well, enough of that," she said. "I should give you something to eat, and we must compare our respective conclusions about Henry's papers. Besides, I suspect we may be discussing this subject tomorrow evening chez Gresly *père et fils.*'

[CHAPTER 4]

SYLVAIN DE GRESLY LIVED IN A SMALL EIGHTEENTH-CENTURY *hôtel particulier* on rue de l'Échaudé, one of the many ancient streets in the *6ème arrondissement* that run from the Seine to boulevard St-Germain: rue Visconti, rue Saint-Benoît, rue Appollinaire, rue de l'Abbayé . . .

Ghislaine and I strolled along these streets the following evening as we made our way to the writer's apartment. Rather than arriving too punctually, we dawdled through the tiny, darkened place Furstemberg with its sunken garden and the studio where Delacroix once worked, then along rue Cardinale and into rue de l'Échaudé where, almost opposite us, was a half-open porte-cochère giving onto a courtyard and a fine eighteenth-century staircase. The concierge directed us to the stairs that led to the first floor. On the half-landing, a handsome pewter jug filled with blue cornflowers had been placed in an alcove.

"My favourite flower," Ghislaine said.

A maid dressed in black with a white apron, not dissimilar to the uniform that Madeleine's Jeanne at La Tiemblais had worn, unbolted the heavy door of the Greslys' home and, after taking

Ghislaine's coat, she showed us into a sombre but stylishly furnished room with high ceilings, an oak floor and a dark-red, textured wallpaper. Paintings and drawings filled the walls. In the far corner sat an elderly man with a Blackwatch-tartan rug draped over his knees and a cornflower in his buttonhole. He wore a formal dark-grey suit, a white shirt with a stiff collar and emerald cufflinks, and a dark-green tweed tie. Thick white hair was swept back from his heavily lined forehead, and his hands were joined over a silver-topped black malacca cane. As we approached, the six or seven other guests who stood around his high-backed chair stepped aside. Ghislaine bent down to greet Sylvain de Gresly and took his hand in both of hers. He gazed up at her, straining his misty blue eyes, and addressed her in a very correct and formal, if somewhat antiquated, French.

"So you are Madeleine's daughter. How the years fall away as I set eyes on you. Come closer. But, yes . . . I can see your mother in your face."

The old man looked around at his friends, inviting them to share his delight.

"This is indeed a great pleasure," he said before switching his attention to me. 'And this, would you believe it, is our old friend Henry's grandson from England. I am so very pleased to meet you and so glad that you should have agreed to join our little gathering . . . Yves!" he called out, searching short-sightedly among his guests, "offer them some champagne and then introduce our new friends, please. And see that they are seated on either side of me at dinner."

Yves de Gresly was a man of about forty with an engaging smile. Ghislaine had told me that there was an element of mystery about his identity since no-one was aware that Sylvain had ever been married. He also spoke in a clipped, formal tone.

"Papa has been greatly looking forward to this moment," he said, pouring champagne into two very ancient glasses. There was something instantly appealing about his warmth and ease of manner. "To tell you the truth, I am overjoyed too, for I am usually the sole representative of what I may be permitted to call the younger generation at our soirées. Papa only likes to see friends from the past, and that means" – he gestured around the room with one arm – "dear old *sons et lumières* such as these. They are wonderful people, of course, and they are all very loyal to him, but they are survivors from another age and occasionally I need some fresh air."

Ghislaine laughed and looked around the room. The other guests did indeed all appear to be in their eighties, at least. Expensively dressed and rather shaky on their feet, they clustered around Sylvain's chair, speaking in loud voices. Their carefully constructed syntax echoed a vanished and far more sophisticated age.

Yves introduced us to a couple with bad-tempered, arrogant expressions. "*Le Comte et Comtesse de Mont . . .*" he said, but I never caught their full name, and it was with some relief that Yves then said he would like me to meet another guest, a man dressed in what appeared to be nineteenth-century clerical clothes, who was seated next to Sylvain.

"*Mon père*, this is Mr William Latymer from England," said Yves. "As I told you, he's the grandson of Papa's old friend, the artist Henry Latymer, who was with him at Sigmaringen, and with whom he occasionally corresponded until Henry's death in Buenos Aires last year." Yves sounded well informed, I thought, and I hoped I would have an opportunity to speak to him later in the evening.

We shook hands, and I could feel the priest appraising me through his half-moon spectacles, which he tried to steady with a shaking hand, as if holding a lorgnette. Then, after a cursory glance at Yves, he turned again to Sylvain.

"Père Roy is an old friend of Papa's, too," Yves whispered, "but I fear I've offended him. He's a priest from the old school and I sometimes drive my father to hear the Mass he says daily at a chapel near Neuilly. It's unofficial, of course, but it's the only truly Tridentine Mass you are likely to find in Paris these days. Imagine! Are you a Catholic, like your grandfather? Papa has told me so much about him."

I nodded non-committally, but before I could speak the old priest touched the sleeve of my jacket. He had finished whatever he had to say to Sylvain and was now ready to receive me. He flourished a long-fingered hand, inviting me to sit down beside him.

"So . . ." he drawled in heavily accented but fluent English, "as Sylvain remembers only too well, I did of course know your grandfather. I, too, was with him in Germany in the last months of the war. He was a remarkable man," he said, his dark eyes seeming to bore into mine. "You should be proud of him, my dear. He was a brave man – a man of the old faith and a true European, too. We all aspired to his vigour and optimism, his cosmopolitan style, his undimmed vision of our then potentially glorious future. Alas! It was not to be. But he was also an excellent artist, in my humble opinion. Look, Sylvain has one of his drawings."

Père Roy pointed to a sketch of a turreted castle in an ornate black frame in the far corner of the room.

"Come. Let us examine it more closely. It's rather interesting,

I think you'll agree" said the priest, as I helped him to his feet. He led me by the arm slowly across the room.

The drawing was in pencil and brown ink, and it was signed "H.L. Dec. '44" in the bottom right-hand corner. The words "Schloss Sigmaringen" had been inscribed in the opposite corner. At first glance I thought it was an imaginary castle, something out of a fairy tale, perched on top of a rocky promontory, high above the deep river that appeared to encircle it. It looked as if it was built over a variety of architectural periods. In addition to the three turrets, there were countless windows and Gothic casements on at least seven different levels. Fluttering over this forbidding fortress, what might have been a French tricolour flew from a flag pole.

"What an extraordinary vision of a castle!" I said, and I remembered Madeleine's photograph of the youthful Henry with the name "Sigmaringen" written on the back. "It reminds me of one of those follies built by Kaiser Ludwig on the Rhine. Is that the French flag flying there?"

"It's the Danube, not the Rhine," Père Roy said, "but you are correct, that is the tricolour. The castle of Sigmaringen was, in effect, the seat of French government for a few tragic months. The town was the capital of our France – the capital of *la France allemande*, that is to say – during the final months of the war. It is a period that, understandably, no-one cares to talk about anymore, but this town – more of a large village, really – in Baden-Württemberg, was all that was left of France in the eyes of some of our compatriots in 1944. You should speak to Sylvain about it. I believe it was there that he first came to know your grandfather."

Just at that moment, the maid who had first received us

announced that dinner was served, and Sylvain and Yves ushered us all into a long, narrow, candle-lit dining room, where Ghislaine and I were placed on either side of our host, as he had requested, at the far end of a long, oak table. The other guests faced one another, with Yves at the opposite end to his father. The flickering candlelight from two wrought-iron candle holders obscured our view of the portraits and prints on the walls. A large and beautiful blue-glass dish containing a floating water lily occupied the centre of the table. A *fleur-de-lys* for an older France, I thought.

The Gresly maid, bearing a silver tureen of soup, stood behind Sylvain's shoulders ready to serve him. Before she could do so, however, Sylvain raised a seigneurial hand and requested silence for Père Roy, who rose to his feet, made a slow sign of the cross and delivered an elaborate Latin grace.

"Henry would have been so touched to know that his death has brought you together," said Sylvain. "His own life was so tragically divided, you know. His English side, and his French side. His idealistic nature was so much at odds with the harsh realities we all had to endure, and I know that it distressed him, in his later years, to think that he had lost touch with his family. And with poor Madeleine, too, of course," he said, addressing Ghislaine and squeezing her hand. "It was never his intention to desert her; you know that, don't you? By the time he felt he could invite her to join him in Argentina, it was too late; she had married Ghislaine's father."

Ghislaine smiled and nodded.

"How you resemble her, my dear," Sylvain said.

I could see that Ghislaine was irritated by the old man's close attention. She thanked him for his loyalty to her mother over the years, and then she explained that it had become our intention to try to unravel some of the unanswered questions that surrounded my grandfather's life.

Sylvain nodded gravely. "They can all be explained," he said, then pursed his lips and shrugged. "Your well-fed, pampered generation cannot imagine the times we all lived through." His hand fanned the air, indicating his guests. "We had a decision to make when Hitler's armies invaded France: whether to fight or to try to create a new Europe, free of the pernicious influence of the Israelites and Freemasons . . ."

I could sense Ghislaine bridle. Her eyes glared in indignation.

"Fighting to the finish seemed senseless in 1940," Sylvain continued. "You had only to look at the crippled and mutilated veterans of Verdun and the Marne, the generation of widows and fatherless children they left behind, to realise that our poor France could not risk another all-out war. A third conflagration in seventy years? Never! We had been weakened by an epidemic of softness and debilitated moral fibre that had damaged the time-honoured traditions of this nation and destroyed its old and glorious faith. In desperation, we turned to a leader, a man with natural authority, a father figure who would save us from the abyss, stiffen our resolve, and to whom we could look up. A man who might rid France of the influence of the Communists and foreign immigrants who threatened the purity of our blood, who would safeguard our heritage and who stood for the values and truths we had lost. *Enfin*, someone like our heroic Maréchal . . . the victor of Verdun . . . do you recognise him in our picture? Perhaps you're too young, both of you."

Sylvain had turned stiffly in his chair and was pointing to a large framed photographic colour print that hung in an alcove in the wall behind him. It depicted an old man in French military uniform, with a white moustache, pink complexion, and bright-blue expressionless eyes. In capital letters beneath the print were the words: "JE FAIS À LA FRANCE LE DON DE MA PERSONNE", while above it, in a bold 1940s sans-serif typeface, were the three words: **Travail Famille Patrie**. In handwriting that I imagine was the Maréchal's own, superimposed over the background of the print, were three lines:

J'ai été avec vous dans les jours glorieux,
Je reste avec vous dans les jours sombres.
Soyez à mes côtés

"But it's Maréchal Pétain!" exclaimed Ghislaine, a look of disbelief on her face.

"It is indeed," said Sylvain, and his expression took on a harder edge. "And we have still not atoned for the sacrifices he made . . ." His voice tailed off, and for a moment he was silent. Then, turning to me, he said, "For your grandfather it was a doubly difficult decision. I did not know him at the time. We only met towards the end, in Germany in 1944. He loved France for the reasons we all do: for her culture, her spirit, her noble traditions . . . and her ancient faith, for, as Père Roy will remind you, France is the eldest daughter of the Church. But in taking French citizenship as he did, thanks to the personal intervention of the Maréchal himself, it was said, Henry was also cutting himself off from his own family and from his Anglo-Saxon heritage. I mean your glorious, if sometimes perfidious Albion. Some of us have still not forgiven you, but let us speak no more of that . . . Let us say that Henry put art above politics. He may have been a political ingénu, one has to admit, but he was such a romantic idealist, such a distinguished artist . . . and so charming a friend."

Sylvain gazed at us in wonderment, then his head drooped, and his chin slumped on his chest. For a moment I thought he had fallen asleep. I glanced around me: Yves was offering his guests a 1980 Château Lafite and the maid was serving thin slices of a succulent-looking *rôti de veau* from a silver platter. Opposite me, Ghislaine was conversing in English with a handsome, well-preserved man sitting next to her, who, like all the other guests we met, must have been in his eighties. I caught the occasional word as I pretended to listen to Sylvain, who had recovered and continued to drone on about the war years and the injustice with which the old Maréchal in the framed print had been treated. At one point, I heard an American accent pronounce the name of the art dealer Ambroise Vollard, and I held my breath for a moment. Could this possibly be Robert, the American whom Henry had known in 1939 and who was mentioned in his Paris diary? He looked the part. What was it, I wondered, that linked these old men and women so firmly and still brought them together after all those years?

All of a sudden, a feeling of claustrophobia came over me. I had the acute sensation that Ghislaine and I were surrounded by ghosts, by masked puppets from a bygone age, and I longed for fresh air, for the cool night breeze of the Paris beyond these walls, one that I associated with the young at heart, with gaiety, with life; a Paris that looked forward to the future, not to the murky, morbid past in which these pompous geriatrics dwelt. I looked across at Ghislaine and felt consoled by the alertness of the expression in her eyes. She, thank God, had nothing in common with the other guests. And yet these people had been my grandfather's friends. They, too, had once known laughter and joy, they had experienced yearning and desire; like Henry, they had dreamed of a better, fairer world. They may have lived according to narrow beliefs, held values that would strike my generation as absurd and outdated, but they were values bred into them by a society that observed some sort of moral creed. Where was that morality today? What did our own greed-ridden and insubstantial world have to offer in its place?

Such thoughts sped through my mind as the remainder of the evening spun out its course. It passed none too quickly for me, or for Ghislaine either, to judge by her occasional bemused and exasperated glances at me across the table. After cheese and a glass of white port had been served, we returned to the drawing-room for coffee, and I found myself hemmed in by the sour-faced count and countess Ghislaine had been introduced to before dinner. They kept a flat in Paris, but came from the same part of Brittany as Madeleine, whom they had also known "in the old days". He was a monarchist, he informed me, and he was so far to the right on the political spectrum that the modern world had become intolerable to him. He did not care for the English. "You will forgive my saying so, but your compatriots have been our hereditary enemy throughout history. A remorseless one, you must admit." The count gesticulated with his hands, and then proceeded to denounce the younger generation for squandering the heritage bequeathed them by their parents. He did not expect agreement, or indeed any reaction on my part, and he evidently derived sufficient encouragement from the accompaniment of pecks and sniffs of assent administered by his bird-faced wife. Mercifully, his monologue was soon interrupted by a tap on the shoulder from Yves, who wanted me to meet another friend of my grand-father's.

Relieved to be free of them, I bowed to the unsmiling count and his tittling wife and made my apologies. I now found myself in the presence of the American with whom Ghislaine had been talking over dinner. He was standing by the door, wearing an inappropriate fur coat, and in his left hand he held a wide-brimmed black Homburg-style hat reminiscent of the one worn by Orson Welles in "The Third Man". It was obvious that he was about to leave, I observed with relief.

"Robert Worcester at your service, old boy," he announced, interrupting Yves' attempt to introduce us.

"My driver is waiting, but I couldn't leave the party without paying my respects to the grandson of my old friend." He spoke with the elegant drawl that educated Americans acquire when they have lived in Europe for many years. Well-built, though not especially tall, with small, twinkling blue eyes and a stack of well-preserved grey hair, his commanding and somewhat cavalier manner was that of a man accustomed to being noticed and listened to, and yet his forbidding appearance was counter-balanced by an immediate charm. His nose, I remember thinking, was the shape of a hawk's beak.

"Here's my telephone number," Robert Worcester said, drawing a card out of a black leather wallet and almost deliber-ately addressing me rather than Ghislaine. "Come and have lunch at La Coupole some day. I lunch there on Tuesdays and Fridays. Give me a call. I'd like to tell you about the times your grandfather and I shared in the good bad old days. Make it soon though, while my memory's still intact. Adieu." And with a flamboyant wave he was off. I looked down at the card in my hand. "Robert Worcester," it read, "Fine Art Dealer", followed by an address in Passy.

∞

It was past midnight when Ghislaine and I emerged onto the street below. Out of sheer relief at having escaped, we collapsed into one another's arms and laughed away our pent-up frustration with the company we had been obliged to keep for the past four hours. Sylvain had been infinitely kind, it was true, the dinner had been sumptuous, and his son Yves had done his best to make us feel welcome, but the cumulative effect of those assembled gerontocrats and the nostalgia they evinced for a vanished France was perplexing.

"Mr Worcester, I take it, is not a woman's man," Ghislaine said. "But then neither is Sylvain. And what a bunch of old fascists!" she added. "We call them *intégristes* now, but if they represent *la vieille France,* then count me out. I can't tell you how relieved I felt when the time came to leave."

"And yet, don't you suppose Henry would have been there among them, had he been alive?" I said. "It makes me wonder about my grandfather. Perhaps he's not the mysterious, romantic figure we have been conjuring up in our imaginations."

"It has to be admitted, though, that Sylvain and Yves have the most impeccable manners," Ghislaine mused. "Did you notice their style, their courteous formality? That really is old France. No-one uses their mode of address anymore; at least not in the world I inhabit."

We were walking down rue de Seine, towards the *quais*. A

breeze was blowing up from the river. The streets were now quiet and our footsteps echoed against the old walls on either side of us. Political graffiti from a time gone by could still be deciphered, daubed on crumbling cement. Ghislaine pointed out the spot where the Restaurant Magny had once stood, and where, she told me, the Goncourt brothers, Flaubert, Turgenev and Théophile Gautier used to gather and converse. Then we turned into rue des Beaux-Arts, past the former Hôtel d'Alsace, where in 1900 Oscar Wilde, broken and living in exile, had died.

"Poor man," Ghislaine reflected. "At least our Henry's exile was self-imposed. After all, he could have returned to England and fought for his country in 1939 if he had really wanted to. Mind you, he would not have been half as interesting to his grandson or to his . . . step-daughter – is that what I am? – had he done the honourable thing, would he? Traitors are always more interesting than patriots. *À propos*, I remember interviewing Graham Greene once. Did I ever tell you that I drank whisky with him at his local restaurant, Chez Félix, in Antibes? We talked for an hour or so about what he called the virtue of disloyalty. It's very much one of his themes, isn't it? I mean Philby and all that. I wonder what he would have made of Henry."

I thought of Greene, whose death in Switzerland a few years ago had made me feel that an era had ended, and I tried to remember which of his novels Ghislaine was referring to.

"But surely that was in the context of a greater loyalty?" I said. "The duty of the writer coming before patriotism; Church before country etc. . . . . Henry did not betray his country, but he refused to fight for it. I wonder about Robert Worcester too: from what I've gleaned, I gather he spent the war years hidden away in Paris. I want to discover what they did in the war. I can't believe they simply existed. And how did either of them manage to survive here without being interned?"

We were leaning against a parapet overlooking the dark waters of the Seine that reflected the shadow of the Louvre on the opposite bank. The branches of the tall, blackened plane trees that lined the *quais* quivered as they swayed to and fro in the night breeze. A pale half-moon danced in and out of the clouds, and, looking up, I tried to identify some of the stars whose names my father had taught me when I was a boy: Aldebaran, Betelgeuse, Cassiopeia, Arcturus . . . names that used to set my imagination racing.

"A penny for your thoughts," Ghislaine said.

"Nothing especially," I lied.

She smiled, and when we walked on, she slipped her arm through mine.

I spent most of the next day at Ghislaine's flat reading Henry's diaries. I also decided to follow up Robert Worcester's invitation to lunch as soon as possible. Ghislaine told me she had to leave Paris for a few days, but she was adamant that I should stay on at her flat. She had to attend a four-day conference in Albi to give a talk on the modern French novel and present a prize on behalf of her magazine to the winner of a short story competition.

"I suppose travel is one of the perks of the job." She sighed "But once you have attended a couple of these gatherings they become a chore. Frankly, I'd much rather be having lunch with you and the dapper Mr Worcester. He intrigues me too.'

"Terrace of La Coupole, William. Tuesday, 12.45 sharp, old chap. The waiter will show you to my usual table," Robert Worcester had said in his elegant drawl when I telephoned him. "Don't be late. I'll order some apéritifs, followed by lunch at one o'clock, sharp. I'm known for my punctuality. As the old French proverb says: 'Men count up the faults of those who keep them waiting,' and I'm a stickler, as anyone will tell you. Mind you, it wasn't always so, as your grandpapa knew only too well." He chuckled down the phone.

And so on Tuesday I set off early to walk to Montparnasse. It was a fine morning and I strolled up boulevard Raspail. Passing the hotel where the Abwehr once had its headquarters during the war, I tried to imagine Paris under German occupation: her silent streets, the forlorn, hopeless atmosphere, the mood of melancholy, the disappearance of her customary *joie de vivre*, the curfew; and not knowing whom you could trust. Such a situation was unthinkable today. Henry and Sylvain's generation of Europeans had suffered infinitely more than my own could ever conceive of, and yet most of them had stood up courageously to deprivation and loss of freedom, and had endured the death or imprisonment of fathers, brothers and sons.

My contemporaries were spoilt by comparison, and surely very few of us would answer a call to arms today. Your country, right or wrong? Patriotism of that unquestioning kind was dead. The notion of going to war without first deciding whether it accorded with one's conscience was something alien to my generation. Would I fight for Britain, or for Europe, if asked to do so today? It would depend on why the war was being fought. Yet that sort of moral justification scarcely occurred to those who joined up to fight Hitler, still less those who took the King's shilling so eagerly in 1914. Yet here I was, obsessed with curiosity about my own grandfather, a man who had abandoned his country and his own family, and who, it seemed, had chosen to collaborate with men eager to appease Britain's enemy in order to avoid a worse fate. Were they cowards? Was Henry really a collaborator, or did he do what he did for the sake of some youthful, idealistic notion of the "New Europe" that his diaries alluded to, and in which he appeared to have invested so much faith?

∞

I did not need to be shown to Robert's table. I recognised my host immediately, sitting on his own on the terrace. Dressed in a three-piece suit and a white shirt and what looked like a college or club tie, he was reading *Le Monde diplomatique* through tinted spectacles set low on the bridge of his nose.

"William, old chap! Bravo! You have the virtue of punctuality, unlike dear Henry," he said, checking the half-hunter gold watch he wore on a chain in the fob pocket of his waistcoat. "We're still in time for a Negroni," and with a wave he invited me to sit down opposite him. "You know La Coupole, of course. Henry used to love coming here, though we preferred the Dôme during the Occupation – it was safer for people like us. These cafés remain much as they were then, thank God, unlike so much of this city."

Robert scarcely drew breath before summoning the waiter. "Jacques," he called, and minutes later two glasses had been placed before us without a further word being said.

"Apart from a few Montparnasse restaurants, and the Val de

Grâce hospital, there are very few parts of the Left Bank that remain just as they were in the old days," he observed, counting on the fingers of one hand. "This beautiful city is being destroyed before our eyes. At least, that's what it seems to old timers like me. I expect you're too young to remember the demolition of Les Halles, but look at what they've erected in its place. Look at La Défense; look at this cursed Montparnasse tower they've built above our heads . . . And it will get worse, I tell you."

Robert shook his thick head of combed silvery grey hair and seemed to fix his gaze on me fully for the first time since I had sat down. His blue eyes peered over his spectacles, and I noticed his gold, initialled cufflinks.

"I know from Henry's diaries that you must have been in Paris in 1939, but when did you first come to live here?" I asked, having first explained how my grandfather's papers had come into my possession.

The American pursed his lips. "It was in '38. And it must have been the beginning of that year, because I sailed over to Cherbourg on a Cunarder in order to see the great Surrealist exhibition in the Faubourg Saint-Honoré. It was my first time away from the States, and I could not believe my eyes. I was *bouleversé*. I'd never seen art like that. There was Dali's "*Taxi pluvieux*" standing in the courtyard as you came in, with two mannequins – a chauffeur and a blonde girl in evening dress – sitting inside the vehicle, surrounded with lettuces and greenery, and – believe it or not – two hundred snails! Dali had installed a system of hoses that showered the interior with water. It was wild, absolutely crazy, and how the critics howled! I had a commission from my college newspaper to interview Dali, but he didn't bother to turn up at the opening. He had gone to London to meet Sigmund Freud. Can you imagine *that* confrontation!"

Robert's eyes lit up as he recalled these moments from his youth. Then, sipping his apéritif, he appeared to shake with pleasure as further memories flowed back to him.

"Inside the gallery there was a long corridor in which twenty or more models had been dressed for the occasion in weird and fantastical costumes by guys like Max Ernst, Man Ray and Masson. Then Duchamps had arranged for what looked like a thousand sacks of coal to be suspended from the glass roof. I remember there was a pond filled with lilies and leaves, and a metal brazier that contained live, burning coals . . . It was sheer, brilliant fantasy, the whole thing, and I was hooked on Paris from that day. I decided there and then that nowhere else on earth would do for me. No matter that France was in a mess after two years of that fool Blum and his Front Populaire, I had made up my mind. That was the year of the *Anschluss* and Munich, you know, and the Surrealist exhibition was a brief glimpse of magic and hope and gaiety before the storm broke and we were all plunged into war. Anyway, the idea of going home to Boston was something I could not bear to contemplate, and so I resolved to find work somewhere, some-how – anything so long as it was to do with art – and live in the proverbial Paris garret. And, somehow, I did!

"Ah! What it was to be young!" Robert looked at me with moist eyes and rubbed his mottled, veined hands together. "What is it the poet says? '*Oisive jeunesse, à tout asservie. Par délicatesse, j'ai perdu ma vie*'" Then he glanced at his fob watch, took another deep sip from his glass, and summoned the waiter to take our order for lunch.

"So you met Henry the following year?' I ventured, trying

to steer Robert's recollections to my grandfather's youth rather than his own.

"Well, I suppose I met Henry in . . . let's see . . . in October '39, it must have been. I had eventually found myself the ideal job working for the celebrated art dealer Ambroise Vollard. Perhaps you have heard of him? He died that summer before war broke out, after a motoring accident. The Paris art world was shocked, for Vollard's reputation was enormous. Though, boy! was he mean with contracts! Anyhow, one day I was sitting in the front of the gallery in rue Laffitte when a young man carrying a large portfolio walked in and asked whether we might care to look at his work. That sort of thing was just not done chez Vollard. No-one familiar with the Paris art world would dare! But I kind of admired this guy's naivety and we got talking. We became friendly, and then he and I used to meet for a drink, for supper, for a walk in the Luxembourg, discussing everything and anything that came to mind: Picasso . . . the Civil War in Spain that had just ended . . . Surrealism . . . different writers, I don't know . . . anything . . ."

Robert paused and took a toothpick. I looked away.

"Spain was the great divider in those days. I had no time for the Republicans and all those pinko idealists in the International Brigades, and I couldn't help admiring guys like Mussolini, like Franco. Not a fashionable thing to admit these days, of course, but they were the kind of strong leaders we needed. I could soon see that Henry and I shared the same shades of political opinion, and we were both crazy about art. Henry actually became a very good artist, by my reckoning. You won't find any of his work around today for love nor money, but if you could, it would sell, I can assure you."

I asked Robert whether he had known any of Henry's friends.

"Well, there was the girl he was crazy about in 1939. Good-looking, sophisticated, very *seizième*, as I recall, though a bit too silent and mysterious for my tastes. Girls were not really my bag, though I wasn't exclusive, if you catch my drift. I remember seeing Giraudoux's *Ondine* with them. Henry was always aiming to sleep with the girl – her name may have been Marie-Hélène – but she wouldn't have any of it . . . Then there was Jean and his sister Chantal, of course. You know about them?"

Robert looked at me, his eyes intent, and his expression grew solemn.

"Henry and Jean were good friends . . . true friends . . ." Robert's voice fell away. He looked around the room. "I don't know how much you've been told, but he was the one who really set Henry up as an artist. All I did was to encourage him. They fixed a show for him in the gallery they owned in Vichy. This would have been before the Armistice and before the government moved over from Bordeaux. Any rate, the show was a success and Henry made some money. He also began to acquire a bit of a reputation, so much so that the Aragos – Jean and Chantal – promised him another exhibition, and that was what prompted Henry to go and live down there. Either that, or else the fact that he had fallen for Chantal. Jean's sister was very beautiful, but I was never sure how deeply Henry loved her. At any rate, his decision was a fortunate one in some ways, because, as you know, Vichy became the seat of government – Pétain and all that crew – and life was far easier in the unoccupied zone. It must have been at about that time that Henry first met Madeleine, and he fell in love with her too. I guess you could say that women were his undoing, indirectly."

Robert sighed and leaned back in his chair. He had left most of his food on his plate, I noticed, and had consumed almost the whole of a bottle of Côtes des Nuits.

"I stayed on in Paris, by one means or another, but that's another story," he said. "In any case, I guess Henry must have become even more politically involved than I ever did. He got to know some of the top officials in Vichy. It was through his connections there – and some of my own, incidentally – that he was able to come and see me in Paris in 1941. He got to cross the demarcation line between the two zones that divided France during the war – the German Occupied Zone and the supposedly 'free' one. That was how he got his naturalisation papers, too. Henry always made good use of his connections. We all had to."

I glanced at my watch, jolting myself back into the late twentieth century. Most of the other diners had left the restaurant. Robert laid his hand on my forearm and kept it there as he continued:

"In those days you could send mail from one zone to another, but that was all. And the mail had to be in the form of postcards with a list of printed messages such as 'I am in good health', or 'Affectionate greetings', which you either ticked or crossed out. There was no contact, no travel from one zone to the other. Nothing. France might as well have been two separate countries. We even had to set our watches to German time in the Occupied Zone. Anyway, through his contacts Henry somehow contrived to be able to send and receive mail – so did I, but only through the gallery where I worked – whereas most people lost touch entirely with their family or friends in the other zone.

"But where was I?" Robert seemed to be tiring, and for a

moment he looked confused, though he quickly picked up the thread.

"After '42, I never heard any more of Henry until the war was over and by that time he had disappeared to South America. No-one knew what had become of him. Some said that he and Madeleine had been deported to Germany, others said he was dead, or that he and Madeleine had separated and he had escaped home to England. It was only much later, when I met Sylvain, who introduced me to Madeleine, that I came to hear about his subsequent life, that terrible period they went through in Germany, and their baby—"

"That baby was my father," I interrupted, a little too curtly.

"Life cannot have been easy for that kid," Robert said, taking my hand in his. "Though how Henry escaped to South America is still a puzzle that no-one has ever been able to explain to me. Madeleine, whom I used occasionally to see in Paris after the war, before she remarried, never liked to speak about the past. You'll have to find someone else to explain that part of his life. Perhaps you'll find something in these diaries you say you have ..."

Robert's interest and concentration seemed to fade towards the end of lunch. I tried to question him further about what he, too, called "the dark years", but he was growing tired and his conversation began to flag. The wonderfully creamy Brillat-Savarin cheese he had ordered for us, as well as the half-bottle of Sauternes, remained virtually untouched by him, and I noticed he was finding it hard to keep his eyes open. I was on the point of enquiring whether I might order coffee, when a young man in his early twenties, wearing jeans and a blue check shirt, and with the looks of a Bellini angel, approached our table. Appraising me before taking Robert's arm, he helped the elderly American to his feet. It was his chauffeur, albeit a distinctly unorthodox one.

"Old chap, it's been a pleasure," Robert murmured, trying to rouse himself. "Come and talk to me again, won't you."

A fleeting image of Zeus and Ganymede slipped through my mind as I watched this old American exile being led to his car. So this was Henry's old friend. So urbane, so much of his time . . . I tried to visualise the two of them in pre-war Paris, their lives and their art before them, victims of a Europe that was about to descend into a convulsion that would affect the dreams and expectations of their generation for ever.

Before leaving the table, I enquired about the bill, but the waiter dismissed my question with a condescending smile.

"Monsieur Robert is one of our oldest and most respected customers," he said, his eyes focussed on a point just above my head. "His guests never pay."

I walked back slowly to Ghislaine's apartment by an indirect route, down rue St-Jacques, past the Val-de-Grâce, along the little rue des Ursulines, into busy rue Gay-Lussac and past the same grey, unprepossessing building where Henry had lived in the autumn of 1939.

Without Ghislaine's presence, her apartment now seemed uninviting. I sat down at the table and, taking an envelope marked "Vichy/Bellerive" from the portfolio I kept containing my grandfather's papers, I tried to piece together and make some sense of these fragments of his life.

⌈CHAPTER 5⌉

A GUST OF WIND RIFFLED THROUGH THE LEAVES OF the drooping branches of the willow trees which at this point were all that separated the grey, gently flowing waters of the River Allier from the tow-path along which Henry Latymer walked on the morning of June 8, 1940. An early riser, scarcely ever able to sleep once the dawn light had pierced the flimsy cotton curtains of his bedroom, this was his daily walk – his constitutional, as he liked to think of it – and it set the tone for the rest of his day. The uneven, muddy track ran along the west bank of the wide river from Bellerive as far as the eye could see, both northwards, towards Moulins, and south, to the mountains and the Allier's ultimate source near Pradelles and Langogne, names long familiar to Henry from the time when as a schoolboy he had read Robert Louis Stevenson's *Travels with a Donkey.*

On the far bank lay the spa town of Vichy, preparing itself for a new day. The traffic and the pedestrians entering the city across the Pont Boutiran had doubled over the past half hour. They were café proprietors, shopkeepers, hotel staff and those who worked in the *salons de thé*, the thermal baths and the casino, for the most part, and they were preparing for the first of the summer visitors, as well as those who, despite the war, continued to take the cure here. Morning mist still shrouded the steeple of the old church of Saint-Blaise on the opposite shore of the Allier from where he stood, sketchbook in hand. To the east, beyond the city, the first rays of sunshine lit up the soft green hills known as the Monts de La Madeleine. An aroma of pine lingered in the morning air. The view he beheld was one he had frequently sketched during the six months he had stayed with Jean and Chantal Arago in Bellerive, a village which, had it not been for the river that separated them, would have been considered a suburb of Vichy, a town made famous by the semi-miraculous reputation of its healing waters, encouraged by the patronage of the rich and the famous over the years, among them Mme de Sévigné and Laetitia Bonaparte.

Henry had left Paris at the end of November 1939 to spend the better part of four weeks at Collioure, the little Mediterranean fishing port and erstwhile artists' colony close to the Spanish border, where he had lived beneath the shadow of the strangely phallic-shaped church, later painted by Dalí, and where he got drunk most nights on *anis* in the company of penniless artists and Republican refugees from across the frontier. He had, however, managed to produce enough supplementary work, mostly portraits or seascapes, to cover the walls of the small gallery that Jean and his sister owned in Vichy. The exhibition had opened just before the Christmas weekend, and over the following fortnight, Henry sold more than half the paintings or drawings that had been on display. Jean, whose belief in his artistic talent was the greatest piece of encouragement Henry had known since leaving the Grosvenor School of Art in London, was overjoyed, and was it not a coincidence that Chantal, Jean's slim and darkly attractive sister, seemed to look upon him in a very different light? Furthermore, as a result of the sales made, Henry could now afford to live off his earnings, at least for the next year.

Even the art critic of the local Vichy newspaper had penned some flattering words, though he could not resist a touch of the anti-British sentiment prevalent during the early months of the war:

> Monsieur Latymer displays in good measure the Anglo-Saxon genius for a type of expressionist realism, no longer in fashion elsewhere, but which is combined in these works with delicate sensitivity and vibrancy of colour.

He had sent a copy of the review to his sister Lavinia in Herefordshire, careful not to give his own address. He doubted whether it would ever be delivered. Since the declaration of war, the postal services had more or less ceased to function.

Henry still thought about England; not nostalgically and not with any regret for the decision he had made to come to France, but there was a feeling of guilt that came over him whenever he read reports of the fighting and of the collapse of the French armies along the Belgian front. It was barely a week since he had heard on the early B.B.C. news bulletin – whenever he was able to listen to it through the crackles of interference on the Aragos' wireless – about the evacuation of British and French troops from Dunkirk. Several thousand men, the announcer had said in his polished and disconcertingly consoling English voice, had been forced back by German

Panzer divisions into the pocket of land surrounding the port and were being driven into the sea, where they were miraculously rescued by a fleet of vessels, small and large, from across the Channel. The much-vaunted Maginot Line had remained intact, but the German armies under von Bock had simply crossed into Belgium and had now brought about the capitulation of that country and of Holland, as well as the surrender of the French First Army at Lille. The war that had been dubbed the phony war, or *drolette*, by the newspapers, was over. Not that anyone would know, down here in the Bourbonnais, Henry reflected, that there was a war taking place.

Ten minutes later he was standing in a small queue at the *tabac* in the main street of Bellerive to buy a packet of Boyards and collect his copy of *L'Œuvre*. It was his daily routine, except on Sundays: a walk, followed by coffee (well, chicory essence) and a cigarette with Jean and Chantal before brother and sister set off across the bridge to Vichy to walk to their gallery in one of the arcades on the far side of the town's park. After they had left, he would settle down to work, usually in the well-lit front room, or else in the tiny back garden beneath an apple tree, or by the river if it was warm enough.

Inspiration, however, did not always come easily, and sometimes, instead of sketching or painting, he read or wrote in his diary, listened to the wireless, leafed through old copies of *L'Illustration* or played through one of several piles of records in Chantal's collection – Lys Gauty, Jean Sablon, Léo Marjane and Charles Trenet were her particular favourites – on the gramophone. Otherwise, he indulged in sensual day-dreaming: fantasies in which he imagined himself in the company of any number of desirable women. Mostly, over the past six months, and ever since they had said goodbye to one another by the fountain in the Luxembourg, he had yearned for Marie-Hélène, but increasingly, in recent weeks, his thoughts were taken up by Chantal.

Chantal had olive skin, dark, almost black hair, brown eyes that were very slightly slanted and seemed to dissolve whenever they caught his gaze, and a body so tantalising that, he told himself, it was surely ripe for love. He longed to paint her, almost as much as he dreamed of kissing her. She had none of Marie-Hélène's self-confidence or cosmopolitan outlook, but there was a natural voluptuousness about her that he seemed to perceive whenever he caught sight of her in repose: at lunchtime, when she and Jean came home for lunch, or in the evenings, at the large wooden table in the kitchen, where every evening they listened to the B.B.C. news on the wireless.

Jean and Chantal's parents had died of tuberculosis within a year of one another while their children were still young. A devoted aunt, Tante Éliane, had nursed the parents in their illness and, after their deaths, she had brought up Jean and Chantal as her own children in a third-floor apartment over-looking the cathedral in the old quarter of Clermont-Ferrand. Jean had attended the local *lycée*, where he won praise for his essays on the Symbolist artists of the *fin de siècle*, and had then continued his studies at the École des Beaux-Arts in Paris; his sister, meanwhile, had been sent to a boarding school run by nuns near Lyon. Their parents, both Jews from Alsace, had left them a certain amount of money, which had been put in trust and had been enough to purchase the house in Bellerive as well as the premises of the small gallery Jean had opened in Vichy the previous summer.

For Henry, meeting Jean Arago had been the greatest good fortune. He and his sister treated him like a surrogate brother and he had never before encountered such warm and open hospitality. Despite the distant war and his sense of alienation from his own family, he felt happy for the first time in his life. He might have abandoned his own family in England, but he had found a new one here with the Aragos on the west bank of the Allier opposite the old and very bourgeois city of Vichy.

In his diary, Henry kept an intermittent record of his own activities as well as of the echoes that reached him of the still-remote war:

June 8, 1940, 41 rue Gabriel Ramin, Bellerive
Jean and Chantal's friend Pascal came to lunch today. He has left Paris, where he was a publisher's editor, and is now looking for work in Vichy. Everybody is fleeing Paris, he says, by any means possible. The day that he heard the French line had been breached at Sedan, he broke down and wept and decided then and there to leave Paris, which he believes will be in German hands in a few days' time. He said Paris looked radiant ("like a bride awaiting her ravisher!") on the morning that he left by train, and confessed that it was the saddest day of his life. The train was packed, with nowhere to sit, and it took seven hours to reach Moulins. His brother, Daniel, with whom he shared a flat, is also leaving and will be joining him in Vichy next week. Jean has said they can both help in the gallery.

Maréchal Pétain has been recalled from the embassy in Madrid and has said that France must sue for peace and that she cannot expect help from Great Britain. His name is being mentioned in newspapers and on the wireless as a possible saviour of the nation, though today's paper reports that Weygand's troops are holding firm.

Played tennis after lunch with Jean, Pascal and another friend of theirs at the courts behind the Hôtel du Parc. Later, I took my easel to the river and in the evening light painted the view of Bellerive from the Vichy shore.

Tuesday, June 11
Italy has declared war on Britain and France. "Il Duce" spoke aggressively and self-righteously on the wireless, addressing swarms of Black Shirts, the announcer said, who had gathered in front of the Piazza Venezia in Rome, ranting about the role History had assigned to his nation, and blaming those who stood in the way of Italian prosperity. Meanwhile, the Paris police have surrounded the Italian embassy on rue de Varenne and the ambassador has been arrested. To think that I was walking in those same streets only seven months ago.

Jean, Chantal and I were all gathered round the wireless set in the kitchen, and when Mussolini had finished speaking there were roars of approval from the crowd and much martial singing. Jean said it was the Fascist Party hymn and that we were all in danger from movements such as Il Duce's. I suggested that at least leaders like Mussolini, Hitler and Franco had a certain vision for their country, which was more than Daladier and Chamberlain had. "Europe needs strong men," I argued, and Jean gave me one of his weary, patronising smiles.

Monsieur Reynaud also spoke on the wireless yesterday evening and said that the battle being fought to the north and east of Paris was "the greatest battle of history . . . the trials that await us are heavy. We are ready for them . . . France cannot die." Chantal held her head in her hands while she listened, then she burst out, clapping excitedly, and exclaimed: "*Bravo pour Monsieur Reynaud! La France ne mourra jamais, n'est-ce pas, Jean?*" and she clutched her brother's arm. Then she turned to me with those wistful brown eyes and seemed to look into my soul: "*Et toi, Henri?* Aren't you patriotic at all? Why don't you show any emotion? If you love France, as you say, you must see that our two nations have to stand up against aggression." I said that there were more important loyalties than patriotism and devotion to one's country, and that for me family and religion came first. Chantal gave me a withering look. "Family! But you have abandoned your family? And I haven't noticed you going to Mass. You don't know what you are saying."

I couldn't tell whether her tone was one of anger or pity. She normally speaks to me with what I've always thought to be tenderness. I said goodnight quickly and went to bed early. I prayed on my knees for my parents and for Lavinia, and for those I knew in England, and I asked forgiveness for my lack of loyalty and faith. The thought occurred to me: does Chantal consider me a traitor?

June 15
On the wireless came the news that Paris has fallen. There are German troops on the Champs-Élysées, there

are machine guns all around the Étoile; swastikas flying on the Arc de Triomphe and the Eiffel Tower. Daniel, Pascal's brother, who arrived this afternoon in his old Renault crammed full with books, clothes and most of the contents of their Paris flat, says he heard German troops in their field-grey uniforms singing "*Lili Marlene*" in the place de la Concorde, and he had seen two German officers in uniform sitting at the terrace of the Sélect, his favourite café.

Chantal, who I'm discovering is very extreme in her emotions, burst into tears when we listened to the news tonight. We were alone. Jean, Daniel and Pascal were still at the gallery, working late, and I put my arm round her shoulders to comfort her. One part of me yearned for her; another held me back.

Suddenly, she stood up and walked to the far side of the room, her figure silhouetted against the window, through which I could see the lights of the house of our neighbours, the Graffin family. "Henry," she said, pronouncing my name in an almost English way. "What do you think will become of us? The Nazis will be all over France very soon and Jean and I won't be safe anywhere. I feel frightened. You know that we are Jews, don't you? I have never told you, but I want to tell you now. You may say one's ancestry makes no difference, but with us it does. We Jews are different, and the world seems to hate us for being what we are. Jean and I have no-one to turn to, no parents, our dear aunt is very old, and we have nowhere to hide. All that we have in the world is this house and our gallery. And friends, it is true . . . good friends like Pascal and Daniel, and you, dear Henry, but you'll want to go home to England one day, when all this sadness is over. We Jews have no homes. For months, people have been saying that there won't be a war, but now it's really happening, and we are lost. France is defeated, and so are we."

She sobbed so violently that her whole body shook and convulsed in wretchedness. A still voice within me urged me to detach myself, but I seized the moment, took her in my arms and kissed her. She responded with such surprising passion and intensity that my whole body was inflamed with an ardour I never knew myself capable of. Her hands gripped me and suddenly she was tearing at my shirt. Our bodies seemed to throb and pulsate with urgency and, despite myself, I followed her as she led me into the bedroom. She locked the door, then she took both my hands and held my gaze in hers. "I never know what you're really thinking, Henry," she said. "I feel I want to trust you and give myself to you, and yet there's something that holds me back." I said nothing. "Do you love me?" she asked, kneeling in front of me on the bed, her dishevelled hair fanned out over her naked shoulders. "We may not have much time."

I don't remember what I said, but I knew I was lying when I told her that I loved her, that she was beautiful and that I would never abandon her. She laughed and kissed me. "Wait for me," she said, and she opened the bedroom door and disappeared into the bathroom. When she returned, she had only a towel wrapped round her, which she discarded as she slipped into the bed. For a blissful hour or more I felt that we belonged solely to one another and that nothing else anywhere on this earth mattered. A part of me wanted those moments to last for ever. But another part of me gloried in the power of possessing her as she lay in my arms afterwards. Later, as I looked into her eyes, I knew I would betray her: she was a victim, she was at my mercy, and yet I desired her. I stroked her smooth, olive-brown skin, her breathing rising and falling rhythmically. She looked so vulnerable. Then I heard Jean's key in the front door and I started up guiltily. Chantal clasped me to her and said, "Why go? It was beautiful," but as soon as the house was silent again, I kissed Chantal and crept back to my own bedroom. I could not sleep, and so I turned on my bedside light and, from memory, sketched Chantal in the position in which she had been lying, her eyes closed, her lips apart, her expression serene.

[CHAPTER 6]

TWO DAYS LATER, MARÉCHAL PÉTAIN BROADCAST TO THE nation. In trembling tones the old man announced that he had appealed to the enemy for an end to fighting. He spoke of the thousands of refugees who were streaming along the roads of France with their pitiful possessions, and he asked for an armistice with honour "between soldiers".

The code of honour he represented belonged to another, more principled age. Henry and his friends, and anyone of their generation, could see that only too clearly. Maréchal Pétain, now eighty-three, the hero of Verdun, who had heroically put the morale of his embattled men – or those of them who survived – before all other considerations, was a relic of his nation's imperial past, of the France of *la gloire* and the armies that stepped to the tune of the Marche de Lorraine. The world had changed drastically since his day. Adolf Hitler and his Nazis, who confronted France now, were men of a different ilk, men with a very different concept of morality and honour.

At lunchtime, Pascal and Daniel had returned with Jean and Chantal from the gallery. They were joined in the kitchen by Monsieur Caussanel, an elderly neighbour who earned a few francs each week by keeping the Aragos' small garden tidy, and he was in tears as he listened to the Maréchal's sombre voice. He was a former soldier himself, a *poilu* who had fought with Pétain in the disastrous Artois offensive in 1915.

"*Ce pauvre Maréchal,*" he reflected sadly when Jean switched off the wireless, was "a fine soldier and a man of honour, but as a politician capable of dealing with the likes of Hitler and Ribbentrop . . ." He shrugged and held out the palms of his hands. "It's unthinkable."

His voice tailed off. Everyone sipped the hot chocolate that Chantal had made. Then, without any warning, the old man stood up. His bent body adopted an erect military posture. His eyes shone and he saluted. "They will try to take Lorraine and Alsace from us again, but they shall never have them. *Vive la France!*" He stood stiffly to attention and saluted, his eyes closed. Then, without another word, he went back into the garden.

∞

These were fateful days for France and for Europe. In Paris, people queued in the streets for bread and there were severe food shortages; for those who had decided to remain in the occupied capital rather than flee to the provinces, life became very hard. Within a few alarming days, the Prime Minister, Paul Reynaud, had resigned and Maréchal Pétain had been summoned and asked to form a new government based in Bordeaux. He offered France "the gift of my person" to attenuate her suffering and he told his people that the fighting must stop. For those of his Verdun generation, and for those who shared the deeply conservative values and militaristic traditions that he represented, he now appeared, almost miraculously, as the knight on a white charger: the saviour of France, a modern Joan of Arc, ready to restore the honour of his nation.

The following morning, gathered once more around the crackling wireless set, Henry, the Aragos, Daniel and Pascal listened to the voice of a former junior minister in Reynaud's government, Charles de Gaulle, broadcasting from London on the B.B.C. and calling on the French people to rally to him in Great Britain. "I, General de Gaulle . . . the flame of French resistance can never be extinguished" were the only words that anyone could make out through the interference.

"One brave man, at least," Jean said. And turning his soft brown eyes on Henry: "This will be proof of our famous *entente cordiale*, my friend. Now we shall see what such sentiments really mean."

"But it's all very well this arrogant, jumped-up officer abandoning ship and accepting the hospitality of our hereditary enemy," Daniel interrupted, "but if one's country is occupied and one's army is defeated, what choice do we have? Personally, I rather sympathise with *le vieux* – he knows from bitter experience what war means – but much will depend on what our navy does. It's even more powerful than your own, you know – if you still regard the Royal Navy as yours," he added, with a dark look at Henry. "And remember, we have an empire too. If our colonies also agree to an armistice with the Germans, then we have no option."

Those June days were fateful ones for Henry and Chantal and their embryonic affair. In Vichy and Bellerive, if one ignored the newspapers and radio broadcasts, little had changed. On either bank of the Allier, people went about their daily tasks untroubled by the cataclysm that was steadily breaking over Europe.

In the late afternoon sunshine, after Chantal had returned from the gallery, she and Henry walked arm-in-arm by the river. Henry was obsessed with her youth and her beauty, her smooth skin, her unfathomable, sad brown eyes and her slender body. Her apparent innocence was contradicted by a sexuality that drove Henry wild with a fierce longing. He begged her to let him sketch her or paint her portrait whenever an opportunity arose: sitting reading at the long table in the house at Bellerive, for example; or leaning over the parapet of the bridge over the Allier, a wistful look in her eyes; sitting astride a rock, skirts hitched up to her knees, in a gully by the river . . . One such drawing may have been the preliminary sketch for the portrait he planned to paint of her that would "commemorate our discovery of one another", as he put it in his diary on June 21:

I want my drawing of Chantal to be the best portrait I have done. I want it to reflect our passion – I hesitate to call it love for I believe I'm incapable of that – and I also want it to express my feelings for France in her hour of distress. Somehow I want the essence of all I love about this country, in peace and in war, to be incorporated into it, which is why I've added a church spire which was not actually visible, and a rather idealised paysage. I want it to convey the personal ecstasy of this actual moment, when France's fortunes have never been so low and my own have never seemed so high. I want it to possess sexual energy, too, if that were possible . . .

The political situation grew bleaker by the day and, as it worsened, so Henry's political views shifted, moving as they did with the tide of least resistance. In his diary, he provides some revealing and informative insights into his life during the summer of 1940.

June 23, midnight
On the news came the announcement of the armistice signed between Germany and France. It took place in the same railway dining carriage in the Forêt de Compiègne where Maréchal Foch had signed the armistice with the defeated Germans in 1918. It will come into force from midnight tomorrow, with certain terms and conditions attached. So . . . France has capitulated. Perhaps it is the lesser evil, and perhaps it will bring peace quickly. A new and united Europe will rid us of the Reds, and those who seek to weaken us. The *Massillia* has sailed from Bordeaux for Casablanca, with Mandel, Mendès-France and Daladier among those on board. Others, like Pierre Laval, who has just been appointed to the Cabinet, say they could never abandon *la patrie*.

This morning, Pascal and Daniel's parents arrived from Cabourg on the Normandy coast and are staying in a nearby hotel. Their father looks like an older version of Jean Gabin. They had driven through the night and appeared broken and distraught. I watched as he greeted his sons: "My dear boys, our beloved France is finished. She has been ravaged. Only the good God can give us peace now." He was in tears as he hugged them both. Their mother, who is more composed and has a proud and aristocratic demeanour, gave a vivid description of the planes (Messerschmitts, she said) patrolling the coast, and the grey tanks rolling into Caen, their tracks making sinister imprints in the tarmac. Swastikas flew everywhere, she said. She described how she had watched a young German with blond hair, stripped to the waist, gazing out arrogantly from the turret of his tank, shouting out Teutonic expletives at the horrified citizens on the pavement as he passed.

Chantal came to Mass with me this morning. It's the first time I've been to church since I left Paris, and I confess I did so both because I am a coward and because I feel distressed by the sense of doom Pascal and Daniel's parents have imparted. As we walked home, we took a roundabout route, past Mme de Sévigné's house and we lingered in the narrow streets. Chantal said she had felt an intruder in church and she irritated me by saying that she was sure I would marry a nice Catholic girl one day, and that "finally, mon chéri, we come from different worlds, you and I". I laughed and said that nothing could be certain in a time of war. But she stared at me sadly and said: "I'm not right for you, Henry. I will only make you suffer." I replied that I now felt French as much as I did English, and that she could only make me happy. Afterwards, I felt morose and disenchanted: it was like the first intimation of pain after ecstasy. I wish Chantal were not Jewish . . .

France is now split into two zones according to the terms of the Armistice: two-thirds of the country, including Paris and the Atlantic coast, will be occupied by the

Nazis; the rest is a "free zone" over which the French government will have sovereignty. Here in Vichy we are in the free zone, thank God, but only just: the "frontier" stops short of Tours and Dijon, and then loops down to Moulins, about seventy kilometres to the north of us. French radio stations have been suppressed – only for the time being, we are assured.

Chantal and Jean are worried by the political re-emergence of Pierre Laval. He's an Auvergnat peasant at heart, Jean says: "He should retire to Châteldon and look after his cows." Laval was born in the village where his father kept the café, and he bought the château there after he resigned as prime minister in 1932. I saw his photograph in the local newspaper, which these days is being printed only intermittently, and I must say there is something devious about his expression. Jean says Laval despises the "perfidious" Anglo-Saxons especially! On the other hand, I sense that he may be the right man to deal with the Germans and the morass into which we all seem to be sinking.

July 2

This past week has been spent at my easel. Jean has told me that work to be shown at my exhibition must be ready a fortnight from now – not later – because there will be summer visitors here taking the waters who may be inclined to buy. Better still, to everyone's astonishment, the Government has now moved here – first they evacuated to Bordeaux, then Clermont, and now all the ministers have come to Vichy – so we are on the map, and I may have rather more opportunity for my pictures to be noticed. The ministers' motor cars began arriving this evening at the Hôtel du Parc as well as at the town's other big hotels, which have been requisitioned for government offices. I was with Jean at his gallery yesterday evening and we went along to watch the procession of officials filing into the Hôtel Majestic, where they were informed of where in town they are to be housed. "It's an invasion of clerks, and all because we have big hotels in Vichy," Jean said. Monsieur Laval arrived on foot, however, for his car had broken down on the way from Clermont. He walked past us with a wave to the crowd. He was wearing a white tie and looked solemn, pompous and bovine. How extraordinary that this quiet, elegant resort should have its peace shattered by such events! As we walked back home, across the park and over the bridge to Bellerive, the atmosphere seemed livelier and more cosmopolitan than at any time since I came to live here. Fancy Vichy becoming the centre of elegance and fashion!

Occasionally, however, I admit to feeling uncomfortable at the thought that I, an Englishman, whose country is at war with Germany, should find myself living less than two kilometres away from what is now the seat of power of a nation whose capital is occupied by Hitler's troops. These are mad and desperate times and, if I am honest, I don't know whether to rejoice or to be frightened.

July 4, 1940

Jean came home for lunch bringing the desperate news that the Royal Navy has bombarded the French fleet as it lay at anchor at its base at Mers-el-Kébir in North Africa, and hundreds of deaths are reported. It seems a cruel and hostile act against a supposed ally in time of war, but Jean explained in his usual, pragmatic way that if the powerful French fleet were to fall into enemy hands, Germany would have little difficulty in controlling the seas. The British delivered an ultimatum to the French, he told us – conveyed by a mere captain – to either sail with them, which would be an infringement of the terms of the Armistice, or to scuttle their ships. Admiral Darlan refused, and so the Royal Navy opened fire. Within minutes, Jean said, hundreds of sailors were swimming for their lives, many of them drowning in the process. He mentioned a friend of his from the Beaux-Arts, a very promising sculptor, who was a young serving officer aboard the destroyer *Mogador*, one of the ships that was sunk. He wondered whether he was still alive.

I feel ashamed and saddened: our two countries are meant to enjoy this supposed "*entente cordiale*", yet throughout history, it seems to me, the English have always treated the French with arrogance, while the French have looked down on the English with intellectual disdain. How can good relations ever be restored after such a desperate act?

This evening, Chantal and I walked to the café just by the Pont Boutiran. Chantal introduced me to the proprietress, Madame Chapart, saying that I was "an artist and a good friend", and she took my hand in a casual yet possessive gesture that I feel sure was meant to indicate that we were friends despite what has happened at Mers-el-Kébir. At least, I like to think so. We sat outside, drinking the cool, thin local white wine, smoking and watching the reflections of the last of the daylight playing on the water as the sun set behind us. Madame Chapart gave us a freshly killed chicken, *pour la famille*, which Chantal cooked for the five of us. Pascal and Daniel's parents left yesterday to drive south, so the house does not seem quite so crowded. There are also fewer mouths for poor Chantal to try to feed, since cooking duties fall mainly to her. The father, Monsieur Amiot, looked haggard and drawn. "In case we should not meet again in this world, I want to embrace you all," he said, and he and his wife wept as they bade us farewell, kissing us one by one on both cheeks.

In the morning I worked on the portrait of Chantal that I have adapted and copied from the sketch I made the other day. I believe I have caught that elusive, ethereal, vulnerable quality she has, as well as her silken flesh that continues to drive me wild whenever I think about her. I captured her enigmatic, gently mocking smile, too. It's as though she knows I will desert her one day. Will I? I no longer know. One part of me yearns to be with her for ever; another tells me to flee. Shall I show the canvas at my exhibition next month? Perhaps . . . and yet I feel I want to keep it (and her) to myself. I even begin to ache with jealousy whenever Daniel addresses what could be construed as slightly intimate or flirtatious remarks to her. Both Daniel and Pascal use a lot of slang expressions and talk in nuances, and although I pick up most of the inferences, I sometimes feel mildly excluded, just as I do whenever the brothers remind me that I am truly an expatriate now.

P.S. Hélène de Portès has been killed in a motoring accident near Sète. I remember Robert telling me in Paris that she was the most beautiful – and the most influential – woman he had ever met. Robert always did have a network of acquaintances, especially in the art world. It's how he gets by. I wish I could see him again.

Sunday – midnight, July 7–8, 1940
I set eyes on Maréchal Pétain for the first time today. I went into town to go to Mass and decided to walk across the park and past the entrance to the Hôtel du Parc. As I approached, a liveried chauffeur at the wheel of a Delahaye, its sun-roof down, drove past at a sedate pace, and there were Pétain and Madame la Maréchale perched regally in the back. The Maréchal looked straight at me as he passed, and he was so close that I could observe the haughty expression in those intensely blue eyes. As the car drew up in front of the former hotel and they alighted, a crowd of women and children gathered around, some cheering and singing. The Maréchal is now bald, with a long moustache, and he has a very upright walk for an old man. His face is pink with a well-scrubbed complexion, and he looks uncannily youthful. He was wearing a grey lounge suit, and he strutted as he entered the hotel

with his head held particularly high. He stopped to shake hands or stroke a child's cheek, or to hold up a hand to the crowd in a gesture of greeting. "*Mes bons amis . . .*" he muttered each time he touched anyone. His wife, a much younger woman, dressed in a floral-pattern dress followed unsmiling behind him. As they walked up the steps, voices in the crowd began to chant the words of the song that has become his anthem:

> *Maréchal, nous voilà!*
> *Devant toi, le sauveur de la France,*
> *Nous jurons, nous, tes gars,*
> *De servir et de suivre tes pas.*

At lunchtime, I told Jean, Chantal and Daniel (Pascal had gone fishing) about my encounter and about the priest's sermon at Mass. "Let us give thanks for the deliverance of France," the abbé had urged the packed congregation, and he went on to praise a government that invokes God, believes in family values, and has given the monastery of La Grande Chartreuse back to the monks. "*Grâce à Dieu*," he said, "a little authority has at last been restored." Jean says that the Church is being influenced unhealthily by Action Française ("France for the French" etc.) and by Charles Maurras and his friends, who believe the only enemy is Bolshevism. I hear a lot about this Maurras.

Daniel told us that his great-uncle had, like Monsieur Caussanel, served under the victor of Verdun at some stage of his military career, and that although Pétain had been a strict, even severe general (his nickname was "Précis-le-sec"), he was also a celebrated womaniser who had numerous affairs, which I said I found surprising given the upright moral image he imparts.

"Not at all, it's typically French –" Chantal reacted heatedly – "the idea that we should all be supposed to revere the sort of man who regards women like that: it's horrible. He treats women as if they were dispensable, just like his soldiers. Whoever dubbed him *'le soldat trop connu'* was quite right. I don't know why you find him so admirable." She glared at us and walked out of the room without another word. Another of Chantal's sudden sulks.

I spent the afternoon painting and I did not see Chantal again until supper time. She had changed into a red sleeveless dress, and I thought I had never seen her look lovelier. Pascal cooked the fish he had caught in the Allier. We ate on the terrace and, not realising that politics has become a subject best avoided in this house nowadays, Pascal referred to Pierre Laval, whose open-roofed car had passed him as he was cycling home on the road from Charmeil. "You can't mistake him," Pascal laughed. "A white tie around his neck and a caporal between his lips. And then he looks so malevolent. He reminds me of a toad – a dark, slimy Mongolian toad. His daughter Josée was with him. She's not bad-looking, though I can't see where she gets it from."

"The wretched man can't help his looks," Jean responded, "and he may be the type of man we – France and Europe – need at this time. Pragmatism and calm are what is required. If men like Hitler and Mussolini are going to run Europe, a narrow-minded patriot like Monsieur Laval may be the only politician available with the necessary tough, peasant-like qualities to be able to stand up to them. The Maréchal can only be a figurehead; he needs ambitious people like Laval around him—"

"Jean, how can you say things like that?" Chantal interrupted, flaring up as she so often does. She was shaking and she had the same angry look that I had noticed in the morning. "Laval is a Germanophile, that's obvious, and a man who sides with Adolf Hitler will certainly not have our interests at heart." Chantal glared at her brother for a moment. "Can't you see that?" Then she turned to me. "And you, Henry. I saw you nodding in agreement with what Jean says. Sometimes I worry about you, you know. You desert your own country when she needs you, and you seem to believe all this talk of a National Revolution. Do you really think that tired old men and clowns like Hitler and Mussolini – probably Laval, too – are the sort to bring about genuine revolution? Don't make me laugh . . . They are power seekers, ruthless men who will crush anyone who opposes them."

I paraphrase her actual words, but Chantal – my beloved Chantal – was overwrought again. I had not seen such a degree of inner fury before, and simultaneously I admired her courage, while recoiling from the liberal political beliefs she seems to support. She went up to her bedroom without saying goodnight to me, and I write this not having been able to sleep or read since.

I woke up after a disturbing dream in which I was

riding out to sea on a horse I could not control. Less and less do I like the way I see myself reflected in others. My heart leads me in one direction, my head in another.

July 9
Painted on the back of a military lorry, the words: "*Vendu, pas vaincu.*" Many people I overhear in cafés and in the street think that the Maréchal will betray the country. I believe he may have saved France.

July 10
My birthday. Twenty-eight and I should be "in my prime", as Jean put it when he and Chantal presented me with a box of exotic dried mushrooms – gathered from the forests near here last autumn, and tied with a red ribbon – at breakfast this morning. Chantal kissed me and apologised for her outburst last night. I worked hard all day in my atelier, touching up and framing pictures for the exhibition (which is now announced on posters in the gallery for the first week of August). Then I took Jean and Chantal out to dinner at the Chante Clair. The cooking is still good there, despite the food short-ages, and the price was reasonable, even with a very good Chambertin '37. I paid with one of the last of the hundred-franc notes I earned from my exhibition last Christmas which I still had hidden away.

At dinner, Jean pointed out Albert Lebrun, the Président, dining by himself in a corner of the restaurant. He looked morose in his baggy grey suit, picking at his food, and hardly tasting the wine that was served to him.

Jean predicts that he will be the last president of the Third Republic and that the Maréchal will be given full powers any day now. He said that all French men and women will be confronted with "the hour of choice": collaboration or resistance.

July 14
Bastille Day. Chantal and I walked past the memorial where Maréchal Pétain ("Philippe le Gaga" is how Pascal refers to him!), resplendent in his Verdun uniform, took the salute and paid tribute to all those *morts pour la patrie* in the Great War and during the fighting of the past two months. Poor old Lebrun is gone – just as Jean prophesied the other day – and the Maréchal is now *Chef de l'État français*. The Republic is dead. There was no dancing in the streets tonight though, and the people gathered in the park looked subdued. Tino Rossi's tenor voice drones out all day on Radio-Vichy: Chantal gives me what I like to think is a special glance whenever he sings "J'attendrai . . ."

∞

Henry's passionate feelings for Chantal appear to have reached a zenith during the last fortnight of July 1940 and, in the process, generated the seeds of their destruction. Inspired by her love for him, he prepared for his second exhibition at the Aragos' little gallery that August with a determination to excel, to sublimate himself, with all the guilt and passion and energy that had been consuming him over the past year, in work which would exceed anything he had done hitherto.

He worked by day and devoted himself to Chantal by night. There was little else to his existence. On the wireless, the reports from the B.B.C. that he still managed to listen to suggested the fighting was escalating, and the French press, which increasingly reflected a neutral view, predicted that a Nazi invasion of Britain was imminent. In the local newspaper, the Bishop of Clermont-Ferrand called for "penitence" and for recognition of the faults that were responsible for the present disaster: moral lassitude, materialism, de-Christianisation. In the weeks that followed, food rationing was introduced – so far there had only been shortages – and conditions had become more harsh. In the Occupied Zone the German vice was tightening: in Strasbourg, place de Broglie was renamed "Adolf Hitler Platz", while place de la République was in future to be known as "Bismarck Platz"; in the shops of Alsace and Lorraine prices were now printed in Deutschmarks and transactions had to be carried out in German currency; priests were forbidden to give their sermons in French at Sunday Mass, while at schools in the provinces lessons in the German language were now obligatory.

In Vichy, however, the mood was less sombre. The nation's saviour, in the eyes of many (though by no means all), the old and venerable Maréchal, was in full control; his newly formed government included such solid and dependable citizens as General Weygand, Admiral Darlan, Pierre Laval and Raphaël Alibert, and his Révolution Nationale had been launched with unconcealed relief. "France has been delivered after sixty years," Paul Claudel wrote, "from the yoke of the anti-Catholic Radical party (teachers, lawyers, Jews, Freemasons). The new Government invokes God and gives back La Grande Chartreuse to the monks. There is hope of being delivered from universal suffrage . . . and also from the evil and stupid domination of teachers, who in the last war covered themselves with shame. The restoration of authority." Charles Maurras and his Action Française movement agreed: "A great good fortune has come to us in our immense misery," read an article in that summer's *La Nouvelle Guyenne*. "God had prepared for us a great leader. Maréchal Pétain has gathered up France in the very hour of her distress." The nation – in the eyes of some of its citizens at least – was being reborn. A new France based on the ethics of *Travail, Famille, Patrie* was in the process of arising. (Or *"Trahison, Famine, Prison"*, as Jean Arago joked.)

Following the destruction of the French fleet at Mers-el-Kébir, there was much more hostility directed at Britain than towards the German aggressor, and Henry took the utmost care to conceal his identity. "I'd lie low, *mon pôte*, if I were you," advised Daniel, "and above all, don't let anyone who knows you're English see you with Chantal until this madness settles down."

Not that Henry was dismayed by such remarks. Perhaps, in his heart, he already regarded himself as a French citizen. Recalling in his diary the evening of his *vernissage* at the gallery, he was in his most positive and confiding frame of mind:

August 8
I have to admit that I enjoy being the focus of attention. However dissatisfied I may feel about my work, its lack of originality and its sameness, other people appear to approve of it – and even buy it, despite the shortages and present economic hardships. I have sold eleven of the twenty-five paintings and drawings that Jean showed,

including four of the seascapes I did at Collioure, which had remained unsold from my last show, and with this money and the little I still have left over, I should have enough to last the year. I feel more liberated than at any time since I arrived here and I want to be less dependent on the Aragos. I have also made some useful contacts in high places . . . for I may need to apply for citizenship and will need help sorting out my papers. If I play my cards with care, I may be able to move a little more freely.

But I am thinking ahead instead of describing the *vernissage*, the high point of my year. There were fifty or sixty people present – far more than at Christmas – not including Jean and Chantal, Daniel and Pascal, or the tame critic from the local paper, whom I rather like. And there were several members of the Maréchal's entourage, it appears, for when Jean showed me the guestbook later he pointed out four names: Henri du Moulin de Labarthète, who had been at the Madrid embassy with Pétain and is now head of the Civil Office; Dr Ménétrel, who is the Old Man's personal physician and as anti-Semitic, apparently, as the Nazis; the writer René Gillouin; and Raphaël Alibert, who is the Minister for Justice and reputed to be the Maréchal's right-hand man. It was Alibert who shook me by the hand as he was leaving and, to my shock and astonishment, told me that "in spite of everything I was very welcome here". Jean took me aside and whispered: "I shouldn't trust him if I were you, but he's a man of influence and is well known for his Action Française views. Let's hope he buys something!" And so he did, I assume, because a woman, who

Jean assures me is his secretary, asked Chantal to put a reserve sticker on my watercolour of the old barn in the field by the river, and she left the Minister's personal card for me.

Daniel also introduced me to a girl whose easy smile, blue eyes and fresh complexion have remained in my thoughts ever since I set eyes on her. She was breathtakingly lovely and appeared to be on her own, but no sooner had we exchanged greetings than she announced that she was obliged to leave because her parents were expecting her. Her name is Madeleine, but neither Daniel, who chatted to her in his insouciant, charming Gallic way, nor anyone else, knows a thing about her ... Jean checked the guestbook, but there was no record of any Madeleine, and he reckons she is the daughter of one of the government clerks or *fonctionnaires* who have moved to Vichy in recent days. Daniel says that she is certainly not local, to judge by her accent, and that she has the social manner of a *Parisienne du seizième*. I MUST SEE HER AGAIN, but I can't tell Jean, who would immediately suspect that my feelings for Chantal are cooling. (I can tell he assumes we shall marry once the war is over.)

After the guests had left, the four of us from Bellerive, together with Jean's friend Jo Bonnard and his fiancée, squeezed into his Renault and set off for dinner at an inn in a pretty village on the road to Roanne. We consumed a large *pôtée auvergnate* between us, and rather too much wine in my case, but I felt light-headed anyway, what with the exhibition and thoughts of Madeleine (even with Chantal sitting close beside me in the car). The conversation became heated and far too political. Jo, who is an anglophile and is slightly older than us, teaches English at a nearby *lycée*. He had the nerve to tell me I was a "Mosleyite" and that I should be wearing a black shirt. He's well built, with dark, flashing eyes and a rather imposing, antagonistic manner. He said that I was "*perfide*" in not defending my own country and he could not understand why an artist with an evidently well-merited reputation should be wasting his time mixing with the "worthless timeservers who have washed up in Vichy". He said, "You British have much more to be proud of in recent years than we do, so why remain in France when your own brave people are fighting for the freedom of Europe and the civilised world?" Apparently the Luftwaffe is bombing South Coast towns such as Portsmouth and Southampton. He said he was sure that it could be arranged for me to escape, and that he had useful contacts if I should need help. Jo believes that the present Armistice will not last. He reckons the Germans will demand Alsace, and perhaps Corsica and Savoy for the Italians, and that a new Franco-German frontier will be drawn along the Meuse. He says that the French must not behave too cravenly towards the Germans, for they will never respect collaboration; he also thinks that we should pay no attention to the propaganda for a National Revolution. I argued back as best I could. I told him that I believed in what Pétain was trying to do and that a new Europe would emerge after the war. I said that I was moved emotionally at the thought of what was happening in my own country, but that if I were true to myself,

I could not be a patriot. Quoting an editorial that I had read in *L'Œuvre* that morning, I tried to suggest that our future depends on the defeat of the Communist peril and the advent of a community of European nations, but he was like a stone wall. Jo is superior and a touch insensitive, especially for a man of the Left, as he describes himself. His attractive fiancée, Mireille (they are to be married next year), nodded in agreement with everything he said. "Not Communism, my friends," he said, wagging a peremptory finger as he puffed on his Sherlock Holmes pipe, "the true danger to Europe is Fascism: Hitler, Mussolini, Franco, Salazar and all those strutting military comedians in uniforms. Democracy is the only solution, liberty the only prize. We may have to go underground, but we shall conquer (*'nous vaincrons'*), and there will be no place for those who have helped *les Fritz*." Later, much later, and slightly drunk, he stood up and gave a bleary rendition of the Marseillaise, until the owners came over and threatened to call the *flics* and we all managed to shut him up. Jean drove Jo's car back to town, for he was too far gone, and Chantal – who listened to Jo in rapt admiration, I observed – made up a bed for him and Mireille on the floor of the front room.

Next morning when I awoke (all this happened three days ago) a letter was delivered to me by special messenger. It seems to have been sent through an official channel, for there were no postage stamps, simply a series of initialled rubber stamps, the largest of which was marked "*Vichy-État*". To my astonishment, it was from Robert Worcester.

I found Robert Worcester's four-page letter tucked into Henry's diary and I believe it is worth reproducing, firstly because Robert has already been mentioned in this attempt of mine to make sense of my grandfather's life, and secondly because of the vivid picture it conveys of Paris under the Occupation.

I want to say at this juncture that I personally had never considered Ghislaine's and my investigation of our forebear's past as anything more than family research. As far as I was concerned, it provided light relief, a welcome contrast to the enclosed, often stifling world of classical music in which I earn my crust. I find myself fascinated – even, on occasions, disturbed by my grandfather's naive political views – views that would be dismissed by most of my friends today as fascist – and by his tendency to make use of people and treat every experience for his own ends.

Ghislaine, on the other hand, believes that Henry is an historical curiosity: a talented artist, a rare, perhaps unique example of an English supporter of Vichy, with pro-Nazi sympathies, who may (I can find no proof of this, though Ghislaine confirms that her mother says that it is so) have been granted French naturalisation at the personal request of Maréchal Pétain, and a romantic francophile who yearned for a France that was disappearing before his eyes. Ghislaine has also told me about the Sigmaringen diaries she has been reading and she describes life there as "a phantasmagoric nightmare". She has been in touch with Sylvain de Gresly and questioned her mother further, and she now believes she has some idea about how Henry made his way from a Germany in ruins in 1945 and came to settle in Buenos Aires, where he lived until his death.

For all these reasons, Ghislaine believes we have a duty to try to bring Henry's story to a wider audience. "Being in the literary world, Will," she wrote to me, "I am fortunate in having connections that may make this possible." She believes that for our putative readers' sake, and for clarity, we should treat the events described in the diaries as narrative, only reproducing my grandfather's actual entries where they help to illustrate aspects of his character. So it was that we set ourselves the task over those months – she in Paris, I in London – of deciphering and reconstructing the remaining material. Only in this way, Ghislaine says, can she detach herself from the fact that the woman who occupies centre stage in Henry's pathetically sad Sigmaringen diaries is none other than her own mother, who is alive and well and living in her family home to this day . . . But I digress, here is Robert Worcester's letter:

[CHAPTER 7]

31 RUE BUFFON, *5ÈME*
Paris, August 9, 1940

Dear Henry

I can imagine your surprise at hearing from me after such a long silence. Communication, however, between the two zones of this divided France is, as you must know, not easy unless one has connections . . . In truth, I am prompted to write because an old friend (let's call him Hervé), a *polytechnicien* who spent a year at Harvard back in 1935 and is now employed by the government, has told me of your exhibition and the success you are enjoying in Vichy. Bravo, old pal! Not that I'm surprised, I knew you had talent from the day we met . . . Between ourselves, Hervé is rather well placed in government circles, and though I prefer not to mention his name at the moment – one has to be ever so discreet in Paris nowadays and so I am mailing this to you via an "inside track" – he could be useful to you in times to come, should you encounter difficulties – as I myself have done – with the authorities.

Life here has scarcely been easy since you left, and no-one could have prepared us for those terrible days in May and June when I felt civilisation was coming to an end. For me – and for you too, I suspect – Paris represents all that is most beautiful and worthwhile in this world, and witnessing what has happened here has been like watching a beloved friend being humiliated, his pride stripped naked, his dignity assaulted; the city's old stones and her historic streets now resound to the brutish tramp of grim-faced Nazi soldiers who have no inkling of where they are, nor of the barbarism they are perpetrating. I have never known the morale of people to have sunk so low.

It seems a year ago already, but in reality it is barely two months since I walked to rue de l'Odéon to call on Sylvia and Adrienne (who send you their best, by the way) at Shakespeare & Co. Sylvia was in tears. We knew that Paris was being bombed as we spoke; not the centre, thank God, but the *15ème* and the *16ème*, where the Lycée Molière (where your friend Marie-Hélène went to school, I remember her saying) has been destroyed, as have Billancourt and the Citroën factories on the Quai de Javel. God, it was awful, Henry! People were fleeing in every direction, their possessions piled onto handcarts. Children were being evacuated – all joy has vanished. Even the birds have deserted the city; the effect of the bombing of the petroleum storage tanks, which were set alight as the Germans approached, and the air becoming poisoned.

Knowing me as I was a year ago, you may be surprised to hear that I don't venture outside much anymore. The streets are silent, even in the Quartier Latin; people queue for basic rations at shops; a curfew has been imposed; the cafés are empty: Paris has lost her soul.

When I do pull myself together and try to see friends, I go to the movies – Greta Garbo in "Ninotchka" at the Kursaal last week – but even then you are aware, in that silvery-blue light, of German soldiers sitting there in their sweat-stained green uniforms, guzzling uncomprehendingly on their Esquimaux. I tell you, Henry, it really *is* like the end of civilisation (and I only dare say such things because I am confident of the dependability of my messenger!). Then, yesterday, I went to the Luxembourg, where last fall you and I talked about the new Europe, and about Marie-Hélène, and love, and art, and literature – and Drieu's books, remember? Well, dammit, there was a German band playing there. You could just as well have been walking down Unter den Linden or sitting in the Englischer Garten in Munich. The tunes were full of that sentimental ersatz Bavarian rusticity, and the musicians even had clusters of bells attached to their instruments. As if that were not bad enough, I walked home to my new apartment opposite the Jardin des Plantes and passed the Lycée Henri IV on the way. There, in large graffiti, were the words: HEIMAT, SÜSSE HEIMAT! And even at night, before the curfew's enforced, you can't escape the cyclist patrols – *hirondelles*, the Parisians call them – and those insolent, blond Aryans whistling "*Lili Marlene*" as they speed by. The blood boils!

Henry, I am guessing you may be surprised at my tone. Knowing my political views, which I seem to recall you shared in some measure, you may wonder at my anti-German attitudes. Let me reassure you: I still believe in the new Europe. But we shall all have to suffer for it – and wait. I, too, used to believe that the way ahead lay with the new Fascism, in the vision of men like Hitler, Mussolini and Franco, because they were the only ones who have sufficient courage to resist the Communist menace. However, I did not envisage that it would be necessary for Hitler to invade and plunder Paris to achieve his ends. Something has gone badly wrong! War will solve nothing and can only bring suffering. Being August, the city is even emptier than usual. Hervé (my friend in high places) and I spent last week in the *midi*. We stayed in Aix-en-Provence, that very beautiful spa town – do you know it? – at a dream of an eighteenth-century *hôtel* off the Cours Mirabeau. My window overlooked a charming fountain that depicted four dolphins gently spouting water. Every morning we would set out under azure skies – Hervé wearing his *beret basque*, I in my panama hat and blazer – to sit for an hour at Les Deux Garçons under the shade of the chestnut trees before the heat of the sun became too intense. I do believe it's my favourite café in the whole of France. There we would take our coffees and our bread (no longer *beurré*, alas), smoke, and read *L'Œuvre* until 10.00 or so before setting off in an old Simca, lent to us by a university friend of Hervé's who lives in Aix, to explore the region. Thus have I seen, in the space of one week, Cezanne's Saint-Victoire from an infinite variety of angles, the Pont du Gard, the Maison Carrée at Nimes, the amphitheatre and Saint-Trophime at Arles, the flamingoes and the white horses on the Camargue . . . to name but some of the glories. And down there, apart from the food shortages, you would never have guessed there was a war going on! After that week, we caught the train back north. It chugged painfully slowly – the railway system has virtually broken down in both sectors – through what will always be the land of my heart: those rivers, mountains, canals and fields that enshrine everything that your old Maréchal in Vichy invokes when he speaks of "*la France eternelle*". I thought I had never seen this country look so beautiful or so forlorn . . . Then, at Moulins, we stopped at the demarcation line and German officers in uniform boarded the train. Although we had our papers in order – thanks to Hervé, who got off at Bourges to visit his mother before returning to Vichy – the train was for some reason put on a deviation that took us so far out of our way that we did not reach Paris until close on midnight (Central European time, which is what we are obliged to conform to up here). No dining car, of course. I was famished, I can tell you!

Somehow, while we were in Provence, I had forgotten that Paris was occupied . . . that she had been invaded and disfigured by this foreign presence. A glance in any direction is enough to remind you forcibly of the ubiquity of this *Deutsches Herrenvolk* in the capital: the swastika flies on all municipal buildings, and each day the soldiers parade up or down one or other of the *grands boulevards*. Only yesterday, on the Champs-Élysées, they marched past in perfect, clockwork unison, goose-stepping and singing their "Horst Wessel" song. Passers-by watched expressionless: Paris is already accustomed to being enslaved. I heard yesterday that the Grand Palais has been commandeered as a garage for military vehicles, and that the École Normale – would you believe it? – has become a barracks!

I had, I admit, some hopes of this German occupation. I think that most of us who had witnessed the depths of apathy to which this nation had sunk imagined that a dose of German efficiency, vision and *realpolitik*, combined with the Maréchal's determination to restore those traditional French values that he represents, would result in a cleansing, a *tabula rasa* of kinds, a revitalising of the spirit. These are early days, but already I'm not so sure; these Nazis are thugs by any other name. This became very clear to me earlier this week when I walked along the Quai Malaquais and suddenly noticed that the statue of Voltaire that used to stand there – remember? – had disappeared. I asked a shopkeeper what had happened and, after looking about him to make sure we were alone, he confided: "*Ce sont les boches, monsieur.* They took it down during the night, just as they have destroyed other fine statues in our city. It seems they use the bronze for munitions – "*là-bas*", he jerked his thumb – "in Germany".

As if that were not bad enough, there is insidious propaganda: the *métro* is full of posters depicting famous men such as Victor Hugo and Renan, beneath which are printed quotations, taken from one of their works that include some favourable allusion to Germany or to

German culture. There are others that show photographs of foreigners (like you and me – you must get yourself naturalised, if you have not already done so: Hervé can help!!) who have been shot for espionage. This is a warning to anyone tempted to resist the Occupation.

Yesterday, on my way home, I had just turned into the narrow rue des Saussaies, when a bicycle pulling a small seat on wheels (they call them *vélo-taxis*) drew up almost beside me, and two Oberbannführers in full uniform alighted, trampled their cigarettes in the gutter and marched into a doorway. I mentioned this in the gallery today and I was told that it was well known that the building was the secret police, or Gestapo, headquarters.

Where will all this lead to, Henry? To the Europe you and I looked forward to so eagerly, or to its subjugation by tyrants posing as revolutionaries? There is so much I want us to talk about. So many questions I want to ask. Are you still a Catholic? Are you a *Maréchaliste*? Do you believe in destiny? Is God watching over France? Is St Louis, or Joan of Arc? Not much sign of them here . . . Should we consider ourselves traitors? (It's worse for you, old boy; at least America isn't involved in this goddam war.) Will you be interned if and when you go home, or will you remain an exile for ever? (Me? I'm not going back. This is my home now, for richer, for poorer.)

We can still discuss these things – or rather, we could if you were prepared to come to Paris. That's not as difficult as you might imagine. Hervé knows Alibert, one of your ministers down there, and he assures me that an *Ausweis* for travel in the Occupied Zone can be facilitated in special cases. You may even be able to travel on the "blue train".

What do you think? The art world has all but collapsed, with German officials helping themselves to virtually anything they want at "special" prices. I am earning rather less for the work I buy and sell, and although I go to the gallery daily, there is little happening. So I can't promise you an exhibition, not even a small one, but there are still some people with money around, including some high-ranking German officers who are only too eager to be thought of as cultured Francophiles. Much as I resent them being here, one has to live . . . You see what a double-dealing hypocrite I have become!

Think about my invitation and try to make it to Paris this fall. (I *repeat*: ask Hervé for help; with letters, with communications, travel, even naturalisation papers; the secretariat at the Hôtel Thermal will know exactly who he is.) I have a spare room, some good books, a bottle of black-market Scotch to make up for the curfew, and some U.S. cigarettes. The Seine is five minutes' walk, so is the Gare d'Austerlitz; the Jardin des Plantes is my front garden. Paris is still worth a Mass, even with the swastika flying over it. How can you resist? Collaborate, I say, and live for the day. It's the only way. A message delivered to Hervé will be forwarded to me. You can count on total discretion.

A très bientôt, alors

Your friend,

Robert

[CHAPTER 8]

ON THE AFTERNOON THAT HENRY LATYMER'S "BLUE" train arrived at the Gare d'Austerlitz he was wearing the *francisque*, a silver brooch depicting a double-headed axe with a marshal's baton, on the lapel of his thick, grey serge suit. Considering it was mid-November, the weather was unusually mild and he wished he had dressed more appropriately. The truth of the matter was that he expected to meet influential people during his stay in the capital, which was why he had packed his one and only suit, a relic from as long ago as his last year at his public school, where he had been required to wear "formal dress" at Mass on Sundays.

The station was crowded, and the smoke from the engines seemed to invade his lungs, more accustomed to the pure air of the Bourbonnais. Railway officials, porters in uniform and women carrying small children bustled to and fro, paying little attention to the armed German soldiers in field-grey uniforms. Henry made his way among them, a canvas bag and a portfolio containing recent work in either hand, down the concourse to the station's exit.

"*Salut, mon pôte!*" a voice boomed out behind him. Then it

dropped to not much more than a whisper as it spoke in English: "Welcome back to Paris! This is the one train in the country that is never late. You're privileged, my friend, the journey normally takes eighteen hours. So glad you could come."

An arm had embraced Henry's shoulder before he could see where the soft American drawl was coming from. Simultaneously, the portfolio was removed from his left hand.

"Let me carry this . . . I had your message yesterday, I knew you wouldn't be able to resist. This may not be quite the city we once knew and loved, but what the hell, it's still Paris."

Robert was wearing grey-flannel trousers, a neat navy *canadienne* with a white shirt and a tie decorated with a motif of Greek letters against a maroon background, which Robert later told his friend denoted membership of his former college fraternity.

At a café on boulevard de l'Hôpital they drank Viandox and each gave the other brief accounts of all that had happened in the year or so since they had last met. For Henry, it was a reminder of what in retrospect seemed a brief period of pre-war bliss. For Robert, it was a rare opportunity to pour out his soul in his native tongue, as long as he kept his voice low. The November sunshine warmed the *terrasse*, and a light breeze off the Seine blew a collection of leaves and litter in gusts around their feet. A few passers-by, eyes to the ground, walked past their table. The streets were strangely quiet.

"Poor Paris," Robert said. "She'll come through, but she'll never be the same for us. Just as we never knew the city of Baudelaire and the Belle Époque, so our children will never know the Paris we had come to love. Do you realise that, Henry? I feel as if our youth has passed with this war. Those Parisian kiosks," he said, pointing across the pavement to the woman wearing a headscarf, just visible above her display of magazines and newspapers with their array of bold, typographical front-page headlines: *La Gerbe, Le Temps, Le Figaro, L'Œuvre, Je Suis Partout, Le Petit Parisien,* and *Gringoire,* the Maréchal's favourite weekly. "And those barges that meander down the Seine, the taxi cabs with their klaxons, the *bals musettes,* the *quais* with their tramps and lovers, all that gaiety and invention that brought us here in the first place, it'll go, you know, and neither the city nor its people will ever be quite what they were again. Of course, new generations will come along and they'll see a different Paris, and I guess that what they never knew, they won't miss. Meanwhile, we shall just have to cope with the German presence and get along with them – or, in our case, avoid them."

Robert shrugged, inhaled his Celtique, and blew out a cloud of bluish smoke.

"I've never known you so gloomy, Robbie. Is this what the Occupation has done to you all?" asked Henry.

In contrast to his friend, Henry looked the provincial he had become. A lock of his fair, wavy hair, parted to the right, fell over one eye and he threw it back with a toss of his head as he laughed.

"And yet you look healthy enough. What about all the shortages and scarcity? You're hardly looking famished. But, in any case, I don't agree. We're still young, this war will be over in a few months, Robbie, and Paris will recover, I'm sure of that. Some good may come out of it all, too."

"Ah, if only you were right." Robert shook his head sadly and lit another cigarette. "But the people here are destroyed, don't you realise? France is a broken nation, I'm telling you. These pedestrians, this waiter here, the little people of Paris who have always made her what she is: superficially they're the same folk you knew a year ago, but something has cracked inside. They're no longer thinking of the future, their careers, their kids, and they don't care any longer. All the they need to be sure about is whether they'll survive the winter, whether they can eat, whether they can afford to live. They don't even bother about an Allied victory; in fact, they'd prefer Britain to be defeated because they would then feel less humiliated. This was a proud nation, Henry, but it has been trampled beneath the Nazi jackboot and it will take a great man to raise them up out of the mire now, war or no war."

"In my view, France already has such a man, Robbie," Henry said. "Down there in Vichy, where I've been living, I've watched the way old Maréchal Pétain has answered his country's call and I've observed his strategy in dealing with the Germans – even the meeting with Hitler at Montoire last month – and I'm impressed, I really am, as I'm sure the Germans are. His National Revolution, if it bears fruit, will mean that France will have its first truly Christian government in 150 years. Out of the ashes of the Third Republic . . ." Henry paused as he caught a look of disbelief in Robert's expression. He drained his Viandox. But Robert said nothing.

"Don't you agree? Why don't you speak?" Henry put his hand on his friend's sleeve.

Robert smiled and slowly shook his head. "'To France I make the gift of my person,'" and he mimicked the Maréchal's sad, sombre tone of voice. "Henry, I'd like to be able to agree with you, but, as I said in my letter, I'm not the idealist I was even a year ago. Sure, something has to be done. France is defeated and she must learn the lessons of defeat. Many people do see your Maréchal as a saviour – a new Joan of Arc, as he no doubt thinks of himself – but the guys he's surrounded with ... *quelle galère!* All those Maurassiens and Action Française types, they're trying to turn him" – and here Robert gestured towards the badge, the *francisque*, on Henry's lapel – "into a version of the king they guillotined the last time they had a revolution. And to give him even greater powers. Anyway, all this talk of true French stock and the purity of French traditions that he bleats on about; this emphasis on discipline and hard work, and diligence which you proclaim when you wear that badge. The Vichy slogan of *Travail, Famille, Patrie* and the 'old values', is that really the sort of France you want? I tell you, there's no room left for the imagination – for artistic freedom, surrealism, for men like Picasso, Breton and Aragon: all those guys you once professed to admire – in a system like that. It's regression, Henry. It's stepping backwards into a pre-1914 world."

"Robbie, this isn't what you were saying a year ago," Henry protested. "You've done a complete political turnaround. I thought we had the same ideas."

"I guess we once did, but people change, thank God! Besides, I've seen the writing on the wall in more senses than one. You can't fail to do so living in a city occupied by a foreign power. And I now sense the danger to personal liberty in the policies of these authoritarian nationalist leaders – Mussolini, Franco, the prattling little Austrian corporal ... Remember I'm an American, old boy – even though I've chosen not to go back to the U.S. of A. – and as a boy, I was taught to learn by heart the words of the Gettysburg address. You know: "government of the people, by the people, and for the people, shall not perish from the earth". Those were great words by a great man. I tell you, Europe badly needs a man of the calibre of Abe Lincoln right now."

"You quote Lincoln," Henry replied, "and I shall reply with the Maréchal. I believe he's a man ordained for the situation France finds herself in. I don't think you respect him enough. Listen: the 'New Order', he said the other day, should not be some servile imitation of foreign experiments. Every nation has a duty to develop a regime appropriate to its particular genius – or words to that effect. Frankly, Robbie, America doesn't concern us here. Europe's problems are our own, be they French, British, German or Italian, and we must resolve them as best we can, without the intrusion of sinister international conspiracies dreamed up by Communists, Jews, Freemasons and international bankers."

Robert raised a peremptory hand and paid the waiter before he spoke. "Old boy, we've only just met after all this time. We're getting too heated and involved. I never imagined you still felt this way. Let's change the subject and go back to my apartment. It's just round the corner. And you probably want to wash and change your clothes, or take a nap after your journey. By the way, I wouldn't repeat any of our conversation – not that you would – to Hervé, or to Alibert, who I gather was at your show, or, indeed, to anyone else. They might suspect me of being an *attentiste*, or disloyal to your venerable Maréchal. As a foreigner employed by the gallery I have to be very careful, just as you do, for there are informers and fifth columnists everywhere. So, not a word. Promise?"

They left the café and set out on what was by now a chill afternoon to make the short journey back to Robert's flat.

A few evenings later, Robert took Henry to see Jean Anouilh's "pink" play, *Leocadia*, with Pierre Fresnay and Yvonne Printemps, at the Théâtre de la Michodière. Their political differences had been set aside temporarily and they had both felt tears well up when Printemps, eyes a-fluttering, had sung *"Les Chemins de l'amour"*.

After the play, Robert and Henry walked through the dim, empty, litter-strewn streets to rue Lamennais, where they reckoned they would have time to dine at Chez Benoit and still be home before the curfew began. Considering that menus were limited, the restaurant was full and the atmosphere lively. They were shown to a corner table close to a window, where an eighteenth-century oil painting of a bacchanalian feast being consumed in an Arcadian landscape hung from the wood panelling, but they were a little too close for their liking to a noisy party of German officers. On the far wall of the room hung a portrait of Maréchal Pétain in his Verdun uniform, beneath which sat a man (surely an actor, to judge by his extravagant mannerisms, but his back was turned towards them) accompanied by a woman in a red dress with striking black hair and dramatic facial features, whom Henry recalled having seen in several films during the months he lived in Paris. He could not place her precisely. Was it Arletty? He was not sure, and so said nothing.

At another table, Robert drew Henry's attention to two other men, one French, the other German. The Frenchman was the writer and political columnist Pierre Drieu la Rochelle, whom Robert had pointed out to Henry when they had seen him at the Closerie des Lilas a year earlier. The other was Otto Abetz, the former art master and youth leader who was Hitler's ambassador to Paris and commissioner for the Occupied Zone, and whose self-confessed Francophilia had made him a figure of fun in Robert's view.

"I don't know Drieu, though I've read and admired *Gilles*, as I think I told you, and I used to like his *Nouvelle Revue Française* pieces," Robert confided in a low voice, "but his notion that a single French political party under German protection will help bring about a social revolution is wishful thinking. I don't really understand their friendship, for Abetz must know that Drieu is a romantic intellectual with no concept of *realpolitik*. Yet one constantly sees them together."

Henry nodded. "I shall always be in your debt for introducing me to Drieu's ideas," he said. "I've become familiar with his journalism since then and I'd say that he represents my own views almost exactly. He knows that Europe is decaying. He sees the dangers that Stalin represents, he has a vision, and he accepts the necessity of collaboration. I don't see how one can disagree objectively."

As Robert dictated their order to the waiter, Henry looked across the restaurant to where the ambassador and the writer were sitting. The buzz of conversation was too loud to hear anything that was being said, but the German was clearly the more excitable and impassioned of the two men, gesticulating as if he were a stage Frenchman, while the author of *Gilles* and *Le Feu follet* listened morosely and puffed on his cigarette, his proud, disdainful, domed head nodding from time to time in movements of assent or disagreement.

"We're all destined to be either dreamers or men of action, don't you think?" said Robert, who, having tasted the 1937 Crozes Hermitage the sommelier had poured, now pointed out to him, a little too disdainfully, Henry thought, that the wine was corked. A further bottle was brought.

"Thought or action," he said, "Drieu or Abetz. There you have them, close enough to hurl bread at if you felt so inclined. It's a toss-up. A year ago I was for action, and if I had not already been involved in the art world, I reckon I might have become a politician. Not in America, you understand, but somehow, one way or another, here in France. At least, that was the way I thought before the Occupation. Now it's too late, although, strictly between ourselves, I have applied for French citizenship and my papers are now at last in order."

"Supposing America declares war?" Henry said.

"America's no longer my concern, despite what I said about Abe Lincoln. I've left the land of the free behind. Sure, my old ma may shed a tear or two, but I have to follow my heart, and my heart has always been here, even when I was a kid at high school. France is my destiny, Henry, it's in the stars." Robert's face shook with fervour as he chuckled and drained his glass.

Meanwhile, the restaurant had grown even noisier with the arrival of a second party of Germans who joined their compatriots at the adjacent table. They had ordered more wine and one of the original diners was encouraging his companions to sing and was having to be restrained. Their loud voices jarred with the elegance of the surroundings and with the blank expressions of the waiters, venerable men in their sixties or seventies for the most part, who paid minimal attention to the uninvited foreign guests.

"As I've said to you already, you should try to do what I've done, Henry, and apply for French citizenship. Only the other day I heard about an Englishwoman who was arrested on suspicion of being a spy. She was a French citizen, married to a Frenchman, who happened to speak to her husband in English at some café or other. Someone reported her to the German authorities. Which is why you and I have to be very careful. But Hervé would help, via Alibert. Tell them that you're disillusioned with your own country and that you love France. Not like Fitzgerald or Hemingway and those sentimental, expatriate types. They were mere romantics who used France to their own ends. I don't think we're in quite the same mould, are we? I doubt they would have turned their backs on their own country, would they? Or have been disloyal, as we have been. And I'm not ashamed of that. It all depends on your view of the world. What was Browning's line? 'We called the chess-board white, – we call it black'."

Henry said nothing. Perhaps he changed the subject. Later that night, however, after they had been stopped a few yards from Robert's flat in rue Buffon by a patrol of German soldiers at two minutes past midnight and reprimanded for breaking the curfew, Henry used the words "betrayed" and "opportunist" in his diary when describing his feelings about his friend.

∽

Paris in November 1940 was moribund. Her citizens – those who had not fled at the approach of the German armies – were apathetic and gloomy, and they led quiet, abstemious and uneventful lives; they lived as though they were imprisoned, put in chains by the invader.

Basic commodities were short and, with winter approaching, housewives queued not just for bread, meat and fresh vegetables (one kilo of butter, if you could get it, cost a thousand francs; a kilo of potatoes, forty francs), but also for the coal and paraffin that would keep them warm in the months ahead.

Despite Maréchal Pétain's proclamations of a National Revolution and his dream of a new Europe born out of the ashes of the Treaty of Versailles, the divided nation was being forced into ever closer collaboration with the Reich. In October, the provinces of Alsace and Lorraine had been annexed: two Gauleiters had been appointed, and the inhabitants – "children of divorced people who have always been torn between their parents", in the words of Pierre Laval – were abandoned. The Bishop of Strasbourg was forbidden to enter his diocese and the Bishop of Metz was expelled from his. There was little the Vichy government could do to protest, let alone resist. "This silence," said Pétain's comrade-in-arms, General Weygand, a man increasingly at odds with his leader, "makes us accomplices of the Germans." He was relieved of his ministerial rank and named as Proconsul in North Africa.

At the same time, the old Maréchal had even more serious problems with his president, Pierre Laval, whose pro-German stance was scarcely in keeping with the conciliatory image of himself that the Maréchal cherished. "He is the man whom I despise most in the world, but I still have need of him," he confided to those who would listen. "Later I shall get rid of him."

General de Gaulle, broadcasting from London on the B.B.C., which Henry could hear quite clearly on the wireless during the two weeks he spent in Robert's apartment, attacked Vichy: "If France lies prostrate," he declared, "it is the crime of this puppet government." All very well, thought Henry, if you are safely tucked away in Carlton Gardens, or Plymouth, or wherever that upstart of a colonel and his so-called Free French were supposed to be. A true patriot, he believed, stayed at home to face the music. Unlike himself.

Following these B.B.C. broadcasts, graffiti in the shape of the letter "V" – and denoting "*Victoire*", rather than the "Victor of Verdun" as some imagined – began to be daubed on walls and *métro* stations, and on beer mats in cafés and bars.

In September 1940, Frenchman had fought against Frenchman, each convinced they were defending their own national interests, as Gaullist forces attacked the North African port of Dakar, which was guarded by troops loyal to Pétain. For Hitler, such news was entirely welcome: a divided France meant a weakened France, and he needed even closer alignment in order to defeat Great Britain and gain full control of Europe. In October, both the Führer and the old Maréchal had proposed a personal meeting at which each could air his expectations and grievances. At the same time, separate negotiations were taking place, unknown to Pétain, for Laval to meet his opposite number, Joachim von Ribbentrop. In the event, Laval had met both Hitler and von Ribbentrop on October 22 in a railway carriage at the otherwise insignificant village station of Montoire, near Tours, where two days later the Maréchal, dressed in his Verdun tunic and wearing only the Medaille Militaire as a decoration, was received by the Nazi leader.

On October 30 the Maréchal had broadcast to his people: "It is in all honour and in order to maintain the unity of France – a unity of ten centuries within the framework of the constructive activity of the New European Order – that I am today pursuing the path of collaboration . . . Until today I have spoken to you in the language of a father. Today I speak to you in the language of a leader. Follow me. Put your faith in *la France eternelle*."

For many French men and women, Montoire was a step too far.

In Paris, German soldiers continued to file like tourists among the hallowed aisles of Notre-Dame, beneath the Eiffel Tower or photographing and sketching the white dome of the Sacré Cœur. The presence of the *boches*, the *Fritz* or the *Fridolins*, as they were variously called, was unrelenting; they were sensed as much as they were seen. They patrolled the streets in the centre of the city in groups, often in military vehicles, always armed, sometimes stopping passers-by with requests for identity papers or a night pass. They took over certain restaurants and cafés, reclining on the terraces and ogling the passing Parisiennes with a gloating air. They paid their bills in German currency, they smoked German cigarettes, and they read German newspapers, except for those with cultural pretensions, who might also read the collaborationist French press.

Meanwhile, those Parisians who remained in the city lived warily, travelling about on foot, or by bicycle in the darkness of dawn, which came late now that clocks were set to Berlin time. They queued patiently for basic provisions, suspicious of their neighbours, who might hitherto have been friends, lest they denounced them to the occupying powers for listening to the B.B.C. or for harbouring undesirable aliens.

That November, while Henry and Robert were celebrating their reunion in Paris, 66,000 citizens of Lorraine and 120,000 Alsatians were crammed into trains and despatched into the "free zone", where they were met at the Gare de Perrache in Lyon by Raphaël Alibert, Pétain's minister of the interior and a man who believed that the future of France lay in the restoration of the monarchy. "There is only one thing to do," Laval was reported as saying, "and that is to be nice to the Germans."

∞

Whether Henry Latymer, sequestered in his friend Robert Worcester's cosy enclave in rue Buffon, was fully aware of just how profoundly the dignity of the nation he loved was being besmirched we cannot be sure. If Robert's experience of the harsh realities of occupation had opened his eyes to the danger of fascism, to the folly of Vichy's self-proclaimed "National Revolution" and the dream of a new world order, Henry, by contrast, seemed to be stubbornly determined to uphold the values enshrined in the old Maréchal, who, in his view, represented the true glory and proud traditions of the nation he loved. If he, Henry, was a traitor to the land of his birth, he felt he was at least loyal to his adopted country. Duty, patriotism, heritage, family values, the "old faith", tradition, moral decadence – these were words or terms that occur surprisingly frequently in his notebook or diary entries from this time, and yet there is also a sense that his strongly held political beliefs were a façade and that all that really mattered to him were his painting, his friends, particularly Robert in Paris, and Jean and Chantal in Bellerive. Although his affair with Chantal appeared to have lost its flame before his stay in Paris, he was clearly anxious to retain what he described as an "*amitié amoureuse*".

∞

November 12, 1940

Yesterday afternoon Robert and I went to the Champs-Élysées, where crowds had gathered to observe the anniversary of the 1918 armistice and to place flowers on the tomb of the unknown soldier, the corpse of the victim chosen from among seven coffins that lay in the citadel at Verdun after the slaughter of 1916 had finally ended. On the orders of the German soldiers present, French police officers were instructed to pick up all the flowers which passers-by had laid in tribute. Huge red and black flags fluttered outside the Hôtel Crillon as we passed, and more flags and sentry boxes lined the wide avenue whose cafés and restaurants were today framed by white fences. Further along the Champs-Élysées, we heard the sound of machine-gun fire and we watched in horror as soldiers with fixed bayonets charged a group of students as they stood on the pavement. Apparently, someone had uttered an insult, and this was the Germans' response.

We caught the *métro* back to the Left Bank, and at Duroc, where we changed, we saw a young beggar – a blind accordionist, with his white stick by his side – sitting on a stool, his head propped against the tiled wall, his sightless eyes gazing upwards, playing the Marseillaise. He had a little tricolour fixed to his accordion and on his hat he wore ribbons shaped into a cockade. The centimes piled up. It was as if people were somehow expiating their guilt . . . On the train, a German officer stood and politely offered his seat to any of the three women who had just got on, but no-one accepted it and the carriage was filled with an awkward silence.

In the afternoon we decided to go to the Luxembourg. We walked past the Odéon and up rue Monsieur le Prince. Robert claims it is his favourite street in all of Paris, and as we strolled past the old houses with their grey shutters and portes-cochères, mostly mournful and grubby on this dank November afternoon, my mood lifted for the first time since I arrived here from Bellerive. For a moment, it seemed to become once more the city I had known in 1939 – carefree, gay and impulsive – and something approaching *joie de vivre* briefly filled my heart. Robert pointed out a particular house, in which Pascal had written his *Pensées*, and another, where an actor who had given drama lessons to Marie-Antoinette had once lived. He talks so authoritatively, and with that American fluency and articulacy that I lack. He is able to direct his thoughts and say exactly what he means, whereas I hesitate and mumble and speak in nuances and half-meanings. Our conversation ranged so widely and I felt closer to Robert than I have done to anyone (except Chantal) since I left home. I described my show at Jean's gallery in the summer, and I told him how strongly Chantal and I had felt about one another. Robert nodded and said: "I worry for Jews in this climate." I was puzzled by his remark, but because I was determined to avoid any more political disagreements, I did not pursue the matter. Robert then spoke to me openly for the first time about his life in America: how he had been a scholarship boy at an Ivy League school called Amherst, who had gone on to graduate school at Harvard, where he was taught by a remarkable professor who continued to inspire his early feelings for France and for French art and history; and he talked, too, of his broken home life. Robert's father separated from his mother when he was eighteen, and his mother's bitterness towards the husband who deserted her was extended to her son, whom she has never forgiven for leaving America.

Rain came on, so we drank some real – not ersatz, for once – coffee at the Tournon until the weather improved. Robert says they serve the real stuff because it is a café frequented by top-ranking German officers who have commandeered the Palais du Luxembourg. Sure enough, at that moment, a tall figure in Nazi uniform left the table at which he had been sitting drinking beer with several other German officers, strolled over towards us, looked Robert full in the eyes, clicked his heels and gave a short bow.

"Heinz von Klamm" – or a very similar-sounding name – "*à votre service, Messieurs*," he announced. "We met, I believe, at one of Otto's parties in rue de Lille."

He exuded an immediate charm and freshness, and the pine scent he was wearing brought to mind Bavarian forests and mountain streams. Robert seemed momentarily confused; then he invited the German to join our table.

"Allow me to present my friend, Henry," he said," a talented painter whom we represent and who is spending a few weeks with me in Paris to refresh his muse." And he laughed nervously.

"*Enchanté, Monsieur.*" The German bowed again, and sat down next to Robert. "I should like to offer you a glass of something a little stronger with which to toast our fortunes, if you permit," he added, and, without inviting a response, he summoned the waiter by clicking his fingers. He ordered schnapps, and when the slim glasses of clear liquid arrived, he raised his, held our eyes with his steady gaze and pronounced "*prosit*", before drinking to "Franco-German friendship". From his manner, I was relieved to see that von Klamm clearly took me for a Frenchman who also spoke English. I still find this flattering, but in this instance it was vital that he should do so, for I would have had some difficulty explaining my position. He talked about the party given by Otto Abetz, the Reich's ambassador to Paris at which Robert had indeed been present, and where he had also been introduced, he told us proudly, to Coco Chanel, Sacha Guitry and Yvonne Printemps. At one point, the German addressed me directly:

"As a painter, you must know, Monsieur, that it is above all art and culture that have forged common links between our two nations. In my opinion, little else matters. This war . . . " – he shrugged – "it will soon be over. Until it is, I shall continue to see myself not simply as a representative of the occupying power, but as an ambassador from the home of Goethe and Dürer in the land of Racine and Delacroix . . . For us" – he corrected himself and, smiling broadly, held up his glass again – "for some of us, it is an honour and a privilege to be here."

There was something at once false and alluring about the quality of the German's voice and his patronising manner, and I was reminded strangely of a gramophone record that my mother used to play at home when I was a child, of a German tenor singing Schubert's "*Erl-Konig*". He then spoke of the films he had seen – "*Les Visiteurs du soir*" and "*Quai des brumes*" – and, taking out two visiting cards from his wallet, he asked us to get in touch should there ever be anything he could do for us.

"*Au revoir, cher maître, et à bientôt peut-être*". He smiled charmingly and bowed his head first to me and then to Robert, muttering something I did not quite catch, and mentioning names that meant nothing to me, before returning to his table. His colleagues turned to glance at us. I felt distinctly uncomfortable.

"One has to admit, the *boches* are very *correctes*, in the French sense, as long as your papers are in order," whispered Robert with a nervous laugh as we walked to the *métro* before returning to his flat.

∞

Thinking about this encounter as I write, there was something about the intimate way in which the German addressed Robert that suggested complicity between the two men. Robert never alluded to the incident again, other than by quoting Shakespeare that evening – "Sweet are the uses of adversity," he said, giving me a searching look. I decided it was best to pry no further.

Slipped in loosely at this point in Henry's diary, there is an undated note on blue airmail paper headed "Another German encounter":

Friday

After lunch, Robert took me to a church somewhere near the Buttes Chaumont where we listened to a performance of Charpentier's "*La Descente d'Orphée aux enfers*". There was no stage, but the singing was so beautiful that we forgot about the War and Occupation and the New Order, in spite of the fact that three German officers were sitting across the aisle from us in the front row. I found myself staring at them, watching for the least evidence of any emotion. They were listening intently and it struck me from their expressions that they were probably men who were well versed in music, brought up, as so many Germans are, on Bach and Brahms, Beethoven and Schubert. It was certainly hard to think of them as the enemy with this sublime music resounding around the old walls, and I wondered whether men like these could sense the hatred that their uniforms inspired in the hearts of so many Parisians, or whether, as the *Herrenvolk*, they felt it was no more than their right to be hated.

On our way home, just by the Pont de la Tournelle, in the late afternoon, we saw a man and a woman being cross-questioned by German soldiers. They were both wearing the star of David, as Jews are obliged to do now, and Robert said that you could tell from their uniforms that the soldiers were from the Gestapo. He says that Jews go in constant fear of arrest: some shops are forbidden to them, and they are only permitted to travel in the last carriage of the *métro*. I could not but think of Chantal.

In Robert's flat that evening, we listened to "*La France*

Libre" on the B.B.C. Robert says he used to know the presenter, Jean Marin, before the war.

I could not sleep. Waking at the "hour of the wolf" – that uneasy period shortly before dawn, when our resistance is lowest – I got out of bed and pushed open the shutters. Paris lay sleeping, but the moon was covered in thick cloud. It was a night without stars.

[CHAPTER 9]

THERE WERE ALMOST TWO YEARS BETWEEN HENRY
Latymer leaving Paris in late November 1940, to return to his
existence as an artist in Bellerive on the River Allier, and the
resumption of his diary. They were years of hardship and shame
for many French citizens, years when the illusions most of them
had nourished about constructive collaboration with the invader
were gradually and cruelly shattered. The overall pattern that
the war was following in Europe suggested a German victory
as more nations fell to the Axis forces: in April 1941, Romania
and the Balkans were occupied; Crete fell in May, and in the
following month Hitler declared war on Russia.

In the summer of 1942, resistance to the occupation within
France began to take a more active and desperate form: at the
Barbès-Rochechouart *métro* station in Paris, a young man by
the name of Pierre Georges, later to become famous by his
code name Colonel Fabien of the Francs-Tireurs et Partisans,
shot and killed Midshipman Moser of the German Kriegsmarine
as he stood in the open carriage of a train. It was the first in
a sequence of political assassinations, all of which provoked
savage reprisals.

Henry took up his intermittent diary again only in October 1942, and there is nothing among his papers that alludes to the previous twenty-three months. What does become clear from this later diary is that at some stage during those months a profound change had come over him. He had evidently deserted Chantal and moved out of the Aragos' house in Bellerive; he appears to have lost any inspiration to paint or sketch; he had found employment in a government office as some sort of *fonctionnaire*, working, at least initially, in a department run by Madeleine's father in one of Vichy's former hotels that had been expropriated to become government offices in the summer of 1940. Using his own connections – or possibly Robert's – he had also acquired French nationality. "I do my duty as a French citizen. I am respected. I earn a decent living, and I have certain privileges. I can afford to take Madeleine out to a cinema show and dine chez Ricou once a week," he notes, all of a sudden the epitome of the self-satisfied, petit-bourgeois clerk.

Although his diary in the autumn of 1942 provides a useful commentary on political events, Henry's own political and artistic idealism seems to have been replaced by a ruthless efficiency, and his main preoccupations are to do with Madeleine – whom he had met again at a gala held in April in honour of the Maréchal's birthday, at which she had sung – and with the secretive nature of his office work. The entries are starker, less composed – it is as if his innocence had been lost, as if he had succumbed to the easy option and allowed security, self-preservation and emotions to govern his decisions – though occasionally they illuminate the twilight world in which he moved, as well as his relationship with Madeleine.

October 10, 1942

Saw Claudel's *L'Annonce faite à Marie* with Madeleine.
Miracles and leprosy in the Middle Ages. Is France in
defeat becoming a Catholic country once more? At Mass
last Sunday the priest spoke of "the new France" and how
she had returned to being "the elder daughter of the
Church" under Pétain. I doubt it. I fear he may have lost
what control he had. They still cheer the old man and
sing *"Maréchal, nous voilà!"* etc., but he seems merely a
symbol now. If there is a future, it will belong to Monsieur
Laval. Only he has the courage and wherewithal to deal
with the Germans. The picture is certainly not as bright
as it was in 1940 . . . Would I have settled down here as
I did in Paris in 1939? Probably not. But at least I have
Madeleine now.

October 13, 1942

Saw Jean walking towards me as I crossed the park this
morning, but he appeared not to notice me. He had a
cigarette between his lips, both hands sunk deep in his
overcoat pockets, and he looked lost in thought as he
shuffled through the autumn leaves. He (deliberately?)
changed direction before I could hail him. Met M. for
lunch and we stole an hour together in my room afterwards. I left her sleeping, the sunlight through the blind
caressing the soft down of her thighs, her hair streaming
over my pillow, and I returned reluctantly to the office.
For a second, I had a longing to sketch her body, but
I've lost the desire to draw or paint. If only she could be
there when I return every evening!

Increasing number of "V" (for *Victoire*) signs on walls and hoardings. I'm told that these signs are put there by Resistance sympathisers, encouraged by the B.B.C. propaganda broadcasts. I even saw "*Vendu*" scribbled beneath a poster of Pétain the other day.

Later: Disillusioned with my work this week. Checking lists. Madeleine's father called me into his office yesterday to explain Vichy's policies. Too many Jews are fleeing France and doing us harm, he said. Foreign Jews must be arrested. Monsieur Bousquet's orders. It is what the Germans insist upon and we are in no position to protest. Virtually all of Europe is now German, he said, "from Finistère to Stalingrad". But what constitutes a foreign Jew? I wanted to ask. Aren't they all French? And where are they being sent to?

October 15

Poupetière, a colleague whom I dislike, looked intently at my lapel during our coffee break this morning, and asked: "But why are you, Monsieur Latymer, *un anglo-saxon après tout, et donc notre ennemi*, wearing the *francisque*?" I told him that I had been naturalised and was therefore a Frenchman just like him, that I had equal rights. I did not tell him Hervé had given the medal to me. He shrugged with a sneer. Was I aware that there was now a denaturalisation law? he asked, adding that it was fortunate for me that I was not a Jew, because anyone naturalised after August 1927 could have his new nationality removed!! Poupetière is an enemy in the making, I fear, and could be dangerous. He reminds me of a weasel.

Madeleine laughed when I told her about this and said she would complain to her father about the man.

October 22, 1942
Supper last night with Madeleine and her parents. M.'s mother, clearly concerned about her daughter's future, asked whether I would take up painting again once the war was over? I think they may regard me as a potential son-in-law. Jean de L. said he admired the British and that France had no quarrel with *le peuple anglais*, but M. Churchill had betrayed his ally, he went on, and it was not for nothing that the English were known as perfidious. Madeleine reminded them that I was now a Frenchman. "He's one of us, Papa," she said, taking my hand, "and he loves our country as much as you or I do."

According to her father, the Americans and the British are expected to launch an attack on Dakar any day now. "Liberty, what crimes are committed in your name," said Madame de L. histrionically, throwing up her hands in mock horror (she was an actress in her youth). She then asked whether I had studied the French Revolution at school.

Madeleine and I walked down to the river before supper. Scarcely anyone in the streets. We lay by the banks of the Allier, which looked wide and forbidding, and snuggled beneath the greatcoat I brought with me from England in 1939. We looked at the moon and the stars through the new binoculars I have been given. The starlit night suddenly made me think of Chantal, but I quickly dispelled the memories. Seeing Jean in the park last week reminded me of his parting words to me when I left the house at Bellerive: "You're a moral coward, Henry. You have wounded my sister more than a man as egotistical as you can ever realise. Something I would never have believed of you. You have betrayed Chantal, and you have betrayed my trust. You can never be my friend. Adieu."

October 23

When I enquired today about the lists of names and details I am being asked to check, I was told that they all relate to foreigners who are refugees and have entered this country illegally. Throughout France, these people's credentials are being checked and the majority are being arrested, sent to the camp at Drancy, in the suburbs of Paris, and then to Metz, after which they are forced to join labour camps in Germany.

"The *Fridolins* are not winning the war as easily as they thought," said Jean-Marc, a man I play chess with occasionally and who, like me, also works as a clerk at the Hôtel de Lucerne. "They need all the workers they can get. We chose to collaborate, and so we have no option but to do as we are told and not ask questions that may be awkward."

The vile Poupetière has been sent to work in another department at the Hôtel du Parc. This is because M. spoke to her father, but I worry that he may still make trouble for me. There was the usual sneer on his lips as he removed his files and emptied his desk drawers this morning.

Alarming reports of assassinations and reprisals in the Occupied Zone. German soldiers shot at a cinema, and an incident at the Marbeuf *métro* station in Paris; for each German shot, there are dozens of French men and women murdered in revenge. Franco-German friendship is increasingly strained. Meanwhile, the attacks on North Africa are expected daily.

Madeleine told me that her mother had asked her whether I was a Catholic. "Are you still a believer, Henry?" I did not know how to reply. Am I? I said that I was, if not a very devout one, but that I go to Mass every Sunday at St-Louis. Her father is furious with the cardinal in Lyon for daring to criticise the government for what he termed "deportation methods against Jews".

M. came to my room today for our *heure intime*, as she calls it, and pulled out one of my old sketchbooks. She wants me to take up painting again as she feels that it will provide a balance to the monotony of the work I do at the ministry. She happened to open the pad at a preliminary drawing I had done of Chantal, the one I later developed into a full-length portrait and which was bought by a retired banker at my exhibition two years ago. But she made no comment. Bad mood for the rest of the day: my conscience still pricks me . . . Thank God I have Madeleine.

Monday, November 9
The war seems to have entered a new phase. Radio-Vichy announced yesterday that American and British troops had landed on the coast of Morocco – bloody fighting

and many deaths. Troops loyal to Darlan are holding off the enemy in Algiers. The Americans are desperate that the French colonies in Africa should not be seized by Hitler, and that must be why Mr Tuck arrived at the Hôtel du Parc in the afternoon with a letter for the Maréchal. Will the Germans now oblige us to break off diplomatic relations with Mr Roosevelt?

Jean-Marc says terrible fighting is taking place on the Eastern front, with the German and Russian armies locked in a desperate struggle. I feel as though we are on a merry-go-round, whirling madly and out of control. The mood in Vichy is one of excitement and fear, and the streets are livelier than they have been for months. On my way home this evening, I called in at the little convent chapel: a choir and school children were being rehearsed. "*Sauvez la France*," they were singing, "*au nom du Sacré Cœur*." I was moved to tears, and spent several minutes on my knees.

November 11

Today is Armistice Day, but it's a sad one for France. This morning there came the news that the Wehrmacht have broken the demarcation line and are marching south to occupy the free zone. Von Rundstedt called on Maréchal Pétain, and at lunchtime we all listened on the wireless as the old man addressed France and the French Empire and saluted the memory of those who had died in Africa. He asked us to put our trust in him, but it seems clear that his power is diminishing and that Monsieur Laval's voice is the one that matters now.

Madeleine was depressed when we met this evening. She is having further singing lessons, but she says there will be no future for her as a serious singer in France and that if it were not for me she would be suicidal. What future did we have together, she asked, and what would become of us? I said that we would do whatever was necessary for our own happiness and that our only ambition should be to remain together. At breakfast, her father explained that what had happened today meant that Vichy was now finished and that Pétain and Laval no longer have influential roles to play. Quite simply, he told her, we have backed the wrong horse.

Next day. M.'s parents invited me to supper this evening. According to her father, the Germans are already moving into Vichy, and the Carlingue[1] has taken over a building in blvd. des États-Unis. Fighting is continuing all over North Africa and more than 2,000 French troops have been killed. Strikes in Paris. The Resistance people continue to broadcast from London, while the Maquis shoot innocent citizens.

Jean de Launay's remarks set me thinking about my future here (our future, for it is irrevocably with Madeleine) and the direction of our lives. We may have to leave: I sense my position in the ministry is uncertain. If the German authorities discover that I acquired French nationality only a year ago, they may take a different view to those here, where I am protected through my connection with M.'s father. I fear that Poupetière, who, I am told, now exercises some authority at the Hôtel du Parc,

1 The Gestapo in Parisian argot. W.L.

recognises that my heart is not in my job, and would get rid of me given the slightest opportunity.

By lunchtime today, when we met in my room, M. was much more her old self. We made love – hurried and frenetic; we need a calmer existence . . . Then we listened to Charles Trenet and Jean Sablon records and, since it was my half-day, we took the bus out into the country and walked for two hours in the hills beyond Le Vernet. The trees glinted gold and yellow in the late-autumn sun and for the first time in many months I wished I could have caught that magical light on canvas. On the bus on the way home I told M. that we may have to be prepared to leave at a moment's notice; she said she would follow me *jusqu'au bout du monde*. I adore her.

The traitor Darlan has ordered a ceasefire in Algiers and has come to an agreement with the Americans.

November 14, 1942

Walking down the Passage Giboin after work, on my way to meet Madeleine at our usual café, I bumped into Daniel, one of the two brothers who had stayed with Jean and Chantal at Bellerive during my first summer here. We had not seen each other since then and I had no idea that he and his brother were still in Vichy. I asked if he would join me for coffee. Daniel is now working for his uncle at his perfumery in Grasse; he is here on business. Pascal is an editor at a publishing house that moved out of Paris just before the Armistice and has set up an office in Arles.

I told him that I had taken French nationality and he looked astonished. "I suppose you did so for political reasons," he said. "Did you change your name too? It can't be easy to have an English name these days, especially now that the Americans have attacked our forces in Africa. I'd change my name, if I were you, my friend." Then: "I see you even wear the *francisque*," and he pursed his lips and raised his eyebrows in one of those Gallic gestures of mock surprise.

He asked about Jean and Chantal and I told him that I no longer saw them. Briefly, I explained about Chantal and myself, and I lied when I told him that our affair had ended by mutual agreement. He said that he was sorry because he thought we were a good match. "And Jean thought highly of you as an artist too," he said. It occurred to me later that he looked rather cold and disapproving. He gave me his visiting card, and shook my hand, saying "*À un de ces jours, si Dieu le veut.*" I found the encounter disturbing. Madeleine arrived at the café shortly after he left. She was wearing a red dress that had belonged to her mother, and her beautiful hair was pinned high above her neck. I had never seen her like that. For a moment, she looked older and unfathomable. Sitting opposite me, she suddenly seemed a stranger, and I could not help grasping her by the shoulders and gazing into her eyes and asking her whether she still loves me. Her features broke into a smile and she took my hands in hers and told me not to be so stupid.

After I walked Madeleine home, I took a roundabout route back, through the narrow streets of the old town. A girl, hand in hand with her lover, just as I had been, moments before, with M., was singing in the street: "*On ne danse plus le java chez Bébert . . . on est swing jusqu'en haut du bas.*" I recognised the catchy tune, but can't remember any more of the words. There was something about the girl and the way she moved her head as she sang that reminded me of my sister Lavinia. I don't often think of life at home, but I did then for a moment.

Who am I? Where am I going? I no longer know . . .

November 15

Went to early morning Mass today and I lit a candle afterwards for Madeleine and our future, and also one for my family in England whom I have treated so badly. The priest in his sermon asked our prayers for those "who guide our earthly fortunes". I prayed for our leaders, but what has become of them?

Bought a baguette on my way back to my room and ate it with the damson jam M.'s mother had given me. That insufferable old egoist Sacha Guitry was singing on the wireless. He sounds so conceited . . . then he was drowned out by the music of the Sambre et Meuse march being played as a troop of young men in black berets marched by in military fashion beneath my window. Everyone wears berets here, but they only make me think of Jean Borotra, the bouncing Basque, whom I saw playing at Wimbledon when I was still at school.

Madeleine has gone with her parents to have lunch with an old family friend at Riom, so I have spent the day alone. Meeting Jean-Marc to play chess at the Grand Café this evening.

November 16, 1942

Beat Jean-Marc for only the second time last night. Used Capablanca opening. Distracted during game by disturbing expression of self-important-looking man at table near ours. Jean-Marc told me that it was Bernard Ménétrel, the Maréchal's personal physician and his confidant. He's apparently the favourite at court and J.-M. says that he's well known for his anti-Semitic views.

"When the subject of Jews is raised, Dr Bernard sees red," he whispered, as if to distract me just when I was consolidating my strong opening by castling. "I expect he's a monarchist. He loathes Freemasons and Protestants too. Most of them do, you know," he confided. "They're all Action Française types . . . admirers of Charles Maurras and Léon Daudet. They're the ones responsible for the mess we're in today."

I like Jean-Marc, if not his political views. After our game, he asked me if I would like to help him finish the *pôt-au-feu* he had cooked at lunchtime. He's stocky and short, built like a rugby prop forward, with black hair, sharp, fine dark eyes and a Southern accent. When we converse, I have the impression he listens to every word I say, and notices every nuance and inflection in my voice. He lives in a single room in rue Leprugne, where we sat eating off our laps, drinking a rather sour local wine, and listening to the Brahms Violin Concerto on his gramophone records. He is from Montpellier, where his uncle is a professor of physical education. He himself trained as an architect, but there's no work available anywhere these days, which is why he's come to Vichy. He has a menial job (for someone of his qualifications) at the ministry. He told me that he thought "you, the English" and the Americans would win the war by the end of next year. Like me, he still trusts the Maréchal and believes in the idea of a New Europe, but since the handshake at Montoire, he has lost faith. "I never thought I would see a marshal of France – the hero of Verdun no less – shaking hands with that little Austrian corporal," he said. "Nor a prime minister say that he hoped for a German victory in order to bring about the collapse of Bolshevism, which is what Laval said. Where is our pride?"

Dreamed last night of Lavinia. She has been on my mind, for some reason, for several days now. We were both young children again, playing at making sandcastles, which we topped with Union Jacks, at some southern English seaside resort that might have been Bournemouth, or perhaps Weymouth, where we once spent a family holiday. Suddenly, a massive tidal wave submerged the whole beach and I was carried out to sea, still clutching my flag, but I wasn't frightened. As I disappeared beneath the waves, I could hear my mother desperately shouting: "Lavinia, where's Henry? You must rescue him." I tried to wave, but no-one could see me. Then, the moment before I was about to drown, I woke up. Madeleine says one doesn't have to be Sigmund Freud to interpret that sort of dream. "It's fairly banal, no?" she said with a superior little smile. I do adore her.

Sunday, November 27, 1942

At Mass this morning, the priest asked us to pray for "the sailors of France, wherever they may be". It was announced on the wireless that the ships of our proud navy – la Royale – or what was left of it after Mers-el-Kébir, had been scuttled in Toulon to prevent the fleet falling into German hands. The German soldiers – the *"verts-de-gris"*, Jean-Marc calls them – arrived there just in time to see the *Strasbourg* being scuttled. As if the Navy has not suffered enough already. It has been another tragic and terrible day for France. Where will this humiliation end?

Lunch with M. and her parents. Everyone gloomy.

∞

For the first time during the four years in which he had lived in France, Henry felt anxious for his own safety and he took the precaution of hiding his diary. Worry and doubts had begun to disturb his sleep and in his notebook he recorded a series of threatening dreams: "Bad dream (Chantal)"; "terrifying nightmare of pursuit (Poupetière)"; "dreamed of Lavinia again"; "can't stop thinking about Jean and Chantal – appalling guilt" that left him feeling exhausted and reluctant to go to work the following morning. When he met Madeleine for their lunchtime trysts, or in the evening, he was frequently out of sorts and uncommunicative.

The office was in part to blame. Within the past six weeks, it is clear that the nature of Henry's clerical work had altered and that he had begun to feel increasingly alarmed about the lists of names and addresses of people whose ethnic origins and dates of naturalisation and entry into France he was being asked to confirm. According to his superiors, these people had no legal right to be living in France. From comments overheard and from files that had been passed through his department, however, he had reason to suspect that many of those whose names and addresses were delivered to the police department were being arrested and were being put onto trains and sent to work in Germany.

When, on his first day back in the office after Christmas, Henry decided to raise the subject again and ask further questions as delicately as he could, his immediate superior, M. Duval, had shrugged unhelpfully, as if what Henry was asking him was of no concern to either of them.

Philippe Duval was evidently a local man, proud of his peasant roots and ambitious for promotion. Henry had jotted down on a note inserted in his diary, "He is about thirty and he wears the same badly cut grey suit, with a *francisque* in the lapel, every single day without fail." Answerable to Madeleine's father and responsible for a staff of four clerks, including Henry, he seems to have been meticulous in his punctuality and in the precise, clipped tones with which he addressed instructions to his staff.

"It is not for you or me to question what our superiors have decreed, young man. The Law of October 4, as you may know, states clearly that 'Foreigners of the Jewish race may be interned in special camps, or be placed in forced residence, by a decision of the prefect in the *département* of their residence.'

"Not French Jews, of course," he went on, "it's the foreign ones, the ones who have taken over our banks and infiltrated our financial and commercial systems. People like Stavisky – you remember him? – and Mandel, who are traitors . . . enemies of *la génie française*, of the virtues that our nation has always stood for. And, in any case, our German partners need our help in the labour camps. They cannot be expected to suffer the burden alone. It's normal . . ."

Monsieur Duval held out the palms of his small hands as if to emphasise that what he was saying was self-evident. He then went on to say that in Paris the Jews were obliged to wear a yellow star, and that this law would soon be enforced in the former free zone.

∞

Ever since Henry had left Bellerive and stopped seeing Jean and Chantal, it is clear that there had been only two people who provided some relief from the tedium of his bizarre life in Vichy, with its large hotels and phantoms of a more glorious age: Madeleine, his beloved, whom he saw virtually every day, and Jean-Marc Mercier, his chess-playing friend, who worked in another department in the same ministry.

Jean-Marc was a free, independent spirit who had little or no respect for authority. He told Henry that he worked purely to live, and, as far as he was concerned, Duval was a pitiable coward, the sort who used war and misfortune as a stepping-stone to power. "An arriviste, *au pied de la lettre*," he scoffed, "and I'm told, by the way, that he was a member of the Cagoule before the war and knew Deloncle," he confided to Henry over a game of chess and a bottle of rough, purple Languedoc one evening. He was alluding to the founder of the notorious secret society, which had been responsible for various political assassinations and attacks on Paris synagogues. "He's the worst sort of miserable petty bureaucrat, in my view," and he spat out the words with venom.

"What'll you do if this war goes on?" asked Henry. "Have you thought of trying to get out over the Pyrenees and into Spain?"

Jean-Marc shrugged and drained his glass.

"What can one do? I haven't the guts to try to escape, let alone join the local Maquis. I've an uncle and a cousin who still live in Montpellier, where I studied and which I think of as home, but otherwise I've no close family left. You see, I'm Jewish, though whisper it not in Gath or I may be done for in the present climate," he said, winking conspiratorially at Henry. "Mercier isn't my real name, it's Meyerson. Yet although my parents came from Galicia – well, Poland, nowadays – I feel as French as any pure-blooded Frenchman and I love this country in good times or bad – '*dans la joie ou la douleur*', as our Charles Trenet sings. In fact, I'm a bit like you, Henry, no?"

"Me? I no longer know where I stand," said Henry. "I'm a traitor to my own country. I left home because, like you, I needed to breathe, and I love France and all that she represents ... civilisation, imagination, respect for liberty – well, the values that matter. I used to believe that a new Germany and a new France would together lead Europe to a modern-day renaissance, to a fresh vision of itself, and to a Europe based on the old values. Now, I'm not so sure. I don't seem to know where I belong or where my allegiances lie anymore. I studied painting in London and at the Beaux-Arts in Paris, but for two years I've scarcely picked up a paintbrush or a sketchpad. Sometimes I despair of myself, and were it not for the girl I live for, I would try to get out of France. Yet only two years ago, I felt as if I were in heaven and that the world lay before me—"

"You see, we're outsiders, my friend," Jean-Marc interrupted, grasping the sleeve of Henry's jacket. "I'm a Jew, you're an Englishman, and yet we both possess French citizenship. But ask your average *Maréchaliste* what he thinks of Jews, foreigners, Freemasons, gypsies, freethinkers – well, anything that does not accord with his petty, circumscribed notion of what France represents – and he'll say they should be sent home, kicked out, *foutus à la porte* . . ."

It was past eleven o'clock and the owner of the Grand Café, where they had been playing chess, two streets away from Jean-Marc's room in rue Leprugne, had begun to look agitated. His son was hoisting chairs onto table tops prior to sweeping the floor, and the last customers had left some ten minutes ago. In Vichy, no-one was about after eleven o'clock at night.

The moon, just past its plenitude, shone down from a starlit sky and a chill wind ruffled the canvas awning of the café as the two men left. Henry buttoned up his overcoat against the cold, but when Jean-Marc suggested they walk a little before retiring, he agreed readily.

They crossed the place de l'Hôtel-de-Ville, followed a long street whose trees were daubed with posters displaying the face of the Maréchal and the Révolution Nationale, and walked westwards before entering one of the narrow, covered arcades that gave onto the Parc des Sources, the tree-lined public gardens around which most of Vichy's sumptuous hotels, now converted into shabby government offices, were situated. In the window of one of them, the Hôtel des Ambassadeurs, Henry caught sight of a man in shirtsleeves. He wore braces and was smoking as he wrote in his notebook, and he was knocking back quick mouthfuls of liquor from a tall glass, impervious, apparently, to all around him. Jean-Marc said he was an American journalist.

In front of the imposing doors of the Hôtel du Parc, two uniformed guards, their rifles held out at an angle in front of them, stood on duty, while a series of official black limousines were parked on the street outside. The hotel was otherwise quiet now, and only the occasional light shone from one of the upper windows, where hard-pressed civil servants worked late into the night.

"By what absurd congruence of the planets did this old spa town, where that cultured old gossip Mme de Sévigné came to take the waters and write her letters, become the seat of government?" Jean-Marc looked up into the night sky as they turned the corner towards the Casino. "It's a world turned upside down, something out of *Alice in Wonderland*, don't you think? *À propos*, did you hear about Darlan? Apparently, the man who shot him in Algiers has been arrested, but where will it all end?"

Henry could only nod blankly, uncomprehendingly, at the news that Pétain's former deputy had been assassinated, but Jean-Marc grew more impassioned.

"In a Nazi Europe, I should imagine," he said, answering his own question. "There's little *le vieux* can do now. His power is waning like the moon above us, obscured in cloud. He may be a man of honour, but he's dealing with a different breed, with men who don't know the meaning of that word. That's why he needs the peasant Laval, who at least talks the same language as people like Hitler and Sauckel, though as far as I'm concerned, he's nothing but an opportunist, a self-seeker, no more and no less. Besides, he has actually said that he hopes for a German victory."

They had reached the Allier. The ruffled, fast-moving waters of the broad river shimmered in the intermittent shafts of moonlight and there was a scent of pine on the brisk easterly breeze. Somewhere in the distance the whistle of a train blew. A pair of lovers, arm in arm and warmly clad, were walking slowly towards them, oblivious to all but their own desires. Though he felt secure in his love for Madeleine, there was something about the girl that reminded Henry of Chantal. How blissfully happy he had been in the Aragos' comfortable home on the other side of the river, he reflected, where life had seemed so relatively simple. It bore a different aspect now. Not that he was unhappy, exactly; it was merely that his expectations had receded, his ideals had crumbled. With Chantal he still had the world and its prospects before him, within his grasp, or so it seemed; with Madeleine the future lay only with her: there was nothing left to aspire to.

∞

January 2, 1943

I have never known a New Year dawn so mournfully. Madeleine and I saw it in with her parents, and her father opened a precious bottle of champagne he had been keeping. He asked me to sing "Auld Lang Syne" ("but not too loudly, in case the *boches* are listening"), some of the words of which he had learned on a visit to Scotland before the war. The streets outside, however, were virtually deserted. Vichy was not in the mood for celebration. Then he raised his glass to us and said: "*Mes enfants*, let us hope with all our hearts for a change of fortune. The horizon is dark, the events in Russia have meant that the tide is turning against us, but nil desperandum?" M. told me that her parents are frightened and they have said to her that they are considering leaving Vichy. The government is in disarray, but since her father has been involved at a senior level in the administration and as a journalist, there is no question of him being received by the Maquisards. He has committed himself to Pétain and to the Maréchal's vision of France. But it was the wrong vision, he now concedes, and all he can do is to try to escape or attempt to switch sides, as so many are doing.

We, and all those who had faith in the Maréchal and a National Revolution, those who had such a shining conception of Europe as it ought to be, have been wretchedly disillusioned. We feel betrayed. We see conspiracies everywhere. We blame and suspect our neighbour. But the simple truth is that we have opted for the wrong side.

January 5

Back to work, thank heavens! At lunchtime today, when I delivered the latest packet of approved lists to the Thermale, I saw M. Laval himself descending the steps. He was wearing his white tie, and a cigarette was glued to his lips. There were Gardes Mobiles with bayonets protecting his approach to his car, and a few people had stopped to watch. He glared around him, looking ever more like a toad, with his hooded eyelids and surly expression; there was a brief wave, a puff on the cigarette, and then he was off to his château in Chateldon. He's no longer quite the suave, smug figure he was a year ago!

Special cakes in the patisserie on the corner for the Epiphany – the *Fête des Rois* – tomorrow, but no-one is in the mood for exchanging presents or giving thanks to God. What for, after all?

The purpose of our Commission for Jewish Affairs, it appears increasingly obvious, is not to help Jews, but to send them in their train-loads to be "treated", or "taken care of" (to use the official phraseology), in Germany. My lists of *Israélites* are divided into sections headed "Drancy", "Pithiviers" and "Beaune-la-Rolande" (*triage*, meaning "sorting", is one of the words the Commission uses), but I have reason to believe that the instructions that came to me from M. Duval emanate ultimately from Germany, and thence, by way of M. de Brinon's or M. Bousquet's offices in Paris, down here to Vichy! We are being asked to surrender French citizens – but only citizens of Jewish origin – to "camps" from which, Jean-Marc believes, they will never return.

January 27

Jean-Marc, spruce and dapper in a tweed suit that he told me proudly was made for him in Ireland, came to say goodbye to Madeleine and me this evening. He has been asked to resign his position at the ministry, for reasons he does not fully understand (though I begin to see the rub), and he is going to try to find work in Montpellier or elsewhere. He spoke angrily about the evils of the government. He took us to Chez Rosalie and bought drinks, and he raised a glass to M.'s and my future happiness. He also said he hoped that we would meet again once the war is over. I feel sad to lose yet another friend. Life is comfortless enough as it is.

When Jean-Marc rose to leave, he embraced us both and then, to my surprise, he handed me a small package. It was a present, he told me, which I was to put in my pocket and not open until after he had left and I was on my own. Later, alone in my room after taking M. home, I unwrapped a slim, plain-covered book entitled *Le Silence de la mer*. The author's name is simply Vercors. On the fly-leaf, J.-M. had written: "For Henry, a friend of the dark days, to help his resolve – his fellow *fonctionnaire* at Vichy – Jean-Marc". He had added an epigraph from Santayana: "Those who cannot remember the past are condemned to repeat it", which has been perplexing me ever since I first read the words.

M. reckons that Jean-Marc is a "*cryptomaquisard*" and is not to be trusted. I told her I disagreed and that I counted him as a loyal friend.

Reports of reprisals being taken in Marseille because of an attack on Wehrmacht soldiers in a brothel in the Vieux Port.

February 2

Now I know the worst. Today my eyes were opened to the full reality of what is happening here, and all over this country – *my* country. But I cannot live in France any longer. Neither can I face myself and what I am being asked to do.

February 3

The last three pages of Henry's diary for this month have clearly been torn out. W.L.

[CHAPTER 10]

APART FROM HENRY'S DIARIES AND NOTEBOOKS, THERE were a few other items in the thick packet of papers marked "Occupation" that Ghislaine and I had taken away with us from La Tiemblais to add to the picture of the man that was beginning to take shape in our minds. There were some press cuttings, most of them folded inside a copy of *Vers l'Europe nouvelle*, bought at the Rive Gauche bookshop, whose green sticker had been gummed on the inside cover, and these included a report of a speech by Maréchal Pétain and a photograph of him in uniform kissing a child who was being held up to him in the outstretched arms of a woman in a crowd; there was an editorial from *L'Œuvre* on the menace posed to France by Freemasons and Jews, and an article (no date is visible) from *La Gerbe*, by the collaborationist writer Drieu la Rochelle, whose ideas certainly appealed to Henry and whom he had observed ("bald and palid, with bulging eyes") both in 1939 and, as we have seen, with Robert, in the Paris restaurant in November 1942, dining with Otto Abetz. Underlined in ink is the following: "Why are we hesitating? For Germany is Europe for us, even if we are entering this Europe humiliated and with a rather sad face."

At one stage, Henry must have considered learning German, for I found a receipt from the École Berlitz for three German lessons. Otherwise, there were some letters from his parents dating from before, or during, the early months of the war, two more from Robert, and one from Sylvain de Gresly, with *"autorisé"* stamped on them; a couple of theatre programmes, an unredeemed *Ausweis*, the official permit needed to travel from Paris to Vichy; a December 1942 copy of the *N.R.F. (Nouvelle Revue Française)*, edited by Drieu himself, and with articles by André Gide and Jean Giono; and one of those official pre-printed wartime postcards that were the only form of written communication permitted between the two zones. It was postmarked *Vichy-État Français* and addressed to Henry at Robert's flat in rue Buffon. It read simply: *"Affectueuses pensées/ baisers – M."*

∞

Two months passed. Following Sylvain de Gresly's party and my meeting with Robert Worcester at La Coupole, I had returned to London, where lengthy rehearsals followed by a series of three concerts at the Barbican, a recording session, and a ten-day tour of the Scandinavian capitals kept me occupied. I ached to be back in Paris. I missed Ghislaine badly and, if I am to be honest with myself, I could not stop thinking of her, be it in the middle of concerts, in the loneliness of bleak hotel bedrooms, or in my flat. She dominated my conscious moments, my subconscious ones too, and still I did not feel I could express any of this to her. I was "family", after all, her cousin, and her "nephew", as she sometimes joked, her mother's illegitimate grandchild, to put it more bluntly. Then I was also her colleague, her fellow investigator in this quest for my grandfather, the man who had been her mother's lover; it was unimaginable that she should ever consider me a candidate for her affections. I felt inadequate, unsophisticated, ill-equipped to cope with the intellectual and literary world in which she moved. Yet I yearned for this woman who had invaded my imagination and my dreams; I was fixated by her face, her eyes, her body, and by thoughts of such voluptuousness – of "carnal passion" and "the flesh" (to use words that recurred in Sylvain de Gresly's novels, albeit usually applied to the opposite sex) – that at times I felt tortured by my mental images of her.

The best I could hope for at present, however, was the occasional telephone call or letter, such as the one I received in early October requesting my agreement to her making use of the diary and documents in her possession relating to the months Henry and Madeleine had spent in Germany, at Sigmaringen, by presenting some of the material as an extract from a work in progress. As she explained in a letter, and as she had previously intimated to me in Paris, her life in the world of French literary journalism was so demanding that she could only afford the time to delve into Henry's diaries and documents if there was some way it might lead to an article, or even a book. It had always been expected of her that she should be published, she explained, and she had frequently been approached by enthusiastic editors from Paris publishing houses urging her to write a novel. Her by-line was already respected in the city's literary circles, a world of gossip-ridden and influential coteries, and Henry's life and what had become of him had provided her with the framework for a book. "This Sigmaringen business fascinates me," she wrote in her letter, "but, as I once told you, I find I can only treat it objectively if I try to view Henry and my mother as fictional characters and treat the episode of their semi-captivity in Germany as an article or a short story. As I'm sure you understand, I would be too emotionally restricted if I were constantly being reminded that Madeleine is my own mother. I feel I need a little fictional latitude to extend and invent facets of their characters which are not necessarily obvious to us. Besides, there are whole gaps in our story, Will. How did Henry and Maman get to Germany in the first place? Where were they in the months before arriving there? Did they have to leave France for fear of recriminations against them? Was it because Henry was more involved than we realise with the Vichy regime? And how did he and Madeleine later escape to Denmark, with Germany collapsing all around them in 1945 and Maman pregnant with your father? How does one explain Henry's sudden reappearance – just like all those Nazis – in South America? And why did Henry not do his utmost to persuade Madeleine to join him in Argentina with the baby? These questions remain unanswered. I know there are pieces of the jigsaw that we can still put into place, but if I write this as fiction, then I am free to imagine what we don't yet know."

∞

I agreed immediately with Ghislaine's proposal and rang to tell her so. It must have been a week after her letter reached me that I decided I should try to get in touch once more with both Robert Worcester and Sylvain de Gresly, the old *Maréchaliste*, and, with or without Ghislaine, question them further while there was still time. They were both in their late eighties, and I realised that their knowledge and memories would go to the grave with them unless I were able to delve a little deeper. I said as much to Ghislaine during one of our subsequent telephone conversations, when, out of the blue, she asked me what my present commitments were. As it happened, after a fairly hectic period, my diary was virtually blank for the next few days, and there was nothing that could not be easily postponed. Our chamber group had no further engagements until late November, when there was a series of concerts in Scotland and the North of England, and there were no other commitments to keep me in London. Professional and emotional uncertainty is one of the drawbacks to a musician's life, but occasionally it provides compensations.

"Because if you've got the time, Will, I'd like you to do a little more research and I'll get on with writing – perhaps what I've set out to do should be a joint effort," she added. "Listen, I'm leaving Paris again shortly. A friend at the office has lent me his house in Provence for two weeks over the Toussaint, and I plan to start writing down there. The article first; then, if I can, something more substantial. There's no telephone there, no Parisians, no books to read or review, no gossip, just the bare essentials for a writer's needs: solitude, silence, and room to think and breathe. You could use my apartment."

"I'd love to," I said, and added, somewhat to my surprise, "but I'd much prefer it if you were going to be there with me."

There was a pause before Ghislaine spoke again. Was it my imagination, or was her voice a tone softer?

'Oh, it's not possible. I've said I'd go to Provence.'

She then agreed that it would make sense to try to see Sylvain de Gresly again ("and don't forget his son") as well as Robert Worcester. She even encouraged me to visit Madeleine in Brittany ("after all, she is your grandmother"), although she emphasised that her mother had said she did not want to be reminded of the "bad old days" and had already said all she intended to say about the war years. In early December, Ghislaine planned to come to London, where she was due to take part in a conference at the French Institute. If I was free perhaps we could spend a little time together, she suggested, and compare notes and discoveries. It seemed an ideal plan as far as I was concerned, and one that restored some hope to my undeclared love for her.

I would go to Paris, I decided, and, if invited, to Brittany. I would also try to elicit as much information from my own mother as I could. She had been infuriatingly vague earlier, when I had brought up the subject of my father's childhood, but now that I was better informed myself and was becoming more closely acquainted with the revelations about my grandfather's past life, perhaps she would be prepared to divulge whatever else she remembered. It would depend on her mood; my mother could be exhaustingly frivolous, although her family and close friends have always known that this superficial veneer disguised a high intelligence and a powerful ability to control life in difficult circumstances. It was a frivolity she had adopted, I should add, following my father's final illness, almost as if she were determined to compensate for her misfortune by displaying an obstinate light-heartedness that would protect her from the intrusions of the outside world. Our chamber group's November tour would provide a useful opportunity for me to spend a couple of days with her in Scotland, and I would endeavour to raise these matters.

I wrote a letter in my most careful French to Sylvain's son, Yves, who, I remembered, had seemed well disposed towards us at the dinner party in rue de l'Échaudé. I asked whether it might be possible to call on him and his father during my forthcoming trip to Paris, to ask them certain questions relating to my grandfather "in the interests of family research". By the same post, I sent a card to Robert Worcester inviting myself to lunch again.

I did not have to wait long for a response. Three days later, just as I was getting ready to drive to the Wigmore Hall, where an old friend from my music college days, Dinah Sutherland, was due to give her first London piano recital, the telephone rang and a gruff American voice asked for "Mr William Latymer, if you please".

"I'll be glad to help in any way I can, old boy. Give me a call when you get to Paris. We'll meet at the *terrasse* of La Coupole." Robert Worcester spoke haltingly, pausing for breath every few words. "But call me as soon as you arrive. I've not been too well lately. And at my age . . ." There was a hollow laugh down the telephone.

The following morning a letter arrived from Yves, written in fastidious handwriting on the most elegant stationery I have ever seen – thick, deckle-edged cream vellum with a watermark, tucked inside a purple-lined envelope – with a rather formal invitation to lunch on November 4. "This is the only date that is convenient for my father, for we shall be leaving on the 5th for Umbria, where we are accustomed to spending the late autumn, but we look forward to receiving you." It ended with the customary old-fashioned Gallic flourish: "My father begs me to transmit his most cordial memories of your last visit. Please believe, dear Monsieur, in our most distinguished wishes." etc. Something about the resonance of this highly formal use of the French language brought back the dark and, as I recalled, claustrophobically oppressive atmosphere of the Greslys' apartment, with its Second Empire furniture and its airless, gloomily lit drawing room.

∞

To my mind, London is at its best in the autumn: the quality of the light, the sweetly pervasive melancholy of the shortening days, the faded colours in the parks, and that sudden chill that ushers in the first intimations of winter. All at once, it is as if life has to be taken seriously again: Londoners shake off their summer slumber and finally revert to their normal way of life following the lotus-eating of the holiday months; Parliament returns after the recess, and the city gradually re-adapts to its natural pace and rhythm. It is a time to take stock, to re-equip and revitalise oneself, a time for resolutions.

During the four or five days I had at my disposal before my departure for Paris, I was determined to avoid all social commitments and I did little but read books about France during the Occupation and leaf through my grandfather's diaries and letters once more. I sat on damp park benches, wrapped in a long woollen scarf and my ancient Loden coat, and I read until the light began to fail or it grew too cold. I telephoned Ghislaine three or four times before she left for Provence. I ate alone, in cheap restaurants or at home, and I saw no-one. To protect myself further from outside distraction, I dictated a message into my answering machine to the effect that I was unavailable until mid-November. Only Ghislaine, my mother and a few friends knew that I was in London.

Gradually, a fuller picture of Henry Latymer was forming in my mind. The France that he cared for so passionately, and which seemed to be collapsing all around him in 1939 and 1940, also assumed new qualities. Henry clearly had an idealised notion of France; for him it was forever the France of the Belle Époque, the France of the artistic communities that patronised Le Lapin Agile and Le Bœuf sur le Toit, the *douce France* celebrated in those marvellously sentimental songs that men like Charles Trenet and Jean Sablon had sung, which my parents used to play on their ancient wind-up gramophone when I was a child. It was certainly a very different country now: Henry's Paris is hard to imagine today, and the *vie de province* that he experienced before the true misery of war set in, during the months he stayed with Jean and Chantal Arago at their home in Bellerive, seems like a breath of wind from the past, an intimation of an existence that has been extinguished by the storm of consumerism and cultural homogeneity that has swept through Europe during my own lifetime. And yet the spirit somehow survives, as it always does: just as you cannot destroy a people, as Hitler and Stalin attempted to do in the death camps and gulags, so something of the sense of the past lingers on, sustaining and firing our imagination, even when we have betrayed all it ever stood for by creating the most soulless of futures.

For all his personal failings – and Henry was hardly a man to admire, I realised – his worst political error was to have identified his deeply personal concept of France with the men who clustered like drowning rats around the pathetic figure of Maréchal Pétain in May and June 1940, when the German armies swept around the vaunted Maginot Line and descended like ravenous wolves on Paris. Apart from the brief spells of success he knew as an artist – in Vichy, and, much later, in Buenos Aires – the rest of Henry's life seems to have been spent compensating and atoning for the sins of his youth, only for him to die eventually, a lonely and tortured ghost of the man that emerges from the diaries, in a distant South American city.

Yet why should any of this matter to me, to Ghislaine, or to anyone else? Why did the scant details of the life of a man whom I had never known, of whose existence I had been virtually unaware until a few months previously, continue to exercise most of my conscious moments? I cannot explain this save by suggesting that, truism though it may be, we are all a part of our own forebears' atavistic memories. History and memory are inextricably bound, and it must surely be our duty to interpret our past if we are to give any meaning to our present lives. And then, of course, it was because of Henry that I had discovered Ghislaine.

∞

So it was that on All Saints' Day, 1999, I boarded the Eurostar to Paris, taking with me a half-bottle of Meursault, a Gruyère sandwich and some plump Italia grapes, and sat and watched the landscapes of Kent and Picardy glide past until I dozed off and awoke at around six o'clock to find the train edging smoothly into the Gare du Nord.

At Ghislaine's flat, there was a note left for me by the telephone on the small table in the hall instructing me to make myself at home, to consume whatever was left in the fridge, and to get in touch with Madeleine in Brittany should I wish to escape from Paris at the weekend. It ended: "Maman would be delighted to see you. *Je t'embrasse fort.* G."

I did as she bid, unpacked my bag, and then called Robert Worcester. The telephone seemed to ring interminably, but the American's rasping, breathless voice eventually answered. "I was expecting you, old boy. Meet me for an apéritif at La Coupole on Friday, 12.15 sharp, don't be late. Then I'll take you to the best restaurant in town. My chauffeur will drive us there. You won't eat better anywhere in Paris, I can promise you." It was the day after my invitation to lunch at the Greslys, though I did not mention this to Robert on the telephone.

∞

Three days later, on a fine, bright November morning, having attended Mass at the abbey church of Saint-Germain-des-Prés, and taken an hour over breakfast at the absurdly expensive Café de Flore, where I sipped coffee and struggled through *Le Monde*, I was strolling happily along the same narrow streets where Ghislaine and I had walked only six months previously, making my way to the Gresly apartment in rue de l'Échaudé.

Yves answered the door. He looked less dramatic, less darkly Latin, than I remembered. "My dear William," he murmured, grasping my hand in both of his, "my father will be so very pleased to see you. You know, he has been a little poorly lately and we have had to postpone our visit to Italy. He tires easily these days, so I propose that we take lunch quite early. By the way" – his voice dropped to a whisper as he guided me down the book-lined corridor – "it is his birthday today. He is ninety-two, but you would hardly believe it."

It took me a few moments to acclimatise myself to the

darkness of the salon, which now seemed smaller than the room with its red walls and Second Empire furniture that still hovered uneasily in my memory. Yves took my coat, asked me to sit down and assured me that "Papa" would join us shortly. He, meanwhile, was going to fetch "something a little special" to celebrate the occasion.

I gazed around the shaded, silent room. The atmosphere was sepulchral, yet also womb-like: the sort of salon in which you could happily escape the world outside. The daylight that filtered through the closed shutters was just sufficient for me to be able to glimpse the canvases and drawings that hung at evenly spaced intervals along three of the four magenta-red walls. Opposite the door through which I had entered, bookshelves stood on either side of an ornate, white-marble fireplace above which hung a large, gilded mirror. A bronze bust of a naked boy, whose sensuously muscular shoulder blades were reflected back at me in the penumbral light, stood in isolation on the mantelpiece. A young man in eighteenth-century clothing stared arrogantly out of a large canvas facing the closed shutters, while a number of late-seventeeth- and eighteenth-century drawings, including what I felt sure must be a Rembrandt sketch, adorned the spaces on either side of the tall, austere window frames. I had not remembered any of this from our previous visit and I ascribed it to my nervousness at the time.

A high-pitched chime, like that of an angelus bell, tinkled in an adjoining room, and I heard the sound of shuffling footsteps before another door opened and Sylvain de Gresly inched his way towards me. He was wearing a dark-grey suit, a white shirt with a stiff collar and cufflinks and a paisley pattern tie. Over one arm he carried the same Blackwatch tartan rug that he had

had with him on our previous visit. With his other hand, Sylvain supported himself on a silver-tipped black cane. I rose to my feet, helped him to his chair, and wished him a happy birthday.

"Try not to live to my age," he said, smiling and shaking his head ruefully. "The modern world grows more and more distasteful, and one is so plagued by memories, I find. Last night, it may astonish you to know, I dreamed of my own father. He, too, lived until he was ninety, and I have inherited his longevity. Do you know, he fought at Sedan? Between us, we span one hundred and eighty years," he chuckled. "Once, on a visit to England in 1892, he set eyes on your Queen Victoria. He was walking in the park near Windsor when her carriage drove past him. He waved, and she rewarded him with a regal *levée du main*. He often told the story. Perhaps it's one reason why I'm still a monarchist at heart."

Sylvain nodded to himself and sighed, and at that moment Yves walked in with a bottle and three crystal glasses. I tried to read the tattered and dusty label.

"This is white port," he announced. "It is rare and very good, I am told. We shall drink to Papa with it, but it is a vintage, I must tell you, that represents a sad year for us. Do you know why?"

I shook my head.

"Nineteen fifty-one is the year that the Maréchal – Philippe Pétain – Papa's former commandant in the army, and our saviour, as you no doubt know, both at Verdun as well as in the dark night of 1940, died in captivity, disgraced and dishonoured – to the eternal shame of France – on the Île d'Yeu."

Yves looked at his father, who bowed his head, then recovered himself and spoke: "We must try not to dwell too much in the past. It is one of my weaknesses. Let us not drink to my absurd age, nor to the shade of the poor Maréchal, but instead to the memory of my old friend, and our dear William's grandfather, Henry Latymer – an artist and a gentleman."

Sylvain leaned forward in his chair to reach for his glass, and, as he raised it to toast Henry's memory, I noticed his cufflinks. Made of silver, they incorporated a marshal's baton with a double-headed axe. It was the *francisque*, the emblem of loyalty to the Vichy regime.

We raised our glasses, and the occasion seemed opportune for me to enquire further about my grandfather. I explained how Ghislaine and I had become curious as to how he and Madeleine had spent the war years, how it had come about that their child, my father, had been born in Copenhagen, and, finally, the circumstances in which he had gone to live in Argentina.

"I shall tell you as much as I can remember." The old man's eyes peered into mine. "But you know that Ghislaine has persuaded her mother, our dear Madeleine – who still telephones me every fortnight, bless her heart – to break her self-imposed vow of silence and record her memories of Sigmaringen on a tape recorder for her daughter. A charming young woman, as I recall from our last meeting. Madeleine's memories will be clearer than mine – and, of course, she and Henry were deeply in love – of that you can be quite sure."

We finished our port and Yves summoned us to lunch.

Sylvain said grace, after which Yves proceeded to present each of us with a half-lobster and to fill our glasses with Alsatian Sylvaner. "We always drink this wine on my father's birthday," said Yves, turning towards me. "He pretends that it's named after him," he joked, before toasting the old writer, and we raised our glasses to his continuing good health.

Sylvain placed his hand on my sleeve, his moist eyes unblinking, and spoke softly: "You are asking me about a period in my life and that of your grandfather that we try to forget today. It's more convenient that way. What's past is past. The war years were a shattering experience for France and the full truth may never emerge. How can it, even now? The personal suffering, the shame, the guilt . . . It is something our leaders have done their best to conceal, for it hardly accords with the idea of France that they would wish to present to the world. They have done their best to re-invent our history and shape it to an image they believe to be more honourable. Most Frenchmen of my generation tell of the glorious and heroic deeds of the Resistance. No doubt, there were many brave men – men such as Jean Moulin – who died in order to free our nation from the Nazis, but you must remember that in June 1940 those like myself and Henry – who although he was English became a naturalised Frenchman, as you must now realise – and countless others, who may have subsequently denied or concealed their involvement, rejoiced in what we earnestly and fervently believed would be the dawn of a new Europe. We did what we did because of our desire to restore *la vieille France* – the France we grew up in and loved, its religion and its glorious heritage – and we saw Philippe Pétain as the person to lead us along that road."

Sylvain paused and held up one hand before resuming. "We were mistaken to place our belief in a man as unworthy as Adolf Hitler, but it is easy to criticise with hindsight. There was a certain allure to this new Germany that pulled itself so nobly out of the ruins of the effete Weimar Republic, and many young men and women of my generation saw it as something thrilling and noble. Out of the old, decadent, weary Europe of the 1930s, in which only the Jew and the Freemason, with their modern, liberal notions, seemed to prosper, a new, shining Europe would once more arise. We would be the vanguard of a moral and patriotic crusade that would cleanse and purify, and that would hold firm against the Communist menace—"

"But Papa, history is cyclical." Yves looked intensely at his father, eyes ablaze, as he interrupted the old man. "You make it sound as if all is lost, but I believe that even now, in France, we can continue to honour men like the Maréchal while moving towards a new future. But first we have to make this country fit for Frenchmen again."

"I devoutly hope you may be right, my son, but it will not happen in my lifetime," Sylvain said, nodding his white head as he picked at a lobster claw.

I listened, spellbound, simultaneously repulsed and fascinated. Here was one of the last of a generation who could speak with any authority about events that were receding into history, and someone who could do so with lucidity and charm, however unacceptable his viewpoint was to those of my generation. Sylvain continued his apologia, and his words, spoken in his old-fashioned, infinitely appealing French, seemed to fill the stillness of the afternoon. We had finished eating and were now sipping the last of a half-bottle of 1970 Château de Malle, a "delectable Sauternes" that Yves had spoken of with reverence. I felt lulled towards sleep. For an instant, I closed my eyes and tried to imagine myself as the young man that Henry must have been; a sudden sense of fused identities seemed to overcome me and these sensations were followed by the rising claustrophobia that I had experienced on my previous visit. The bell I had heard earlier was tinkling once more. I glanced at my watch. It was four o'clock.

"Henry was my friend and, in my eyes, a model citizen of the new Europe to which we both aspired. A man at ease in any company. A gentleman of the older, more anglicised style. I always wished I had known him earlier, as his American friend Mr Worcester, whom you met at our dinner party, had the good fortune to do. He had his faults, but he also had such polish, such *joie de vivre*, you know; people adored him. And so handsome . . ."

Sylvain's eyes gleamed and he shook his head thoughtfully before looking away. From outside, through the drawn shutters, I could hear the bells of St-Germain-des-Prés striking the hour, half muffled by the thick silence that seemed to droop around us like a heavy curtain.

I glanced at Henry's drawing on the wall. "How would you rate him as an artist?" I said.

The old writer appeared not to hear me. His chin had dropped onto his chest and he seemed lost in memories. Yves smiled sweetly at me and shrugged, his dark eyes and his expression affirming that this was what happened in old age: *Si vieillesse pouvait* . . . He proceeded to answer my question himself in a gentle whisper.

"Those who knew his work in France at the time rated him highly. I'm talking of people who are supposed to hold unchallengeable opinions on such matters." Yves smiled and gazed into my eyes. "People like Yvonne Zervos and Dunoyer de Segonzac, who were very impressed by his work, so I'm told. But Henry had to be careful. People always spoke of his excellent French, but he was a foreigner in our country, after all; an Englishman who was pro-Vichy was a rarity and it must have been difficult for him to survive, let alone develop his career, in those wartime days when nobody knew whom they could trust. And remember, the English were very unpopular in certain circles in France."

Yves continued. "From the few works I myself have seen, I would say he was an exceptional artist. In our house in the Sarthe, Papa has an oil painting of a female nude and a pencil drawing of a view over the River Allier looking towards Vichy. They are both outstanding, to my mind: delicate, sensitive, and the oil has – how can I put it? – a distinctly voluptuous quality. Had he remained in Paris, and had he been able to work with Robert and come to know the influential gallery owners and dealers, perhaps his name would be celebrated today. He was a casualty of the war, you could say."

"My son is right. He would have been an important European painter," Sylvain broke in, suddenly recovered. "But you must remember that by the time we met in Germany – and you should really rely on Madeleine's memories of this period – it was 1944 and all our dreams and aspirations truly had been dashed. Sigmaringen, that bizarre little town on the Danube, represented the final collapse, the final dishonour, our nemesis. There was no-one to speak up for us; only Destouches with his lunatic ramblings. You know his work?'

"You mean Céline, Papa," Yves intervened helpfully.

"Yes, Céline – his nom de plume was Louis-Ferdinand Céline." Sylvain turned towards me. "Whatever people say, he was a fine doctor, and for some, a great writer. How curious life can be."

Sylvain's head slumped forward again and he seemed confused. Yves was quick to come to his aid.

"William, you will forgive me, but I think Papa should take a rest now. He normally retires to his room after lunch, but today has been special. All these memories of long ago, our little celebration and the excitement of seeing his old friend's grandson have exhausted him."

Yves helped Sylvain up from his chair and led his father out of the room. "Such a pleasure," the old man murmured, turning his profile slowly as he shuffled away. "You will come again, won't you?"

∞

As it happened, I never saw Sylvain de Gresly again. Two months later, in January 2000, he died at home in his sleep. There was a brief mention in the London *Guardian*, but in one of her letters Ghislaine enclosed three long articles about him from the French press that referred to his early work, his insufficiently recognised importance as a witness to our century, and his lifelong commitment to the Catholic Church. None of them, however, mentioned his years as a silent collaborator or the period of dishonour following his return to France, initially under an assumed name, in 1947.

∞

Despite Henry's classically English good looks, he was easier to visualise in Paris or provincial France than as a young art student in the London I knew, or in distant Buenos Aires, where he had lived out the remainder of his post-war life. Robert Worcester, whom I met again at La Coupole the following day, filled in further gaps.

The American was at his customary table. He was dressed in a tweed jacket, a white shirt and the same tie he had worn when we had met there earlier in the year, and highly polished black brogues. He looked older than he had done at our last meeting only a few months ago. His hair was longer and whiter, and he took a little time to recognise me.

"William, old chap. Come and sit on my left. I'm getting a touch deaf, you know."

Robert ordered two martinis. The waiter nodded from a distance. A yellow *papier maïs* Gitane lay crushed in an ashtray. He glanced at the gold fob watch he carried in his waistcoat pocket and turned to me with watering eyes.

"This city is choking from traffic fumes, don't you find? Between them, the automobile and the city planners are ruining Paris. Myself, I prefer to die from my own smoke than from air pollution. Do you know, when your grandfather and I met here during the war, the streets were empty and so quiet. Plenty of bicycles, of course, and too many Germans." He chuckled. "But it's no use regretting. We can only hope for a little more good sense from the politicians in the next world.

"Take no notice of my foolish prattle, old chap," Robert said, patting my knee. "I'm an old sentimentalist, grown fond and foolish. All my friends – those that are left – tell me so. Drink that down, and my driver will take us to lunch. We'll be there by one o'clock. Are you a gourmand? I think we're going to enjoy ourselves."

We had spent barely half an hour at La Coupole.

Robert took my arm as we left and we turned into rue Delambre, where his driver (no longer the Bellini angel, I noted) was waiting in a black car that must almost have qualified as an antique. I had no idea of the make. A Lagonda? A Facel-Vega? We swooped smoothly down boulevard Montparnasse, along Raspail, past the Invalides and over the Seine, to be deposited outside the discreet frontage of an old-fashioned establishment in rue Lamennais.

"You won't find better food in Paris these days," Robert confided, as a doorman in a green tailcoat opened the door to us. "The chef has been here for thirty years. Only Faugeron cooks as well, in my view. And, by the way, I particularly recommend the *noisettes d'agneau*."

The restaurant was already full and there was a buzz of conversation from the clientele, who mostly looked like businessmen. The large dining hall with its blue velvet wall hangings and oak-panelled walls, covered with unidentifiable paintings of provincial and rural scenes, exuded a discreet, cosmopolitan atmosphere. Attentive waiters and sommeliers glided to and fro, and we were shown to a corner table. Since I was Robert's guest, I felt that I could not ignore his suggestion, and so rather than study the menu in detail as my host did, I chose a plate of *queues d'ecrevisses* and the *noisettes* that he had recommended, while Robert ordered *suprème de pigeon* in a wine sauce. We drank a Château Haut-Brion, which Robert deemed was "amusing, but challenging to the palate".

"I take wine seriously, even if I can no longer treat daily life in quite the same way," Robert said as he nudged my arm. "As my friend Liebling used to say: 'No sane man can afford to dispense with debilitating pleasures; no ascetic can be considered reliably sane', and although I sometimes doubt my own sanity, I am certain about my few remaining pleasures. Liebling also said that old friends should always be re-met in fine restaurants.

And so, for Henry's sake, old chap, as well as for our own, I hope we'll remain good friends for a few years yet."

Robert spoke these words in a sort of mock oration. As he finished, he raised his glass and proposed a toast to Henry. It must have been at least the sixth time during the past year that I had drunk to the memory of this man whom I had never met. I reflected that for someone who had been dismissed by some as a traitor and a coward, my grandfather had certainly been held in high regard by his friends.

"Did I tell you about the last time I saw Henry?' Robert tucked his napkin beneath his chin and settled back into his chair. "It was in 1942 – May, I believe – at Arno Breker's exhibition at the Orangerie. I'd procured an invitation to the *vernissage*, and Henry had come up on the blue train from Vichy. That was the special train that took Laval and all the government V.I.P.s back and forth between Vichy and Paris. Ordinary folk wanting to travel north had to have a special pass, but he and I had no problem. Thanks to some useful connections, Henry had acquired his naturalisation papers, just as I had, and, to all intents and purposes, we were Frenchmen. Does it shock you to think of your grandfather as a traitor to the Allied cause?"

I evaded the question, shrugged and muttered something about the rights of conscientious objectors.

Robert sipped his wine. "We were young and we were blind, I guess. I would not have made the same mistake again, I can tell you. I would have fought for my country, but at the time . . ." He held up his hands and sighed. "And we suffered the consequences. That's why Henry ended up in Buenos Aires."

"And you?"

The old American looked momentarily disconcerted. "I clung on here," he mumbled, shaking his head sadly. "I was a ghost for two years . . . life was not easy . . . not easy at all . . . But, I was telling you . . ." Robert quickly recovered his composure. "Breker's exhibition. He was the great Nazi sculptor, though he was already well known in Paris, for he'd lived here before the war. Friend of Albert Speer's. Laval even gave a lunch for him at the Matignon. Anyway, all Paris was there for his opening. Guitry and Cocteau, Paul Morand, Diaghilev's dancer Serge Lifar, Abetz and the top Nazis, everyone . . . Abel Bonnard delivered a speech, I remember, and people walked round and round inspecting Breker's larger-than-life nudes, praising the heroism of German youth, the desirability of health and virility in the moral education of the young, and mouthing all that stuff about how the physical beauty and aesthetic ideals of Ancient Greece were being reborn in Hitler's Germany. Perverted nonsense, of course. Dangerous stuff, too. Art can never serve ideology. But that's how we saw things then."

"Surely Henry didn't admire that kind of work?"

"No. As an artist, I think he must have secretly despised it. Henry always recognised good art, or so it seemed to me. But you must remember that up until that time we were swept along by our idealistic dreams, and if Breker was going to be the fashion, it was not for us to disagree with the master race, was it? Actually, I reckon by that time Henry was already sensing that Pétain's 'new broom' was worn out . . . The old boy must have known that he'd been hoodwinked by the Nazis, and he could no longer have thought of himself as a Joan of Arc. A pathetic comedy, really."

Robert removed his spectacles and rubbed his eyes with

one hand. "What a century it's been," he continued, sipping his wine again.

Our conversation reverted to the excellence of the food. Robert was evidently an authority on the fine art of French cuisine, and he was happier reminiscing about dishes he had eaten and about memorable vintages than he was recalling *les années noires*. He told me that he had once paid his restaurant bills for two years during the 1960s by writing a monthly column for an American magazine at a time when his work as an art dealer was not bringing in much revenue.

"I'm a disciple of Escoffier," Robert declared, "and the one thing I've learned is that a great dish is never eaten twice. Every great cook has his own individual approach. Always find out who the chef is in a restaurant of any standing, get to know him, if you can, and never accept what the *maître d'hôtel* recommends. Those are my rules."

∞

The afternoon wore on and by three o'clock the restaurant was beginning to empty. As soon as we had finished our main course, Robert knocked on the table and ordered coffee and cognac from the ever-attentive waiter. "Two glasses of Hine," he said, "and my compliments to Monsieur Claude."

I chose the moment to bring the conversation back to Henry and to ask about two of the people most frequently referred to in my grandfather's diaries, and who particularly intrigued me: Jean Arago and his sister, Chantal.

Robert's expression hardened when I mentioned these names and he removed his spectacles to rub his eyes again. He shook his head slowly from side to side.

"I hoped you wouldn't ask me about them, old chap. They were true friends to Henry, and his success as an artist in those years could be attributed to Jean's belief in him. Henry would never have had the self-confidence to succeed without Jean's encouragement and enthusiasm.'

"What became of them?"

"I suppose you knew they were Jewish?"

"Yes, I've come to realise that."

"Perhaps you have heard of Drancy. It's one of the most infamous names in recent French history."

I nodded.

"Well, tens of thousands of Jews were deported from France in those terrible years, mostly to Auschwitz or Ravensbrück. It's not something people care to talk about, even today. But before the Jews were herded onto the trains which, as we now know – but didn't know then – were bound for the death camps, they were sent to Drancy, which was a sort of transit place just north of Paris. You see, after the Germans took over the free zone in November 1942, French Jews began to be arrested in the same way that Jews of foreign extraction had earlier been. They were rounded up, shoved into trucks and trains, and some were tortured and murdered even before they reached Drancy – and not just by the Gestapo, but later by Darnand's band of thugs in the *milice* as well. Poor Jean and Chantal – she was such a beautiful girl, to judge by Henry's remarks. They disappeared one night in 1943, I believe. No-one knew what had become of them at first. We learned later that they had perished at Auschwitz."

Robert paused for breath and inhaled his cognac.

"Could Henry have done nothing to help them?" I said. "He had been in love with Chantal, after all.'

Robert looked me in the eye.

"William, we shall never know the whole truth, but I reckon Henry must have known something of the fate in store for his friends. Let us hope he was unaware of what was happening in Germany. I had no knowledge of what was going on – none of us did. Once Henry broke with Chantal, he produced no further paintings, at least not for two years or more. He needed money, and so, once he had his naturalisation papers, he worked for Madeleine's father, who was employed by the Vichy government. I believe that this work involved compiling dossiers of the names of Jews for the Ministry of the Interior. These were eventually delivered to Theo Dannecker."

"Who was he?"

"Scum." Robert spat the word. "One of the most evil, vain and arrogant men imaginable. He was one of Eichmann's minions. It was he who issued the orders for Jewish arrests."

"And Henry was one of those who provided him with the information?" I asked.

"No, not exactly. You see . . ." Robert held his chin in the palm of one hand, brushing his fingers across his face in a characteristic gesture. "By that time, Henry had fallen in love with Madeleine. His affair with Chantal had come to an end. Henry had moved out of her brother's house at Bellerive, and soon afterwards Chantal stopped working at Jean's gallery and joined one of the Chantiers de Jeunesse, the youth camps set up by General de la Porte du Theil. He was a patriot who believed in Pétain and eventually stood up bravely to the Nazis. All young French people in the unoccupied zone, who were over the age of twenty, had to work in them for six months or so. The aim was to teach demoralised French youth how to become model citizens. You know, *mens sana in corpore sano* and all that. My friend Hervé – he was shot by the Resistance at the end of the war – knew Jean and Chantal a little and he used to see her occasionally in Vichy. She told him about her decision to leave the running of the gallery to Jean and to support the aims of the Maréchal by working at one of the local camps. Hervé used to come to Paris on government business, which is how I know about the Aragos, and I remember him proudly showing me one of the posters for the youth camps: a young man dressed in green knickerbockers and wearing a cloak and beret, and behind him, in silhouette, a Gaul with a helmet and a double-headed axe. You get the picture?"

I confess I was confused by these further aspects of a regime that I was only beginning to comprehend, but I said nothing to Robert.

"At least those guys still had a vision of France which they tried to keep alive in those early days, before the Germans over-ran the unoccupied zone. All those allusions to the noble Gaul, to Joan of Arc, the heroes of Verdun and the eldest daughter of the Church, and all that nostalgia for the monarchy and military glory. Like de Gaulle, the Vichyssois had their 'certain idea' of France – or they did at that stage – and they thought they were creating a national revolution, a new political structure, in which God, the family and the moral order were paramount. I think Henry, and, to a lesser extent initially, Jean and Chantal too, all fell for the ideal. Most of us did. The Maréchal had a vision of an eternal France: a ruling elite and a noble peasantry that might have come out of a Giono novel, and a "*retour à la terre*" – that was the phrase – back to the land. It was romantic nonsense, of course, but somehow it rang true at the time. And Pétain had a Légion des Combattants whose job it was to spread the principles of the revolution: *travail, famille, patrie*. It was created by Xavier Vallat, the man who a year later was heading the commissariat for Jewish affairs."

"Did Henry know him?"

"He didn't know Henry, but Henry must have been aware of him. Vallat wasn't quite the villain he's made out to be. Sure, he was an anti-Semite – so were many prominent Frenchmen in those days – but he was a patriot, and he so annoyed the Nazis with his delaying tactics that finally they had him removed. He wanted to limit the power of Jews and Freemasons, but he didn't intend to destroy the Jewish race. His successor, a monster by the name of Darquier de Pellepoix, was much more to the Nazis' liking."

Robert paused, drained his cognac, checked his fob watch and continued. I noticed that his voice had dropped to a loud, confidential whisper and that occasionally he glanced surreptitiously around the few neighbouring tables still occupied. Outside, in rue Lamennais, it had begun to rain.

"As I was saying, through Madeleine's father Henry was given work compiling dossiers for Vichy. Jean's gallery still functioned, I suppose, but there wasn't much of a living to be made from being a painter any longer and it may be that Jean felt understandably angry at Henry's treatment of his sister and had distanced himself. I don't know. It could just be coincidence, but the terrible thing was that within two months of Henry starting to work for the government, Jean and Chantal had vanished, as had many other Jews in the vicinity. Disappeared overnight, *bei Nacht und Nebel*, under cover of night and fog, just like that. A car would arrive outside the victims' house in

the early hours of the morning. The Jews were given ten minutes to pack an overnight bag and were then led away by men
in uniform. They were loaded onto trains and taken to the
transit camps, to Pithiviers, to Compiègne or the Vél d'Hiv,
and eventually Drancy, and from there they were deported to
the German frontier and thence to Poland."

Robert reached his mottled, wrinkled hand across the table
and grasped mine for what seemed like several minutes.

"We can't be held responsible for the mistakes and failings
of our friends, William – or those of our grandparents. There is
no proof, only hearsay. Nothing more. Nothing to prove that
Henry betrayed his friends . . ." he added in his educated drawl.

Then, quite suddenly, Robert summoned the waiter, asked
for the bill, which he signed, and we left the restaurant in
silence, the elderly American leaning heavily on my arm. His
car was outside and the rain had stopped. Minutes later, his
chauffeur drew up outside Ghislaine's apartment in rue des
Saints-Pères. I thanked Robert warmly, got out, and as I did so
he opened the car door, called me to him and clasped me in his
arms. His head slumped on my shoulder and his body seemed
to be trembling.

"Dear Henry." His voice was choked in a sob. "My poor
friend . . . If only our allotted span of years were longer so
that we could learn from our errors." He sighed, then quickly
recovered his composure, drew himself up in his seat and gave
instructions to his chauffeur. "Goodbye, old chap. Come and
see me again, won't you?"

[CHAPTER 11]

I SPENT THE FOLLOWING WEEKEND IN BRITTANY. STAYING
in Ghislaine's flat, surrounded by her books, her belongings, her
pictures and photographs, only made me long for her efferves-
cent company and, since she was unattainable even by telephone
at her Provençal bolt-hole, I resolved to ring Madeleine and
ask if I could come and stay for a night. It would be as close
to Ghislaine as I could get in the circumstances, and Madeleine
was, after all – as I kept having to remind myself – my grandmother.

"But, my dear, you have only to ask. This house is yours,
William, whenever you want to come here. You really must
think of yourself as family now."

The T.G.V. from Montparnasse reached Dinan in about
three hours. Madeleine had sent her gardener's son, Bruno,
to meet me in an ancient black Citroën. The smell of the
old leather upholstery and polished-wood panelling transported
me into some undefined past, not the past of Vichy and the
war years that so preoccupied me, but a more immediate past
that excluded all those anxieties and concerns of our present-
day world, analysed in such painstaking detail in the *Monde*

Diplomatique that I had brought with me for the journey.

At La Tiemblais, Madeleine was seated in the same arm-chair, her black and white spaniel at her feet. A fire smouldered. A Mozart piano quintet was being broadcast on the radio and an early novel by Sylvain de Gresly lay open on the table beside her. She greeted me warmly when Jeanne announced me; more affectionately, in fact, than I had thought possible.

"You have so often been in my thoughts – and in my prayers," she added, rising slowly to her feet. "Jeanne and I prayed to the Holy Virgin and to St Anne, our patron saint here in Brittany, to bring you back here before it was too late for us. You cannot know how happy it makes me to see you again. Your friendship with Ghislaine – and I often wonder whether it may be more than friendship – has meant a great deal to me and my secret hope is that your relationship may develop. Like any mother, I worry about my daughter."

Then she embraced me.

"Jeanne will show you to your room and we shall meet for dinner in an hour's time. You must forgive me if I disappear the moment you arrive. I like to attend vespers at our little church, and Bruno is waiting. You must make yourself at home."

I was given the same bedroom at the top of the house, the one with the four-poster bed and the smell of varnish and turpentine furniture polish I had occupied on my previous visit. Purple and red asters drooped from a green pottery jug on the chest of drawers. On the bedside table lay a copy of Céline's *D'un château l'autre*. I picked up the book with its worn paper covers and examined its bold, now dated typography, and I ran my eye over what appeared to be a continuous sequence of unfinished sentences, punctuated by marks of omission.

I unpacked my night bag and lay down on the bed. The linen sheets, no doubt ironed by Jeanne, smelled of starch and lavender. The shutters were still open, and through the window-pane I could see the first evening stars.

I stood up, opened the window and let the cool air envelop me. These stars in the clear, unpolluted night sky brought back memories of my father and of the rare occasions when I had felt close to him. I remembered the night before I was despatched by train for the first time to the boarding school that both Henry and my father had also attended. That evening, he had taken me by the arm and led me outside, into the garden. It was dark, but the heavens were ablaze with stars. He handed me his most precious possession: the pair of binoculars that he kept in a brown leather case in his study. It was the first time I had ever been allowed to touch them. They were German glasses, he told me, the very best available, made by Zeiss of Jena. I have them to this day.

"They are the only memento I possess of my own father, a man I never knew," he told me. "They'll last for ever and one day they'll be yours." (Did he have some intimation of his early death, I used to wonder.) "Look, directly overhead, below the planet Jupiter, that's Aldebaran, it's always been my favourite star." He placed the binoculars around my neck and then, with his hands on my shoulders, he guided me through the brightest celestial bodies in the night sky. The Plough, the Pole Star, the Pleiades, Sirius, Orion and his belt, Rigel and Betelgeuse, Castor and Pollux, Arcturus, Stella Capella, Cassiopeia . . . Such magical names, and on winter nights such as this, I can even identify some of them.

I remembered, too, the sense of helplessness and desperation

I felt bidding my parents goodbye the next morning. As the train prepared to pull out of the station, my father and I shook hands and my mother kissed me and waved wildly as she struggled to hold back her own tears. Then, all at once, as the train gathered speed, they were gone, and I was left to deal as best I could with the peculiar conventions of life at a Catholic public school in England. On the first evening after I arrived, perplexed and alarmed by the throng of boys teeming noisily along a maze of corridors that reeked of detergent and sweat ("Pilgrims to Parnassus", the priest who welcomed the new boys had called us), we were obliged to attend a service in chapel, held at the start of each school year, known as *Bona Mors*. It consisted of a lengthy series of chanted litanies to which three hundred or more apparently healthy and boisterous teenagers responded, praying for the blessing of a peaceful or good death: one of the Jesuit priests or novices, attired in a black robe, called out the Latin antiphons from the altar, and the boys' voices, high-pitched, recently broken or deeply booming, according to their age, sang the response in forbidding unison. "*Ab omne malo*," the priest intoned. "*Domine exaudi nos*", we answered. "From all evil": "O Lord deliver us". "From that dreadful day of judgment": "O Lord deliver us". The dirge-like litany would continue for twenty minutes, during which every saint in heaven seemed to be invoked for the protection of our still comparatively innocent lives, now dedicated, as the initials A.M.D.G., which we were obliged to inscribe daily at the top of every exercise or piece of homework, reminded us, *ad maiorem dei gloriam*, to the greater glory of God. The service was no doubt intended to subdue our spirits, dampen any immature lustful instincts and prepare us for the hardships ahead. That night, I sobbed myself to sleep, imploring the gentler, softer Jesus whom I felt I knew from my prayers at home, to spare me from these shades of death and spectres of the night. I wrote a letter the next day asking to be brought home and it was my father who replied. He too remembered the terrors of *Bona Mors*, but one came to value such traditions and as I grew older, he wrote, I would come to realise that there was some valuable point to these formative rituals. Life was a mystery, but it was also a gift, he went on, and I was fortunate to enjoy the love of a family and a privileged start to life, which many others did not possess.

My reverie was broken by a gong being struck. I swiftly changed and hurried downstairs. Madeleine had dressed for dinner. "One has to maintain standards nowadays, so few people make any effort," she said when I complemented her on her dress. The old lady said grace, after which we sat in solemn dignity at either end of the long mahogany table. Jeanne came in with a silver tureen of soup, which she held for us each in turn, coming back a few minutes later to offer a second helping.

"Jeanne's family came from Montauban originally," Madeleine said, when her old servant had left the room, "although she has lived in Brittany all her adult life. She learned all the cooking she knows from her mother, and so we are given a preponderance of southern dishes here."

When Jeanne removed the soup plates and brought in a pot of cassoulet, I poured us both some wine, a good Côtes de Beaune, from a delicate, fluted-glass decanter.

"William, to business. This matter of your grandfather and his affairs seems to perturb you and Ghislaine so much. I must say, I never expected anyone to show such interest. As you probably know, Ghislaine has told me of her plans and, though

I found it an ordeal, I have dictated into her little tape-recorder all that I can recall of the last months we spent together in Germany, at Sigmaringen, and the very short time we had in Copenhagen before we were parted. It was a sad and terrible time, but I've thought long and hard and I've tried to come to terms with it. Now, at my age, it seems silly to go on trying to bury the past. It makes no sense. The past doesn't belong to us, so why try to disguise or evade the truth, as so many of my compatriots have done? We suffered in the war, some of us unimaginably so, but we also did foolish and desperate things that we may regret and feel guilty about, but which we have no right to hide. I've also talked to Ghislaine at length – in fact our conversations have brought us very close to one another lately – and I've given her my permission to make whatever use she can of any of this material."

Madeleine paused. Through the windows that adjoined the conservatory where Ghislaine and I had had breakfast, I could see the planet Jupiter. A half-moon was rising in the eastern sky.

"You must try to understand, to forgive us for what must seem to you and to Ghislaine unpardonable acts of treachery and negligence – sins I've confessed many a time, I may say. 'God will understand,' our young priest says comfortingly, but he's so young and so innocent I wonder whether he can possibly understand what was at stake. Our world was so very different in those days. It was a Europe which in 1945 was in a state of collapse after that devastating war and, you know, the France in which I grew up would, I expect, be unrecognisable to the average inhabitant of this country today – those privileged young men and women whom I read about in newspapers and see on my television screen – and I have to admit that in many ways I prefer the old world, with all its faults. Of course, no-one wants war, but the world that gave us the choice of a Pétain or a de Gaulle to lead us still had values, and whatever the rights or wrongs, it was at least a world that we could comprehend. We had ideals then, but I see little idealism and few examples of unselfish courage anywhere these days. Greed and self-interest prevail nowadays.

"But I don't want to sound like a prophet of doom. After all, it's not every day I have my only grandson to myself. So you must tell me what you want to know. Ghislaine never stops asking me questions, so why shouldn't you?"

After dinner we returned to the drawing room. Madeleine placed two logs over the embers of the still-glowing fire and then proceeded to speak of Henry and of her love for him with a frankness and affection that I found very touching in the circumstances. She had the ability to conjure up the periods of the war that they had spent together. She spoke of her first meetings with Henry, of their early days in Vichy when the war had still seemed unreal and when prospects in the unoccupied zone had for a time seemed optimistic. She spoke of her parents and of her decision to leave home and follow Henry.

"We had become resigned to German occupation," Madeleine said, "but at least the Maréchal had succeeded in preventing France from becoming a battleground once more. All that changed, however, in November 1942, when the Germans invaded the unoccupied zone. The supposed sovereignty of Vichy was shown to be a fiction. For the first time, we began to see the Nazis for the power-crazed tyrants they were. All those European ideals expressed at Hitler's meeting with

Pétain at Montoire about a collaboration founded on mutual agreement were seen as a ruse. 'Put your faith in *la France éternelle*,' the Maréchal had told us, and we stood firmly by him, Henry and I, and my parents too – remember, my father worked for the government – fully believing in the new European Order he spoke of so confidently. But after November 1942, when the remains of our empire in Africa had been lost and what was left of our fleet had been scuttled at Toulon, there was no longer any hope. Stalingrad marked the turning point, as we now know. I remember my father describing the Maréchal's meeting with Hitler's emissary, von Rundstedt, who had come to tell him of the Führer's decision to occupy the free zone. Pétain was in his Verdun uniform, wearing his Croix de Guerre. Papa said he looked so weary and so desolate. It was the end of Vichy. The end of our aspirations.

"After that things moved from bad to worse. There were continuous food shortages, the Maquis had begun their resistance work; there were assassinations and even worse reprisals. Once the Allied forces had landed in North Africa, Pétain's and Laval's positions became impossible. Frenchmen began killing Frenchmen. Can you imagine? It was the most shameful period our country has ever known."

The old woman paused and sipped the *verveine* which Jeanne had served us. For a moment she appeared to have lost the thread of what she had been saying, then she pressed both hands to her face and drew her open palms slowly downwards. Her eyes remained half closed. Outside, a cloud had obscured the moon and a wind had risen, rattling the shutters of the house. Only Madeleine's lightly fluting voice and the heavy breathing of her spaniel lying at her feet broke the silence.

"You know, if I had not been the dutiful daughter I was, Henry and I might have been spared some of the indignity and suffering of the next two years. To speak frankly, I have deliberately obliterated much of that terrible period from my memory, and it is only now that certain moments return to me. You see, I loved my parents very much. I was their only child, and they depended on me. When Henry decided that we should leave Vichy, early in 1943, I told my parents everything: that we were deeply in love, that I was no longer a virgin, that we wanted to be married once peace came, etcetera; but I promised my father that, wherever we were, we would keep in touch and we would not leave France. Because Papa worked for the government, as indeed did Henry, I was able to send letters to him from anywhere in France, using a special official code, and Papa always managed to get messages back to me until the Vichy government collapsed. In the last communication I had from him, he made me promise that we would follow them to Germany. It was a big mistake."

"But how did you both survive in the months between leaving Vichy and reaching Sigmaringen?" I said.

"For over a year, Henry and I travelled in various parts of Southern France, wandering here and there, like gypsies, avoiding the police, the Germans and the *milice* as best we could. We lived on very little. We worked on farms, in vineyards, for four months we both had jobs in a glove-making factory in Millau, earning only a few francs in return for a roof over our heads. We had a room in a house by the River Tarn that belonged to the manager of the tannery. He had family who lived near Vichy and he told me that he had heard me sing at the Maréchal's birthday celebration, and that he had also seen paintings by

Henry Latymer at Jean's gallery. He seemed to take an interest in us and we felt quite safe there from police patrols. I learned how to cut the lamb or kid leather we used, but poor Henry's job involved trimming any remaining flesh off the animal hides and salting them. It made him feel ill, he said, and his hands were often covered with blood when we met in the evening, he exhausted.

"When winter set in, we became restless and I felt the need for sun and warmth. Henry wrote to his friend Jean-Marc, who had escaped from Vichy and had gone to Montpellier. He invited us to join him, but he warned us that as a Jew he might have to leave town at any moment.

"Jean-Marc became a good friend. Because he had left Vichy before Jean and Chantal were arrested, he never knew what Henry had witnessed and his terrible sense of guilt."

"I can understand my grandfather's remorse," I said, "but it must have been so difficult for you."

"Yes, it was, but not because I had any doubt about his love for me, only because of his distress over what occurred at the station. Their love affair had already come to an end, remember. In retrospect, I realise Henry had treated Chantal badly, and I suppose you could say I supplanted her. He had been instrumental, he felt, in allowing a woman he had once loved, and a man who had been vital to his career as an artist, to go to their probable deaths.

"Anyway, we didn't stay in Montpellier for long. Jews were being rounded up in all the larger cities of France, and so Jean-Marc proposed a plan for the three of us. 'I know that as a Jew I am most at risk,' he told us, 'but once the Pétain government has collapsed – which it most certainly will, I assure you – then anyone who has worked for the regime will be at the mercy of the Resistance, the Maquis, whose numbers are growing.'

"He told us about a friend of his, Fernand Autran, who owned a vineyard in the very remote Maures hills, in the Var, north of Toulon. This man, who was about Jean-Marc's age, had offered to shelter him, and any of his friends who were at risk, in the almost impenetrable forests of the area.

"I remember the distinct perfumes of that part of the *midi* – that fusion of pine, mimosa and lemon, the colours of the oleander and bougainvillea. We travelled in the back of a truck lent to Jean-Marc. We left Montpellier early in the morning, lying on deep straw matting to protect us if it was cold, with a canvas tarpaulin to cover us in case we were stopped by the Italian troops who had occupied eight of the *départements* of the south-east in November 1942. But each time we were waved on with a smile and a *va bene* – they were very different from the Germans. By eight o'clock in the evening, when the curfew came into force, we had reached Cap Nègre on the coast east of Toulon. Next morning, Fernand came to meet us in his *camionette* and we started climbing along rough, spiralling roads high into the hills."

"You make it sound like a holiday adventure," I said.

"Well, perhaps my fading memory has romanticised those days, William, but apart from a few alarming moments when Italian, and later German patrols drove along the only road – the route de la Crête, I think it was called – we were blissfully happy. The war seemed far away at Fernand's home, we were in love; the scenery, the scents, the light, the silence, the colours – you see, I'm repeating myself . . ."

"Please go on."

"We were hungry at times. We survived on the occasional chicken, rabbits which Fernand shot, even squirrel, which wasn't bad; bread and pieces of meat whenever he drove down to the market at Rayol and queued. We had grapes, chestnuts, oranges. Henry, Jean-Marc and I helped with the vineyard and the *vendange*. We had to make sure no lights were visible after the curfew at eight in the evening in case planes flying overhead spotted a sliver of light. Fernand had black-out curtains, even though his house was completely hidden by vegetation.

"On the rare occasions that we met anyone, we were careful not to talk about ourselves, our past, or how we came to be there. Fernand was able to find the B.B.C. on his radio set sometimes. I had only basic English in those days, but I can't tell you how wonderful it was to listen to a trusted source and to hear the truth."

"So why did you ever leave such a paradise?"

"Jean-Marc stayed and I believe he lived out the war in the Maures hills. But Henry and I decided we must move north. I suppose we really left because I had begun to worry about my parents. I missed them too. But it was also due to Laval's decree that young people should work in Germany – the *Service de travail obligatoire en Allemagne*. The young were fleeing the towns and taking refuge in abandoned farms and in the forests, and local gauleiters had begun pursuing them into the hills. Villas were being destroyed along the coast and mines laid on the beaches in case the Allies landed. And the Germans had disarmed the Italian troops and taken over.

"At some stage in the spring of 1944, I had received a letter from my father, passed on through Jean-Marc's contacts. In it he said that he and my mother had decided that it was safest for them to remain with their government colleagues in Vichy and follow them to Belfort, and subsequently to Sigmaringen, an episode that I have told Ghislaine about in as much detail as I was able.

"We bid a tearful farewell to Jean-Marc, I remember, and kind Fernand drove us as far as he safely could. Somewhere past the ruins of the Carthusian monastery of La Verne, past Digne, Gap and Grenoble on some very tricky roads, and he dropped us at a railway station not far from Lyon, I think. We embraced Fernand and thanked him for all he had done for us. We took with us a rug, a change of clothes, our ration books, Henry's pencils and sketch pad, some emergency food and first-aid things, all tucked into our rucksacks. We stayed in monasteries, convents, abandoned buildings and even in the open air, and we travelled on foot or on local buses. Love kept us going, I suppose.

"Many years later, long after the war, Ghislaine's father and I spent a summer near Le Lavandou. We drove up into the Maures and I recognised that beautiful landscape. It was still as impenetrable as when Henry and I hid there. I mentioned the name of Fernand Autran to various people we met, but the only person who remembered him was someone called Marius Viout, who had lived nearby and who had also sheltered Jews and Maquis heroically in 1944. I remember we drank some delicious rosé wine that he offered us.

"Oh, and one other thing you might want to know, for it proved very useful: we had hidden our passports in the lining of our rucksacks, and because Fernand owned a printing press and a camera for preparing his wine lists, he suggested he make us false identity cards bearing the surname Rossi. He thought it wise to let the authorities think we were Italians, and so it proved when we encountered any patrols, at least until we were over the German border. He also thought we should pretend we were man and wife, and so Henry found a piece of copper wire and plaited it into a wedding ring of sorts. We held a mock ceremony before leaving. Fernand joined our hands together and uttered some words in Provençal, and Jean-Marc was our best man. We made our vows and Henry gave me the ring. I've kept it all these years because I couldn't bear to part with it, but I feel you should have it now. Who knows, you might even want to offer it to Ghislaine," she added with a knowing smile. "It would be bringing the ring full circle, you might say."

Just then Jeanne knocked and entered the room to ask whether Madeleine needed anything before she retired for the night. Hoping she might reminisce a little longer, I took the opportunity to put another log on the fire and poured some more *verveine*.

"That's Jeanne's way of ordering me upstairs," Madeleine whispered, as her old servant closed the door. "She likes to look after me and she strongly disapproves of my going to bed a minute after ten o'clock. But this is a special occasion, for it's not every day . . . Where was I?"

"You were leaving for Germany to be with your parents," I said.

"Ah! yes. But, William dear, is this boring you? After all, it's not your country, or your history . . . though I suppose it does concern *your* grandfather. Perhaps you too share something of his devotion to our nation."

Madeleine leaned down to pick up her handbag, which lay at the foot of her armchair.

"*À propos*," she murmured, "I discovered another old photograph that I thought you might like to see. I found it this morning, tucked into a book."

It was a sepia and white print of a young couple sitting at a table on the terrace of a café. The woman's head was thrown back. She was laughing, her eyes sparkled, and the lined contours of her lips revealed a perfect set of teeth. Sitting to her left, holding a wine glass in his hand, was a man of about thirty, a lock of fair hair had fallen over one eyebrow and he was wearing a waistcoat and a white shirt and tie. He was smiling and looking directly at the camera, a quizzical expression hovered about his forehead and his wide-apart eyes. His right arm rested confidently on the woman's padded shoulders.

"Is it you?" I asked.

"And Henry. It was taken in Germany. Look, I see that I scribbled the date on the back: Sigmaringen, December 1944. It must have been taken at Café Schön and, if I remember correctly, I had just given my first recital there, if you could call it that. I used to sing, and twenty or thirty of the French community would gather to listen to me. I must have been quite a success, because afterwards they asked me to sing every two or three weeks."

Madeleine took the photograph from me and looked at it again.

"Not bad, were we? We were still so very much in love." She shook her head and there was an expression of wonderment on her face that was both wistful and wise, but which bore no trace of nostalgia. "And I must have been pregnant by then, I suppose – with your father."

She sighed and took my hand in hers. But by now she

was tired, and she made as if to get to her feet. I helped her up.

I longed to ask her further questions, but the opportunity was gone.

Madeleine placed a guard in front of the fireplace, whereupon the spaniel woke and stretched its limbs, ready to follow its mistress upstairs.

"All these memories can be a little too much for an old lady, you know, and to tell you frankly, they can be upsetting. I vowed to bury them once, and after talking to you and Ghislaine I shall do so again – for good this time. There are some memories one can do without . . . Now, tomorrow it's Sunday, and I must be up for Mass at ten o'clock."

I opened the door for her, switched off the lights, and we walked together to the foot of the stairs, the dog following. I noticed Ghislaine's handwriting on a postcard on the hall table and I longed to read it. Madeleine kissed me goodnight.

"You go first, William, the stairs take me a little time. Goodnight, my dear. Good-night."

∞

I rose early the next day and took breakfast on my own. The wind had dropped and it was a cool, misty morning. Jeanne had left coffee, two brioches and a copy of Saturday's *La Croix* on the dining-room table. Once I had finished, I walked across the terrace, over to the lawn that had been allowed to become overgrown, past a greenhouse and up to the old asphalt tennis court, now disused and flecked with moss. A frayed net, dipped and gathered in the middle, still hung between the two posts. In the little pavilion were some well-used wooden rackets, but it was evident that no-one could have played here for several years. Had Ghislaine in her youth, I wondered? I tried to visualise her at the opposite end of the court, svelte and long-limbed, dressed in white. Had La Tiemblais once been alive with the cries of young people enjoying themselves? Would she have had friends and cousins to stay? Boyfriends? It was hard to conceive such a scene now, yet the house was certainly large enough for the kind of country house parties that I imagined might have taken place here. What would she have looked like aged seventeen, say? I felt a sudden longing to have known her as a young girl, to have her here and now to myself, to tell her openly and candidly that I was in love with her and that for me there was now more to our relationship than this delving into history that had so fortuitously brought us together. My obsession with the past was developing into a quest for a future that I wanted to belong to both of us. But at the same time, another voice told me that these were unattainable dreams. Ghislaine was a modern, professional woman with an established position in the Parisian literary world. She was also several years older than me, so why should she bother to concern herself with a musician who had never previously been able to form any lasting or worthwhile relationship and whose prospects were scarcely inspiring? Besides, she was my "aunt", as she sometimes reminded me; my grandfather's mistress' daughter! There were degrees of consanguinity. The whole thing was unthinkable.

The bells of the village church began to chime and, before they had finished, a loud voice from the terrace broke my introspection.

"*Monsieur William, Madame est prête!*" It was Jeanne,

summoning me to say that Bruno, the chauffeur, would be leaving in three minutes to take Madeleine to Mass. I had decided to accompany her.

The little church was barely two minutes away by car, but I could see that as the chatelaine, Madeleine felt it incumbent on her to arrive if not by diligence, then at least in her elderly, but chauffeur-driven car – and on time. Tradition dies hard here, and I reflected that were it not for our clothing and the fact that the decrees of the Second Vatican Council required the priest to face his congregation, we might have been in a nineteenth-century Breton village. I could sense the curious glances of the twenty or so parishioners as we walked up the aisle, past shrines to St Anne, St Yves and St Samson, to the family's pew at the front of the church; no sooner were we in our places than a bell was rung and the priest and his server appeared at the altar.

The Mass lasted barely forty minutes. There was a brief sermon on the theme of Advent, Madeleine took Communion, followed by the entire congregation. As we left at the end of the service, Madeleine nodded in greeting to left and to right as she walked down the aisle. At the church door, the young priest shook my hand warmly when she introduced me. I was dismayed to learn, however, that he and a local couple had been invited to lunch.

The formal Sunday lunch and the polite conversation precluded any further discussions. By four o'clock, when her guests had finally left, it was time for me to depart as well. I had decided that rather than return to Ghislaine's empty flat in Paris, I would catch the night ferry to Portsmouth from St Malo and keep my Eurostar return ticket for another occasion. The port was barely half an hour's drive away and Bruno agreed to take me there.

In the dusk light, Jeanne was already standing at the top of the front steps, ready to bid me goodbye. She was still wearing the black dress and white apron in which she had served Madeleine's guests at lunchtime. Bruno parked the old Citroën on the gravel drive. I was on the point of embracing my grandmother when suddenly she hesitated and asked me to accompany her into the little salon. I stood waiting as she rummaged through the drawer of a desk before producing an envelope which she held out to me.

"William, this is a letter I have never shown to anyone, not even to Ghislaine. It's the last letter your grandfather wrote to me before he left Europe in 1945 to begin his new life in Argentina and it's the only one of his that I possess from those days. He was still in Denmark. I had returned to France. Your father – our child – had been taken to England by Henry's sister. It was probably the lowest point in my life, and probably in Henry's, too.

"I find it hard to believe even now, but I never heard from Henry again, directly, until the recent communication from Buenos Aires that you have already seen arrived earlier this year. This letter I'm giving you now may help to explain some of the things I still prefer not to talk about and, in particular, it may help you to understand why I have never been able to bring myself to speak freely about the baby, your father, whom I never saw again, and why I felt I could never set foot in your country. England has always held a terror for me for this reason."

She took my arm as we walked back towards the front door.

"My child, you must think me very heartless . . ." She

faltered, then gave a curt, dismissive wave of the hand, as if in self-reproach.

"I give you this on one condition," Madeleine said, tucking the envelope into the inside pocket of my jacket and clasping me in her arms as she did so. "You must promise not to read it until you are safely at sea. After that, you will know virtually all there is to know, but I do not wish to discuss this period of our lives again, ever. It's over and there's nothing any of us can do to make amends. Now, goodbye dear William. God bless you and all your endeavours, and come back soon."

The old lady and Jeanne stood on the porch above the front steps, waving, as we set off for St Malo.

Bruno did his best to make conversation as he drove. I told him that I was collecting information about my grandfather's life. When he told me that his own grandfather had been a fisherman who had perished at sea off the coast of Shetland in the great storms of 1928, I thought of *Pêcheur d'Islande* and how Loti's novel had been one of Henry's favourite books. Then an image of Madeleine sitting at her piano came to mind and that little Breton song she had sung when I first met her with Ghislaine. How did it go?

> *J'aime Paimpol et sa falaise*
> *Son église et son Grand Pardon*
> *J'aime surtout la Paimpolaise*
> *Qui m'attend au pays Breton*

Later that evening, with the rocky, indented coastline receding into darkness and the ship's engines gathering speed, I felt heavy-hearted as I stood on deck beneath the arc lamps and took out the letter Madeleine had given me. It was written in French in faint but still-legible handwriting on faded, yellowing notepaper, several pages long, and addressed to Mlle Madeleine de Launay, 16 rue Cortambert, Paris XVIe.

[CHAPTER 12]

4 NIELS HEMMINGSENS GADE
Copenhagen,   8 July 1945

My Madeleine, my darling, my only love –

Lavinia arrived yesterday to take our little Theo to
England. She was overjoyed at the sight of him and came
with a carrycot, blankets and baby rations. She will be a
good mother to him until you are ready to take him back,
of that you can be certain.

She travelled here on the ferry from Harwich to
Holland, and then, with some difficulty, by train and
ferry to Denmark. Her trip took two days and a night. I
wish I could have contributed to her fare, but she assured
me she has enough money and that she has been able
to make savings during the war. I saw her off again at the
station two hours ago and I gave her my old Zeiss binoculars as a farewell present. I have nothing else of any
value. It will be a long journey for them both and I will
not feel calm until I have a telegram from her telling me

they have arrived safely. How I wish we could have spent more time together. A few hours, after an absence of six years, with the only member of my family likely to want to have anything to do with me, is not enough. I so wish you could have known my sister. You might then have felt less anguished about entrusting little Theo to a stranger.

The war has torn me from my family, from you, and now from our little boy, and though it's over now, I fear I shall not be at peace with myself until I can escape from Europe and live free from suspicion. The war has dishonoured people like us – like your parents and me – my darling, and we shall have to suffer the consequences for many years, I fear.

I plan to leave Denmark within the next few days, as soon as I have my papers in order. There is a steamship company with boats that leave Gothenburg every week for the Atlantic ports of South America. There, either in Buenos Aires or Montevideo I expect, I shall start a new life in a new land. And as soon as I am able to earn a decent living and can convince myself that I still have some talent as an artist and can provide a secure home for you after our gypsy life of the past two years, I shall send money and summon you both. Believe me, it is all I long for.

It broke my heart to be separated from little Theo – just as it must have broken yours when you left us to return to Paris. But Lavinia will care for him in England and give him the love he needs, I know she will. He will be safer with her. She is a saintly person, my darling, and I am quite unworthy of such a sister. She is honourable, loyal and kind, and I sense that she loves me too, whatever the wrongs I may have done. She is forgiving and tolerant, unlike my parents.

I roam around this watery city, which I should have loved to sketch, in a haze of melancholy, as if in a never-ending daydream. I think of you and of all we have endured, and I'm haunted by memories. The shops here are full of enticing cheeses, eggs and butter, there is a semblance of prosperity and a buzz in the air; people walk the streets looking well dressed and with a sense of purpose, as if they have woken up after a lengthy sleep. They look you in the eye. There are no soldiers or peasant farmers peering at one suspiciously anymore. And there is a mood of hope, something I have not experienced since 1939. With money, we could live well here one day, but life is expensive and what savings I have are barely enough to keep me for another month, after which my residency permit expires.

Do you have news of your parents? Where are they living? We must pray that your father will not be tried in France for political crimes – I fear there will be much vindictiveness and bitterness towards those who served the Maréchal.

Two days ago, walking past the Christiansborg Palace, I bumped into Destouches – the doctor/writer who lived in the Löwen at Sigmaringen with his wife, Lucette, and their very fat cat, do you remember? – still wearing his blue canvas cap. They got out of Germany in March and now they share a room (with the cat!) in a house on the Ved Stranden, where we walked by the canal the evening before you left. He looked exhausted and seemed depressed, but he's still the same manic, sneering fellow to whom so many in Sig. owed their health. I had to remind myself that it was he who delivered Theo into the world. He told me that his publisher Denoël had been shot dead in a Paris street and that he could not return to France because there was a warrant for his arrest and the "slobbering hyenas" would try to get him extradited. "*Faut dire, mon ami, nous sommes tous foutus. Tu verras,*" he said, tapping me gravely on the arm before he hobbled away. I can't help liking him, despite his gruffness and his virulent opinions.

Thank you, darling, for your consoling letter. It was a relief to know that you are safely back in France and I pray there will be no repercussions. You and your mother have, after all, done nothing wrong. In fact, your singing, in Vichy, and especially in Sig., raised the spirits of our compatriots in Germany, whose only sin was to have put their faith, as we all did, in the Maréchal. You have a beautiful voice, Madeleine, and a great talent, and it will be the making of your future – our future, as soon as we can make arrangements for you and Theo to join me. Please try to have singing lessons. Why not track down that fellow Ulmer whom Sylvain mentioned? Perhaps he can give you advice about having your songs recorded.

I am close to despairing when I think that I shall not be there to sustain and encourage you. Instead, I must serve my exile in a distant land, expiating for the wrongs I have done. Now that I am able to look back on my recent life with some objectivity, I accept that I am escaping to Argentina because I cannot live in my native country, or my adopted one, without risking arrest. My conscience is clear on this: my decision to leave England and to adopt French citizenship was taken in full cognisance of what I was doing. When I speak of wrongs, I mean the work that I carried out for your father's department in Vichy in relation to the "*Statuts des Juifs*". I never spoke to you about my work. I was somehow too ashamed, but also frightened. Neither did your father talk at home about what his department's duties actually entailed.

At this point, before I say anything else, I need to unburden myself to you, my dearest treasure, of a matter that afflicts my conscience mercilessly: the memories of what happened bedevil my innermost thoughts, my waking moments, my dreams and my nightmares. It is something I have never faced up to until now.

Attached to this letter are some pages I tore out of the diary I kept in February 1943. I was terrified in case you should ever happen to see them and so I hid them inside a book.

The pages referred to are weathered and, in places, barely legible. I have reproduced them as best I can. W.L.

I have at last recovered my composure, but my life can never be the same again . . . I need to make my confession, but no priest will ever give me absolution, and no-one can ever forgive what I have done – what I have failed to do.

February 5, 1943

M. and I have made secret plans to leave Vichy. We shall live like outlaws or tinkers, if need be, should the worst come to the worst.

I can't stay. Yesterday evening that suddenly became horribly clear to me. This is what happened:

Yesterday morning, as I checked through the latest lists that M. Duval had passed on to me, I was astonished to see the names "Arago, Jean and Chantal (Aronovich)", followed by their Bellerive address, printed at the top of the first column of the alphabetical list of names of those (not only foreign Jews any longer) who were required to be transported to Drancy the following day. On the same list, further down, I also saw the name "Meyerson, Jean-Marc", and the address which I knew he had left early last Thursday morning.

I now know for certain that these Jews, whether "foreign" or "French", are being sent away against their will, in fear of their lives. Some say that they are being treated humanely and will soon be allowed to leave, but others say that once they arrive in Germany they are sent to camps from which they will never return.

I closed my eyes, and my head felt as if it was bursting. I wanted to run away, there and then. Instead, may God forgive me, I initialled the lists, as I am required to do, having checked the addresses, before making a dash to the bathroom where I was violently sick.

Duval called me in later and prefaced his remarks by informing me that he was well aware that I had only been naturalised in 1942 and could not, therefore, call myself a true Frenchman. He also intimated that I was being treated with special consideration on account of my "intimate" friendship with M. de L.'s daughter, but that I could not expect such a situation to last indefinitely. He himself, he said, had long ago made his commitment to *la patrie* manifest by joining the L.V.F., the "Légion des Volontaires Français contre le bolchévisme", and he was prepared to fight shoulder to shoulder with our German friends to purify *nos terres* and rid our land of those who continue to corrupt it. Pressure was now being put on all of us, *vous comme moi, jusqu'au Président Laval lui-même*, to cooperate more fully and more efficiently with the German people in the cause of the struggle against the Bolshevik menace that threatens our liberty.

Then he instructed me to be present at Vichy railway station the following morning to check the list of "refugees" whose names are on our lists and to ascertain that they were on board the train to the north. When I pointed out that this was not part of my usual office duties, he rose to his feet and spoke sternly: "Ours is the land of Vercingetorix and Louis XI, Monsieur, and it is led by a saintly man who has twice saved France: first at Verdun, now at Montoire. We all have a duty to serve him. Those being transported," he said, "would be lined up on the platform prior to departure. Their names would be called out and it was my job to ensure that everyone had boarded the train and that no-one was missing. (I knew in advance that one man would be absent: Jean-Marc Meyerson. I hoped and prayed that he had not been arrested before he could leave Vichy.)

At six o'clock next morning, the northbound platform of the station was thronged with people, some in police uniform, shouting orders in loud voices, but the majority were men and women, young and old, dressed in winter coats, scarves and furs. Some carried travelling rugs over one arm; all of them stood with a single suitcase at their feet. They were eighty to a hundred citizens of Vichy, its municipal district (including Bellerive) and its outlying villages, who had been roused from their beds in the early hours of the morning, ordered to pack and gather their possessions, and conveyed in trucks to a large warehouse building adjacent to the station, where they had waited to be summoned to their train. They looked shocked, but resigned.

I took up my position by the entrance to the first carriage, my list of names in one hand, my pen in the other. In the early morning light a breeze was blowing from the north, and it was very cold. As I waited while the refugees milled over the platform, searching for friends or relatives, the station lights were switched on. The noise was terrifying: children crying, women wailing, men protesting, some speaking in foreign languages, some in French, as the steam from the train's engine hissed and rose into the early morning darkness; officials were barking orders, while others meekly accepted instructions in silence.

Then I heard the names I dreaded hearing. "Aronovich, Jean et Chantal", the man in uniform standing a few paces from me had bellowed. Not Arago, I noted. I could hardly bear to look up. I ticked their names on my list and I waited until I felt they must have boarded the train, but I could not stop myself looking into their carriage. As I turned to my left, my gaze met the eyes of Chantal through the thick, grimy windowpane. She was standing, staring at me, her eyes expressionless, neither sad, nor imploring, neither reproachful, nor accusing, but her gaze seemed directed at me. Her body was bent slightly to one side. Her hair was dishevelled and she wore no make-up. I recognised a dark-brown overcoat she wore when we walked on the banks of the Allier. In her right hand she held a black suitcase, while her left arm rested on the arm of a seat. A file of bodies pressed against her as they were forced through the carriage. Perhaps our eyes met for a matter of seconds, but it seemed an eternity. Then she was pressed forward in the half-light, a gloved hand on her shoulder guiding her from behind. It was Jean's hand, a man whom I have known ever since I had first come to Paris, a man to whom I owe whatever reputation I once had as an artist, whose hospitality and generosity I accepted and abused, and whose pure, innocent, beautiful sister I had loved, rejected and betrayed. I watched Jean's face in profile. As always, he was immaculately dressed: a black hat and the dark-grey suit he always wore in the gallery. His overcoat he carried over one arm and he, too, had a suitcase. His head was held erect and he looked neither to left nor to right, but I sensed somehow that he had seen me and that he was aware of my presence. I also knew it would be the last time I would set eyes on either of them.

The man in uniform continued to call out the names – "Bernstein . . . Blum . . . Clausemann . . ." – as the platform slowly emptied. When he reached the letter M, I held my breath and hoped I would not hear Jean-Marc's surnames, either the one he was born with or the one his father had adopted. Neither were called. Thank God he has left town. One friend, at least, will not be bound for Drancy, or for Germany . . .

Later

I am resigned to departure, and, I fear, a life of guilt and despair after what I witnessed this morning. My mind is numb, my conscience burns. I think how I might have saved them. Jean and Chantal were my friends; Chantal, my beloved. I could have removed their names. I could have pleaded with M. Duval or tried to intercede with M.'s father. Something. Anything. I did nothing.

∞

There, dearest Madeleine! I have told you what I most needed to confess – all that I can bring myself to say. I accuse myself alone. I should have spoken of this long ago, in front of you and in front of your father, whose orders I helped to carry out. He and I have played our parts in the Nazi crimes. And so have the French, or some of them. Worst of all, I have betrayed my friends.

I tell you this not to hurt you, my love, but because I must, at last, confront myself – my cowardice, my inadequacy, my failure to act.

I live in the past now because I fear the future. And yet that future once appeared so bright. I think of Paris in

1939 and of how, in spite of the threat of war, my friends and I felt alive with excitement at the prospect of a new Europe. The stagnancy of the years in which we had grown to adulthood would be replaced with new ideals, new values that would restore France and all that it represented. And even after the Maginot Line was pierced and France was defeated, we still believed in a Europe based upon the combined genius of two civilisations. How wrong we were! How entirely deceived!

Do you remember me talking about one of my friends from my time in Paris, the American art dealer, Robert Worcester? I don't believe you met him, but I should like you to get in touch with him. He may be of help to you and he may remind you of the person I feel I once was before all this.

He's a tough, realistic, unsentimental fellow who always reminded me of a character in one of those Hemingway stories we used to read, and which I used to translate for you on exercise books in Sigmaringen. He and I corresponded occasionally, which was difficult in those days, but the last time I actually set eyes on him was in the autumn of 1940, when I stayed for several weeks at his flat opposite the Jardin des Plantes. I no longer have the address, but there's a well-known art gallery in rue Laffitte (it used to be Vollard's), where he worked, and someone there may be able to tell you where he now lives. I doubt that a man like him would ever return to America, for he, too, was a "deserter", and he had friends in high places in Paris and in Vichy. He also had private money.

Then there's Sylvain, who must be back in France by

now. He was fond of you and I feel sure he will remain a good friend, someone you can always call on, unless he is obliged to live in exile. Before we left Sig., he and I went for a long walk along the banks of the river. The stars were so bright that night that they were reflected in the water, I remember, and the silence was so magical that we forgot about our troubles and the misery of war. I told him of our plans and I made him promise that whatever became of me, he would keep a watchful eye over you. He reassured me and we embraced. Later, I made him a present of that drawing I did of the castle from the river bank where you and I used to sit sometimes. I like to think of it as a token of the promise he made. He's a good person, my darling, and dependable and well connected, too. He has done nothing except write a handful of harmless novels – unlike Destouches – and if there are to be the purges that some say are taking place already he will surely go free for he is blameless.

These shadows, these long summer nights without you here in the stern and pitiless North . . . How strange our lives have become! I try to imagine you in the Paris I once knew. I think of Lavinia and our Theo, and what sort of life awaits the boy, and then I pray that one day I shall be able to bring both of you out of this devastated Europe into a new existence in a new world.

I shall stop before I start to feel sorry for myself. I shall take a walk. It is a fine, warm July afternoon in Copenhagen and I can smell the sea air through my open window. I shall seal this letter with a hundred kisses and then I shall catch the five o'clock post and wander about this fine city before my rendezvous at a bar on the Nyhavn, where I am to meet a man by the name of Mikkelsen, who will advise me about the boats that sail from Gothenburg to the River Plate. Afterwards, I shall come back, light the oil stove, draw those tattered curtains, heat the remains of the soup I made from last week's vegetables and fall asleep to dream of you, my dearest one. Before that, however, I shall write to Lavinia to enquire about little Theo and to thank her for her kindness to her wretched brother. Should anything ever happen to me, you must ask her too for help. She is another truly good person whom I have treated shabbily.

I kiss you tenderly, dearest Madeleine. You cannot know how I long for you, but God willing, we shall be together soon. Meanwhile, you will always be with me, in my mind, in my heart, wherever I am. H.

∞

I tucked my grandfather's letter into my coat pocket and walked over to the ship's railings. The lights of St Malo were still visible on the horizon. A gentle, south-westerly wind was blowing and the phosphorescence of the sea lit up the waves that lapped at the ship's hull. The occasional siren sounded, passing vessels could be seen on the horizon, but there were no stars visible.

My grandfather remained an enigma, but a clearer picture of him was at last beginning to emerge. For all his faults and self-confessed crimes he had, as far as he was able, atoned for his guilt and he had forced himself to confront his past. Like many another creative artist, he lived primarily for himself, treating other people and using his own experiences simply as mileposts on his journey to some imagined greater destiny. I do not mean to suggest that he had not loved Chantal and Madeleine – and he was certainly loved *by* them wholeheartedly – but, egotistical and self-absorbed man as he was, even they had ultimately been adjuncts to his journey of self-discovery.

He was also, I could never forget, a man with the blood of friends on his hands, the blood of a woman he had once loved. Had he remained in Europe, it is most probable that he would have been tried and executed.

∞

There was a letter from Ghislaine when I arrived back at my flat. I immediately recognised the stationery, the sloped, looping hand, and the Carpentras postmark. I avoided opening it immediately. I poured myself a whisky and put on a recording of Shostakovich's 2nd Piano Concerto while I went through the rest of my post. But I could not concentrate.

It was not Henry and his past that filled my mind now: it was Ghislaine, and this even before I had opened her letter. Somehow, and especially since leaving La Tiemblais, I knew that she had become essential to my happiness and that I wanted very much to spend my life with her. In the relatively short time I had known her, the focus of my world had shifted, and it was as if I now saw everything through a new lens. Ghislaine had added an impetus to what I did; with her intelligence and practicality, but also her capacity to dream, she had given a purpose and a direction to my existence.

In my musings, I found myself trying to imagine how Henry had first wooed Madeleine; I wondered what words he might have used, whether he would have spoken to her awkwardly or passionately, brazenly or, like his grandson, timidly.

I dozed; then I poured myself another drink. I opened Ghislaine's letter: it was short, but it was the most affectionate letter I have ever received. With it was an article from a French literary magazine.

[CHAPTER 13]

A SEASON IN SIGMARINGEN: A memoir of *"la France allemande"*, assembled from private sources and written and translated from French by Ghislaine de Valcros (reprinted by agreement with *Les Lettres*, December 2000)

My mother, Madeleine Lambert (to give her back her former stage name), enjoyed a certain success as a popular singer in Paris in the immediate post-war years. She sang at a number of cabarets and café-concerts, such as Le Tabou, Les Trois Baudets and Le Quodlibet, and you could hear her records played regularly on the radio up to the early days of Radio Luxembourg. Her best-known songs, *"À nos amours"* and *"Laisse-moi t'oublier"*, however, were written and first performed in Vichy, where she lived with her parents during the years of German occupation, and where her father was a senior government employee in the ministry of information. One occasionally comes across her old 78 r.p.m. records in flea markets and junk shops, but only those with a sufficiently long memory can attest to the qualities of her sweetly magnetic, faintly husky but youthful voice, and to the power of her yearning and often sentimental lyrics. At Sigmaringen, where she, her English-born lover and her parents saw out the end of the war among the colony of collaborationists marooned in the German forests, and where the remnants of the defeated Vichy regime endeavoured to maintain their own idea of France, Madeleine must have brought a ray of light into the dismal existences of the two thousand or more of her compatriots who were obliged to live there, in pathetic exile from their homeland, for the simple reason that there was nowhere else for them to go: their pasts had caught up with them.

In 1944–45, the time of which I write, Madeleine was young, she was attractive, as surviving photographs of her at that period attest. The politics of collaboration or the rights and wrongs of the Vichy regime were of little consequence to her. She was a woman who lived purely for the day, longing only for France to be free again, and to be able to share a normal life with the man she loved and whose child she was expecting.

The object of her infatuation was a handsome British artist, Henry Latymer, a francophile who may have been the only one of his countrymen to be accorded French nationality by the Pétain regime. She first met him at a public concert in 1940 during the early months of Vichy rule. Latymer, too, had acquired a certain reputation for his paintings at that time; he appears to have had useful connections and his work had begun to attract a discerning market in the early months of a period in our history with which we are only now coming to terms.

My mother is still alive today. She is in her early eighties and lives in seclusion in a remote corner of her native Brittany. She has not sung in public since 1949, shortly before she met and married my own father and moved to Algeria, where she lived until the death of her husband, who was murdered by the F.L.N. She returned to France with her young daughter in 1961.

Henry Latymer died a year ago in Argentina, far from the Europe he had escaped in 1945. He lived in a suburb of Buenos Aires where he had shaped a new life for himself. Like so many guilty of collaboration (and there is reason to believe that in his work for the Vichy government, a job arranged by my mother's father in the department he headed, he was involved in the deportation of Jews to Drancy and to Germany), Henry and Madeleine had fled to Germany as General de Lattre de Tassigny's army edged ever closer to *la France allemande* in Sigmaringen. After several months in Baden-Württemberg, they were given a pass to cross into Denmark, where they lived in near penury in a single room in Copenhagen. In February 1945, their son Theo – my own late half-brother – was born, brought into the world by no less a figure than Dr Destouches, better known to us nowadays as the novelist Louis-Ferdinand Céline. For the sake of their child's future, they arranged for him to be smuggled to England, where he was brought up by Henry's sister, Lavinia.

Madeleine had previously returned to France to face the relatively minor consequences of her disloyalty, though this was not the term she would have used: she would say in the words of one of her songs that she had merely been "following her heart". Henry sailed from Gothenburg in the summer of 1945 aboard a Swedish cargo vessel bound for the River Plate and he lived out the rest of his life in Buenos Aires. The picture that emerges of him from letters and other accounts is of a tragic figure, a man cut off both from his native land and from the country he had adopted so enthusiastically in 1939, as well as from his own family, the woman he loved and the son he had scarcely known.

About a year ago, Henry Latymer's "archive" – it was the word he used – came to light. In his will he asked that two boxes of his diaries, correspondence and printed ephemera should be delivered to my mother, or, as he put it, "my former common-law wife Madeleine de L., if she is alive and her whereabouts can be ascertained, for disposal according to her wishes". My mother, perhaps understandably in the circumstances, did not wish to be reminded of a turbulent and emotionally fraught period in her life and declined to investigate the contents of this legacy so long after the events concerned. Instead, she delegated responsibility for these mementoes to me, her daughter, and to her grandson, as she is now happy to refer to him, the English musician William Latymer, the son of Henry and Madeleine's child, Theo (who died in 1988 having never known his mother).

Contemporary literature is well enough endowed with accounts of the Nazi and Vichy periods; my purpose in this short recreation, based on detailed records and my own research, is simply to throw some light on one of recent history's stranger chapters and to evoke something of the flavour of those bizarre months my mother and her English lover spent in the shadow of that Kafkaesque collaborators' castle on the banks of the Upper Danube at Sigmaringen. I do not wish to condemn them or romanticise their plight, merely briefly to illuminate them before their story sinks into the vestiges of history.

Ô saisons, ô châteaux,
Quelle âme est sans défauts?

They arrived on the little train that runs along the branch line, rumbling over the winding single track that, ever since Erfurt, has twisted along the wide, tranquil banks of the River Danube. The steam-driven locomotive is one of the oldest still in service in war-torn Germany, and the slow, rhythmic throb of its pistons lulls them into fitful but much-needed bouts of sleep, so that they are oblivious to the pastoral scenes passing by on either side of the grime-covered windows, just as they are to the hum of voices all around them. Out in the countryside, among those peaceful, sun-blanched meadows and the forested foothills of Baden-Württemberg, with the scent of pine wafting through the open windows, they could forget briefly about war and about their safety. Only the occasional drone of enemy aircraft flying overhead reminded them that the cities of Germany were being bombed inexorably into submission. Half waking, as the train grinds to a stop at yet another insignificant-looking country station where nobody either gets on or off, Henry gazes gratefully at the girl who is asleep, wrapped in an ill-fitting military greatcoat, legs huddled beneath her, in the seat opposite his before he drifts into slumber once more. She is his consolation, his sustenance, his sole joy left on this earth, his one *raison d'être*, his Madeleine.

Only at Ulm station was it obvious that they were unwanted exiles in a country that is still at war; foreigners in a nation whose citizens are enduring intense hardship, many of them close to starvation; a nation that is contemplating the grim consequences of defeat for the first time in five long years of war. Soldiers, hollow-eyed from lack of sleep, their uniforms crumpled, wander listlessly to and fro over the dimly lit station concourse and push their way through crowds such as Henry and Madeleine had not seen in months of wandering. Inside the railway carriage, the atmosphere was heavy, the gloom oppressive as the little train ground its way along the tracks. Out of the window, they glimpsed the black and pitted outline of the Gothic cathedral spire that was once the tallest in Europe and which was all that remained of the ancient city, bombed to near rubble by British and American aircraft. To their astonishment, they heard French being spoken for the first time since they had crossed the Rhine at Seltz, and it was at once shocking and consoling, alarming yet reassuring, for them to realise that the majority of the passengers on the train, weighed down by their few possessions, are indeed French. Men, women, some children, too, exhausted, starving, and wearing a look of resigned desperation; they were her compatriots – and his, too, ever since he had acquired French citizenship – people speaking their own beloved language in a variety of accents.

∞

What wild product of a Piranesian imagination could have conceived of such an unlikely structure? It's a joke: a castle out of a nineteenth-century operetta, an extravaganza, some mad creation of Walt Disney's. Those fairy-tale turrets and gargoyles, that unlikely confection of architectural styles and periods piled one on top of the other, a Promethean kingdom perched on a massive rock overlooking the River Danube. Can they be real? Here is the tower from which Sister Anna loosed her coils of hair; here Bluebeard's dungeon. Were the river broader and less sluggish, you might think of Ludwig, the mad king, of Wagner's "Nibelungen", of Lorelei, the siren who lured sailors to their deaths, or even of Kafka's metaphorical castle. But this is the Danube, not the Rhine; their tutelary gods are not the same.

Seen from the charming little railway station at which Henry and Madeleine, and a hundred other French men and women, alighted in November 1944, Schloss Sigmaringen must have appeared as some sort of vision. How had that poor wretch Destouches described it in his novel?:

> . . . stucco, bric-à-brac, gingerbread in every style, turrets, chimneys, gargoyles . . . unbelievable . . . super Hollywood . . . every period from the melting of the icecap, the narrowing of the Danube, the slaying of the Dragon, the victory of St Fidelis, down to Wilhelm II and Goering.

But we should say nothing to criticise the much-maligned doctor/novelist. Neither should we forget him. Without him, his kindness and attention to duty, where would Henry and Madeleine be? Without his medical adroitness, those evening consultations at the Löwen, no fee, how could little Theo have survived, born as he was in such unpropitious conditions, in a hotel bedroom in Sigmaringen? Charlatan, racist, Nazi scum . . . that's what people used to say about Docteur Destouches (or Monsieur Céline) in Paris . . . still do, even today. . . Some revile him, others revere him . . . a cult, you might say . . . critical studies, symposia, international conferences . . . *des conneries* . . . how darkly he would have laughed. And let us not forget his wife Lucette . . . or their cat Bébert . . . has any cat played a more heroic role in all of literature? Or their actor friend, Robert Le Vigan. Perhaps Henry may have encountered him in exile in Argentina, during the years that lay ahead of him? Le Vigan died there in 1972. To remind yourself of what he looked like, you only have to watch films such as *"Quai des brumes"* . . . such charm . . . such originality . . . such panache!

∞

The original fortress of Sigmaringen, the ancestral home of a branch of the Hohenzollern family, was built in the tenth century by Sigmar de Pfullendorf. Inside its lugubrious walls are floor upon floor of stately halls, galleries and staircases, and a myriad doorways and labyrinthine passages. Suits of armour, halberds, crossbows and an array of hunting trophies are paraded along the corridors, and rows of disdainful Hohenzollerns glare down sternly at you from the heavily framed portraits on the wood-panelled walls of the castle's statérooms.

In September 1944, with the Allied troops sweeping through France and the end to the war in sight, Hitler was obliged to provide sanctuary here for the 88-year-old Maréchal Pétain and the ill-assorted remnants of his inglorious Vichy regime. So it was that for a few brief but nightmarish months in 1944–45 Schloss Sigmaringen became the capital of *la France allemande*, the "new France" that some still deceived themselves into believing would emerge after a German victory. For them and those who had shared their aspirations, there was no other hiding place. Later, a historian would record:

On September 7 the journey to Germany took place. The fighting was approaching Belfort: it was known that de Lattre's army was at Strasbourg. At 6.30 a.m., the convoy set out accompanied with considerable military strength . . . The Marshal crossed the Rhine at 11 a.m. They halted at Fribourg-en-Brisgau. Due to the emotions aroused by leaving, Laval had forgotten the overcoat in whose lining, ever since November 1942, had been kept the poison, which he used in prison a year later. A car retrieved it for him from Belfort.

On September 8, in the morning, the Marshal resumed the journey; Laval resumed his on the morning of the 9th.

The Marshal's car drew up at the foot of an enormous castle built on a crag of rock at a bend in the Danube. There was no reception ceremony.

On September 9, Laval arrived with his wife, and former ministers, Bichelonne, Bonnard, Gabolde, Déat, Brinon, Bidoux, Darnand and Marion.

But it was not only the old Maréchal and Pierre Laval, their wives and the phantom cabinet – in which Pétain refused to play any further part – who came to Sigmaringen. Fearing reprisals and possible death in liberated France because of their collaborationist activities, hundreds of French refugees had made their way across the border, or from the work camps in Germany, seeking refuge in the hotels, boarding houses and cafés of the little town, thus expanding the small and understandably hostile local population, who had felt themselves sheltered from the realities of war for four years amid the encircling hills and forests and the muddy waters of the meandering River Danube.

Within the labyrinthine passages and corridors of the castle, its former state rooms and private apartments, a semblance of government – a *Commission gouvernementale pour la défense des intérêts français en Allemagne* – was formed; it had neither Pétain's nor Laval's support.

At Sigmaringen, Pétain and Madame la Maréchale resided on the seventh floor, accessible by the castle's only lift, where they were attended by the ever-faithful if somewhat sinister Dr Bernard Ménétrel, whom some believed may have been the old man's illegitimate son. Here, in these former Hohenzollern state rooms, aloof from the manic world evolving on the floors below, Pétain read Talleyrand's *Mémoires*, attended Mass in the old family chapel, ate voracious quantities of *Stammgericht* (a local speciality composed of cabbage, turnips and swedes, served on silver platters), reflected on the vicissitudes of fortune, and planned his defence for the trial that he knew would await him. The daily outing in his black Citroën 15CV along the banks of the Danube, escorted by two Gestapo cars, provided him with the fresh air he needed. Nearing ninety, a survivor who had outlived his time, whose pride and dignity had been tested beyond endurance, he remained a symbol, nothing more. For the hero of Verdun there would be no return from Elba.

Below, in the sixth-floor apartments that had once belonged to Princesse Josephine, Pierre Laval and his plump and homely wife, Jeanne, fumed against the Germans, chain-smoked Gitanes, scoured the columns of *Le Petit Parisien* and polished the silver they had carefully removed from the Matignon palace before their hurried departure. The luxury of these rooms only embarrassed the former prime minister and his wife: he, after all, was a peasant – as he was fond of saying – and all he now wanted was to return to Châteldon and his cattle, savour a proper Potée Auvergnat again and sink down *un bon coup de rouge.*

"Don't you know Châteldon?" Laval would ask with a sigh. "There's no place like it in the world."

Here, in Sigmaringen, the diet of boiled potatoes and indigestible vegetables made him ill and gave him an ulcer, which the morbid doctor/writer, Dr Destouches, did his best to control. Like the Maréchal, Laval also brooded as he listened to the lunatic Hérold-Paquis on Sigmaringen's own French radio station and leafed through the community's own newspaper. *"Je suis dans la merde, jusqu'au cou"* (I'm in the shit, up to my neck) he would say later, in his defence. And like the Maréchal, who refused to speak to him, Laval regarded himself as a prisoner of France's collaboration partner, and he would have nothing to do with the so-called "cabinet" his fellow Frenchmen had created.

Along another sombre passageway, five of the castle's more sinister residents would meet to discuss affairs of state and fantasise over their illusory powers. Fernand de Brinon presided at these sessions: aristocratic and tough (he had "the eyes of a toad", according to the wife of one of his junior colleagues), it was he who had been one of those most responsible for promoting Franco-German friendship in the early years of the war. Also present was Joseph Darnand, a soldier and man of action, who was in charge of the ten thousand members of the *milice* now stationed at Ulm. With his pencil moustache, he was thought in his facial features to resemble Hitler. They were joined by Jean Luchaire, a former journalist and a friend of Otto Abetz, the man in charge of the day-to-day organisation of this outpost of France, and who had only recently been

Hitler's overweeningly francophile ambassador to the Quai d'Orsay; Luchaire was editor in chief of *La France*, the community's daily newspaper, and he also ran the local radio station, which broadcast music, football scores and harmless gossip: the exiled population had to be protected from too much political or military reality. The fourth member of these little gatherings was General Bridoux, former Secretary of Defence and pro-German to the core; it was he who had handed over France's munitions once the unoccupied zone had been ceded to the Nazis. Lastly, and perhaps the most alarming of them all, there was Marcel Déat, stout as a small bulldog and habitually dressed in a black jacket and striped trousers, who wore a beret and around his neck a white scarf. Déat, the son of a policeman from Clermont-Ferrand and editor of the former Paris daily, *L'Œuvre,* had been a socialist who had swung to the right after the German occupation. "French peasants have no wish to die for Polacks," he had famously declared in September 1939.

Others, too, played a more passive role in the affairs of this "German France". Men like Jean Bichelonne, youngest and most able of the former Vichy ministers. With his marked limp, the result of a motoring accident, he was a well-known figure in the maze-like passages of Schloss Sigmaringen. Then there were the intellectuals: men like Maurice Gabolde and Abel Bonnard, who spent most of their time in the well-stocked Hohenzollern library; and Paul Marion, who still dreamed of saving France from anarchy and liberalism and integrating her into a new European economy.

∞

And there was my mother, and there was her handsome English lover. I shudder to think of how they fitted into this bizarre little community, participating in this nightmarish "dance of crabs", as Destouches/Céline called it. My poor mother, so elegant, so soignée and sophisticated, how could she have survived all this "*boche baroque*", this Gothic fantasy, this world turned upside down? Reading Henry's diaries, I piece together fragments of their life there; I try to imagine them wandering the streets of the little town with its quaint wooden houses and trim window boxes. I gaze at her photograph in *Le Petit Parisien* and I try to imagine her performing for all those "ghosts, monsters and fanatics", which is how Henry describes them (January 12, 1945), or singing "*À nos amours*" at the Deutsches Haus months before she and that song became a post-war hit in Paris, or sitting in Café Schön, with its framed portrait of the Führer, drinking ersatz coffee and listening to old records of Charles Trenet singing "*Mes jeunes années*". For a moment I can glimpse the strangeness of their lives together, as Germany fell apart, their world crumbled and the future turned black; a picture takes shape in my mind, for an instant it gleams as if illuminated in the beam of a projector, and then it is gone.

"It is at Sigmaringen that the heart of France beats," runs an article from *L'Écho de Nancy*, clipped inside Henry's tattered diary, "it is at Sigmaringen that the future of our country is being prepared". The notes of the "Eroica" still boomed out every evening from Radio Berlin. "England, like Carthage, will be destroyed," Jean Hérold-Paquis ranted hysterically night after night on Radio Paris, and the population of *la France allemande* did their best to believe him. Yet how could they have been taken in by such nonsense? All hope had evaporated.

Leclerc and his Senegalese troops were edging closer by the day. The game was up. It was preposterous.

From Henry's sketches, I can visualise the lugubrious castle, perched on its rock over the Danube. I can imagine those neat, tidy streets, ringed by hills and forests, and that river that could never have looked "blue" in a thousand years. But I cannot believe that my mother would have had any time for that fiction of a "new order", the charade of a "new Europe" that some still dreamed about. Could Henry really have thought that the old Maréchal, imprisoned in his seventh-floor apartments, any longer cared? Perhaps Henry did; perhaps a desperate hope was all that was left to him; for why else would he have attended a talk by the Belgian Fascist leader, Léon Degrelle "resplendent in his black S.S. uniform and wearing an Iron Cross"? And how strange it must have been for this English renegade to watch those Lancasters and Flying Fortresses, droning through the night, as they prepared to blitz the now defenceless city of Ulm! There was even a note of optimism in Henry's diary entry for December 19, 1944: "The tide may at last be beginning to turn; heard on the wireless that Von Rundstedt's Panzers had made advances in the Ardennes." And a few days later, in January, he wrote: "Recent news is cheering. At the Schön, last night, where Sylvain and I played chess (Scotch defence, weak opening), we talked till past midnight. Sylvain believes that Germany is invincible, and that only Hitler can control the spread of what he called the 'usury and bolshevism that contaminate our century'." He was clinging to the wreckage of a sinking ship.

Sylvain, with his "effortless, high-flown manner and voice", is, of course, the novelist Sylvain de Gresly. If ever there was a friendship built on shifting foundations, this was it. They must have first come across each other at the Gasthaus zum Alten Fritz, where they all lodged: Henry and Madeleine, her poor mother and father, loyally continuing to work for Luchaire in the Ministère de l'Information, and Sylvain de Gresly, dapper and insouciant even then, according to the photographs, and surely the only man in Sigmaringen to be seen wearing a suit and a bow tie. Henry's looks would surely have appealed to this self-confessed "*inverti*", and Sylvain's erudite, civilised manner must have afforded some consolation to the Englishman. Sylvain appreciated art, as is clear from his novels, and he would have been able to discuss the artists, French as well as English, whom Henry admired: Vuillard, Balthus, Penrose, Ben Nicholson etc. Sylvain had also lived in England, where he had once spent a term attending lectures on Milton at Oxford in the 1920s. He could talk fluently about Shakespeare and Racine, about Valéry and Eliot. In this nightmarish Götterdämmerung, amid these frightened puppets with their *façons barbares*, he felt grateful for this "man of parts", as he put it. And Sylvain was someone with whom Henry could converse and play chess, and who could respond to his carefully rehearsed Scotch Defence with shrewdly devised gambits of his own.

Sylvain appears regularly now in the spasmodic, exasperatingly random entries of Henry's diary during these last painful months. He was his *camarade*, his confidant, his loyal friend. We read of them discussing the impact of the French Revolution as they amble along the frosty banks of the Danube one December morning. A few days later, we find Sylvain teaching Henry the German words of "*Lili Marlene*" and of another popular song, "*Ich habe eine Kamarade*", and then, at Christmas, Henry and Madeleine join Sylvain and "half the inhabitants of this little town at the old church by the Friedhof for Midnight Mass.

'Silent Night' was sung: the French and German voices blend-ing together so sublimely. Softly, almost silently, I mouthed the words to myself in English. Not even M. heard me."

In January, Henry accompanied Sylvain to Mass again. It was the Feast of the Epiphany and they went to the little Hohenzollern chapel, hard by the present-day entrance to the castle:

I longed to follow Sylvain when he rose from the pew and joined the congregation as they approached the altar to receive Communion. So reverent they looked, these simple German peasants with their coarse red faces, and I felt so unworthy by comparison. "Domine non sum dignus . . .", I repeated, dimly remembering the Latin intonation, as the priest beat his breast before taking the host himself, and I felt as I had at school occasionally – moments of sublime conviction that transported me to another plain – when I would feel myself being drawn willingly into a spiritual vortex that overshadowed all human resistance . . . I think I must have been overcome with emotion, because Madeleine, who sat throughout Mass because she feels uncomfortable kneeling and because the baby has begun to kick sharply, touched me on the arm. "*Qu'est-ce qu'il y a, chéri?*" She looked genu-inely anxious; her beautiful eyes gazing into mine with what seemed to me adoration. I looked up at the altar, and as I did so, I saw the old Maréchal making his slow way back to his pew. The victor of Verdun on his knees before his Creator in a Hohenzollern chapel amid the forests of Baden-Württemberg! What comedy is this?

∞

There's a newspaper cutting, too [*La France*, November 9, 1944], with a photograph of Madeleine and a caption alerting readers to this "talented *artiste* who lives among us and whose charming songs have helped restore a little of our beloved France to the fabric of our daily lives. She can be heard this evening, in a programme interspersed with songs on gramophone record by Charles Trenet and Lyna Margy, immediately after the broadcast of "*Içi la France*" at 20h.45."

By day, Henry worked at the Ministère de l'Information at number 3 Karlstrasse, Sigmaringen's principal street, to earn the wherewithal for their rent at Zum Alten Fritz and to obtain vouchers for their food, which they cooked on a tiny gas ring in their bedroom. Henry was one of 220 clerks, under the direction of the *commissaire*, Jean Luchaire, who were given jobs in the overstaffed ministry. His particular task was to compile information that was then printed in the community's daily newspaper, *La France* (4 francs or 20 pfennigs), or else broadcast on Radio Sigmaringen's *Içi la France* programme, which went out every evening.

Henry rose each morning at 7.00 a.m. He washed in cold water and then took Madeleine her breakfast of black bread, jam and water, followed by a spoonful of Dr Destouches's tonic for pregnant mothers, which she loathed. It was a short, pleasant walk from Zum Alten Fritz to Karlstrasse, past the Café Schön, with its pathetic array of cakes, the Fidelis inn, with its stags' heads and beer steins hanging on the wooden walls, and the Deutsche Haus, before he reached the "ministry". He was at his desk in his first-floor office by 8.30 a.m.; he took a break for a cigarette and ersatz coffee at 10.30, and at 12.30 he began his lunch hour. There was a canteen of sorts at the ministry, but more often than not Henry would meet Madeleine, who brought him rolls filled with whatever she could procure from the grocer's, and they would walk past the half-timbered houses with their pointed roofs, down to the Danube. There was a rusty green-metal bench directly beneath the soaring castle rock where they sat and made plans for a future that seemed bleaker by the day. In the afternoons, while Henry assembled information for M. Luchaire to print, or for M. Hérold-Paquis or others to broadcast, Madeleine practised her singing, tried to write new lyrics, or visited her mother at Hotel Löwen.

∞

Meanwhile, in newly liberated France, the *épuration* was in full flow. "Fascists" and "collaborators", former members of the *milice*, peasants, shopkeepers and company directors who had had dealings of any sort with the enemy – even those who had helped with re-building after Allied bombings – were being hunted down, suspected of aiding the enemy, of being *collabos*. Some were sentenced to imprisonment or executed. Others were summarily shot. In Metz, an acquaintance of Henry's referred to only as "André" killed himself with an injection of strychnine on the day he heard that Paris had been liberated. Many now openly paraded their previously unsuspected resistance sympathies. Young women, known to have slept with German soldiers, had their heads shaved and were dragged ignominiously through the streets of France's towns and villages; *les tondues*, the shaven ones, they were called. Those who could do so escaped; some managing to slip over the border into Switzerland, others to Italy or Spain, many never to surface again in their former identity. Approximately ten thousand

French men and women were executed for collaborating. Many thousands of others held their breath.

In Sigmaringen the citizens of *la France allemande* became increasingly inured to the consequences of German defeat. As their prospects grew bleaker, they seemed to become ever more French in their personal mannerisms, behaving like self-caricatures – the grim-faced Breton; the Pagnol-type of Marseillais; the tough, acerbic Lyonnais; the Parisian lad with his cheeky humour – as they wandered through the silent streets of Sigmaringen, beneath the Teutonic firs in the forest, or by the banks of the slow-flowing Danube, some still chic in their pre-war Chanel suits, their silk scarves, their natty correspondent shoes. But, as 1945 wore on, the last of the rats prepared to desert the sinking ship. The war was lost and their illusions had vanished.

∽

Henry and Madeleine's baby, Theo, was born on February 24. A fortnight beforehand, Henry describes how he, Madeleine and her mother, Diane, had gone for a drink with Dr Destouches after he had come to examine her:

> M. in good shape. Diane never leaves her. Destouches is pleased with progress and told us not to worry. He is so busy tending the sick at the castle and among the French community here that much as I should have liked to discuss his writing with him, I have never wanted to waste his time. However, it was he who suggested a beer at the little café round the corner from the Löwen, where he lives. When we were seated, he looked me in the eye

with that weary, slightly cynical expression of the Parisian who's seen it all and said: "You're English, aren't you? One can always tell. A perfidious, treacherous race, my friend, it is well said. Your compatriots left the French people to be massacred. You have always hated us. It's the fault of your Israelites, all those Jewish bosses in the City and the House of Lords." He's a puzzling, rather frightening man, with a receding hairline and a piercing gaze that fills me with unease. I prefer to spend time with him in the company of his wife Lucette, an attractive woman with whom M. gets on well, and I like it most when the conversation is restricted to the subject of cats! Dr Destouches venerates his enormous, plump, tortoiseshell cat, whose name is Bébert. It sometimes accompanies him on his rounds (though not today), travelling in a bag or in a sack with breathing holes in it carried round his neck. Bébert has his own passport, which the doctor proudly showed me: "Bébert, owner Dr Destouches, 4 rue Girardon, Paris", and there's a photograph too. He advised me to leave Germany as soon as I could. "Leclerc and his Senegalese are nearly here. Get out while you can. Go north. Don't listen to deluded idiots like Degrelle," he said. "He's only fit for the noose of a rope. Like me." He talked, too, about the Lavals, who had invited him and his wife to the castle for dinner once, and he described how Monsieur Laval had appointed him to be Governor of Saint-Pierre-et-Miquelon. Laval was a *sacré con*, he said. For a medical man, Destouches swears rather a lot. M. says he frightens her, but she can sense he's a good doctor. And no-one ever seems to pay him. Sylvain told me that his novels are *bien vus,* but that he incurs public wrath with his anti-Semitism.

∞

Theo's birth was drawn out, but not painful. Madeleine still remembers the comforting reassurance that Dr Destouches gave her, and the kindness of Hildegarde, the German nurse who delivered the baby. Henry had been pacing the river bank, unable to bear the sight of his beloved's suffering, and Madeleine's parents only appeared once, after time enough had elapsed for everything to have been tidied and cleaned. The baby was baptised a few days later following the weekday-morning Mass at the Hohenzollern chapel, courtesy of "Monsieur Otto" and the other authorities at the castle, who were pleased to accord this privilege to such an industrious servant of *la France allemande* as Madeleine's father. He, his wife Diane, Henry and Madeleine, Henry's friend Sylvain, and a woman he refers to only as "Mademoiselle Cécile", a dressmaker from Nancy, were present. Cécile and Sylvain were the godparents.

∞

Henry, Madeleine and their infant son left Sigmaringen in the early days of March 1945. The little train that ran spasmodically from the railway station built along the contours of a bend in the Danube, would have taken them either eastwards to Ulm, whence they had arrived barely five months earlier, or, conceivably, north to Stuttgart. Madeleine cannot remember. Their journey must have been the stuff of nightmares, for the Allied bombing raids had created havoc in the cities and industrial centres of the Reich. People went about their daily lives amid piles of ruins, making their way along streets in which bomb craters had appeared overnight, in towns where gas pipes, electricity and telephone lines had been blown up and where the windows of shops and houses had been ransacked. Retribution was being taken on a defeated Germany.

Chaos and confusion reigned. Madeleine remembers being told that in Dresden, on the night of February 13 alone, 650,000 incendiary bombs were dropped on the ancient city, and a million and a half tons of high explosives rained down on a population that had been swelled by the arrival of thousands of refugees from the East. Some met their deaths burning like torches as they ran through the streets, while those who were fast enough plunged into the waters of the River Elbe. Bodies were burned on public pyres. The destruction had disrupted the transport systems, and anyone travelling by rail or by road did so at their peril. It was Armageddon.

∞

Henry's and Madeleine's journey to Denmark with their baby must have taken at least a week, for Henry's passport, which was included among his "family archives", was stamped March 9, 1945 at the Danish customs post at Rodbyhavn. Wending their way northwards, they spent nights in cold, blacked-out railway carriages or in damp, dingy station waiting rooms, making connections where they could, their progress hampered by air-raids and explosions, by tracks blown away by the bombing, by destroyed bridges and by the panic of civilians in the maelstrom of impending defeat. The following day they arrived in Copenhagen.

[EPILOGUE]

His heart was formed for softness – warped to wrong:
Betrayed too early, and beguiled too long.

Byron – *Corsair* 3, 23

"I WONDERED WHETHER YOU WOULD EVER RAISE THE subject, dear Will," Ghislaine said when I finally summoned up the courage to declare my feelings to her. "I've felt we somehow belonged together from the time we were in Brittany, but I'm afraid I'm far too unsure of myself to think of any other life beyond my job."

I had persuaded Ghislaine to come to London for a weekend in the early spring. She stayed at my flat and it was there that I proposed. Scarcely anyone in London or Paris knew about our engagement. There was no formal announcement and neither of us wanted any fuss; a few friends came to an impromptu gathering at a Kensington pub much frequented by musicians and we celebrated, but it was hardly Ghislaine's scene.

Before we left London on our flight to Buenos Aires, I had telephoned my mother in Edinburgh. Since my father's death, she had retreated into a calm and matter-of-fact world of her own and she accepted the news serenely. All that puzzled her was why we were going so far away to "do the deed".

"But don't they loathe us in Argentina, darling, after that horrid Falklands business?" she protested. "I do hope you'll be safe. Bring Gillian – is that her name? – up north as soon as you're back, won't you? Promise? I do wonder what your poor father would have said about his son marrying his own half-sister – his aunt, for goodness sake ..." She paused, and then added tactfully: "I'm sure you'll be very happy."

As for Madeleine, she could not have been more thrilled ("my prayers have been answered, dear Will," she said to me over the telephone) and she did not appear in the least deterred that her beloved only daughter was marrying her grandson. She declared our union to be "entirely appropriate" and told Ghislaine that she had secretly hoped for such an outcome ever since my first visit to Brittany.

Two factors had influenced our decision to be married in Argentina. First and foremost was the short tour that my agent had been able to arrange for our quartet: a reasonably lucrative series of concerts in three Argentine cities over the course of a week. Secondly, Ghislaine had been commissioned by her newspaper to write two features: an article on Argentine literature post-Borges, and an extended interview with the elderly novelist Ernesto Sábato, the man who had heroically led the National Commission on the Disappeared following the military dictatorship of the 1970s. Better still, an Argentine friend of hers who had left the country at that time had offered to lend us the tiny apartment he still owned on Viamonte, in the heart of Buenos Aires.

It was as if fate or Henry's shade were summoning us to Buenos Aires, and so I made the necessary arrangements for Ghislaine to join me on the flight to Argentina.

"But after we're married and we've laid Henry's ghost to rest, Will, I want us to start afresh," Ghislaine declared at the airport on the morning of our departure. "Frankly, I'm more than a little tired of all this living in the past. I feel as if I must escape from it all, wash it away. And yet whenever I try to concentrate on my job, I sense myself being lured back. It's that old devil Henry, rather than my mother, who is responsible. Maman recounted everything that she remembered into my tape recorder, and I know she talked to you too, but for her all that Vichy business and its aftermath really is buried now. 'Each of us has to find a way of dealing with the dreams and nightmares of our youth,' she said, 'no-one else can help you.'"

∞

I was astonished by the sophistication of Buenos Aires. It's a vast, humid, sprawling city of broad avenues and bustling streets, skyscrapers, parks and statues, and elegant cafés; "a crucible of souls and races", in the words of the great Argentine writer Borges, and it's a city of many different moods, too, according to which *barrio* you find yourself in. European influences – Italian, French, British – are reflected everywhere. Although Argentina was going through a serious financial crisis that had brought chaos and rioting to Buenos Aires, with massive demonstrations in the Plaza de Mayo that had led to the resignation of the President, we were fortunate to have arrived during a period of relative peace.

∞

After several days spent roaming the narrow, exhaust-polluted streets of the city centre before the first of my concerts, waiting for the necessary papers from our respective consulates, Ghislaine and I exchanged vows at a simple ceremony following the midday Mass at a church overlooking the palm trees and formal gardens of a pretty *plaza* in the northern suburb of Olivos. It was a hot, humid day, without a breath of wind, and we had travelled on a dusty, rattling 1950s vintage train from Retiro station. I wore my only suit, and Ghislaine had bought a simple pale-blue dress and a hand-painted scarf to wear over her head, if necessary. Rosita Suarez, Henry's faithful housekeeper – and, as we later came to realise, his erstwhile mistress – to whom I had written prior to our arrival, helped make the arrangements with her own local parish priest, who had agreed to give us a blessing. She was one of the witnesses and her brother Manolo, who was also present to sign the civil register, the other. It was at his house, on Mariano Pelliza, a street a few blocks away from the church, that a reception of sorts took place afterwards. Rosita had made varieties of *empanadas*, and Manolo proposed a dignified toast – "to our two new friends, their health and their happiness, and in memory of our dearest Henry".

There were three other guests whom Rosita had invited to this impromptu celebration: a woman and two men. All were of a certain age. None of them had been present at the church, but they were waiting for us in the front terrace of Manolo's house. The woman must have been in her eighties; she had light-brown eyes and tinted grey hair, and she was dressed in a camel-hair overcoat. I had no idea who she was, but I somehow sensed she was French, and I remember there was something pleasantly reassuring about her presence and about the warmth with which she embraced Rosita. The two men looked less appealing and reminded me of conspirators in films about the mafia. They were dressed for a funeral rather than for a wedding party. Both of them wore dark suits and ties. The balder and taller of the two had a moustache and exuded an aroma of bitter aloes. He was Ernesto Garay, the owner of the gallery at which Henry's paintings had been exhibited during his early years in Buenos Aires. He walked over to greet us, embracing me as if I were his own long-lost relative. He bowed stiffly to kiss Ghislaine's hand and spoke in a strongly accented English.

"My friends," he said. "How proud dear Henry would have been and how we wish he could have been here today. It is an honour for us, as his old friends, to welcome you to our country and to wish you many years of happiness together." And he bowed again, with a pained smile, before raising his glass to us.

Rosita introduced the other guest as Henry's physician and a faithful friend over many years. Dr Jacques Bouteillier had left France as a boy, "after the war", he said, and had practised as a doctor in Buenos Aires until his retirement. He lived in the prestigious, leafy suburb of Belgrano now, though he had come originally from the spa town of Châtel-Guyon.

Dr Bouteillier bowed and he too kissed Ghislaine's hand. I asked him when he had last been in France.

"A long time ago. I was very young when I left. My life has been in Argentina. We started afresh after the war. My parents wanted to wipe the slate clean, as they say."

He sipped his champagne.

"We are Argentinians now to all intents and purposes; my wife is from Uruguay and she and our sons converse in Spanish, not French. My grandchildren, too. Europe is another world for us. It represents the past, a different way of doing things, and for me personally it was a past that I recall with too much grief. My parents left all those memories of war behind them when we came out here. Just as Henry did. We are citizens of the New World now." He smiled at Ghislaine as he looked her up and down.

I took a particular dislike to Dr Bouteillier, who enquired after Madeleine.

"She was a beautiful woman, your mother," he said to Ghislaine. "I heard her singing on the radio once, shortly after the Liberation, before we left France. Ah! But, as I told you, no-one speaks of those times anymore. The war with Germany is long forgotten," he mused, turning to face me. "A few ageing Nazis out in the provinces who make the headlines from time to time, I suppose, but they're dying off now. Besides, what do the young care? They have their own battles. Your grandfather was the only friend I had in B.A. who knew anything about that period, but he, too, preferred to forget the past. No doubt there were many who went underground, so to speak, but most of them are now dead."

Dr Bouteillier paused, offered his glass to Manolo to be refilled, and then continued:

"My wife has never been to Europe; neither have my children or grandchildren. Of course, they know about your British royal family, the names of a few football players, pop singers and film stars, but they are ignorant of history and what the old Europe meant . . . and, as I've told you, they think of themselves as Argentine."

Dr Bouteillier droned on. There was a whiff of mothballs emanating from his clothing. His presence rekindled memories of the mood that had come over Ghislaine and me on our first evening in Buenos Aires, when we had walked through the streets and plazas of the central city, and sat down in a smart café called the Biela, opposite the Recoleta cemetery. Perhaps it had something to do with the climate, or the wind that blew off the muddy waters of the River Plate, but whatever it was, I was overcome by a mood of melancholy that I shall forever associate with the proud stances of those men with distant, arrogant expressions on the many statues erected to the memory of nineteenth-century heroes and liberators – José de San Martín, Manuel Belgrano, Domingo Faustino Sarmiento, Bartolomé Mitre, and my particular favourite, that of the brave Almirante William Brown – that adorn the charming, well-shaded parks and squares. It was a mood that was evoked, too, in the poignant airs of the tangos – brimming with pathos and unfulfilled yearning – first sung by *"el inmortal"*, Carlos Gardel, whose songs are still played in bars and restaurants all over the city. In spite of what Dr Bouteillier had said, Argentinians lived in the past more than most of us, perpetually awaiting that golden future so long forecast, but which never quite dawns.

The art gallery owner, Ernesto Garay, proposed another toast to us. Then, in the briefest of speeches, I thanked Rosita and Manolo for their kindness, as well as our three guests, and, in my inadequate Spanish, I toasted the memory of Henry. Rosita raised her glass again too, repeating what everyone present had said at least once: namely, that Henry would have been overjoyed by the appropriateness of this happy event. "It would have meant so much to him," she said, her voice cracking a little.

Before the party was over, the elderly woman with the camel-hair overcoat took Ghislaine and me to one side and spoke to us in English. She was returning next morning to the *"campo"*, as she referred to the provinces, but she would be delighted if, before we left for Europe, we would visit her at her estancia, some four hundred kilometres from the capital, not far from Necochea, in the south of the province of Buenos Aires.

"You can reach us by train, and either my son or our foreman will come to meet you. It would help give you a truer taste of this immense country. Here, take my card – it is my late husband's actually – and be sure to telephone me this week. Please, no excuses, I want you to come. Besides, we have much to talk about."

She passed the card to me and patted Ghislaine on the shoulder as though to emphasise her wishes. Unlike Dr Bouteillier, to whom, Ghislaine later observed, she did not address a single word, Señora Volkov spoke to her in a formal, timeless French that was redolent of another age. I could not help noticing her almond eyes as we parted. As she bid us goodbye and climbed into the car waiting outside, I glanced at the visiting card: Señora Basilio Volkov, it read, and I wondered what the nature of her friendship with Henry could have been.

The answer was not long in coming. Once the art dealer and Dr Bouteillier had departed, Rosita and Manolo suggested we stay a little longer because she had some information to impart. Manolo ushered us into the small back garden, where we sat beneath the shade of two dark cypress trees while he went to prepare tea. There was a scent of lemons. Rosita came outside to join us. I thanked her for the efficient and thoughtful way she had organised our little wedding party. She smiled and said it was only normal and "what Henry would have wished". With her dark and heavily made-up complexion, Rosita Suarez was plump, scarcely over five feet tall. She must have been in her early sixties. Her dyed black hair gleamed and her brown eyes danced as she gesticulated and spoke proudly about my grandfather.

"He transformed my life, you know. He made me what I am, what I have become. He gave me whatever education and understanding of life I possess. Thanks to his paintings, which I sold with his permission, I have money to live on nowadays – and a little self-respect, too. When we first met, some time in the 1950s, I think, I was virtually on the streets; an innocent provincial girl from Entre Rios, living in one of the poorest *barrios* of the city. I knew nothing about life. Nothing!" she reiterated, gesticulating with her small hands which she brought up to her face, pressing them to her cheeks and covering her eyes for a few seconds.

"No-one knew him here as I did. I was his *querida*, not his wife, of course, but there was no shame in that. Not in a country where, when I was young, a so-called 'actress' like Evita Perón could become the president's wife! I looked after Henry: I cooked, I swept and cleaned, I mended his clothes, I soothed him when he was sad and nursed him when he was ill. But I did not live with him. I came to him every day, and stayed only when he asked me to do so . . ."

Rosita seemed close to tears. Ghislaine, who was sitting beside her stroked her hand.

"There was only one other woman in Argentina who revered him as I did, who knew all the secrets of his past life, his guilty feelings about the war and about his family and friends in Europe, and that was María Elena, the lady who has just left. She is a saint, I must tell you. A woman in a million, a truly civilised and wise human being. I owe her, too, a great deal, and

I do not just mean money. Henry respected her as he did few people in this country. She's a widow now, her husband died three years ago, but she telephones me every month, and we meet whenever she comes up to town. You must visit her on her estancia if you have the time. She told me she planned to invite you; it is an honour, and it would be a great pity if you did not take advantage of such an opportunity. You will find echoes of an older Argentina there – as it was before our terrible military regime, before Perón and Evita even – as it was in the thirties, in the days of hope. And it is so beautiful." Rosita wrung her hands and sighed.

Moved with emotion, Rosita leaned over and embraced Ghislaine, who then asked the question that had been on my lips. "Señora Volkov comes from France originally, doesn't she?"

"*Claro!* A French woman from head to toe. She has such style, don't you think?"

"Did you know her when she first came to Argentina?"

"I met her shortly after I knew Henry. She was an émigrée, like so many Europeans who came here after the war. I was very young, and I couldn't say exactly when it was. Henry had known her – intimately? Well, I was never really sure – but before I met him in 1952, I was a poor *campesina*. Naive, uneducated and still a virgin. Henry was a celebrated artist and he offered me a job. With the money I earned, I was able to keep a roof over my head. Señora Volkov – Henry always called her Marie-Hélène, not María Elena, and they would speak in French to one another – used to come to lunch whenever she was in town and could escape from her husband, who was Russian and evidently a bit of a martinet, as Henry used to say. They would meet every two or three months. He would either take her to the English Club on 25 de Mayo, or to Pedemonte, his favourite restaurant, to eat a *bife de lomo*. Or occasionally he would ask me to prepare something at his flat and they would spend the afternoon together. I was never jealous. It wasn't like that. My love for Henry was pure, never possessive. I accepted what I had been granted by the good Lord. I wanted nothing more, and therefore there was never any question of jealousy. His love for her was to do with the past, whereas his love for me belonged to the present, and, as I used to think, to the future." Rosita dabbed her eyes with a small white lace handkerchief.

"Afterwards, he would accompany her to the railway terminus in time for her to catch the night train to Necochea. They were truly devoted to one another."

"Didn't her husband mind her absences?" I asked, as Manolo laid out the teacups.

"Don Basilio? No, I don't think so. He was a proud, authoritarian man, but as long as he had all that he needed, she was allowed out on her shopping sprees. She usually spent a night or two in town, at the City Hotel, before it was closed. And she always brought something back from the big shops: European clothes from Harrods or Gath y Chaves, or the latest French or English novels from the Librería Mackern. Basilio was rich and very eccentric, and I think the idea that his wife enjoyed a close friendship with another man rather pleased him. Up to a point, at least. It gave him the freedom to call on his own girlfriends, and to get drunk, which he regularly did. The estancia had belonged to Basilio's father. It was said that they had smuggled gold and jewellery out of their town house in St Petersburg before the Bolshevik revolution and that his family owned vast estates which they had to leave behind in Russia. Volkov was not his real name. Perhaps he was an aristocrat. He was certainly handsome, and very Russian, as you will see from photographs, and his son, the young Basilio, has inherited his looks – *es un diós!*" Rosita kissed the bunched fingers of her hand to add emphasis.

After another hour of Rosita's reminiscences, we took our leave of her and Manolo, promising not to lose touch. Then, we caught the train back to Retiro, and walked back to our apartment on Viamonte. After a short siesta, we spent our first evening together as man and wife at a restaurant on the Costanera, where the speciality was a fish called *pejarey*, and we toasted one another with a soft and mellow white wine. After two hours, we took a deliberately indirect route home, strolling arm in arm. We heard the bells from the church of St Catherine of Siena striking midnight. A cool breeze blew in from the River Plate. The Southern Cross shimmered in the night sky and, on this occasion, the city's customary mood of melancholy was tinged with one of expectancy and desire.

∞

It was, admittedly, a bizarre thing to do on our honeymoon, but we spent the following morning in the Chacarita cemetery, looking for Henry's grave. It was Sunday. The bright sunshine flooding through the flimsy curtains had persuaded us to rise at 7.30 and, following Rosita's precise instructions, we travelled through the empty and as yet unpolluted streets of the city on a *colectivo*, one of the municipal buses, at a terrifying speed that was inappropriate for a modern metropolis. At Chacarita, florists' stalls lined the railings on either side of the ornate and imposing central gateway leading to the vast burial ground. Ghislaine bought two large bunches of mimosa.

"My mother's favourite," Ghislaine said, holding up the bright-yellow buds to my nose as we walked along the cemetery's central avenue. "She always bought it whenever she could find it. Its perfume intoxicates you for a few hours; then it's gone. Like passion – like life, too, I suppose," she added, her fair hair falling over her shoulder as she put her arm through mine, "but not like love. Not our love, anyway, *n'est-ce pas,* Will? This mimosa with its wonderfully sensual perfume shall be Maman's tribute to her lover – and your grandfather."

The grave was situated at the furthest end of the cemetery, beyond the massive, brooding, Argentine-baroque mausoleums in which the nineteenth-century bourgeoisie had buried its dead. A very old *ombú,* a tree native to Argentina and one of its national symbols, spread its boughs above our heads. A simple stone cross in white marble bore the inscription HENRY LATYMER and, beneath it, the words *pintór, caballero, ciudadino del mundo*: artist, gentleman, citizen of the world. On the plinth, in small letters: "*le cœur a ses raisons . . .*" A few flowers, now withered, were in a plastic urn at the foot of the grave. Ghislaine and I stood holding hands, and I muttered a prayer to myself for the repose of my grandfather's soul. A gust of wind rustled the branches of the ancient tree and the whistle of a train sounded in the distance. On the far side of the path from us, a gardener knelt, tending a flower bed, a burned-out cigarette butt in his lips. As he worked, he listened to the excitable voices of two football commentators on his transistor radio, reliving the excitement of the River Plate football team's match the previous evening. Suddenly, his cigarette fell to the ground: "*Gó-ó-ó-l.*

G-ó-ól de Ri-i-ver" the commentator crowed in jubilation, and the gardener pumped his fist in celebration.

I wondered who had been responsible for the wording on the tombstone. Artist, certainly; gentleman, more doubtful; but "citizen of the world"? Henry's travelling had scarcely been done of his own volition. And that epitaph?

"It's Pascal," Ghislaine said. "How would you say it in English? The heart has its reasons of which reason knows nothing. Something like that."

"But how typically enigmatic. Who do you think had it done? Not Rosita, surely?"

"No," Ghislaine agreed. "But perhaps it was the French-woman whom Rosita told us about."

"Señora Volkov, do you mean?"

Ghislaine nodded. Then she added: "And Will, à propos, now that I think of it, wasn't there a Marie-Hélène in Henry's diary of his early days in Paris? And didn't Robert, the American, speak to you about her? The girl Henry liked so much when he was first in Paris, whom he took to the theatre with Robert, but could never get close to? The one with the almond eyes. I'm sure this is the same woman."

∞

We took a taxi back to the centre of town, as far as the Plaza de Mayo. Then we walked up the narrow Calle Florida, mercifully free of traffic, but full of gaudy, modern shops and bustling with crowds strolling gently to and fro, dressed in their Sunday best. We stopped to have tea and a cake in the more sedate, faded confines of the Richmond Tea Rooms.

Literary creature that she is, Ghislaine informed me that

it was here in this old-fashioned tea-house, frequented by the British residents of the Argentine capital during their heyday in the 1930s, that Dr Plarr in Graham Greene's novel, *The Honorary Consul*, had met his mother, a woman who was particularly partial to cream cakes.

"Typical of you British! You always have to transport your way of life around the world with you," she teased, giving me a mocking smile and glancing round the dimly lit room. "Tea rooms, Harrods – it's gone now, by the way – Hurlingham. And tomorrow you're taking me to lunch at the English Club. Honestly! We French were so much more discreet in the way we colonised." She took my hand under the table and squeezed it.

I reminded Ghislaine that it had been the British who had been responsible for the city's commercial wealth, but Ghislaine shrugged. She would have preferred a further sampling of Argentine beef to lunching at the English Club where Henry had been a member for forty years. The very idea of such a place depressed her.

"I thought going there might help to provide a few more clues about Henry," I said apologetically. "He lunched there regularly, you know."

Ghislaine shrugged again, pouting in a way I find tantalising. No further words were needed; we spent the rest of the afternoon in bed, before getting dressed and setting out again at eight o'clock. We sat on a bench in the Parque Lezama, watching the evening gather momentum. As darkness set in, we strolled to the San Telmo district, where we sat and drank gin and tonic on the terrace of a café while tango dancers performed on the pavement.

The English Club revealed little that we did not already know. The secretary said that he remembered Henry Latymer, but he only seemed to do so after consulting his list of members, whereupon he invited us to take lunch and led us into a large, empty and somewhat forbidding dining hall and directed us to the table by the window where Henry used to sit, he assured us, whenever he lunched at the Club. He then asked us to wait a moment while he disappeared through a swing-door into the kitchens, returning seconds later, accompanied by an elderly man in a waiter's black and white uniform, whom he introduced as Fernando. He stood erect and spoke deliberately slowly in a mixture of Spanish and heavily accented English.

"Señor Latymer" was "*un caballero inglés*" – an English gentleman – Fernando told us, a much respected artist ("*muy estimado*"), and a man who was always courteous and honourable. He was "*de estilo antiguo*" – old-fashioned – and also (here the old waiter lowered his voice and looked at me as if he were imparting confidential information) "*muy devoto*" – a very devout man. In the months before he died, Fernando recalled seeing him frequently at the church of St Catherine of Siena, a few blocks from where we were, kneeling in prayer before the statue of the Virgin, known as Nuestra Señora del Mar – Our Lady of the Sea. "In any case," he declared gravely and with a slight bow, it was "an honour to be accorded the privilege of meeting the relatives of such a man".

"Did he come here alone?" Ghislaine said.

"Usually alone, but sometimes with Señora Volkov, an old friend who lived in the *campo* – the country," the old man answered discreetly. They were very old friends, and very attached – "*muy cariñosos*".

Two days later, I met my colleagues from our quartet at Ezeiza airport and, during the week that followed, we rehearsed and performed a series of concerts that had been arranged for us by the British Council. A packed hall in Buenos Aires itself, where I had to plead for Ghislaine to be allowed a ticket, gave us an enthusiastic reception, and it was much the same, though on a smaller scale, at concert halls in the cities of Rosario and Córdoba. The "Malvinas" or Falklands war seemed to have been forgotten. During the three days that I was on tour, Ghislaine remained in the capital researching her article on modern Argentine literature. She travelled out to the suburb of Santos Lugares to interview Borges' contemporary, the novelist Ernesto Sábato, a man she admired greatly, not just for his political courage during Argentina's military dictatorship, but for what she reckoned to be one of the great overlooked novels of our time, *On Heroes and Tombs*. I had hated leaving her – more than I imagined possible – but it was worth the pain of separation just to see the expression on her face, easily spotted among the crowds at the airport, when she met me on our return from Cordoba three days later.

Early in the morning following my return, we caught a train to the seaside resort of Necochea to spend our two last days in Argentina at María Elena Volkov's estancia at Mechongué, several hours' journey south of the capital. Her farm manager, or factor, met us at the railway station in an ancient 1950s Land Rover, and for nearly three hours we drove in virtual silence across the flat pampas, a land inhabited, so it seemed, solely by cattle, llamas and the occasional ranch worker or *peón* on horseback. The rich agricultural plain extended indefinitely westwards, without undulation, until it reached the distant Tandíl hills, now tinged reddish grey in the late afternoon sunlight. At last we turned off the narrow tarmac road onto what was little more than a dusty track, and, ten minutes later, we arrived at the estancia, to be met by a flurry of barking sheepdogs that leaped up menacingly at the vehicle. The main house, set in its own parkland, must have been built in the 1930s. Low and single-storeyed, a straw-roofed veranda hung with pink and red oleanders ran along the three inner sides of the building's U-shaped structure. The manager took our luggage and led us through a chained curtain into a cool, shaded room, its floor paved with black and white tiles like some huge chessboard.

"Señora Volkov," our driver, a taciturn man named Luís, announced, "is engaged for the moment. She begs your forgiveness and says she will join you shortly."

Through the open windows that looked out onto the veranda and the inner courtyard and were partially covered by wicker blinds, the evening sun was dipping below the now purple-coloured hills on the horizon. The dogs lay panting outside, but the silence was broken by the sound of women's voices from along the corridor that led into the room in which we were standing. A fountain trickled in the centre of the courtyard and cicadas sawed among the branches of the tall eucalyptus trees that stood guard over the farmhouse.

A heavy, sedate mahogany desk and an ornate chaise longue covered in a dark-red taffeta dominated the oblong room. Glancing about her, Ghislaine reckoned both pieces of furniture to be nineteenth-century and probably Russian. She pointed to the oval portrait that hung over the desk. A handsome-looking man of about twenty-five, wearing a high military collar and with a slightly drooping moustache, gazed superciliously towards the far side of the room, where a small cabinet – on which stood bottles of J&B whisky, Gordon's gin and Noilly Prat – occupied the space between the two French windows.

"He is certainly Russian, and an aristocrat, I'd say." Ghislaine pointed at the painting. "1880s or 90s. He reminds me of the well-known portrait of Lermontov."

I shrugged impatiently. Apprehensive about our hostess' imminent arrival, I felt mildly irritated that Ghislaine should appear so relaxed and always be so tiresomely bookish in the associations she made.

A door opened behind us and Señora Volkov, or Marie-Hélène as I now thought of her, entered, accompanied by a young maid.

"Dear Will and Ghislaine. We are so pleased to welcome you to our home." In the Argentine manner, Marie-Hélène gave each of us a single kiss on the cheek. "My son, Basilio, will be back for dinner, but meanwhile you must be tired after such a journey. Anita will show you to your room. Please take a shower if you wish. Some guests who are keen to meet you will be joining us, and so I must hurry and get ready, but tomorrow we shall have a little time to ourselves." She smiled warmly, summoned her maid and gave a little wave as though she were dismissing us.

Our bedroom overlooked the park. In the last of the dusk light I could just distinguish the outline of the trees and what looked to be a *mirador*, or summer house, on the far side of the big lawn. I opened the shutters and a scent of eucalyptus wafted through the now chilly evening air. While Ghislaine took a shower, I undressed; then I sat down on the bed and glanced at the titles of the books on the shelves above our bedside table. I was reminded of my two visits to Madeleine's house in Brittany. There were books in Russian, English, Spanish and French, but there was little that was not pre-war: Pushkin's verse, André Gide's *Journal*, four volumes of Osbert Sitwell's autobiography, an Albatross anthology of English verse, the ubiquitous (in these parts) *Far Away and Long Ago* by W.H. Hudson, who, we were later informed, had spent part of his childhood on a farm not far from here, and *Eight Bells*, a history of the Royal Mail shipping line. I picked them up one by one, leafing through them, sniffing their musty bindings and yellowing paper. Most of the other titles meant little to me, but there was one that caused me to catch my breath for an instant: it was Pierre Drieu la Rochelle's posthumously published *Journal secret*.

In a flash, fleeting images of the world that Henry had recorded in his diaries, that world that Madeleine, and Robert, and Sylvain de Gresly, had all evoked in their different ways, were conjured up again in my imagination: the wretchedness of those war-torn years, the debris and ashes of the old Europe, that world of victors and vanquished, of heroes and villains – and, of course, of collaborators. My grandfather had certainly been one of them. Why else did he end his days here in Argentina, along with those Nazis, who had gone to ground and whose progeny now blended into their South American backgrounds? Not just the Mengeles or Eichmanns, not the murderers with the blood of Jews on their hands, but those ordinary men and women, all elderly now, who had simply accepted the *status quo*, taken the path of least resistance and realised too late that they had opted for the wrong side. What was the line of Browning's that Henry had quoted? "We called the chess-board white, – we call it black". It was a matter of perspective, wasn't it? They, too, might once have been confused idealists, like Henry and so many others – intellectuals, artists, writers – attracted by the lure of revolution, longing to change society radically, to wipe the slate clean, searching, then as now, for the European ideal.

I flicked through the final pages of Drieu la Rochelle's journal.

Yes, I am a traitor. Yes, I worked with the enemy. I offered the enemy French intelligence. It is no fault of mine if this enemy was not intelligent.

Yes, I am no ordinary patriot, no limited nationalist: I am an internationalist.

I am not only a Frenchman, I am a European.

You are Europeans too, whether you know it or not. But we played and I lost.

I demand the death penalty.

This was treason of a different order to Henry's, surely, yet there was a certain nobility in Drieu's stance, that of a man who was true to his ideals and not afraid of public vilification.

At that moment, Ghislaine emerged shivering from the bathroom, her body wrapped in a large pink towel, her hair in a smaller one.

"Will, do close the windows. It's freezing in here. And pull the shutters to, and draw our curtains if you don't want all the gauchos and *peónes* on the estancia to see me stark naked."

I drew the curtains and walked over to her. I held her close, and for a long moment we neither spoke nor moved. I felt supremely happy. The towel that was loosely fastened above Ghislaine's breasts slipped to the floor and we moved unerringly towards the bed. Our bodies dissolved into one another and, as we came together I tried to imagine ourselves as Henry and Madeleine: my grandfather; Ghislaine's mother. Time and space divided us – so too did history – but had the intensity of their love been so very different? Had they not once been as happy as we were now? I felt as if a journey of sorts had been accomplished, a circular one that somehow reconciled the past to the present and, for the first time in my life, I felt as though I could finally accept myself as the person I am. It was as if, in that sublime, spontaneous moment when we existed uniquely for and through one another, in surges of sublime passion, our bodies had fused into theirs. The dingy student rooms in wartime Vichy, the miserable hotel bedroom in Sigmaringen, Henry's and Madeleine's last night spent together in a second-floor flat overlooking a Copenhagen canal, had all merged into this guest bedroom in an estancia on the Argentine pampas.

∞

We were roused some twenty minutes later by a gong summoning us to dinner. We dressed hurriedly. As we crossed the courtyard, where the fountain was still trickling, I could see the shadows of several guests moving to and fro behind the Venetian blinds.

"There you are at last. We were beginning to wonder whether you had fallen asleep after that tiring train journey." Marie-Hélène stepped forward to greet us, laughing and ushering us towards the end of the room where her guests were drinking and talking. She had changed into a navy-blue dress. She handed each of us a glass and, alluding to us as "Henry's grandson and his wife", she introduced us to a tall and strikingly handsome dark-haired man of about forty who bowed and kissed Ghislaine's hand. It was Basilio, her son, and I could see from Ghislaine's expression that she responded readily to his easy charm and his unusual appearance. He bowed to me from the neck, and his slightly slanted green eyes fixed mine with an intense gaze before he turned to engage Ghislaine in conversation. The notion was absurd, but for a fleeting moment I wondered whether Henry could have been his father. I dismissed the thought.

"Basilio took over the running of Mechongué when his father – my poor husband – died three years ago," Marie-Hélène explained, taking my arm in hers and leading me to the other side of the room. "He works even harder than his Russian grandfather who created this farm from virgin land back at the turn of the century. He's the gentleman you may have noticed in the painting in the ante-room as you came in. Basilio's the image of his grandfather, I think. And, like him, incidentally, a *coureur de jupons*. My son has always had an eye for a pretty woman." She whispered her last remark, giving a covert wink in Ghislaine's direction. "Not that he shows any sign of wanting to marry any of them, mind you! And now, William, I want you to meet someone else."

Conversing easily and with the poise of a much younger woman, Marie-Hélène paused to greet Luís, her factor, the surly fellow who had driven us from Necochea, and his timid wife, Laura. Then she led me to the other side of the room, confiding to me in a whisper that the woman I was about to meet had been an old friend of Henry's.

Like Marie-Hélène, Señora Loeb must have been in her eighties. With her profusion of white hair, her pronounced forehead, protruding upper jaw and disdainful expression, her appearance was forbidding, but her features grew more animated and gentler in conversation. She was sitting by a window, apparently lost in contemplation, when Marie-Hélène introduced me. She gazed up short-sightedly before asking me to sit down. I drew up a chair and within minutes Esther Loeb began relating how she had first come to know my grandfather.

"We met in B.A. aboard a British Royal Navy cruiser – H.M.S. *Superb*, I think the ship was called – which was here on a good-will mission after the war. Frankly, I never understood how Henry contrived to get an invitation, because he was rather *persona non grata* at your embassy. He was, after all, a naturalised French subject, as I expect you know. He took French nationality in 1942, a personal gift from Maréchal Pétain, so it was rumoured. Some of the older members of the British community actually shunned him when it became known that he had spent the war years in France, and one old boy at the Club actually called him 'a chum of Adolf's' to his face, I remember. Nevertheless" – she patted my arm – "he was a fine artist and he had great charm. I, for one, could not resist him."

Esther Loeb chuckled softly and sipped her dry martini before continuing.

"Incidentally, it was I who put him in touch with Marie-Hélène. He had not seen her since he was an art student in Paris in 1939. Can you imagine? But I was telling you . . . My husband and I came here in 1947. We were Jews from Alsace who had both been in the camps – he at Ravensbrück, I at Auschwitz; two of the few to survive – though it's not something I like to talk about," she added, waving an imperious hand to dismiss the memory. "Sidney, my husband, was on good terms with an Englishman whom he had met at the Belgrano Club in B.A., and who, by way of thanking him for a useful business introduction, had procured us an invitation to the reception on board ship. It was all so formal, and very British. Nobody talked to us and we knew no-one. Then Henry approached us in that wonderfully open way of his, and told us that he recognised us from a photograph that had appeared recently in the social pages of the *Standard*, one of the English-language newspapers we used to take, and the next thing I knew he and I were alone on deck, for Sidney had begun talking to someone else. It was the beginning of a great friendship. For some reason I had mentioned our experiences at Auschwitz, and he then told me about a young woman he had once known by the name of Chantal Aranovich, who had perished in the camps. She was French and, by an extraordinary coincidence, I had known her. Chantal was one of my closest friends in those ghastly days, although it is difficult to associate anything as human and God-given as friendship with the horrors we endured. I survived; she was murdered. A throw of fate's dice. I still feel guilty whenever I think about her. Why her, and thousands of others, and not me?" The old woman wrung her hands. "It's something you never really forgive yourself for: surviving."

Esther Loeb seemed momentarily distracted. "It's history now, Mr Latymer . . . all so long ago. I try to forgive, but we can never forget, you understand. But you're young, you and your wife – *tan linda* and *si simpática*, as we Argentines say –

and so I wonder why you bother delving into your grandfather's past, as Marie-Hélène tells me you are doing. Why should all that business of war and suffering and retribution mean anything to your generation? You are children, *por Diós,* you have the whole world and a lifetime before you. You should look forwards, not backwards."

"I feel I have to learn all I can," I said. "And not just about Henry, but about another woman he loved, Madeleine, who was my own father's mother and who later became my wife Ghislaine's mother after her second marriage. I also wanted to find out the truth about what happened to Chantal and her brother, Jean. You have confirmed what we have only recently discovered. From Henry's diaries, it was clear that he loved Chantal very much. Yet he deserted her and betrayed her. You could even say that he was indirectly responsible for her and her brother's deaths."

Señora Loeb shook her head and was silent for a few seconds. Then she said:

"He was a complex man. I got to know him well, but I think it was only in later life that he came to a self-realisation, and finally an acceptance of the person he had once been. I believe he expiated for his sins in the only way he could as a Christian: by finally confronting them and repenting. He did feel guilty about his years in France. I know this, because he spoke to me once about his office work in Vichy. It was fairly menial stuff; he was not much more than a clerk, but in his heart of hearts he believed he could have saved Chantal and her brother. As you may know, he had the job of providing basic information – names, addresses, ages, race – to the police, who then compiled an individual report on every Jew, before each of them was shipped off to Drancy or one of the other transit camps, and thence to the death camps in Nazi Germany. The conditions at Drancy were pretty terrible, but as nothing to what we found when we arrived at the camps in Germany and Poland. How much did Henry know about any of this? Very little, I imagine. Who knew what was going on? None of us did at the time. Politically, he was naive, and he was a romantic. A weak and egotistic man in many ways, but to me, for all his faults, a loveable person, and he was a wonderful painter. Because of the fact that I knew about Jean and Chantal, I became a sort of confessor figure for him. In my heart I forgave Henry long ago for the sins that so tortured him. Where does guilt lie, Mr Latymer? What good does it do for us to hunt down and pursue even the worst criminals? Why, in a society that both Judaism and Christianity teaches us should be compassionate, do we hound old men to their graves? An eye for an eye? *Quien sabe?* I don't, and I'm Jewish."

Like so many of her generation, Esther Loeb dropped Spanish words and phrases into her English conversation, but she was too old and too dignified for this to seem affected.

"Was Henry anti-Semitic in your view?" I said.

She shrugged and looked away. "I don't think so. Or if he was, he was never really conscious of it. So many were, of course, without realising it. But then my generation tends not to classify or make judgments about people in quite the way yours does . . . By the way, you should ask Marie-Hélène to show you Henry's painting of Chantal. It's unforgettable, to my mind. And ask her to tell you how she acquired it."

At this point Marie-Hélène's son Basilio ushered us into the dining room and I did not speak to Señora Loeb again until after dinner, and it was then only to bid her goodbye.

"Come and see me in Tandíl one day," she said to us outside as she wrapped a vicuña coat around herself. Her chauffeur held the car door open She squeezed my hand tightly, then settled herself into the back of her very old Bentley ("a relic of kindlier days," she murmured). Then she was off, the tyres of the car sending a flurry of dust over the moonlit pampas.

Her departure created an empty space within me and was like a wrench to the soul: I longed to spend more time in the company of this woman who had experienced and witnessed the worst depravities of our century, but who could nevertheless forgive. Like Marie-Hélène, she bridged two worlds for me. Yet at the same time I knew that Ghislaine and I now had our own future to face. The past had to remain in the past, as so many people kept telling me, and perhaps we had spent too much time there for our own good.

∞

Next morning, after breakfast, Basilio took us on a tour of the estancia on horseback. I had not ridden since childhood, but Ghislaine immediately looked the part of the experienced horsewoman, and I felt both impressed and inadequate as she cantered ahead with Basilio, while I struggled in their wake, finding it impossible to induce my horse into more than a jolting trot. On the way, we stopped at one of the bungalows belonging to the *péones* or farm workers so that Basilio could pay his respects to Ramón and Inés, who had just returned from hospital with their first child. His father, he informed us, had always maintained that a successful farm was dependent on the owner's good treatment of his workers, and he intended to follow his father's example. He produced an envelope from his pocket containing cash: "a small token to celebrate the baby's safe arrival". We were invited inside their small house, and *maté* was prepared. The sweetened *yerba* tea, drunk through a silver strainer with a pipe and a mouthpiece, was passed around in a communal gourd and filled at intervals from a pan of water from the kitchen range. Ten minutes later, looking every inch a latter-day Tsarist landowner, Basilio stood up to leave, and our tour of inspection continued.

These flat, empty spaces and wide horizons were a tonic after the narrow, traffic-ridden streets of central Buenos Aires, but I regretted that we were not spending longer at the farm with Marie-Hélène. She was probably one of the few women alive who had known Henry both as a young man before he left Paris and in his post-war reincarnation in Argentina. She had been genuinely fond of him, to judge from Rosita's account, and she appeared to bear no grudge against him for what he had thought of as his "sins". If anyone could shed further light on my grandfather, she could.

When we finally returned from our ride, Marie-Hélène was only too happy to talk about the past. Later that afternoon, she invited us to join her in what she called the library, a room overlooking the courtyard, which was lined with books on two sides and was hung with nineteenth-century engravings and lithographs. She poured coffee and offered us biscuits that she referred to as *alfajores*.

"Having you here for such a short time has been a special treat for me," she said, once we had sat down in the cosily furnished room. "Every time I look at you, William, I am so much reminded of Henry as a young man, and of the long conversations he and I used to have. Although he never knew either of you, he did speak about his family: his parents, from whom he so regretted having cut himself off; his sister Lavinia – he had been devoted to her; Madeleine and the baby – your own father, I now realise – whom they had abandoned. You know, most of us who came out to South America after the war, for whatever reason, wanted to forget the past and that old war-weary Europe that had brought so much grief. People like my own parents wanted a new life and a chance to begin again. But Henry was not like that. It's strange, because in one sense he was a pragmatist. He had an artistic temperament, of course, and he was a romantic where affairs of the heart were concerned, but he was never sentimental. He did whatever he did, or had to do, because it was the simplest way, the most straightforward."

Marie-Hélène paused. "The path of least resistance, I suppose. He was an enigma yet in the end he knew he had to stand up and be counted. I think he died reconciled to himself. He was a brave man in many ways, don't you think? – for all his weaknesses."

It was Ghislaine who responded:

"Yes, and I think I am beginning to see what it was about him that attracted my mother and the other women in his life. It's not something I can understand from his diaries and the letters I have seen. He seems to have been a man who – unintentionally or perhaps deliberately, who can say? – wounded women in one way or another. My mother has told us as much as she can or is prepared to say, but she prefers not to recall the past any longer. What was it about him, do you think, that appealed to you, to Chantal, to my mother?"

"Yes, that sad and beautiful Chantal. Which reminds me, I

have something to show you in a minute. Esther Loeb rang this morning to tell me not to forget . . . I don't really know how to answer your question. He had charm, and charm can be dangerous. He had a self-assurance that was compelling. He had enormous enthusiasm. But it was more than that. Henry clung to the past, he was a sort of mirror to an outdated notion of France. A France that was vanishing even when I was young. And although his physical looks were those of an Englishman – his hair, his features, those rather fastidious mannerisms – he was French – how can I put it? – in his inner being. He used to tell me that after his first month in Vichy, his French was sufficiently fluent to ensure that he would not be taken for a foreigner. Either there, in the unoccupied zone where it was less dangerous, or, more astonishingly, in Paris, when he stayed with his American friend Robert Worcester. He boasted that he was only ever once stopped and asked for his papers, and, by that time, they were in order. Of course, Robert knew Abetz, and I'm sure he must have sold pictures to him and to some of the high-ranking Nazis in return for immunity or favours. Or that's my theory."

Marie-Hélène took a sip of her coffee. She had not fully answered Ghislaine's question. I looked at Ghislaine, my wife, who was gazing out of the window towards the Tandíl hills, her mind far away.

"In France," Marie-Hélène said, "Henry had rid himself totally of his English identity – his family, his education, his social background – and created a new French persona for himself. I think he loved our country more than any foreigner I've ever known." Marie-Hélène searched for the words to express herself. "How can I explain? Henry's tragedy was that he had his own vision of France, a sort of idealised myth, but, as I say, it was a vision that was already almost extinct, even by 1939, when he first came to Paris. In the end he was deceived by illusions. He was a victim."

"What about his friends?" I said. "People like Jean, and Robert, and Sylvain de Gresly? Were they also deceived?"

"Robert possibly," said Marie-Hélène thoughtfully. "It's so long since I met him, a lifetime, in fact, and then it was only for a few hours. He was an American in the Hemingway mould, a hangover from the days when those American intellectuals he disassociated himself from flocked to Paris. But Robert knew what he was about. He was a survivor, a pragmatist too, but a man for whom the end always justified the means, I'm afraid."

She shrugged. "Mind you, who can cast the first stone? Love, war . . . these things happen. I never knew Sylvain except through hearing Henry's memories of him during the nightmare months he spent in Germany . . . *épouvantable*. I've read some of his novels. They're written in beautiful French, of course, but they seem over-written and somewhat dated nowadays. Jean, I did meet briefly. It was in Paris, just before Henry set off for Collioure to paint and think, and we were living through the phoney war He was a student at the École des Beaux-Arts. Was he deceived? I doubt it. He was Jewish, remember, a highly intelligent man who would have gone far, though I doubt that he had any illusions about what was happening at the time that he and his sister were deported."

"And Chantal?"

Marie-Hélène sipped her coffee. Then she rose to her feet as if she had suddenly remembered something she had to do.

She walked into another room and came back holding a framed canvas which she held up to show us.

"I keep this painting in my study. It has a curious history. In 1953, I went back to France, the only time I've been back. I stayed at the Hôtel du Roi René, I remember, in Aix-en-Provence, the town to which my parents had moved from Paris during the early days of the Occupation. A friend had invited me to a *vernissage* at a local art gallery and there, to my astonishment, on the wall facing me as I entered the room, I saw this dramatic portrait of a young woman. I recognised Henry's line and the tones he used immediately. You know, all those bright shades of red, and that particular way he had of portraying eyes – always so dark and so brooding, so haunted – and I asked the price. The owner of the gallery had, it transpired, known Henry in Vichy in 1942, and later, the following year, when he and Henry and Madeleine had hidden in the Maures hills. They used to play chess together, he told me. Anyway, this man returned to Vichy after the war, and, having recently acquired his own art gallery in Aix, he was looking for new work to exhibit and sell. There was a lot of stuff around in those days, and at good prices too. According to him, this portrait – look, Henry wrote on the back of the canvas, in English: 'Chantal by the Allier, Bellerive, July 1940' – had formed part of the contents of a wealthy banker's house at Bellerive, on the opposite side of the river from Vichy, he told me, and it was for sale. He acquired it because it was by his old friend, Henry. It's very moving, I think, though horribly poignant for those of us who learned what became of Chantal.

"I was so touched by the coincidence that I paid him – oh! I don't know, 5,000 old francs, very little really – and had it shipped back to Buenos Aires with me. I thought no more about it for months other than of the pleasure it might give Henry to see it again.

"But what I could never have foreseen was the effect the painting would have on your grandfather." Marie-Hélène turned to me. "I showed it to him a few months later when he came to stay here. You see, we had only recently met each other again after all those years. At the time, I had been told very little about Henry's war. Remember, we had only known each other for a few months in 1939. He looked at it for about ten minutes and kept asking to see it again throughout the weekend he stayed here. I'd never seen him with tears in his eyes, either before or since. He wasn't that sort of man."

Marie-Hélène set the canvas on a chair and stepped back to stand beside us.

The painting was of a young woman of about nineteen or twenty, with brown, shining eyes, her dark hair piled on top of her head. She was sitting on the grass beside a wide river. On the far bank I could make out the skyline of a quintessentially French provincial town. I recognised it immediately from Henry's few photographs, and I knew Ghislaine had as well. It was Vichy, its roofs and its church towers, seen from Bellerive. The girl was Chantal as she had been in the summer of 1940, two years before she perished at Auschwitz.

∞

That night, after dinner, I stepped outside onto the veranda to breathe in the cool breeze of the pampas before retiring. There was a sense of enchantment in the night air and I regretted having to return to the city next morning. Above me, the constellation of the Southern Cross still lay on its side above a crescent moon in a night that was aglow with stars. The cicadas sawed and a light breeze wafted through the perfumed air. I gazed over the parkland, towards the *mirador*, the tall eucalyptus trees and the pampas beyond, the sky shimmering in the blackness of the night.

I had not heard her approach, but Ghislaine had joined me. She took my arm in both her hands and laid her head on my shoulder.

"Will, do you ever think of stars as the eyes of people? Those who have gone before us. I always used to as a child."

It was as though she had been reading my mind. I kissed her.

"I do too, my darling, but we must start to live in the present now, for ourselves."

The wind rustled the eucalyptus leaves and a cloud passed over the slither of moon. We walked back to the veranda, past the stuttering fountain, and made our way to our room.

Author's Note

I should like to thank Margaret Stead, Adam Munthe, Allan Massie and Christopher MacLehose for their encouragement and advice.

For many of the details about Sigmaringen I am indebted to Henry Rousso's book *Pétain et la fin de la Collaboration*, first published by Éditions Ramsay in 1980 under the title *Un château en Allemagne*, and to Louis-Ferdinand Céline's novel *D'un château l'autre*, published by Gallimard in 1957 and later translated into English by Ralph Manheim as *Castle to Castle* in 1968.

EUAN CAMERON is an editor and translator. *Madeleine* is his first novel. He worked in book publishing and as a literary journalist for many years before becoming a translator from French. His translations include works by Julien Green, Paul Morand, Simone de Beauvoir, Patrick Modiano and Philippe Claudel, as well as biographies of Marcel Proust and Irène Némirovsky. He was appointed Chevalier dans l'ordre des Arts et des Lettres in 2011.